BOOK NOOK
100,000 USED -
Books, Records, CD's,
Comics & Videos
404-633-1328

The Company of a Daughter

THE COMPANY OF A DAUGHTER

Paddy Richardson

STEELE ROBERTS
Aotearoa New Zealand
2000

To Christopher, Simon and Amie ~ with love

© Paddy Richardson 2000

Cover artwork Simon Richardson; design Lynn Peck

Published by Roger Steele
STEELE ROBERTS LTD
Box 9321
Aotearoa New Zealand
Phone (04) 499 0044 – Fax (04) 499 0056
Email rwsteele@actrix.gen.nz

Published with the assistance of

creative nz
ARTS COUNCIL OF NEW ZEALAND *TOI AOTEAROA*

ISBN 0-9583712-8-8
January 2000

Acknowledgements

This novel was written during my residence as 1997 Burns Fellow at the University of Otago.

I thank my mother for telling me the stories of my family and giving me the fragments of Eliza's diary, and my father for teaching me the value of language. While this is a fictionalised account of a family I would like to acknowledge the helpful resource of Murray Gitoos' family history *First There Were Three*. My reference to the voyage of Mael Duin derives from a ninth century Irish tale.

My thanks and gratitude also to Jim for his patient good humour and Helen for her unfailing encouragement.

1

My grandmother Evie was a gardener. At the end of each summer she would gather up seeds, label them and store them safely in cool dry places. In early spring Evie made her seed-beds in the shelter of the verandah, pushing saved seeds into fine dark soil. When I built my own first garden she sent envelopes filled with dry golden husks, memories of past gardens, foreshadowing those of the future.

Evie told me that we are all connected, and that the past must be respected, it is as important as the present. There were times I did not listen well enough to her lessons of preservation and nurture. I knew she loved me unreservedly. I knew by the direct gaze of her eyes, the tautness of skin around her mouth, that she sometimes saw my failings but still loved me. She taught me lessons from her stories, hoping the seeds which she understood would for some time remain dormant, might one day grow and flourish.

The other seeds she gave me were from lavender, foxgloves, violets and delphiniums which grew in her own grandmother's garden in the Hokianga. Evie said her grandmother Eliza's flower garden was small compared with the large space used for growing the necessary vegetables, fruit and herbs but it was her indulgence, her way of implanting a little English refinement into that place of mangroves, flax and kauri.

I think of those seeds from that first garden. Evie crushing lavender in her lean brown hands and holding it out to me. As I breathed in that sweet pungency, she told me about Eliza's garden in the Hokianga.

Perhaps that is why I'm making this journey. Perhaps those seeds from past gardens, Eliza's pretty indulgence and the spread of colour and flourishing growth of Evie's garden, have caught up with me. Because I'm on this train, retracing the journey up north I made so often when I was a child. Rather than flying away somewhere exotic, I am travelling towards a place I visited in my childhood which is part of the myths and stories of my life. Now, when I'm no longer sure of anything, I'm making a journey which may seem without purpose, but which I'm drawn to make.

The reason may unfold. Perhaps it's escape. All I know is that my life, despite my son, my lover and that occupation I used to call my career, seems hollow and the idea for this journey has nudged and pursued me. In the end, I finished up my work, made my arrangements and got on a train.

When I was a child, at the end of each year my mother and I took the train from Christchurch through to the ship at Lyttelton. I remember the acrid smoke, the taste of soot and the winding darkness of the tunnel. At the end of it my mother gave me my kiss, my ticket, my money and asked if I had everything I needed.

I put my suitcase in the cabin then ran back up the stairs onto the deck to look for her. She stood on the wharf with the wind tugging at her hair, waved when she saw me, then turned and walked off towards the train before the ferry chugged slowly out. I stood on the deck watching the hills. The sky was generally grey, the wind icy and the sea dense green oil. I always felt cold there in the early evening on deck watching the hills disappear.

When I woke there was a trickle of early sun on the water as we glided through the Wellington heads. I did not need to look for Evie. I knew she would be there, but each year a heady joy sent me running up the stairs to stand on deck, clutching my small brown suitcase, long before we were due to berth.

The expectation of Evie's level gaze, her cool hand on my forehead, the calm voice which reminded me of sun and warmth and gardens, a cushion of love I would settle myself into. My mother was winter and the city and school. Evie was summer and gardens and the hammock on the verandah.

This early morning sun has multiplied into five perfectly round golden discs diminishing in size which hover to the right of the train then hurtle up at us above charcoal and purple hills. There are pines looming, and small ice-covered ponds and paddocks like dark waves. The sky is milky, edged in aquamarine, and now the sun is transformed into a red-edged golden eye. There is mist rising off grass, then shadows on the shingle around the Waimakariri with its sombre depths. The voice over the loudspeaker translates, *Waimakariri, cold waters*.

The bell peals an alarm and we click-clack through a town. I see a billboard and smile: *Do You Need Direction In Your Life? The Bible Has The Answers*. There is a stone church, behind it the cemetery, *Remember man that you were dust and to dust you will return*. Then we are out again rollicking past a grey-white river, a symmetry of square paddocks, edged and enclosed by pines, another river surrounded with shingle, poplars, hills scooped out to let in the sky, the change to tussock, the gentler landscape and there suddenly is the sea.

Do You Need Direction In Your Life? The Bible Has The Answers.

I chose to make this journey by train, ferry and bus so I could sit, stare out and reflect. This was not the time to be gathered up, blindly whisked above clouds to arrive miraculously, minutes later. I watch the sea, the iron-grey sand, the cliffs we creep so close against you could stretch out your hand and touch rock. The scallops of coast, cobalt sea, edgings of rock, the dark curve of road beside the tracks. Everywhere there are contrasts of shadow and light. Evie talked about contrasts. She talked about the confusion of trying to see through the dark. About darkness — the anguish and the necessity for it. About direction — the journey of the spirit.

The stories are like scrolls rolling forwards and backwards and interweaving. Evie told them as if they were happening here with us in the present, there in the upstairs bedroom, in the kitchen, down below us on the beach under the ridge or over beyond the house in the gardens, orchard and the bush.

The stories. The garden in the Hokianga. Hannah, the daughter Eliza yearned for. Hannah, Evie's mother, her good-angel, mild nature, her fair hair shining in the sun, her hands holding a violin. Evangeline. Evie, the gardener, who married then all too soon buried her charming Irish lover. Evie, the mother of Grace. My mother. And me. Zoe.

Recently forty, I am the same age Eliza was when she gave birth to her only daughter, Hannah; eight years younger than my mother when she died. Perhaps my story is not even halfway over. Like Evie, I may live until I am almost ninety. But, unlike her, I am aimless and lost.

When I was a child I attended Sunday School because a girl I knew at school went with her sister and said I should come. My mother let me; it was a way of entertaining me for part of the weekend. Going to Sunday School involved certain preparations and rituals. I had to learn my verse for the week and colour in a Jesus picture. There was the donning of the best dress, clean white socks and polished shoes.

I persuaded my mother to buy me a hat like my friend's. It was a sailor's hat, white-painted straw. Artificial flowers were poked in behind the turned-up brim and satin ribbons hung down my back from a large bow. I found a Bible in our bookshelves which, I believed, added authenticity to my role as a Christian child. Our Sunday School teacher had powdery eyes and a face which glowed. She wore white gloves, a navy dress and a straw sailor's hat, but without flowers or ribbon. She told us she had committed her life to Jesus. She spoke of heaven and the type of person who would be welcome there; about the unfortunate endings of people who were not. Spreading the Gospel, she said, was the best way to earn yourself a place.

When I told my mother I had committed my life to Jesus and intended to become a missionary in China she laughed and said I was ridiculous.

I have entered on a new scene, left the parental roof, and the friends and guides of my youth, to become a wife. I have forsaken my native land and embarked for a distant clime as the helpmate of a Christian missionary.

When Eliza arrived in New Zealand after the five-month journey from England with the husband she scarcely knew, the ship was held back for a further five days by what she describes in her diary as a foul wind. Her husband had fallen out with the ship's captain in the early part of the voyage — *William finds it difficult to command his temper.* The ship was infested with cockroaches and since it was a whaler the deck was frequently awash with blood. Eliza was the only woman on board and obliged to spend much of the journey below decks.

Eventually they anchored in the Bay of Islands and the captain ordered the guns to be fired. The ship was rapidly surrounded by canoes. *Before the anchor had been dropped half an hour, more than a hundred Natives were on board — they made a great clamour — I was completely encircled by them. Some got into the rigging and examined my countenance and dress with great earnestness.*

Eliza, almost nineteen, was seven months pregnant and had somehow to be got across the island to the mission station in the Hokianga. There were no tracks suitable for horses but there was a foot track, steep in places. She settled herself on the covered sedan and was hoisted up and carried the distance by two young men — *they were as careful over me as they probably could be.*

That first child, a son, was stillborn soon after her arrival. The next, a daughter, was strangled during birth by the umbilical cord wrapped around her neck. Two weeks after the birth Eliza was called out in the night to act as a midwife for another settler's wife. She was rowed across the river — *a female in a boat, late at night, on a large river in a thick fog with only New Zealanders for my companions — but I felt perfectly safe.*

She birthed the child then tended the mother and newborn girl — *I found my dear friend ill, and after a severe time she was safely delivered of a fine girl. I dressed the little stranger, sat on a while with my friend, then returned home.*

She took the slippery, blood-covered child in her arms, gently washed and dressed her, then wrapped her in a new, soft shawl. For a long while she held and rocked the baby in her arms as the mother slept.

Every wound in my bleeding heart was opened afresh, and I was obliged to give vent to my griefs. None but a mother bereaved of her children in a foreign land can conceive how deeply, how acutely I felt when holding this precious babe in my arms.

Eliza's life was tough and frequently troubled, but led with faith in her Master and a self-effacing dedication to the cause. She busied herself with the conversion and education of Maori girls and young women. She learned their language and set up a school. She miscarried a third child, then at last gave birth to two sons. When her husband was accused and found guilty of immoral relations with Maori women she removed her goods and chattels from the *large and commodious* mission dwelling and resettled the household in the raupo house near the top of the hill. Her Maori became fluent but she was never allowed to preach, even though the Maori listeners to the Good News were unable to understand its English-speaking deliverers — *I heartily wish I could lend Brother my knowledge of language and almost feel a wish that it were common and proper for Women to preach.* She attempted to curb her habit of voracious reading — *I fear if fictitious works were often in my way I should be overcome with temptation — I have many struggles with this besetting sin.*

Eliza's diaries are bound in black leather, wrapped in tissue and kept in William's oak desk which faces on to the living room window looking out over Evie's garden. Sometimes when I held those diaries in my hand and looked down on the regularly formed, black-inked words, I'd imagine I was Eliza.

I saw an endless expanse of dark waves beyond the porthole, felt the surge of the sea, smelt salt and blood, felt a rush of bile in my throat. I paced my cabin for the five days before the ship could proceed into the Bay of Islands, aching for land but fearing it. I saw dark bodies, tattooed faces, felt the loss of friends, brothers, mother and father. I felt the cold fear pierce my belly as the men carrying me slipped in mud, saw dense bush, heard the sounds of alien birds. I felt the agony of childbirth without anaesthetic or medical care, the loss of the children I'd carried in my belly, the betrayal by my older, difficult husband.

I see Eliza walking down the beach in her trailing dress buttoned to the neck and arranged over petticoats and boned undergarments. I see her striding over stones, shells, the coarse sand, gazing out to the sea. She longed to bathe during those hot Hokianga summers but because of her modesty could not. I see her tears for the husband she had trusted and believed in, for the children she lost, for the strangeness of the place and the family left.

But I know, also, of her love which grew for the place, for the beauty of sea and land and the people she lived with — *I can sit down with a party of*

Natives with as much comfort as though they were a party of my English friends, and I believe the Anger of the Fiercest Chief might be allayed by a basin of sweet tea.

In the portrait above the mantelpiece in Evie's house, Eliza's hair is pinned back from her small, pointed face. Her eyes gaze candidly towards the artist and her smile is demure but teasing.

Eliza first encountered William when he was in England on leave from the mission station, and looking for a wife. She saw him in her local church. He preached about lives led in devotion and commitment to Christ. He spoke of his mission life in New Zealand. Volatile, tall and formidable, he was passionate about his subject. Eliza, in response to the calling she had experienced on seeing and hearing William, knelt beside the iron bed she had slept safely in all her life and dedicated the remainder of it to the missions. She was the answer to William's prayers.

Eliza's diaries affirm that her sense of duty and faith remained strong. Any impatience is with herself — *I know not one Native woman who has derived any real benefit from my instruction — please God allow me the grace to perform my duty with better patience and humility.* Her response to William's adultery was not of anger but compassion —*my deep concern is for the welfare of his most precious soul.*

Once I was impatient with that sense of duty, commitment and purpose, seeing it as limiting, blinkered. Now I've come to envy it. To believe implicitly in something, anything at all, seems beyond me. I'm too cynical, questioning, old. It's too late for me to sit in a church, to hear the satisfactory rustle of satin ribbons on my shoulder, to hold securely onto a Bible recovered from a dusty shelf and feel the fervour of a faith larger than self.

Eliza built her garden at the back of the mission house, clearing the ground, digging, raking and feeding the soil with the peelings from her kitchen. At the far end of the plot of earth she dug in fruit trees. Then she planted the largest portion in vegetables, mainly potatoes and kumara. Beside the vegetables she made a herb garden and in the strip nearest the house arranged flower beds. She planted a briar rose and a honeysuckle vine, violets, hollyhocks, larkspur, foxgloves and an edging of lavender.

She cared steadfastly for her garden. Despite the deaths of her babies and the homesickness which threatened to engulf her, despite her husband's indiscretions, despite exile from the mission house and William's antagonistic estrangement from their neighbours — *He waved a cutlass at William and shouted that were it not for his wife he would bring large guns and blow the mission station up.*

She tilled the soil and carried water from the well. She fretted when her plants died, felt joy when they flourished. She cared for her husband and sons, tended to what she described as domestic drudgery and her Christian duties. From the fruit trees in blossom, the haze of lavender against the larkspur, the briar entwining with honeysuckle she gained deep satisfaction.

In the early 1900s, many years after Eliza built her garden in the Hokianga, a church official inspected the property. Taken up the harbour by boat, he walked up the steep slope to the abandoned buildings and the gravestones beneath the oak.

The estate is in a state of dilapidation, overrun with gorse and sweetbriar. There is the solitary Norfolk pine, a gift of gratitude to Mrs Eliza White and imported from Sydney, on the crest of the hill above the site of the old mission church. Pressing on our way through the tall tea-tree, we came upon the dwelling, still well preserved, the privet fence, and fencing posts, inside of which had grown the pohutukawa, puriri and karaka. In the scrub could be seen at intervals several varieties of apple and pear trees, the ginger plant, the gnarled and knotty arm of a briar rose hung from a rotted fence post.

I see Eliza bent over the earth on the ridge, way up above that wide stretch of the Hokianga. Watch her stand. There is mud on her dress and hands, and wet, dark patches beneath her arms on the tight-buttoned bodice of her dress. She turns and stretches her arms above her body, then gazes out over the expanse of inky sea, the ocean which divides her from all that was once familiar, safe and easy.

I know she loved that garden, that small place of ordered beauty among confusion and chaos. I know she tended her garden and longed for the company of a daughter.

In Evie's garden the seeds of larkspur, foxglove, the cuttings of honeysuckle, lavender and violets transplanted from the Hokianga took and sprang into life. Eliza's briar rose sulked for a time then hungrily wound itself around the posts of the verandah.

2

The trees are turning. Sun flashes and trickles through hills of nutmeg, cinnamon, brash yellow-gold. The sea and sky overlap in hazy smoke, blue-grey ash. The hump of hills is a sleeping giant woman's back, hips and spine raised and hunched against the sky. Violet-grey panne velvet winding around her body.

Through the tunnels, out of the dark, the sky is dazzling sapphire, we lose the sea for a time then find it again, a vast spread of crinkly silk.

I leave my bags at the motel in Picton, walk down to the bay and stretch out on warm sand, close my eyes and feel the sun on my face. The phone in my bag rings and I disconnect it. All that can wait.

There are dolphins close to shore. A calf and mother arc into the harbour and in unison dip and glide among the boats anchored near the wharf. Suddenly there are crowds at the edge of the sea and flashing cameras. The dolphins swim on, unperturbed by attention, put on their show of glorious leaps and dives, then follow the ferry, curving in and out of its wake.

During the soft evening I walk along the stones edging the harbour and look across the hills in the direction of Wellington. After nondescript wine and food at a restaurant I try to sleep, moving restlessly around in stiff sheets. So silent here.

More dolphins in Cook Strait as we cross next day. I watch them from the deck, feeling the chill of wind on my face and in my hair. I wonder if it's true that dolphins come to offer blessings for a journey.

The old ferry that used to travel between Christchurch and Wellington was a no-man's land for me, a place which marked the leaving of one world and entrance into another. My mother's friends sometimes asked if it was entirely suitable for a minor to travel overnight on the ferry unaccompanied. Perhaps they envisaged the possibilities of young children slipping unnoticed into the sea or being enticed into unlit corners by seedy characters. But my mother expected me to behave responsibly, and if any emergency should arise it would doubtlessly be dealt with by the stewards who properly supervised the passengers and performed the tasks required of them. My mother had little patience with incompetence and indeed I survived each crossing unmolested and unperturbed. I was used to being left to my own resources.

I shared cabins with an assortment of women with or without children who made clucking noises about my smallness and oddly adult manner as

I unpacked my pyjamas, cleaned my teeth, settled into my bunk and began the book I'd selected for the journey. They asked pointed questions about my mother. I answered them succinctly from over the top of my book, then switched off my light and curled into the red blankets. I felt the motion of the sea beneath me, listened to the clanking and groaning of the ship and the soft hush of water and fell into sleep thinking about Evie, thinking about my mother.

Mother suited her name.

Grace.

Her face was small and delicately shaped. Her hair was dark and lustrous and her skin that pale-coffee colour often associated with Italians. She was elegant in a way unusual in small women; her back perfectly straight and her chin uptilted. Shoes pleased her. She would bring new shoes home, lift one out of the box and place it in the palm of her hand weighing the balance of toe and heel, running her finger across the sheen of leather. Her shoes were high-heeled and narrow — she had small, slender feet — and always impeccably clean. She wore dark, slim skirts and trim jackets which fitted snugly over her arms and shoulders and pressed into her waist. Underneath she wore blouses of flimsy, cobwebby material with a lace collar or an embroidered panel inset into the front and a row of small pearl buttons. She carried a black bag shaped like an envelope and whenever she was going out she pulled on tight leather gloves, smoothed them around her fingers, then sat a small beret perfectly straight at the back of her head.

Grace.

I loved her for her name because gracious was what I believed her to be. I loved her for her elegance and delicacy, the cool cheek pressed against mine when she said goodnight and turned off my light. I would lie in my bed, looking into the blackness and listening to the tap-tap of her fingers on the portable typewriter as she described fashions or recipes or beauty hints for the newspaper's Friday women's page. I'd hear her sigh, imagine her stretching out her arms above her head and flexing her fingers before she started the next page.

From my mother and grandmother I learned about love. From my grandmother I learned about the kind of love which can surround you with a warmth to luxuriate in, love that is tireless, unquestioning and endless. My mother taught me, however, that love may be bestowed with a wary coolness and must sometimes be coaxed and earned by careful and responsible behaviour. Once I resented and grieved at my mother's coolness and failed to understand that my grandmother's love was a rare gift. Now I see the value of both lessons. Now I know that love may sometimes be as expansive as the sky, as solid as the earth and I know sometimes it may be given out in precisely calculated segments. With some love you can be buoyant and irresponsible as though you are bouncing on gold-edged clouds. With other kinds it's as if you have a tiny ancient coin you must shine up, guard and savour. Both types are precious.

I lived with my mother in a brick house joined to another exactly the same. Behind the iron fence, close to the street, a strip of garden crammed with tatty hydrangeas edged the cracked concrete path. The front door had a brass letter-slot I always felt proud of since next door didn't have one. Downstairs was a dim, wood-panelled passage, the small square living room — my mother never said lounge — with narrow windows facing into the street and a kitchen slotted in behind. Then the steep stairs up to a cupboard of a bathroom, my mother's bedroom and my own.

My mother's bedroom was her private place where she brushed her hair in front of the mirror, walked about in lace and silk petticoats with fine satin straps, slept in the wide bed covered with the deep blue quilting and read her books. It was the place where she stood in the window staring out over the lights and the darkness of the city, up into the hills patched with light and puckered by shadows.

But some days, after I opened the front door with the key always left beneath the loose brick, I hung my coat and school-case in my bedroom, took off my shoes and tiptoed into my mother's bedroom. It was cool and quiet.

I opened her wardrobe and took out her dressing gown — it was navy, patterned with small biscuit-red triangles — and carefully inserted my arms into the satiny sleeves. I drew it around me, shivering as the fabric encased me, feeling the heaviness at my wrists and my neck and smelling the sharp sweetness of my mother's perfume.

I lay on her bed or rather burrowed into it, hiding my face in the pillows and crawling into the mounds of quilting. I lay silent and still until the street-lamps switched on and I knew she'd come home. I hung up her dressing gown, straightened her quilt, placed my homework books on the desk in my room and went down the stairs to peel the potatoes.

Those were the years when I didn't have Evie, when I didn't have that other world of garden and ocean and verandah. I remember a city of harsh streets, the nosing traffic beyond our windows, the sounds in the early morning of cars starting and factory whistles and distant trains, the bells and rhythmical shunting. The evening buzz and hum of voices, the sudden rise of laughing and shouting from the pub on the corner.

When I was very young my days were governed by a strict routine. The morning rush of quick-Zoe-quick washing and dressing and the small mound of porridge drowned in milk and brown sugar I spooned quickly into my mouth as I crouched over the one-bar heater. Mornings with the smog catching in my throat as my mother hurried me down the street. I listened to the click of her heels on the pavement as I struggled to keep up with her. The shortcut across the park to the lady with the fluff of curls over her head who looked after me until my mother came back. Every morning we went to the shop for the bread and, if I was good, on to the park with the swings and the slide. In the afternoons I played with the dolls her own little girl had played with years before.

Sometimes I slept. Sometimes I played in the back garden. I had a secret home beneath the blackcurrant bushes. Sometimes I would stop whatever I was doing and want my mother, and the lady would give me what she called a sweetie or a bikkie.

My mother came for me and we walked briskly across the lamp-lit park. We ate cheese on toast, eggs on toast, meals that were flung together, easily made. I listened to the sounds of the radio and my mother's typewriter as I went to sleep.

The special times were valued because of their rarity. My mother read me stories from the thick *Grimm's Fairy Tales* with gold lettering on the front and delicately tinted pictures inside. I would lean my head into her body as she read, her voice rising, falling, pausing. Her voice was sweet and clear when she was Snow White, grating and full of menace when she was the witch. Occasionally my mother took me into the Square to the pictures or took me shopping and we'd have egg sandwiches and chocolate éclairs at Beaths.

In summer we sometimes took the bus out to the beach at Sumner. My mother wore a black bathing suit without straps. Mine was red with white spots with a tight top my mother said was made of shirred elastic. Sitting together on the sand we would watch ships on the horizon. We walked through Cave Rock and I felt the black sand cool and firm underneath my feet. We jumped the waves together. My mother held me and swam with me. I lay on my back, feeling her arms securely around me, the sun warming me, the gentle bob of waves.

Sometimes at night my mother sat on my bed and told me the story which did not come from a book, the story of Mael Duin and his wanderings and adventures. She told me of the end of his journeying, when he and his seventeen men came to the island where they found the great adorned house and the queen and her seventeen women. She told about Mael Duin's love for the queen and the words she said to him, the words that were the end of the story.

'Stay here,' the queen said, 'and age will not fall on you, but the age that you have attained. And you shall have lasting life always and what came to you this day shall come to you every day without labour. And be no longer wandering from island to island.'

There is an image which comes into my head whenever I think of us. I am with her but also somehow outside, away beyond my body. I'm watching a mother with her daughter.

The daughter is quite young, almost a baby, not quite four. She is wearing a short, fire-engine red double-breasted coat with gold buttons, white socks which come up around strong plump knees, and black patent leather shoes. Her hair is a fuzz of brown ringlets. She is running along, her short legs pumping to keep up with the swiftly strutting mother with the distracted face who holds her hand firmly in her own gloved hand.

The mother slows and glances down. Smiles. In her other hand the daughter is holding desperately onto a string tied to a bobbing blue balloon.

When I was five my mother took me into the city and bought three shirts with stiff pointed collars, a heavy black tunic which came down below my knees, thick grey socks and black lace-up shoes.

The routine changed. I walked with my mother to the gates of the school. All day I sat in an enormous room filled with hazards you somehow had to recognise and negotiate. There were books and paper and crayons and puzzles and drums and cymbals and flutes you could sometimes touch but other times must leave alone. There were children you could sometimes talk to and play with but other times must not. There were counters you had to place together on pieces of cardboard but mustn't build up into towers. There were marks on paper with corresponding sounds you were expected to know. After, I walked home, found the key and waited for my mother.

I didn't know about other children. About how to talk, play, fight with them. Nor why I didn't have a father. I didn't know why my mother wasn't waiting at home for me, with the chops in a frypan and biscuits and cakes made and piled in the tins with the Queen's head or a picnicking family on the top. With an apple pie and custard for pudding and the fire on.

I didn't know why I had no brothers and sisters but I wanted them, I wanted them so much. For the company, of course, but more than that I thought an added child or two may turn us into something more normal. I understood from school that I and my mother were odd, strange. I wanted to be more like the other children. I couldn't see why my mother wouldn't get more children. Even one would help. When I asked her, explaining that I would be very good and helpful, that really she would find having a baby no trouble at all, I doubted she would even notice it much, she smiled a little but then her face went cold and she stared above me, out of the window.

She said, 'You are as much as I can possibly manage.'

Her world was an enigma to me. I knew she wasn't like other mothers I saw waiting outside the school. They talked to each other with their arms folded on their chests, frowning and smiling and shaking back their heads and laughing. I saw them growling and hitting and kissing and hugging the other children. They wore dresses patterned with flowers and cardigans and flat-heeled shoes. Sometimes they had scarves wound around their heads.

My mother put on her blouses, her costumes, her high heels, asked me if the seams were straight on her nylons and went into the city to the newspaper office. She did fires and court news and meetings but most of the time, she said, she did the women's pages.

In all those years I never once went with my mother to the newspaper. I wonder if the newspaper knew of my existence; perhaps she had to deny me to procure or keep her position. I could only imagine where my mother spent her days. Stacks of white paper to be filled with the words which click-clacked from the typewriters operated by rows and rows of men and women grimly bent over desks. I imagined the paper-boys I saw sometimes calling on the streets, huddled in a corner, rolling the papers into the missiles they threw from their bikes into houses. I saw someone tall and angry and godly, rather like the headmaster of the school, striding along rows, booming out orders.

We were usually alone in the evenings and weekends. When I learned to read and haphazardly tore my way through any book I could get hold of, I discovered my mother and I were actually the stuff of fiction. We were heroines, almost orphans, entirely on our own in this great world. We were without aunts, brothers, sisters, grandmothers, grandfathers, husbands, fathers. All we had was each other.

I explained our heroic status to my mother. That we were like the orphans in books, all alone in the world with only each other and wasn't that a tragedy? Tragedy was a new and much loved word. She only smiled and raised her eyebrows. Despite my mother not understanding our plight, I began to savour rather than despair over my difference from the other children blessed with families.

I was fatherless. I was a Dickensian heroine and I learned to use my disadvantages. When the other girls talked about their families I lowered my head, sighed loudly and attempted an expression of courageous suffering. Someone always put their arm around me. Someone always offered to lend me something valued, or gave me a chocolate biscuit.

Although we were without family, we were not entirely without friends. My mother had an assortment of people who came now and then for coffee on weekend afternoons or drinks on Saturday evenings. Her friends were as unlike the other children's parents as my mother was. The women were elegant and birdlike. I was fascinated by their hands. They had long curved fingernails painted in shades of red, which they waved about as they smoked. They sat in our living room, drank coffee or gin-and-lemon, and chattered in high excited voices.

My mother said I must be polite and stay in the room long enough to offer the milk, sugar, sandwiches and savouries arranged on the silver tray but then I would escape from the chit-chat and bury myself in a book up in my room. My mother's friends laughed at me and said I was so sweet, so quiet, so shy, *just a dear little bookworm, Grace.*

Occasionally in the evenings there were men there as well but I hardly ever saw them. Usually I was in bed and only heard their voices, lower-pitched among the women's. Sometimes I heard my mother laughing. Now and then a man stayed for the night. I'd hear a voice, deeper than my mother's, whispering, as he slipped out early in the morning.

I shied from men but was intrigued by them. I wondered how the pushing, shouting boys at school could possibly transform into the tall aloof men who made my mother laugh in our living room. I saw other girls driving off with their fathers, sitting beside them, talking to them. How could you chatter and laugh with these large gruff beings? I was pleased I only had my mother. I never met or asked about the men who stayed the night, never asked about my father.

Despite being different, and unwilling to join in loud and boisterous games I acquired friends. Until adolescence I was slight like my mother. The other girls liked to think of me as a sad little sister who should be petted and looked after. They took me to their houses after school and I shyly negotiated the perils of parents and older siblings. Once I was taken on a picnic to the Waimakariri River with a girl's family. It was a difficult and miserable experience. All the family went. The rough boy cousins and the grandparents and the aunts and uncles and the glamorous older girls. They blew up tyre tubes and lilos and raced them along the river and played cricket and threw large balls at each other and shouted and cried and ate a great deal of food. They could not believe I had no family, that I'd never before been on a family picnic nor on an outing to the Waimakariri. I heard the mother whisper I was a poor little mite.

Other mothers also said I was quaint. I knew the teachers thought I was clever but shy. I didn't join in, I was quiet and sweet, a bookworm. But it was not the whole story. I had my own inner self — a courageous, strong self, quite different to the poor waif. I was Katy and Jane Eyre and Little Nell and Anne of Green Gables.

And I had a mysterious past.

Perhaps I didn't ask my mother about my father because I'd discovered that the world of reality is most often inferior to that of fantasy.

When the girls at school asked about my father and how he'd died I said it was a secret. I could not immediately imagine anything glorious or dramatic enough to tell them. Another of the girls at our school was also without a father. He had died from pneumonia. That did not seem nearly splendid enough for my own story.

I lay in bed and created my brave, noble father and his sad demise. A sailor, no, a captain choosing to go down with his sinking ship? A soldier shot down in the war defending his own country? All right, but scarcely original. I imagined spies and racing cars and wild-eyed horses and sabotaged aeroplanes. I wanted a story which would be dramatic but believable, a story which would mark me with tragedy. In the end I was so satisfied with the story I invented that I easily convinced the girls and almost, in the end, myself. I smile at it now, but can see why I thought it had a pleasing balance of glamour, heroism and pathos.

My parents were on honeymoon in Africa. They loved each other passionately and had recently married in the cathedral. My father wore a pin-striped suit with a carnation attached to the lapel. My mother wore a white satin dress and a veil which measured twenty-six feet and had six bridesmaids in lilac frocks and two flowergirls carrying baskets of rose-petals.

After drinking pink champagne my parents sailed to Africa for their honeymoon. My father was to photograph dangerous animals for the newspaper. He was photographing elephants when my mother got too close to a calf and its mother began to charge. My father ran, pushing her out of the way and saving her life, but at the same time getting himself gored by the tusks. He was carried, bravely disguising the excruciating pain he was in, to his tent where despite my mother's tears and attentions he died in her arms.

The sweetly beguiling elephant calf; my mother in a cream safari suit, smiling, hovering, straying too far forward; my father, tall and tanned-blond? — yes certainly, his blond hair would glisten in the sunlight as he rushed forward. The pounding, stampeding, immensely frightening beast, the trumpeting shriek and the flash of dagger-sharp ivory, my mother screaming, the crevice of bright blood that had been my father's chest and belly. My father brave and soundless in suffering, sighing his death in my weeping mother's arms. Oh it was true, of course it was true!

My mother returned to Christchurch and gave birth to a daughter who would never know a father's devotion. She never properly recovered from her broken heart. One day she would return to Africa with her daughter to visit a lonely grave.

When I was almost ten I lived a story which was less exotic but much more terrifying.

In the week before it happened I heard my mother vomit. She was usually quiet but now she didn't speak at all. Her face was pale and angry. I heard her whisper urgently into the telephone.

'No. No. That isn't what I want. Don't be stupid. It's unthinkable.'

I came home from school and my mother was lying in her bed. She had never stayed home before. Her face was flushed, her eyes looked strange and she was shivering. She looked too small and frail to look after me.

I made toast for tea but my mother wouldn't eat any. In the night I heard her vomit and moan. In the morning there was blood on the floor beside the toilet bowl. My mother quietly told me I must go to school.

I sat all day with dread in my belly. What if she died? I had no-one, there was nobody else. They wouldn't let me live alone in our house, someone would come and take me to an orphanage, the kind where they were cruel to children. I wouldn't have my mother. She would be dead.

When I got home she was lying very still. Her eyes were closed and her face was yellow. There were stains and smell from blood and vomit. I was afraid to touch her. Dead people were cold to touch, I knew that. I ran down the stairs, my heart bursting and flung myself battering and shouting against the neighbour's door.

My mother. Oh please, my mother!

The neighbour ran up our stairs and called down to her husband, her voice shrill with alarm, *Hurry up, Bob, call the ambulance!*

I heard it coming. The alarm shrilling and the red light pulsing danger. I sat in front of our house on the top step with the concrete cutting into my knees, sobbing hopelessly as they carried my mother out on the stretcher. She was motionless, covered by a red blanket. They took her down the path and lifted her into the back of the ambulance.

I stood up and ran. Ran at the two men who carried my mother. Ran. Shouting, crying, *Is she dead, is she, is my mother dead? Don't let my mother die.*

Is there somebody here to look after the kiddie?

The neighbours took me in, wrapped me in a blanket and fed me sweet milky tea.

For the next week I lived with them. I was numbed by fear. They said I couldn't see her yet. I thought she was dead and they were keeping it from me. They told me she was getting better. I heard them whispering. When I came into a room they stopped.

Think she'd've learned.

One mistake too many if you ask me.

The way she brings up that kiddie.

Welfare. Could bring Welfare into it.

Died. Could've. Could've if we hadn't been... if it hadn't been for...

That poor kid.

Prosecuted, prosecuted if she's not lucky.

At the end of the week the neighbour brushed my hair, tied it into a ponytail, inspected my dress, shoes and socks and took me to the bus stop. We went to the Square then walked through the city to the hospital. Heavy swinging doors. An unfamiliar smell hit me. Disinfectant, sickness and fear. I began to shake. We went up in a lift. I was trembling. The neighbour said, *You getting upset's not going to help mum.* I knew then she wasn't dead.

We walked down the corridor. She was in a high steel bed in a row of women in similar beds. A tube taped to one of her hands was attached to a bottle which hung above her head. She held out her other hand to me and gripped my wrist tightly then closed her eyes. When she opened them again she told me in a slurred voice my grandmother was coming for me.

My grandmother?

My grandmother Evie came for me and took me away from the neighbours and cleaned our house and packed up my clothes into her old black suitcase.

She took me to the hospital to say goodbye to my mother. In all my life I saw them together only three times and each time was in a hospital. My mother held out her hand and touched my cheek with her fingers. She looked up at my grandmother.

'Remember, Mother. Zoe is my daughter.'

Evie came. She knelt down in front of me, placed her hands gently on my shoulders and looked into my face. She looked into my face knowing and loving me and I pressed against her sharp hard collarbone, nestled into her thin strong arms, closed my eyes and rested my body in against hers.

In my head I hear it. The sigh we both made, the long yearning animal sound of knowing and remembering. The sound of coming home and finding what was lost.

3

I sit at a booth close to the window, drink latté, fork pieces of quiche I don't much want into my mouth. In the booth opposite are two women. They lean towards the window, pointing to the dolphins. They have selected lemon sole. The taller woman has taken the vegetable option, the one in glasses has a finely chopped mound of coleslaw edged by a pool of mayonnaise at the side of her plate. They are in holiday mood with their wine and laden plates, their fast talk, gestures and laughter. Perhaps a brief Thelma-and-Louise escape from domesticity. Perhaps they are business colleagues. Perhaps lovers, though they don't brush together or gaze.

The man and woman to the side of me are not lovers, although they very well may be married since there are thick gold rings on their fingers. They gaze grimly about the room and rarely speak.

At one time when I was in the honeymoon period of marital separation and embroiled in one affair or another I'd have felt smug that I was not some sad woman manacled to a soulless man. I'd have felt buoyant and courageous in my own escape and release. But then I believed in the grand passions of opera and tragedy, all-encompassing love, the entwining of souls. While I awaited my destined lover's embrace I simply made do with whatever semi-attractive substitute fate threw my way.

I wonder what observers make of Tom and me. Sometimes we sit unspeaking, gazing idly about, though I'd like to think we appear neither blank nor grim. But I know now that grand passion doesn't translate too well into the paraphernalia of shopping lists, mowing lawns and getting the car fixed. I understand passion is more inclined towards obsession than love. If you can like each other very well most of the time and be kind, consistently, patiently kind, well, you can't ask for better.

I go up on deck when the sea begins to smooth, watch the hills in the distance and stand closer to the side of the ship as we begin to glide through the heads. The sea around the rocks where the *Wahine* went down is so calm today, so mild. I watch cabbage trees, scattered houses, narrow grey ribbons of road binding the hills, all sliding by. The sun shimmers, the water gleams, all is warmth and benevolence, everything the exact right temperature and shade.

Unlike the dank morning when Evie and I waited in our cabin for the ship to moor to the wharf. I felt the sea churn, heard the wind and observed Evie's face for signs of alarm. I'd never been on a boat before. Never left

Christchurch and our house and my mother.

After my mother told me my grandmother was coming for me I rode back with my neighbour in the bus, staring out through the window and sifting through this surprising information.

I had no experience of grandmothers, but I knew from reading about them and listening to the girls at school that they were very old and usually kind, although often opinionated, strict and old-fashioned in their expectations of manners and behaviour. I didn't know what my grandmother would look like but in my mind I saw a dumpy woman with faded hair and rosy cheeks and a face like a round withered apple. I put gloves — white and crochet-edged — on her plump wrinkled hands, then popped the kind of frothy hat usually seen in photos of the Queen Mother on her head. She would take me to the type of house which is neat, square and built out of symmetrical rows of red bricks. There would be cushions on the couches and antimacassars — I had read about those in a book and the name held great fascination for me — on the armchairs, and lace curtains festooning the windows. On the wall above the fireplace was a picture of a shipwreck in a heavy gilt frame. She would insist on cleanliness and fresh air and vegetables. She would bake gingerbread, own a cat named Bubbles and sleep in the afternoons.

I was surprised then, by the appearance of the tall, angular woman with burnt brown skin, silver-dark hair and almost black eyes who stood beside the neighbour's door. She looked attentively down at me, shook the neighbour's hand, listened politely — *poor wee mite, what she's been through, never even knew she had a grandma* — thanked her then walked beside me to my own house.

She waited silently while I found the key, unlocked and opened the door. The house was very cold, very silent and I thought it smelled of dirt and fear and disease. I stood in the hallway chilled and unsure. I looked up into Evie's face certain she would be appalled at the chaos and disappointed in me.

It was then that she knelt beside me.

'Zoe. Ah Zoe.'

She held my shoulders in firm, gentle hands and looked closely into my face and we stayed that way for some minutes scrutinising each other. Her face: the skin hardened by wind and sun, stretched across high, taut cheekbones, eyes like shining black buttons and her mouth with the thin, bow-shaped top, the fuller bottom lip. My rounder, softer face, my skin the same pale-coffee as my mother's, as Evie's but with my mother's blue eyes.

We stayed there looking, beginning the knowing and the understanding then drew fiercely against each other.

We did not say much during those two days before she took me away. She washed the sheets and slept in my mother's bed. She scrubbed the bathroom. She lit the fire. We ate fish and chips out of the paper wrapping, sprinkled with salt and vinegar. I showed her the books I'd been reading and she put on her glasses, looked at the titles, then smiled at me and stroked the covers with the tips of her fingers.

My mother touched my cheek with her hand. I said goodbye and then we were in red leather seats on the Lyttelton train with the smell of the city and smoke and soot filling our mouths. Then onto the ferry and down clanking iron stairs to a little cabin with bunk beds and a round window which looked directly over the sea. I knew from my books it was a porthole but not if it was entirely safe: it looked far too fragile to keep out the ocean. Evie assured me it would not break and that there was little chance of shipwrecks or hurricanes.

In Wellington the hills huddle, encircling the towering buildings and streets with their clutter of shops and cars. Everybody is so busy, so important in Wellington. I drink coffee in a café on Lambton Quay and listen to talk of property and business deals. I always feel a little tatty in Wellington, and somehow incomplete. I run into a shop to buy a jacket since I left my own behind and the sky looks ominous and I am pathetically relieved and grateful when the assistant compliments me on the cut of my shirt. I glance at other women on the street. Perhaps I should have my hair cut, exchange my flat boots for slim, tottering heels. Perhaps I should wear shorter skirts, tighter trousers, buy a snug waist-length jersey with a little zip inserted in the centre in one of the season's colours with lipstick to match. Plum. Or bronze. Maybe I'm letting myself go.

The hotel is smart, olive and cream. There's a small fountain, a pond with water-lilies and uniformed people hovering, anxious to direct and oblige. My room has the usual immense quilt-covered bed and television, phone, laden fridge and jug. The bathroom is complete with fluffy towels, small bottles of fruit-flavoured foams and salts and body lotions on a shelf above the spa-bath.

I listen to my call minder, ring the numbers and leave messages. I finish the article on my laptop and email it off. In this techno-age it is rarely necessary to meet anybody at all. A television, video, stereo, computer, email and cellphone cater for almost all requirements of communication and entertainment. You can switch them off should they prove tedious, rather than have to extricate yourself from some burdensome relationship. If they could somehow come up with a viable technological method of transmitting sexual pleasure you wouldn't ever have to leave home at all.

But I like my civilised comforts. I enjoy the scented, bubbling spa-bath, the clean-smelling sheets, the safe ordinary hum of the TV in the next room as I slip into sleep. Walls of muted textures and safe landscapes. Lamps and entertainment and warmth and good smells and things to eat and drink and a means of financing it, perhaps it's all I should expect.

In the morning we creak out of Wellington's dour station. I'm again settled in a sheepskin seat with a wide window outlook and the handy tray to accommodate the food and beverages from the hospitality carriage.

On that first morning Evie held my hand as we pushed against the wind sweeping into the harbour. She carried her voluminous handbag and the black suitcase. We took a taxi to the railway station and ate breakfast there, bacon and eggs, thick toast and butter and marmalade laid out before us on slabs of white china. Evie said to eat everything up, there was a long way to go.

Evie put her squashy black bag in the rack above us and we settled into the seats with the tiny window beside us. She gave me one of the pillows she'd hired for one-and-sixpence-each from the stall on the platform, tucked her own beneath her head and spread a blanket across our knees. I stared up at the emergency cord at the end of the carriage. *To be pulled in emergency only. Unwarranted members of the public interfering with the emergency cord will be liable for prosecution.*

Liable for prosecution.

I thought about my mother and what the neighbours said.

I asked Evie, 'What's prosecuted?'

'If you do something that's against the law you may very well be prosecuted. You have to go to court. You know what a court is?'

I thought about gowns and wigs, a judge with an angry face and a large wooden hammer.

'You go to court and it finds whether you're guilty of what you're accused of. If it says no you're free. If it decides yes you pay a fine or if it's very serious you go to prison.'

I wondered what my mother had possibly done that was so bad she could be prosecuted and if it had anything to do with me and if that was why my grandmother had to take me away.

My mother was going to prison and I had to be sent away.

I stared out the window. I imagined my mother with her gloved hands clutching prison bars, her little face peering through the gaps. I felt doomed. We were doomed, my mother and I. Orphans. Orphans and prisoners.

Prosecuted.

Prosecuted.

Prosecuted prisoner.

The train said it over and over, and I repeated it in my head.

Pros-e-cu-ted.

Pros-e-cu-ted.

Pros-e-cu-ted.

Pris-on-er.

Prosecuted. I stared out the window.

Evie touched the back of my head. I turned and she looked directly into my eyes. I knew she was reading me.

'What do you know about Wellington?'

'Wellington?'

'Yes. Wellington. What do you know about it? I don't suppose you've ever been here before.'

That was easy.

I recited. 'Wellington is the capital of New Zealand because it is the centre of the country. Parliament buildings are situated in the heart of the city which is one of the largest in New Zealand.'

Evie's mouth didn't smile but her eyes did. 'That's what you've been told, but what do you see?'

I didn't know what she meant. 'What do I see?'

'Yes, what do you see?'

I turned my head again towards the window and looked out but where before my gaze had been dull and glazed now it was sharp and I stared harder at the buildings, cars, hills.

'I see hills. Cars and buildings and streets, houses and hills.'

'What colour?'

'The hills? Green.'

'Only green? That's what you've been told. Hills are green. Look again, Zoe.'

It's Evie who taught me about colours. Evie who taught me to question and probe and see.

So I told her all the colours I discovered that morning, all the shades in the hills, sea and sky. Not just blue, yellow, red, but colours as exact as I could say them. I learned other ways of naming them like violet, jade, mauve, aquamarine, vermilion, amethyst, lavender and taupe.

'And what do you know about Parliament, and the Parliament Buildings?'

'It's where the government makes laws.'

She saw from my eyes I thought all that was boring.

'Where the government makes laws? Well, it certainly is that. But government and laws, Zoe? That sounds so dull. The government are people, and they make their laws for people, all of it's about people and their stories. It's not all formality and manners and tight faces, Zoe, it's passion as well.'

I didn't understand that word.

'What do you mean, passion?'

'Something felt very deeply. Feeling something so strongly you can't stop thinking about it and it takes you over. You feel it so deeply it becomes an obsession.'

I understood that. It was how I loved my mother.

'Love, you mean?'

'Love. Yes. Or anger. Or grief. Or loss. Or jealousy. Did you know, once somebody shot himself there, Zoe?'

I thought about the building we'd passed, so stately and grand, how could anyone dare do that there?

'Really?'

'Yes indeed.'

'Why? Who was it?'

'He was a Member of Parliament, William Larnach. He lived in a castle he'd built for himself way out on a wild peninsula near Dunedin. He'd been married three times. So he could marry his second wife, who was actually his first wife's sister, he had to have a law passed through Parliament. By the time he shot himself he was onto his third wife who was much much younger than he was and very pretty. There's a story that says that at the exact moment he shot himself the horses in his stable all those hundreds of miles away on the peninsula near Dunedin took fright and bolted.'

I thought about that. A far-away cracking shot. The horses that loved him, somehow sensing it. Screaming, wild-eyed, madly rearing up. I wanted it to be true.

'Do you believe that?'

'I do, Zoe.'

'Why did he shoot himself? If he was a Member of Parliament and owned a castle and his wife was pretty?'

'Because he'd lost them, Zoe. He'd lost his fortune and he'd lost his wife. She was in love with somebody else — with his own son, they say.'

This was shocking. I'd never heard a story like it. And this was truth. This was real people.

'His own son?'

'Mmm.'

'What happened to her?'

'Larnach's family ostracised her — do you know that word, Zoe? It means you're left out, nobody will talk to you, you're ignored and rejected. She was left with nothing. No children, no home, no money. Nothing. She came to live in Wellington in a house her brother bought for her. She lived quite alone there for the rest of her life.'

Ostracised. I loved that word. Was awed by it. Ran it around in my head and saved it.

'It was all her own fault. That she was ostracised.'

'Ah, Zoe, no. Not all her fault. She loved her husband but he didn't look after her, he neglected her, and that was wrong as well.'

And so the stories began and I was so caught up with the characters who peopled this Parliament, this place of unexpected intrigue and iniquity that the train wheels' refrain, *prisoner-prisoner/ prosecution-orphan* became lost among the stories of triumphs and failures, comedies and tragedies. Mackenzie with his flaming hair and booming voice. Richard Seddon, the so-called king from the wild west coast. Michael Joseph Savage. Mickey Savage, the one they said was the people's saint. And the women.

'Did you know, Zoe, that New Zealand women were the first in the world to get themselves the right to vote?'

'No.'

'Well, let me tell you about that then.'

The stories wound and sped with us around the rocky fringe of coastline, through light-sifting bush, across land so flat it seemed to roll from emerald into amber ridged with charcoal shading to the edge of an endless world, through black breathless tunnels.

Auckland was habitable then, the station not so frenetic, not so grubby and desperate. Evie took my hand and we collected the suitcase.

'Are we there?'

'No, Zoe, not yet. We're staying the night at your great-great-aunt Alice's house. I daresay your mother has told you about her? No? Oh well, then. Alice was married to my mother's, your great-grandmother's brother. She's a very old lady now.'

I'm propelled back into my present journey by the broadcasted voice telling us we're approaching our destination. It's almost night as we trundle and clack our way through Middlemore, Mount Eden. I watch the lights, the endless snakes of cars, the walls covered with graffiti and tags. The city hums and screams. I take my bag, walk past the green-tiled walls and the ticket offices and wait in the queue for a taxi.

4

Brian is waiting for me in the hotel foyer. As happens when I meet a man I once imagined I loved I'm surprised at the ordinariness of this previously flawless being.

I'm not at all fond of the name Brian, and in that lust-blurred world we shared before he became mortal I didn't believe it was at all worthy of him. The first time we went to bed and were lying dreamily, entwined in sweaty post-coital reverie I tentatively brought up the topic of his name by confiding my own interest in names and how they are acquired.

Brian looked surprised at all this. I suspect he had anticipated the usual after-play whispering of wasn't that wonderful/didn't you love that/you are so gorgeous and sexy stuff but he gamely joined in and told me his mother was a devout Catholic and had insisted on a saint's name. In fact both his names were after saints. His second name was Christopher. I rather liked Christopher. I felt it was vastly superior to Brian. I tried it out idly.

'Chris-to-pher. Chris.'

I was about to suggest a name change. Or at least that my own privileged position would allow me to call him Chris.

'Awful isn't it?' he said. 'Lucky the old man came up with Brian.'

I should have known then that my passion for somebody not only named Brian but who also called his father 'the old man' would not be eternal. I should have made a hasty retreat, but retreats were not my forte. I tended to hang on far too long, clinging to the old and seldom proved love-vanquishes-all philosophy, hoping that such minor details as failures of communication, wives, unpleasant habits, lack of common interests, or undesirable names would simply float away.

Brian is one of my few triumphs. We have stayed in touch, have made that difficult transition from lovers to friends. When I'm in Auckland we see each other. We dine together and speak amicably. He kisses my cheek when we meet. I pat his arm. We don't mention those hours spent in hotels groaning and panting and clinging to each other's wet, sticky body or sleepy soft moments, whispering I love you. Nor do we mention the slammed doors, raised voices, weeping and pain. And indeed, it's difficult for me, as I watch Brian's head bowed over the steak he always orders and always methodically cuts into small pieces, to imagine how it ever could have been so.

This evening, as we walk together out the door of the hotel, Brian explains that he has friends with him, business associates he had arranged to have dinner with before he knew I would be in town. He hopes I won't mind. He's sure I'll like them.

I'm ushered towards a group of people standing beside a large hired limousine. I meet Phil and Jackie, Terry and Sue. I want to invent a sudden debilitating illness, to hiss at Brian that if I'd known he already had an engagement I would've happily eaten alone. I want to slip back behind the hotel doors but as I say, the strategy of the hasty retreat is not a skill I manage well. I tell myself it won't be too bad, it may very well be fun, it's good for me to meet new people.

I smile and repeat the names, 'Hello. Phil, Jackie, Terry. Hello Sue.'

Brian says proudly that Zoe is a journalist. A writer. Maybe she'll write an article about us.

Sue says archly that it isn't going to turn into one of those kind of sordid nights, is it Brian?

Terry says, 'A writer, eh? What do you write?'

'Oh, magazine articles. Anything I can get, really.'

Brian says Zoe is far too modest, she's a very good writer. Well-known too. She's even published books.

I follow Phil and Jackie into the car.

When we are all arranged inside Brian glances cautiously at me and announces heartily that since Phil and Jackie are from out of Auckland and since it's their night out on the town we thought we might all pop into the casino first. Just for a look. I don't mind do I?

They all look at me.

'No, of course not.'

We lurch from traffic lights to traffic lights. Then we're speeding, sparring for a space, pounded by jagged lighting and revving engines and bellowing horns. The central city. Jesus. Everything's lit up. I'm pummelled by the tearing noise, the hammering light.

We walk across the carpark to queue for a lift. Sue explains it really is true, people come here on benefit day and leave their kids in the carpark and spend all their money on the machines. Sue is Auckland. Her dress is short and tight against her gym-trimmed, sun-bedded body. Her nails are the correct colour and shape for the season, her hair is blonde and her heels high. She is at her hospitable best. She points out and categorises the carving in the foyer as a beautiful piece of artwork. She waves at the painting on the wall above us and explains that this is Maui, kind of a Maori god, fishing up Ay-a-tee-a-row-ah.

But she's right. This carving is beautiful. The soft sheen of intricately patterned wood towers above us. Lithe, tricky Maui hooks his thrashing fish.

The rooms whizz with lights, buzz with sound. I stand overwhelmed by the crowds and noise. I avoid the spectacle of people attempting to make cheap easy cash whenever I can. Down aisles of people filling machines with money I find Brian at a table playing a card game. He knows the language, taps on the green felt to signal he wants another card.

'I'm going,' I say.

He looks up then motions with his hand his withdrawal from the game. He stands over me, frowning.

'You're going? Leaving?'

'Yes. I'm tired, Brian. I've got meetings in the morning. I have to be up early. I'll get a taxi. I'll be perfectly all right. Truly. Tell the others I had a headache or something.'

He looks upset. 'I knew this wouldn't be your thing but I couldn't get out of it. I'll find the others and we'll go to dinner.'

'No. I am tired. Really. I didn't realise how much until now. And I do have to work in the morning.'

He's gracious enough to kiss my cheek and send me back to the hotel in the limousine.

And I am tired. I've not enough patience this evening for Brian and Terry and Jackie and Phil and Sue. Or indeed myself in their company. I know, despite his affection for me, that with the combination of wine and male competitiveness Brian will not be able to avoid the temptation of subtly hinting at a previous torrid liaison with this clever writing woman beside him.

I know Jackie will effuse over the Auckland shops, be so impressed by Sue's glamour and sophistication that inwardly she'll be vowing to try that new diet, to take out that subscription for the gym. Sue will chatter in a seemingly knowledgeable way about wine and will hold up her glass towards the men and tip it idly to and fro when it's empty. She'll talk about restaurants, wine bars, shows she zoomed over to Sydney for, and ski holidays. I know that both Terry and Phil will goggle while she crosses one exposed thigh over another and will gaze at her cleavage — Phil out of prideful ownership and Terry out of speculation and envy.

I know I'd become silent, irritable and bored, pop in the odd sly, brittle barb — but smiling as I spoke, pretending what I said was meant to be amusing — I'm such a witty, clever, writing woman-of-the-world! I'd dislike them, feel superior, feel stern disapproval of my own petulance.

But the hotel room is too silent, too sterile. I turn up the TV, make coffee, have a splashing, too-hot shower. I leave the curtains open to the lights I should be out in, the people I should be grappling with.

Evie and her stories always are there. Mine always there. I should live here. Here and now. In this real, tangible, well-lit world of sound and people and easy money and cafés.

Instead, always this leaning back, my head tilted for those whispers from Evie's lost world.

I don't sleep well. I watch the light flicker, listen to the traffic and sirens. I should've played with money at the casino, drunk too much wine, laughed my way through dinner. Should've invited Brian in to drink, to slur secrets and profundities into the morning. I shouldn't have been alone.

But next day I'm pleased by my restraint since I am attentive and creative at my meetings. Then, when I'm at last free I take a taxi over to Ponsonby.

I ask the driver to stop at the corner by the service station. Across the road is a supermarket and wine shop where the corner grocery and the draper used to be. I used to buy half a loaf and, as I walked back to Evie and Aunt Alice, tear the soft white bread from around the crust and cram it into my mouth. I remember choosing buttons, cool and smooth like tiny round stones for the shoulder of the jersey Alice knitted for me.

The street is very much as it was despite the villas that have been replaced with blocks of town-houses with gaping, tinted windows. Lawns and wrought-iron fences, trees edging the footpath. Everything is much smarter, of course. The area is now desirable, properties have been renovated and restored — meticulously presented, the real estate ads say. There are acres of paving and bark chips, double garages, tasteful additions.

I'm almost afraid when I see Number 39 on the fence ahead of me. I force myself to walk on, then stop.

I am flooded with relief and sadness.

The garden is tidied, the roses gone, lawns clipped and contained by a new paved driveway and path. But there is still the walnut with its gigantic trunk and thick, wide branches. We hung a swing from it, Alice, Evie and I. Evie climbed up the ladder — *Glory be, Evie, whatever you do, don't fall* — and tied the rope to the branches with her strong hands. Those hands you always could trust.

It was my idea and it meant an excursion for a plank of wood — it must be strong and safe, Evie said — and rope. The man who helped us find the correct makings drilled holes in the wood for the rope to loop through.

Then we took our treasures back to Alice's and assembled my swing. It was the first thing I looked for when we stayed here on the way home. I never tired of it. Swinging up into the branches looking over the fences and the garden. Evie and Alice drank their tea in the sunroom and watched me from the window.

The weatherboards are painted that same singing white and, oh God, the door and window frames are still grey — darker, but still grey. There are cane chairs and faded cushions on the verandah and if it weren't for the wind-chimes and the new brass locks on the door and all those paving stones and that barbecue, I could be a child again getting out of the taxi with Evie, looking through the gate up into the house with the wrought-iron fretwork edging the top of that wide verandah right along the front then swinging around to the side. I could be that small girl walking up the path hanging on to the hand of my newly-found grandmother about to meet my great-great-aunt who would open the door and stand in the shadows of the hall for a moment looking down at me with her pale eyes. 'Ah, the child. Gracie's girl. Well, let's have a look at you.'

Gracie's girl.

She peered into my face and announced I wasn't much like my mother. Perhaps like Hannah around the mouth. Maybe Eliza's hair. But she favours you, Evie. Your skin, your bones. She definitely favours you.

And so I found my family. I was Gracie's girl. I had Evie and Alice. Hannah and Eliza as well.

I lean against the fence. Alice's house. Her garden and her tree. Alice's old face, framed in a puff of thick white hair watching for us from the window. The tap of her walking-stick on the verandah.

My eyes sting with tears.

That first time I stayed Alice showed me her music box, the one that played "Annie Laurie." We'd learned it at school and so I sang it. I had a clear, sweet child's voice and I was proud of my ability to hit the high notes and sing in tune. I liked to hear my voice rise and hover and I sang Annie Laurie as well as I could to the tinkling accompaniment of Alice's music box. When I'd lingered over the last words, *And for bonnie Annie Laurie, I'd lay me doon and dee,* I grinned and looked at Evie and Alice for their approval. I saw tears in their eyes.

I walk to the shopping centre, have a cappucino then taxi back to the hotel. The room seems less empty this evening. I shower and sit close to the window looking out over the lights, fall into sleep thinking of Evie.

She tucks the sheets around me. I'm to sleep in a high bed with slatted wooden ends and a yellow cotton cover in a bedroom with a door opening into the back garden. I'm in my Aunt Alice's house.

Evie says we will stay another day.

'And then we'll go home, Zoe.'

'Where will we go? Is it a long way?'

'Not too far now. But almost one more day's travelling.'

'Where is it? What kind of house do you live in?'

'Tomorrow I'll show you on the map. You'll see what kind of house it is when we get there and then it will be more of a surprise. It's the house your mother lived in until she grew up and the house your great-grandmother Hannah lived in and for a short while her mother, Eliza. It's the house where I've lived all my life.'

Now I must make that journey alone. But not to Evie's house. Not yet.

I'm at the bus station early. The bus is faded and slightly battered. There aren't many of us on board. Holidays in the far north are not so popular at this time of year. We're on the winter timetable.

When Evie and I made this journey there were long stretches of bush and the road became isolated, edged for miles by cabbage trees and toe-toe. Now we speed through one town after another and the early sunlight bounces off the roofs of the surrounding cars. Every now and then I glimpse scatterings of white crosses beside the road.

Orewa, Waiwera, Warkworth, Wellsford. Kaiwaka. I change to another, more dishevelled bus at Brynderwyn, ask the driver what time we should arrive and he winks at me.

'Some time between two and three. We're on Hokianga time now.'

I eat lunch sitting outside a bakery on a white plastic chair at a white plastic table in Dargaville. The sun is on my face. No cellphones, no cappuccino. My body is looser. I breathe more easily.

I sit in the front and in the end there's only me and the driver and a young man with a pack, sleeping stretched out on the back seat.

'Been up here before?'

'Not for years,' I say.

'Always feel better when I'm up this way. Always wanted to be up here, felt drawn back, always wanting to be back. Hard to explain. Then I found out my family came from up here. I never knew. Funny, eh?'

I say it's the same for me. My family, too, came from here. I felt drawn here, it's why I've come back.

He glances back at me and is silent. I feel awkward, as if I've revealed too much of myself, as if I have been presumptuous. He is Maori. I'm obviously European. Perhaps he doubts what I've said, believing the bonds of family which claim him, drawing him back to this place could not be the same for me. Perhaps my claims are insignificant compared to his. He is tangata whenua. My people are the intruders, usurpers, bringers of the plagues — missionaries and measles. But if I have no claims here, to this earth, this sky, this ocean well then I am placeless, homeless.

He glances back again, grins and repeats, 'Funny eh? Did you know Hokianga means the returning place?'

'Yes.'

'Hokianga. The returning place. It's where Kupe left to go back to Hawaiki.'

We climb through bush, come to the top of the hill and then the slow, creaking, spiral down.

And here at last outspread is this wash of gleaming ocean with the hills starkly rising on both sides, one bright gold, the other covered by dark bush and sparsely dotted with houses.

Hokianga.

5

Hokianga. The returning place.
'At the first glimpse of those heads from the sea, one is white, the other black.'

I stand on the beach looking across at the contrast of light and shade and think of Augustus Earle's description, made as they sailed across the bar into the harbour, as he first caught sight of this land.

This is not only the returning place but a place of beginning since this is where Kupe, our first settler landed. There at the entrance to this vast harbour are the South and North Heads, Kupe's mokaikai, his pets, the taniwha, Araiteuru and Niua, left behind to protect this place for him and to guide other travellers in. There across the water are the ridged slabs of rock forming a dark verge between sea and land. When Kupe landed here he sent his slaves across the hills for these rocks so that mussels would grow on them and be harvested by his people. Here in Hokianga, Kupe left his footmarks on the coast near to the Heads, the bailer of his canoe at Kohukohu, the anchor near to the narrows at Rangiora, his canoe at Rangi Point, the resting place, where it was dragged into a secret stone cave. Here he left his child, Tuputupuwhenua.

These are the stories.

And I am overcome by this storehouse of myth and beauty. By the resplendent sea, brazen in its cloak of sapphire, sad grey-blue and shadings of dark and pale jade. By the sun-slashed sky, by the soar of cloud at the far end of the harbour. By the sandhills, those vast stretches of tawdry copper with their shaded pockets of cinnamon and taupe.

In the evening the sea is slate, the sandhills almond. I watch a woman with a plait down her back fishing from the jetty and listen to the sea slap against the sand. I feel the wind coming in from the harbour soft on my face, smell the salt and taste it in my mouth.

'Aunty. I'm goin' in the pub, Aunty.'

He is standing beside the shop, calling at the door.

She comes outside and stands over him.

'You 'lowed?'

'Cos I've been in there before, Aunty.'

I watch him run across the carpark, push in through the doors.

It's all that is left here now: the store, the pub, the school, the sea, sky and hills, the people and the stories.

At one time there could be thirty sailing ships in the harbour coming in over the bar from the ocean. They came for whale-oil, for loads of timber. Sailed up mangrove-fringed rivers, with the rise of bush so thick on either side the sun could scarcely pierce through. And then, when the kauri was gone they burned the land, blazing away the bush so that the ridges were exposed like bones, the soil burnt the colour of dried blood. This is a place of fortune and misfortune, beauty and grandeur and ugliness and loss. Across the harbour, buried in the sandhills are the bones of the ancestors, scattered in the hills are the ruins of houses and churches, forgotten settlements. The land has been fought and cheated for, burned and pillaged and abandoned. The settlers' vision was the potential wealth to be mined from the land and the sea. The missionaries' concern was with the mining of souls.

I watch the sky streak pink scarlet and yellow. Listen to the silence, the slapping of the waves. See the creeping dark, wonder at the anguish over land and souls, gardens built then abandoned. The births, battles and death.

Now there's a battle over at the pub. They spill out, shouting from the bar and huddle closely at the top of the steps underneath the lights. I see three men scuffle, trying to hold somebody. A woman is screaming.

'Bloody wanker.'

'Leave him alone. Bastards. Fucking leave him alone.'

It all comes to nothing. The held man is shoved down the steps and the others yell at him to piss off, just piss off home. He stands, swaying at the bottom of the steps, moves forward to go back in, thinks better of it then turns and walks down towards the sea, slumps there on a bench.

A woman comes from the pub. She stands beside him.

'I told you. Told you to leave it.'

His head is bent and ashamed.

'I told you. I told you. Stupid bastard.'

He is silent and she stands over him watching.

'What're you doing?'

He looks up at her, 'Just sitting here. Just watching the harbour.'

She stares down, then sits beside him. Her body is upright, removed from his. They are both silent, watching. He takes her hand.

I also watch this stretch of sea. I think of Eliza, five months on ship then journeying, seven months pregnant, through mud and scrub and bush. To save souls.

I think of my own life of desires and loves and losses, of nurturing and neglect.

I have done those things I ought not to have done and left undone those things I ought to have done.
And there is no health in me.

It is a sentiment which fascinated me during my brief sojourn into the premises of Sunday School and the church. I liked to say it, that pleasingly resonant assonance of the not, ought and done. I liked the complicated syntax, liked the idea of myself pleading for mercy, eyes closed, hands devoutly clasped. The small sinner in the beribboned sailor hat.

But the words return to me. The things I have done. The things I have not done.

And there is no health in me.

I'm preoccupied by waste. By the waste of discarded aspirations, forgotten desires, loves. Lost gardens and lost battles. I try to comfort myself with the idea that it's the living of it, the doing, that is most important, but still it's the end product I find myself most concerned with. What am I? Where do I belong? What have I achieved?

Still, I sleep with the mutter of sea beneath my window. Sleep held, warmed and enclosed by Eliza's hills, rocked, lulled by her ocean.

I am the only guest at breakfast. As I eat, the woman who manages the hotel asks if I've been disturbed by noise from the bar.

'No, it's not too bad,' I say.

'It might be bad tonight,' she warns, 'It's Thursday. Benefit day. They come to celebrate. It gets pretty rowdy. We could move you to one of the units around the back if you like.'

But I like my room at the front of the hotel, close to the road and looking out to the sea. The night sounds, sea sounds, the birds.

'No. It'll be okay. If it gets too bad I'll just turn up the TV.'

She looks doubtful, 'Don't say I didn't warn you. You look a bit, uh, refined for the kind of row we have on Thursday night. On holiday are you?'

'Yes. And a bit of research as well.'

She's worried, 'You going to write something about staying here? About the hotel?'

'No. My family came from around here. I just wanted to come back. Find out what I could.'

She looks relieved, 'There's the information place just down the road. They've got quite a lot about the history of the place.' She laughs, 'Thought you might be writing about us. Or about all those marijuana plantations we've got hidden around here.'

'I've heard about those,' I say. 'Is it true people are making their fortunes up here?'

'If they are I haven't heard about them. Seen anyone around here who looks like they might've got a fortune stashed away?'

I think of the rusted cars, the old motorbikes filling the carpark, the modest little houses and shacks lining the road and I shake my head and laugh with her.

'Oh it's there,' she said. 'It's there all right. But nobody from around here makes anything out of it. Nobody I know. They might sell a bit but mostly they just smoke it. I won't let them have it here, though. I warned someone just last week. He was sitting out in the beer garden smoking it and I warned him but the silly bugger wouldn't listen to me so I threw a bucket of water over him.'

She is small, Pakeha. I'm amazed by her daring. The men I've seen around the pub are huge, tattooed, dressed in leather.

'My God, weren't you afraid of starting a riot?'

'Nuh. They respect us. Have to. Nothing worse around here than being banned from the pub. And if there's any trouble the locals support us.'

It's hot again. I take a book and walk along the beach, lie on a stretch of sand and feel it heating my bare arms and legs. I stretch out on my stomach, digging with my toes into the sand, resting my head on my hands and close my eyes.

I came here once with Evie, in a bus jolting endlessly, it seemed to me, over narrow gravel roads. It was hot and the dust rose in clouds from the wheels, filling my mouth. Evie had to ask the driver to stop so I could be sick in the ditch.

We stayed at the old hotel. The imposing old wooden one with the balconies and verandahs that burned down.

Every day we went down to the beach. Evie would spread out a blanket near the edge of the water in the shade of the pines. She sat there reading while I swam and built sandcastles. Most days she came swimming with me — *A dip in the tide* she called it. She wore an old knitted black bathing suit. When it was wet it sagged over her bony shoulders and ribs, around her straight skinny hips. She swam silently and methodically, arms perfectly curved and legs straight, the way she taught me. When she'd swum out to the buoy and back she would turn over and lie motionless with her eyes closed, her hair billowing around her head. I would swim and dive and burrow around her.

My skin burned pink, then a deep dusky brown. My hair was ribboned with bleached stripes from the sun and salt. I lay outstretched on hot sand listening to the sea, watching the clouds. Evie told me about the dolphin, about how he played with the children on the beach, took them for rides on his back. About the crowds of people who came to see him, about how this had only once happened before in Greece and how both dolphins had died.

I looked out into the sea, hoping for a dancing fin, hoping for another miraculous dolphin I could befriend and protect.

I believed in miracles then.

Evie brought me here so I could see where Eliza lived. Where she gave birth to Hannah. I thought it a wondrous place. I considered Eliza fortunate, thought her life to be grand, adventurous and enchanting.

And now I'm here again and so caught up in the beauty of this place I am inclined, still, to overlook Eliza's loneliness, primitive conditions and yearning for home.

When William first arrived in the Hokianga he was ardent to deliver his Message of Good News to the spiritually impoverished. He carefully and eloquently explained the method of the world's creation to his first congregation who listened with quiet patience. When he had finished there was silence for some time until it was politely explained to him that he was incorrect, that in fact Maui had hauled the land on which they were standing from the ocean.

Although I smile at this it also reminds me that myth and reality intermingle, that people set out on crusades in the name of a truth with a hollow centre and that stories are not always to be trusted. I think of the stories I write and how truth can become blurred and stretched and moulded into a preferred fiction. I think about the stories I've lived and believed in.

When I was eighteen I met and lost the love of my life.

That's what I told myself, that's the myth I lived.

The love of my life was dark and tall, just like in the books. His eyes were bright and brown and his hair curled at the back of his neck. His smile was as endearing as his curling hair. When he slowly smiled his lips remained firmly pressed together and crinkles appeared in his cheeks. His walk was a sexy, arrogant strut.

The love of my life was also intelligent, witty, successful and a more than adequate lover.

Or so I believed.

I also believed I was fortunate to have him and accommodated his every whim. Well, every whim I was able to accommodate.

I giggled and dieted and orgasmed — or at least made a good pretence at it. I was romantic, playful, serious, sincere, responsive, sympathetic and empathetic. I consulted endless magazines, the kind that tell you ten tips to drive a man wild and make him yours forever, how you can tell if your man has a roving eye and what you can do to stop it.

I was as beautiful as I could manage. But not beautiful enough since this love of my life left me one night and never returned.

I thought I might've been pregnant.

For years I blamed myself. I'd not been thin enough, pretty enough, exciting enough to hold him. I'd said and done all the wrong things — *I have done those things I ought not to have done and left undone those things I ought…*

How could I have so burdened him with the news that I thought I'd got myself pregnant?

And there is no health in me.

Years later I experienced the event I had yearned for. Quite unexpectedly, I ran into the love of my life at an airport. We gazed at each other. He kissed my cheek, *Zoe*. He was as tall as I'd remembered, his skin still dark, although a faintly orange tinge suggested sunbeds. His smile was as beguiling as ever. His hair, intact, still curled.

Moreover, he had long mourned the error of his ways. I was, in retrospect, also the love of his life. He had thought of me with affectionate lust over the years. He shook his head ruefully, crinkled his eyes down at me.

I was redeemed. I was not merely a body and a giggle.

And he was divorced. As I was. In the present social climate discovering another divorced person when you are similarly disengaged is propitious.

There were long gazes over dinners in candlelit and moonlit restaurants, phonecalls stretching through the night, longing letters, an abundance of flowers.

Except I'd become less accommodating, more cautious. His strut was a pose and his smile a construction. Furthermore he glanced into mirrors and windows, listed the things he owned, the countries he'd visited, the personages he'd met. He had right-wing opinions and Glen Campbell CDs. I stopped gazing and began to yawn. I went away one night and never returned.

While I can grin, albeit ruefully, and shrug it away as one of life's sad little experiences, I cannot forget that for years I longed for him. I imagined as I lay beside my sleeping husband, beside other lovers, that I would meet him at a bus stop, restaurant, airport. He would confess his undying love and whisk me away.

I lived a story with a hollow centre.

And I wonder sitting here on this beach watching the glory of this always-changing ocean if it's better never to know. To never see and know there's hollowness and rot at the centre of a truth. I wonder if Eliza ever questioned the truth so central to her life.

My truth is my duty to my God and to my dear husband.

Oh Eliza, if you believed it, then I envy you. And pity you as well.

I watch the ocean out beyond the bar. No dolphins today.

6

Noise from the bar pulsates through the night. They have a band every Thursday. The regularity of the bass thrum mingles with the rasp and squeak of the microphone, the singing, shouting voices. Cars rev in the carpark, braking and hurtling onto the road and out into the night. I think about the small white crosses I've seen on the roadside. About the one I stopped beside yesterday, a woven headband strung around the top, wristlets and beads hanging from the arms.

No fights tonight. Just the singing. I try to read but the words swim in front of me. I lie on the bed listening until the last songs, the last few voices call from the carpark.

In the morning I ask the manager if there is anyone who does boat tours. I want to go up the harbour to where the mission station was.

'Yeah, probably Dave'd take you. Dave does tours.'

'Do you know what time he leaves?'

'Depends when you want to go.'

I think about the rigidity of timetabled tours elsewhere. Hokianga time.

'How do I find him? Can I phone?'

'Don't think he'd be home. Just look out for him. He'll be around. He's got that red boat, *Hokianga Experiences* on the side.'

I sit on the deck outside my room and eventually a red boat ambles alongside the jetty. A small, wiry man climbs out and walks across to the hotel, carrying a plastic bag.

'Are you Dave?'

He grins up at me. 'Yep.'

'Are you doing any boat trips today?'

'Depends who's around.'

'I want to go to the old mission station up the harbour. Do you know where that is? Would you take me?'

'Yeah I know where it is.' He squints out at the sea. 'Might get rough later on. Could be all right though.'

'When could you take me?'

He holds up the bag. 'Got these to unload here first. Mussels. Want some?'

I shake my head.

He looks down at his watch then looks again out at the sea.

'I'll drop these off and get some coffee. Say around eleven. Half past?'

'Could you leave me at the mission for a while?'

'Yeah. Leave you there and do some fishing. Come back for you if it comes up rough.'

'How much?'

He shrugs and his eyes run over me, no doubt assessing my potential wealth.

'Twenty, thirty dollars? Depends how long we're away. How far you want to go. You want to go anywhere else? Want to have a look around?'

'Yes. All right. I'd like that.'

'Historical tour. Thirty dollars then.'

I find him on the jetty beside his boat around twelve. He says they gave him a feed at the pub, then he had a couple of fellas to see. We climb down into the boat and he starts up the engine. I ask him about a life jacket. He grins as if I'm being unnecessarily awkward and pulls one from under the seat.

'Okay?'

'Yes.'

'We're away then.'

There is the rev and roar of the engine, the sea is choppy and a harsh wind beats against my face.

'How long have you lived here?' I shout.

'All my life. Grew up here. Been away though. Lived all around. Stewart Island. The West Coast. Auckland. Always come back.'

'Can you tell me what you know? Anything. Anything about the places we see. Any history? '

He slows the boat and we chug across to the place where Kupe landed. He voyaged here from Hawaiki, encountered the perils of sea demons on the voyage and on discovering Maui's fish not quite killed, navigated around, gradually killing it as they sailed. We stop and he points to the dark shelf of rock where Kupe ordered mussels to be cultivated. He points up at the sandhills and says Kupe ordered beacons to be kept alight there but the fires got out of control and burnt away the bush. He points towards the hills and tells me it's where Nuku lived. Nuku was told of this place by Kupe and made use of his canoe to emigrate here. And over there is where he drowned, having been swept into the whirlpool, Pipiraueru, here in the harbour.

'This is where Nuku's daughter, in danger from a storm conjured up by her brother and sister as she travelled by canoe from Kaipara to Hokianga, offered up a powerful incantation. Having stilled the raging sea and wind, she chanted the pihe for her dead father. This place is where the bones of the first migrants, the ancestors, are buried and still discovered up there in the sandhills.'

He points out the pa sites. We head out towards the bar and stop beneath a cliff. There was a pa up there, he tells me and when it was attacked and defeat inevitable, the people threw things which were precious and sacred into the sea to save them from being taken by the enemy. It must be true, he says, because a few years ago there were divers around there. One of them found something wedged behind rock, a large greenstone carving. When he began to bring it up to the surface his breathing apparatus blocked. The sea which had been mild and calm turned rough.

'Dark down there, water thick as green ink. You have to watch out. Watch you don't get wedged between rocks. Watch for tides too because it can turn rough. You're in the dark scrabbling in the ledges of rocks, finding something, holding on to it and suddenly you can't breathe. You start to gasp and choke, your head feels like it's going to burst. You're going to die down here in the dark.

'He tried to swim to the surface but he was a long way down and without air he was too weak. He became disoriented. He let go of the carving gripped in his hand and began to breathe again.'

These are the stories.

There are the modern-day tales as well. The booze cruises around the harbour and up the rivers. The Italian tourist who lost her bikini top when she was water skiing off the back of the boat and the British tourists sitting down the back didn't know where to look. The Auckland yuppies who take over the place in summer. And over there in the trees is the mansion where the American millionaire lives for two weeks in the summer. Over there is where that famous film star is thinking about building. Maybe he'll make a film here. Over there is where someone rich from Hong Kong might be building a multi-million dollar holiday resort. Land prices are going to rise. Auckland people are going to start building holiday homes here. This place is gonna boom.

And all the churches dotted around above us. Most of them way at the top of the hills. All similarly small and weatherboarded. High-pitched roofs, porchways, topped by steeples, marked with crosses.

The Anglicans and the Presbyterians and the Catholics and the Methodists. All with their missions and messages. The One True Way To God.

The waves are high, the boat lurches and falls and the wind feels sharper. I look at a mass of cloud clinging closely to the hills.

'Is it going to get rough?'
He looks up and then out to the neck of the harbour.
'Clear sky over there. Should be right.'
He turns the boat and we head towards a jetty.
'Here it is. How long do you want to stay?'
'An hour. Two?'
He looks at me quizzically. 'Right. Be back in about an hour or so.'
'Don't forget about me, will you?'
I am nervous about his looseness, casualness. It's a long walk back to the hotel.
'Never lost anyone yet. Always a first time though.'
I climb up onto the jetty, walk along the water's edge and then up through long grass and patches of boggy dirt to a wire and paling fence and sagging wooden gate.
I push the gate until there is enough room to squeeze through then stand beside the fence looking up.
Above me on the rise is a little wooden church with a high grey roof, a curved doorway leading into the porch and three plain rectangular windows on each side. Further up is a white-painted cottage. The door is set exactly centre with small-paned windows on either side. Two dormers jut out of the roof which extends beyond the walls providing shelter for the verandah along the front.

Eliza was set down from the canopied box supported on poles, directly across from where I am now standing, on the other side of the harbour. She and William were met by another missionary from the station and paddled across in a canoe. The plain wooden chest filled with the linen and china carefully chosen from Home, was carried behind her. She walked up through the mud and flax, gathering up her long skirts in her hands, feeling the child lurch within her, to the little rush house. There was a washing tub set up beside it, a camp oven, underneath which she would daily build fires to bake her bread. The church was already built but the construction of the cottage, the substantial and commodious dwelling was not yet considered a priority. Self-denial and physical hardship were the stuff, the virtue of missionary life.
Whom the Lord loveth he chasteneth.
Eliza waited at the door of her new home while the chest was placed in the room. She stood motionless at the entrance until her eyes were accustomed to the darkness. The room was tiny with drab walls and a mud

floor. On one side was a bare table with two chairs. On the other, a black iron bedstead with a cabinet beside it on which she could place her Bible and her diary. There was a quilt covering the bed, a soft quilt and two pillows encased in embroidered pillow slips. Jane, the other missionary's wife she would come to know and love, had left them there. The quilt, the pillows and a glass jar filled with ferns on the washstand. Eliza went to the bed and stroked the quilt and the pillows with the tips of her fingers.

I am rather poorly in my health after the voyage yet I am grateful for the attentions and kindness shown to me in my new home. I do not think I was ever more happy in my mind.

I walk up the hill to the church. Close beside is a plaque describing the origins of the Mission, which is preserved by the Historic Places Trust. The door is locked of course, but I find fenceposts to stack high enough against the wall so I can pull myself up to peer through a window.

It is plain and sparse inside, the walls varnished timber. A high, arched central window is at the front.

It is where William stood with the sun against the back of his head, lighting up his hair like a hazy halo and the church was filled with his powerful voice. His voice rose, rose higher, warning of the wickedness of drunkenness, immodesty, stealing, violence and the penalties for such ungodliness; hellfire, the removal from God's grace. Then softened as he described the advantages of righteousness. God's forgiveness, His love, eternal life in the honeyed, sunny world of Paradise.

William standing there tall and upright, lit by the light from the window, lit by truth, his voice passionate and thundering, filling his church, filling the ears of his *congregation of poor heathens, so lately savage, now singing the praises of our One True Saviour.*

The congregation whose regular attendance and conversions, so ardently prayed for by the mission, were perhaps prompted not so much by promises of redemption and eternal life but by those more tangible, visually pleasing goodies — shiny beads and spades, the sharp axes and warm, soft blankets.

There was more than belief in doctrine that filled the chapel.

Ah yes, truth.

But I rest against the church, touch the walls with reverence, lay the palm of my hand against the ancient weathered timber and think of William in his black suit gripping his Bible in his hand. And Eliza with her sweet, too-young face and the two little boys pressed to the sides of her Sunday silk dress.

On Saturdays Eliza worked doubly hard since she had to prepare the food and clothing and tend to the domestic arrangements for the forthcoming Sunday. Nothing was to be done on the Sabbath except go to church and attend to Devotional Work.

William strides out on his Sunday walk. He must rid his head of those matters pertaining to anything other than the contemplation of his saviour and his mission to save souls. He observes all around him souls needful of saving. And English souls, which should know better, at that.

I am ashamed to find you at work on a Sunday.
Well, damn my eyes if I knew it was a Sunday.
Now, to make matters worse, you are blaspheming.

I pat the walls, then walk up the rise to the cottage. Eliza's cottage she waited years for, watched being laboriously built. The kauri was felled, sawn by hand, the central fireplaces built from bricks they waited months for, shipped from Sydney with iron for the roof.

The cottage is snug against the ridge yet has had an unsettled history. It's been cut in half and sent away, reassembled to serve as a parsonage in Auckland, sold and hauled by steam-engine up Queen Street to another suburb. Finally it has returned to sit again on this hillside. To settle into the silent tranquillity of this place and watch the Hokianga.

On Eliza's verandah I turn and look as she did over the harbour and hills. The sweep of pale and shadowed sea, rock, coastline etched against the blue then rising to a bank of dark hills shadow-pocketed. All that and the sky. The glitter of sun through a mass of low-hung cloud.

I do not think I was ever more happy in my mind.

The parlour faces out onto the verandah and there's an ample bedroom on the other side of the central door. Behind the parlour is the dining room, the kitchen and the scullery and to the side, two cramped bedrooms. This is where Eliza placed her china, the wedding gift from her parents in England, on the kauri dresser, where she spread the sheets she had hemmed and embroidered on the bedsteads, where she prepared food for her husband and sons and the frequent visitors to the Mission.

It's where she played with her little boys, watched them from her window, where she waited for her husband to return from his visits to other missions. Where she removed her china and linen from the shelves, placed them in a plain wooden box, took her sons' hands firmly in her own and walked through the door, down the verandah steps, leaving home.

He was a great preacher but his weakness was native women.

Eliza takes the blue-and-white patterned teapot from the dresser and rubs her finger across the smooth delicacy of finest china. Her mother gave it to her. It was her own. Her mother stood beside the polished mahogany table which was in front of the window which looked out over lush green lawns and roses. She took up the teapot and a silk cloth and rubbed it hard, held it up to the light, scrutinising it for dust or damage and then held it out to her daughter.

Eliza holds the teapot in her hands and looks through the window to the sea. She thinks of William's long fingers, his long-boned, thin pale body. She thinks of supple, brown flesh. She thinks of her husband's hands coiled and gripped in coarse black hair.

She wraps the teapot in a shawl then carefully places it in her box.

I walk to the back of the house and up the hill. Despite his removal from office William continued to live in the Hokianga, insisting on both his innocence and right to preach, his right to share his wealth, the Message of Good News. And to mill the wealth of kauri which surrounded him.

He and Eliza and their sons moved to land at the top of the hill overlooking the mission. Eliza continued to tend the garden she had built. She took her cuttings and her seeds further up the hill and began another.

The garden which, even now, I discover remnants of.

Rotted stumps, fruit trees with stunted grey branches, kotukutuku clumped in long grass. I find a fragment of lavender, crush the leaves in my finger and smell its pungency. At the centre is a fig tree bent so far over that its branches touch the earth.

Mother cared for a large orchard with a beautiful old fig tree. In one place peach trees grew wild and we went out riding to reach the fruit down from horse-back.

When the land wars broke out the mission closed but William and Eliza and their sons remained. Jane and the other women from the mission left. Eliza longed for the company of women, longed for a daughter.

I walk back down the hill watching the Hokianga.

To the side of the church is the cemetery. In the centre a willow tree has grown so huge that roots have burst through the adjoining graves and stones. I pick my way through the scrub reading names Evie told me, finding broken stones, stones so old and weathered the names have become illegible.

I was confined with a little girl whose feeble voice uttered a plaintive cry, and was silent in death. This stroke seemed for a moment more than my nature could bear.

By the time Eliza held her daughter in her arms she was forty. She had given birth to six previous children, two daughters and four sons. Two sons survived. She called this last daughter Hannah for William's mother, Evangeline for her own, Mary for the mother of Christ and Elizabeth for herself. With so many mothers as namesakes and spiritual guardians, she reasoned, this child must survive.

Hannah Evangeline Mary Elizabeth. Her seventh child. Her own daughter.

I must pray to be saved from idolising this child. I have had many warnings but my treacherous heart still cleaves to the earth. My daughter occupies much of my time and attention.

Eliza takes the child up into her arms. The night is hot and the child is restless and whimpering, her cheeks flushed, feverish with her first teeth coming. She carries her, rocking, crooning, out into the cool air and stands looking up into the night.

She hears the murmur of the sea. Above her the sky is blue-black and the stars ten thousand pinpoints of silver. The pale band of the Milky Way criss-crosses the night. She rocks her daughter in her arms, murmuring, softly singing.

I hear the boat, then see it approach from across the harbour. I walk down to meet it. Dave holds up a bag filled with fish and grins.

'Find what you wanted?'

I nod.

My face burns as we drive against the wind on our journey back.

7

I sit on the deck outside my room watching the sky change. It's pink then violet. Settles finally for the colour of ripe plums.

Below the sea shifts and changes, troughs of pearl and lead. The darkness and the light.

Eliza grieved for her four dead children and unfaithful husband. She was separated from her family, shamed and banished from her house.

Then in the middle of her life, when all seemed bleak, she was blessed by the birth of the daughter she longed for. As a double blessing this daughter was bright and sweet-natured. Her body was graceful, her feet and hands delicate, her hair pale. But it was her eyes you noticed most. They were like sea lit by sun.

This is what Evie told me as we sat on the upstairs balcony of the old hotel.

I watch the huddle and sweep of hills and think about the burning off so they were bare, blackened and ruined. Gradually the bush returned. Small patches, shallow tinges appeared then turned into deep green pockets which grew and spread giving life and flesh to the charred bones of the land.

When Eliza knew she was pregnant again she was afraid, because of her age and because the women from the mission station who depended on each other to act as midwives had left.

When her time came William asked for the women skilled in birthing to come from the nearby pa. Eliza lay on her back in the iron bed covered by a linen sheet. The baby was slow in coming and the pain and fear hard to contain but she did not cry out.

The women took her from the bed and removed the nightgown from her drenched, feverish body. They stroked her hair and her head, soothed and murmured, massaged her back and belly with oil and coaxed her into a squatting position.

She began to pant, to grunt and push down, her feet square on the floor, thighs braced, fists gripping the sides of the bed, the women crouched, hands outstretched to receive the child. Eliza screamed, a long keening wail, the birth cry of agony and exaltation and Hannah Evangeline Mary Elizabeth came swiftly down the birth canal and was triumphantly caught by the waiting hands. They cut the cord and laid her, blue and bloody, nuzzling at her mother's skin.

Before my son was born I was labelled, shaven and given an enema. A doctor probed with his gloved finger deep inside me puncturing the membrane containing the amniotic fluid, my wrist was injected by a syringe attached to a bag of clear fluid and I was told to remain still and flat, lying on my back so that the drip would continue to flow uninterrupted into my veins. When the birth pains began I was injected and when they became stronger the drip into my wrist was removed and I was wheeled to a room and laid out with my feet trussed to stirrups so that my lower body tilted upwards. I was given a mask to breathe into and told to be a good girl and push. My vagina was injected, my son cut from my body and cleaned, clothed and wrapped while the doctor sewed me up and I vomited into a stainless steel bowl.

My son was labelled, placed in a stainless steel bassinet and spirited away. I was lifted onto a bed and wheeled into a ward.

During the following days he appeared at regular intervals beside my bed for feeding — four minutes on both sides and three minutes in between for burping. *Please ensure the babies are not late back to the nursery.*

And God help you if you don't know how to make your baby suck.

The young girl with the long red hair at the end of the ward is crying again, sniffling quietly and helplessly. The nurse holds her swollen breast in one hand while the other firmly grips the back of the baby's head. The nurse pushes, then presses the head onto the nipple. The baby snuffles and gasps, his head writhes backwards and forwards, his body is rigid with panic as he begins to scream.

But progress is inevitable. A short time later medical science discovered the importance of immediate bonding between mother and offspring.

Better not to think of my own stories. Much better to think of Evie telling the stories to my child-self enchantedly listening. She began them all in the same way.

'Ah, Zoe. That reminds me. Have I ever told you …'

And I would be alert, ready.

'No, no you haven't.'

'Let me tell you then. Now as I remember it..'

The wind blowing up from the sea is piercing and the noise from the bar louder. I go into my room and shut the door on the night and the voices and the cars and the stories. I listen to the messages on my answering service and smile as I hear Ben on the phone. Ben my vulnerable child. The young man who now looms above me, and wraps my head against his chest. My boy, barely twenty, on the other side of the world.

'Mum? Mum? No letters, no presents, no phone calls, no money. I hate you, Mum.' I hear him chuckle and I grin. 'Mum, give me a ring. Soon, okay?'

I check my watch. It will be late morning there now and he'll have left his flat.

I make coffee and plug in my laptop, spread my notes out on the table thinking how to start. Begin to tap the words slowly. The article is due by the end of the week. I'll work late, finish it, get it out of the way. Fax it in the morning.

'You think you're clever, don't you?'

I wake and my husband is standing over me, crumpling the magazine in his hand, drunk, dangerous and afraid. Ben is asleep in the bedroom across the hall.

'You think you're too bloody clever for me don't you?'

I close my eyes tightly, shake my head, massage my neck with my fingers, make more coffee, find more words.

I believed words could save you. Words and stories. Naming things. Knowing things.

Perhaps I could have saved him. Us. Saved Robert-and-Zoe with soothing, sugary stories of love, words to deny, promise and soothe. But that was not how I saw my truth.

'Yes. Yes. I am.'

Hear the doors slam. The car starts up, accelerates down the driveway and out into the road.

Now that I'm on a first name basis with the hotel manager she regards me with less suspicion.

'Morning Annette.'

'Morning Zoe. Nice one, eh?'

Annette tells me I'm spoiled with the weather and looking out at the blue-on-blue of sky and sea splintered by light I agree with her.

'Us women deserve a bit of spoiling now and then.'

'Damn right,' she sniffs, 'Tell me about it.'

The tide is on the way out. I take off my sandals and walk along the fringe of sea feeling wet sand, hard stones, the lap and pull of waves around my feet.

I sit on my patch of sand in a pool of sun. Hard to believe that ships have been lost, people drowned out there in that benevolence of spreading blue. Difficult to believe bloody battles have raged amidst this tranquil bush and sea.

Cities, cappuccino, the superiority of one Chardonnay over another, correctly tagged life accessories, all that is so remote as I sit here. I watch as a horse canters down the beach at the water's edge. A grand, glossy animal. The rider sits taut in the saddle, his hair long and streaming down his back. He sees me watching, lifts his chin, bestows a swift white-flashing grin, digs his knees into the horse's flanks and they are off in a measured gallop.

Oh the glory of this place. Of a sleek horse and rider.

Perhaps I could retreat. Buy a little cottage over on the edge of the hill and fill it with my books. Grow my hair. Swathe my body in flowing muslin and swinging beads. Build a garden. Watch the sea.

I'm smiling at myself. I hear Evie observe that I have a romantic temperament and her black eyes crinkle. She's laughing at me.

Just build a garden. Watch the sea.

'You're running away.'

He's standing beside the door watching me, his face grim.

No. I'm not running away. I'm going away. Just for a while.

'If you're leaving for Christ's sake can't you be honest about it?'

'I'm not leaving you, Tom. How could I leave you?'

But Zoe, you can be hard and cold as well. And Evie's eyes no longer crinkle around the edges, no longer fill with light.

I place my hand over her mouth and burrow against her body. I want her to forgive me, to spin and weave her stories so they are a thick, safe net wrapping my body.

'Ah, now my Zoe, that reminds me, have you heard about…'

We sat together in the night. The wind soothed my hot red skin as she told me about Hannah.

At first I disliked Hannah. I was jealous of her. She was too good, pretty, clever. I began to consider her with the kind of suspicion and disgust I'd have for a child's cautionary tale.

I always thought of Hannah as a child my own age. I couldn't believe in her as Evie's mother. I didn't like the way Evie spoke as if she loved her as much as she loved me. Evie was mine. I was her child and she was mine. I would not share her.

And so I hated Hannah until I looked closely at her picture and was compelled to fall in love with her. In Evie's house, the wall above the fireplace in the living-room is a gallery of family photographs. The portrait of Hannah when she was still a little girl is the one I came to love most when I was a child. I loved it, and the story which went with it.

William had business which would keep him in town for some weeks. Since there were household necessities to buy he said we should come with him. We travelled to Auckland, the journey taking two full days and very hot and rough it was in the coach but the child was so good and so quiet never crying nor complaining.

We drove to the hotel, passing down by the wharf being built by the waterfront and came across a wedding party. The bridal cab was so bogged in mud that the party were forced to walk in the street, the bride's dress of beautiful white silk trailing in the mud. The children were enthralled by such a spectacle. James laughed but his sister began to cry so that I had to take her on my knee and comfort her. Our daughter has a soft and tender heart.

During their time in Auckland a portrait, set in a garden, was taken of the family. Perhaps the photographer was innovative enough to suggest the garden of the hotel or of friends as a setting rather than the more formal backdrop offered in his studio. Perhaps Eliza wanted it. I like to think so.

The garden is lush around them. William is seated beside Eliza; together they form the centre of the portrait. He wears a high-necked shirt, a waistcoat and a tail-coat, a black tie sits tightly beneath his chin and a thin strand of watch-chain loops across his chest. His back is rigid, his pale bony hands are clasped above his knees, his hair is thin at the top of his head, he has a thin top lip which does not curve even for the sake of the portrait. His jaw is square and his eyes narrow as he gazes directly into the camera.

Eliza's hair is drawn back from her forehead and hidden beneath the bonnet which closely frames her face. She has on a dark dress edged with a paler satin trim at the wrists and at the high collar with the tiny close-spaced buttons below it fastening the bodice. She also has her hands clasped but there is a slight curve about her mouth and you can see the edge of white petticoat at the hem of her dress and the pointed toe of a black-buttoned boot.

James stands behind, his hand on his father's shoulder. He also wears a suit. Light trickles through the leaves behind him and onto his hair. Luke is in a half-reclining position on the grass. He is younger and wears a boy's paler suit and a wide-collared shirt without a tie. His hair is fair and very short and he leans on his elbow facing the camera, his other hand resting on his knee. His face is narrow with fine features. He squints into the camera with Eliza's dark eyes.

Hannah sits on a small chair in front of her parents. She upstages them all. Her face is round and soft and glowing — *Hannah's skin was like smooth ripe peaches even when she was quite old.* Her hair curls around the top of the lace-trimmed collar of her dress. There is a wide satin sash around her waist, flounces of lace around the hem of her dress and her small feet are buttoned into ankle boots.

You can't help but fall in love with her. Everybody else in the group appears dull and controlled — dour William, the solemn boys, Eliza, so proper and stern. But Hannah grips the edges of her chair, her head and upper body tilt forward and her mouth opens up in a full beaming smile.

The women of my family have been storytellers and writers, concerned with the importance of remembering, of understanding and knowing through memory. Although Hannah, unlike her mother, did not keep a diary, in her later life she wrote parts of recalled stories so they would not be lost.

My father, who was by that time a timber merchant, bought a large piece of ground and built a house upon it for my mother and my brothers. That was before I was born and mother told me at first it was very rough. I can remember visitors to our house and I am sure they thoroughly enjoyed the milk, cream, the turkeys and fruit on my mother's table. One gentleman remarked he thought ours a real English home, the most homelike he had seen since leaving the old country.

In one particular place peach trees grew wild, and we used to go out riding and reach from horseback for the fruit. At other times we often got great baskets of cape gooseberries, and sometimes we gathered from the kotukutuku — the native fuschia, berries which Mother made tarts and pies with.

There was a large orchard behind the house which had in it a beautiful fig tree. One day when the fruit was ripe we were going to play in the orchard and father said we must not touch the figs, but one in particular looked tempting and so I thought I would just touch it. As I did it came off in my hands and I said to Luke, 'Oh, what shall I do?' Luke said he would show me and when I handed it to him he bit into it and divided it into two pieces and very soon we had swallowed it all.

On my sixth birthday my mother had a party, inviting all the children from around the area and we played blind man's buff. There was a tub full of soap suds near where we were playing and I was stepping backwards to avoid the blind man, when I fell backwards into this pail. One of the Maori women carried me off and stripped me, wrapping me in a blanket, while dry clothes were fetched from our house. She would not let the other children laugh at me, which you may be sure they were ready to do.

I must tell you about Meg, one of our favourite horses, and my own pet. Caleb Martin got a new pony called Jupiter and rode him over to our house to show him off. He would have it that Jupiter could beat Meg at galloping and he and I went for a ride. When we got onto the flat he began to spur his horse so I said 'Go it, Meg' and away she went like a bird. Many Natives were there, and when Meg came in first they hurrahed and waved and cheered in a very excited way.

These are the stories I loved as a child because more than those which celebrated her beauty, talent and sweet temperament I loved those which told about my great-grandmother's mischievousness and spirit. That spirit which beams from the darkness of an old photograph with a luminosity which reminds me of my own mother Grace.

Evie would never tell me about Grace although I asked and asked her.

'No Zoe. Grace's stories are her own to tell.'

'But she won't tell me.'

'One day she might.'

Evie taught me how you must respect stories. 'You can't tell other people's stories, without their consent. And always remember, Zoe, that how you tell something can only be the way you see it. One story may have many different tellings, all of them true.'

The wind is sharpening. I haul myself up and walk back to the hotel. My phone is blinking at me again.

'Zoe? This is my third message. I'm waiting to hear from you.'

Tom's voice is controlled but I hear the impatience.

'Are you all right? You must know I'm concerned about you. Give me a ring won't you?'

I sit on the deck and make notes for the next article. I look out over the Hokianga and think about fig trees and ponies and parties, other ways of living. Thinking about other people's histories is always easier than your own. I wait until four-thirty, then pour myself a brandy. With a clear conscience — after four in the afternoon is practically evening and not at all early for alcohol. Even if you are drinking alone. I sip it slowly, jot a few more words, listen to the kids calling to each other, racing across the carpark, waiting for Dad or Mum to come out with the bags of hot salty chips. Beautiful children with firm bodies, glossy hair, eyes filled with light.

I go inside. Pour another brandy.

8

Let me tell you a little tale from my childhood. My mother and the woman who helped her used to do the washing down by the river, leaving the tubs always there. There was a wide deep pool and on the other side a flat rock. I used to think how I would like to sit on that rock. I decided one day that I would sail to it in one of the tubs. I got two sticks for oars, and things went all right until suddenly my boat turned over and sank. I held tightly to my tub feeling the river begin to suck me downstream. All at once Mother appeared on the river bank and strode through the rapids to rescue me. She grabbed me up in her arms and we returned to the bank thoroughly wet. Mother said I must never do such a thing again since I could have drowned but we did laugh at ourselves, so wet and Mother had not taken off her shoes before plunging into the river to save her only daughter.

I wake with the sun coming through the curtains, Hannah's memories in my head.

Another time Luke took me up the river for a picnic. It was a narrow river, more like a creek in some places, and we went for miles until we came to a place where there were kowhai trees in bloom. When the time came to go home we went down the bank and found the boat left high and dry. It was quite late and dark before she was able to be floated off. We got in and heard another boat coming and somebody called out. We found it was Mother coming to look for us.

From Hannah's stories I know Eliza encouraged her daughter to explore and risk but was never heedless of her safety. I know that was a lesson Hannah learned from Eliza and how Evie, in turn, was mothered then mothered her own daughter, Grace. Evie said it's not only a horse must be allowed its head.

We had horses of our own, and used to go out riding, making hurdles of piled up brushwood. We used to have great fun going along leaping and galloping.
   Meg once ran away with me. I thought she was going to jump a wide place called the canal, and I prepared for the leap, but she went on, leaving me behind in the mud. Mother came up behind me and persuaded me back onto Meg's back.

When I first went to Evie's she taught me how to swim, row and how to ride. Those things were essential, she said. Every girl should be able to ride a horse and survive in the water, if you can manage those you can manage most things. At the time I wondered how often in everyday life, or indeed my future, I would be required to join in such activities. I was not a particularly physical child, much preferring books to the team sports we were required to participate in at school. All that running and scrambling to hit or grab a ball seemed senseless.

I'd never before been called upon to leap on a horse, swim rivers or row vast distances nor could I imagine seeking situations which required such skills. Now I understand Evie knew they were skills which required discipline, strength and perseverance. Patience, too, for riding. I was never any good at it.

But I can row with reasonable capability and Annette said I can borrow the hotel dinghy provided I don't drown myself. After breakfast I'm supplied with a life jacket and oars from the shed and go down to the dinghy bobbing at the end of the jetty.

I climb in, untie the rope and shove off staying close to the shore. I don't want the drama of a rescue or indeed my death by drowning being communicated by radio and television around the country to listening friends and associates.

You're going where?

The faces are incredulous above the plates of spinach-with-coriander soup.

'The Hokianga.'

'That's right up the top, isn't it?'

'Yes it is.'

'Why on earth would you want to go there? Its miles from anywhere. There won't be anyone else there. It's off season, Zoe. How long are you staying? Is it research?'

'I don't know. Probably not.'

I spoon soup into my mouth, quite enjoying the horrified attention this aberration in my usually predictable behaviour is causing.

'Well why are you going then? It's dangerous up there isn't it? Gangs and crime. And drugs. Isn't that where they grow all that marijuana? What does Tom think? Tom, what do you think of all this? Zoe running off to the end of the earth?'

He's silent and glances across the table at me. He says carefully that Zoe often runs off to the ends of the earth but always manages to get herself safely back.

'Is this some sort of mid-life crisis, Zoe? Couldn't you choose somewhere more comfortable to have it?'

I say airily, 'No I don't believe it is. Midlife crises were very eighties. They really aren't "in" any more. I don't think I could possibly have picked one up.'

They all laugh and somebody breathes, isn't it awfully ethnic up there? Are you sure you'll be safe, a woman on her own? I say briskly I'm sure I'll be perfectly safe, much safer than I ever am in Auckland and I'm always there and somebody says, but Zoe, what ever are you going for?

Tom says, 'This soup really is superb, Estelle,' and we're all enthusiastically agreeing and talking about the wine and what Brian Edwards' food expert recommended last Saturday morning and the new Italian restaurant that's just opened up and the horrors of the coalition government and the economy and what does everyone think about that ghastly murder case in the news? Did she really do it? Then we're all talking in raised voices about clairvoyants, and Zoe's lack of good sense and discretion in choosing to leave poor old Tom to his own devices for some undisclosed length of time and take herself off to the Hokianga for God's sake is quite forgotten.

That question, *why are you going there Zoe?* remained unanswered, partially through my own caprice but mainly because I couldn't answer it. Now, despite the sun and wind on my face, the movement of the sea beneath me, that feeling of control and coordination and power I have when rowing a boat through water, despite those mysterious, changing hills I have come to love, I still cannot answer it. Not entirely. If coming here was to find the answer to that rather pressing problem I should swiftly and ruthlessly deal with, I must admit the journey so far is futile. But if it was to wait and see, to contemplate and to remember, well then, perhaps I've come some of the way towards the answer.

A story has more than one telling, Zoe — more than one truth — more than one ending.

'Zoe. Listen to me. I don't want this. I'm telling you.'

'How do you know? We never expected it to happen so you've never thought about it. You haven't given it a chance.'

'I don't want it. And if you really thought about it, if just for one rational bloody moment you'd get rid of that fantasy you seem presently to be revelling in, then you'd see you don't want it either. I'm telling you, Zoe. I don't want it and you don't either.'

'Don't tell me what I want. Don't tell me what I think.'

'And anyway, what's the point of discussing this? You don't even know! We're probably going through all this for nothing.'

He's shouting. I'm shouting. We're slamming windows and doors, clenching our fists and striding. Pounding hot anger surges through my body.

Yet there is an amused incredulous self which steps aside. Watching and listening with a cool detachment.

Because this is Tom. Cautious, careful Tom. Nice Tom and nice Zoe. How can they be so angry?

Usually they're so civilised with their sniffings and sippings of wine, their chopping and seasoning and steaming and basting and tasting of food. Their smiles, laughter. Their little kisses and pats and embraces. Oh sometimes they're less civilised. Occasionally their lovemaking is performed in front of the log-burner on the thickly carpeted living room floor. Even against the walls of the shower. But always with adult control. Conscious amusement.

But see now. Here they are swept up by passion. By rage.

'Zoe. I'm warning you. Don't do it.'

'Don't threaten me. I'll do what I want.'

Yes. If I came to see and be silent and remember, I was right to come. The oars slip through water as I row close to the shore around the edge of the harbour.

When I was here with Evie we also borrowed a boat. Evie wanted to row to the mission. She'd been there years before when she was a girl and wanted to go back, wanted me to see it. We rowed part of the way and pulled in for a rest and a picnic on a beach she thought was about halfway to where we were headed. In the end, though, we had to turn back because the wind blew up and the harbour was choppy. There was no Dave. No *Hokianga Experiences*.

But we went into shore, pulled the boat up onto the sand and climbed up to explore the hill. Towards the top among bush we found a double-fronted brick fireplace and part of a chimney, all that was left of what had been a house. Alongside was a hydrangea bush, grown huge and festooned with papery blooms. Evie put the palms of her hands beneath one of the flowers, cupping it.

'Look at this,' she said. 'Isn't this glorious? To think some woman planted this here, way up here on this hill in this isolated place. It's what women do, Zoe. Make gardens. Make homes. Wherever they are, out of whatever they can get.'

I'm unsure of Evie's landing place but I stop at the point about where I think it may have been and heave the dinghy up onto dry sand. I stare up at the hill, start the climb but half-heartedly. Steep and the scrub is rough and dense. Too tough. I'm too tired to push my way through bracken and flax to search for a heap of bricks and a hydrangea bush.

So I walk back down and stretch out in the sand.

You must not give up too easily, Zoe. Sometimes what seems easiest turns out hardest in the end.

All right Evie. I hear you. Not today.

I roll over onto my stomach and burrow my head into my arms.

William died here in the Hokianga around the time of Hannah's tenth birthday. He went out at dawn. When he had not returned long after she'd served the evening meal, Eliza sent Luke for help to search for his father. The men went deep into the bush and it was daylight before they came across his body. There were no marks except for fresh grazes and bruising on his temple which may have occurred as he fell. The doctor was over in the Bay of Islands when it happened. There was no way to ascertain how he had died. Eliza's preferred belief was that he'd been suddenly overcome by a swift, mercifully brief heart attack.

Although William had enemies he was also loved. Maori from the district visited to bring gifts and grieve over their *Waiti* whose body lay for two days on the marital bed resplendent in his best black suit complete with gold fob and watch-chain. Eliza followed in a coach as he was taken to the Symonds Street Cemetery in Auckland — the resting place considered most fitting for an ordained minister, albeit one of doubtful character.

James was twenty years old and already living in Auckland, working in the office which managed the affairs of his father's timber milling business. Eliza stayed on in the Hokianga with Hannah and Luke for some months, then took Hannah to live in the town, appointing Luke, who was almost eighteen as manager of the mill.

Eliza had lived thirty-two years with her husband in the isolation of the Hokianga. She was now obliged to adapt to widowhood and live among the people of this rapidly growing town. She bought a cottage in Herne Bay with dormers pitched high in the roof, facing out to the sea. She set about planting a new garden.

In her later years Eliza discontinued her diary. Perhaps her daughter became the focus for her creative force, perhaps Hannah's story took precedence over her own. But I know because of what Hannah wrote and told Evie that Eliza kept a close relationship with her church and was a regular visitor to the prison, the hospital, the Old Women's Refuge and the institution then called the Lunatic Asylum.

As regularly as was possible, Eliza and Hannah visited Luke who stayed and married in the Hokianga. Luke's wife was Maori. She was baptised into the True Faith on the evening before the wedding, given her new Christian name Ruth and a respectable dress, which had been Eliza's, to be married in. Their first child was born some weeks later which makes me think of those narrow bodices of Eliza's gowns and wonder how the newly baptised Ruth managed to button the one she was given over her belly and so hide her shame. It is not clear whether or not Luke's Ruth followed the example of her optimistically selected Biblical namesake and was dutiful and obedient in her devotion to her beloved. I know she had a great many children. I know she took great care of Eliza's garden.

James courted and managed to win for himself Alice Jane Morrow. After their wedding tour to Sydney — a combination of business and pleasure since much of the kauri from the mill was transported there — they moved directly into the house in Ponsonby where they stayed for the remainder of their lives. Although from all accounts he was a silent and dour man with his father's impenetrable gaze and thin lips, I was assured by Evie that Alice was James' greatest, his only love. The business and other members of his family were merely factors he was obliged to deal with in a measured and responsible manner. He never appeared to care much for anyone else, not even his children. Alice was enough.

'Alice was a beauty,' Evie told me, 'I thought of her as my pretty aunt. Her dresses were always of those subtle pastel shades which showed off the blackness of her hair. That was the Welsh in her. She would come into a room and my Uncle James would somehow unclench. It was as if he was incredibly relieved to find she'd come back to him. And in minutes he'd be standing or sitting beside her. And touch her. Always touch her. Just once. Oh, not hold her hand or kiss her or anything so obvious as that of course. But rest his hand for a moment, just lightly, against her arm. It was not ownership. Not that, but gratitude. She always smiled agreeably back at him. He was an irritating man in many ways. Stern and serious and one-eyed and he had his father's quick temper. But you could forgive him all that because of Alice. He loved Alice with all the passion he had, and I believe she loved him equally.'

James built the house in Ponsonby from kauri milled from the Hokianga. It was his wedding gift to Alice and in a whimsically romantic gesture he had a stained glass window made with a small centrally-placed pattern of their entwined initials set in beside the front door.

Hannah was taught to read and write, to speak French and read Latin, to sing, draw and play the piano both by Eliza and a string of carefully selected governesses and tutors. Hannah was clever. By the time she was twelve she was reading her way through the books which filled the shelves of the tiny back room they called the library. Evie told me she had a quick mind, a flashing wit. She remained all her life informed about the world's affairs and well read both in contemporary literature and the classics.

It wasn't, however, until she was almost thirteen it was discovered that Hannah was not only an able, intelligent pupil, but also gifted with a unique talent. Surely given by God. A newly-employed tutor, Mr Gerald Brownlie, was a violinist of average capability, but certainly capable of teaching. Eliza decided that learning to play a new instrument would be interesting and challenging for Hannah, and the violin, after all, was exquisite.

Hannah ran her fingers lightly across the golden surface, picked up the violin then instinctively settled it in against her body as a mother may cradle her child. Without instruction she fitted the belly to the left of the point on her chin, the neck rested lightly on the joint at the bottom of her thumb. Although in many ways it is a strangely-shaped instrument and usually awkward for a beginner to hold, the violin seemed an extension of her body. She drew the bow across the strings. Closed her eyes.

It was a miracle, Evie said. Immediately, the sound she drew from the violin was tuneful and resonant. She practised constantly and compulsively, loving that relationship she had with her instrument, striving for the most perfect sound that she and her instrument could in unity achieve. She intuitively knew her scales. First attempts at simple tunes demonstrated an immediate control. She effortlessly achieved a high degree of expression, her control of loud and soft notes perfectly placed to enhance the quality of sound.

Hannah's music undulated through Eliza's house. Bach, Vivaldi, Hayden. Mr Brownlie, after a short period of tuition, became so worn out by Hannah's insistent passion and the limits of his own lack of skill he said he could teach her no more. Eliza advertised and a Mr Dieter Braun, a graduate of the Musik Hochschule in Cologne, Teacher of the Violin, appeared at their door. At first Hannah was delivered by coach once a week to Mr Braun's offices but then the visits became twice then thrice weekly. Mr Braun rhapsodised about Hannah's intonation and tone, the intuitive sense with which she placed her fingers, the speed and power of her bowing. They played Mozart. And then finally Beethoven, the Romances and at last when she was ready, the Concerto.

Evie said the sound of Hannah's playing was quite simply the purest kind of beauty. Like iced mountain water over rocks, opulent, liquid fire. And as well as the sweep and soar of sound, you could not help but be moved by Hannah's absorption, her love for her violin.

When Hannah was eighteen she secured a place at the London Trinity College of Music. She was to live with her aunt and uncle, Eliza's brother and the sister-in-law she had never met. Eliza would accompany her initially and enjoy an extended visit with the family she had not seen for years. They were to leave at the beginning of the New Year. In the November before, a company ship carrying a load of kauri to Sydney sank just beyond the Hokianga bar. Because of an accumulation of recent losses the family business was made bankrupt. Luke remained in the Hokianga, burnt off the bush on the land then set about developing it for farming. James joined an accountancy firm.

In December Hannah met Alexandre Andre Guinard and his companion Antoine Duval at a musical soirée celebrating the forthcoming Christmas. Alexandre had been sent by his father, the owner of several sugar plantations in Cuba, to purchase and develop land holdings in New Zealand. Since land was cheap and the climate more moderate, the eventual intention was that the family would re-settle there.

Alexandre became a regular caller. He and Hannah married in late January. Although the marriage was of a short duration it is believed their alliance was comfortable. Alexandre built a house on a hill above several thousand acres of land, seventy or so miles north of Auckland, the house that became Evie's.

Eliza lived there with them. Hannah continued her twice-daily violin practice and sometimes played in the evenings for Eliza and Alexandre and for visiting friends. Alexandre enjoyed his wife's playing although he preferred that she played light and popular tunes.

I push myself up. Stand unmoving for a moment gazing up at the hill. Dense rough scrub. A steep sheer climb. Then I'm pushing through the powdery sand at the bottom, my feet sinking almost to my knees. Haul myself up into the scrubby undergrowth, pushing a way through, forcing my body upwards, clawing, tearing through bush and bracken and fern. I will not stop. My heart is racing. Pounds with a deep hollow thud. Sweat drenches my face. I'm beginning to feel nauseous. Too hot, too steep. The low branches and gorse tear at me.

I will not stop.

Near the top I pause to let my breathing and my heart slow and survey the last climb. It's the steepest part. I'm on my hands and knees crawling upwards through briar so thick I'm in darkness. God what if I got lost or hurt here? Who'd look for me? But I'm there. I heave myself up into the light and stand on the brow of the hill, the Hokianga spread below. For me.

Evie, you were right. You pay too dearly for what seems easy and most comfortable. If I'd remained lazy down there on the beach I'd never have seen this vastness of the ocean swelling and rippling below me. Or the way the hills curve and peak against the ashy sky. Yes. There's always choice.

9

I don't want to leave. I'd like to cocoon myself in this sparse, sunlit room with the sea a background mutter. I think of all the paraphernalia of my life, that array of things I thought I needed. Toys that chop and mince and measure and whip, juice and crush and knead. Things to sleep under and sit on and play with and listen to and watch. A variety of clothing selected to reflect a persona I've adopted, desire to project — *Zoe, you look so elegant.* To say nothing of those decorative objects, once thought so beautiful, cluttering walls, tables and shelves.

I look around this room. A bed, wardrobe, jug, cup, plate. Television. Radio. Nothing extra other than the faded print of almost indecipherable roses, an air freshener disguised as a basket of plastic flowers.

I've a whimsy to stay forever wearing my shorts, jeans, T-shirts walking down there along the rocks. Nothing more important to do than watch the clouds churn above the Hokianga. Listening to the sea lap and fold. No greater test than to haul my way up a hill.

My last day.

Tomorrow I must start again on my life. Make decisions. Make contacts. Put things in order.

But for now I lie late in the morning, luxuriating in this borrowed bed with its faded pink cover. Make coffee. Pull open the curtains. Turn on the radio and read with sunlight patterning the bed. I'd forgotten how simple it is to be content.

I prop my head against the pillow thinking about my last day here with Evie. It'd rained in the morning, so we packed up clothes, washed the salt and sand out of our swimming suits. But in the afternoon the sun began to sift through, gilt streaked the sky, and although it was cool and there were rainclouds above the neck of the harbour we walked for miles along the coast line. That was when Evie told me about Hannah.

'She had a great talent,' Evie told me. 'When she played the violin I forgot she was my mother. I was so overwhelmed by the sound of the music she made somehow she became detached from me as if she were another person. When I was young I didn't like her to play. I'd pull at her skirt and want to be picked up and settled into her lap and have my mother back. It wasn't until later that I realised the gift she had.'

I was thirteen with that wonderful thirteen-year-old absolute knowledge of what is right, what is wrong, and needing to set people right about it.

'It was terrible.' I was bursting with indignity at the injustice. 'Why didn't Hannah go to London? Why couldn't she? Why didn't Luke and James help? What about Eliza's family? She should have gone, surely she could have gone. She married someone she didn't even love. She couldn't have loved him. Her life was ruined.'

Evie was quiet for some time, looking out on the sea. I thought that perhaps I'd hurt her and she wouldn't answer me.

'That's what I mean when I tell you there are always many ways to tell a story. I could tell you about Hannah's life as if it was tragic, as if it was, as you say, ruined and wasted. But lives are rarely ruined entirely. You go a certain distance along a road and should you choose not to go any further, why then you can simply head off down another track. Different, but perhaps no better nor worse. Hannah didn't go to London but she lived in a place she loved among people who loved her. It's not the worst way of spending your life, Zoe. And she chose that way. It may be her decision is difficult for you to understand but you should respect it.'

'But it was wrong,' I said. 'It was a mistake. She should have gone to London. She would have been famous. And rich.'

Evie smiled. ''Being rich, being famous, now Zoe, that's not the most important thing you can be. Being loved? Well that's something else again and Hannah was loved. No doubt about it. And in spite of what you might think of as the limitations of her life she was happy. For most of the time anyway. Not everyone can say that.'

'How do you know she was happy? She was probably pretending,' I was determined to cast Hannah as the martyred heroine.

'You can tell when people pretend,' Evie said. 'Their spirit tells you, that is if you're prepared to watch and listen. When people are happy there's a gentleness about them. Hannah had that. All her life she was tranquil in a way that made you want to sit next to her, be quiet with her. It's something you don't have when you're unhappy. It's something you can't pretend.'

I kicked at stones. Hannah, my heroine, my martyred heroine, lost to the world of music and greatness by misfortune. By other people's selfishness. I was not prepared to give up on it.

Evie said, 'When I was almost grown up I felt the same way. I asked Mother how she could possibly give up London and music to live on a farm? How could she give all that up and not be bitter? And do you know what she said to me, Zoe?'

'No.' I was sulky but curious.

'She said God didn't want it that way.'

I kicked harder at the stones. There was no answer to that. I wasn't entirely sure about Evie's own dealings with God but my own brief association was enough to convince me that it may just be testing your luck too far to say out loud God didn't know what He was doing. God made pathetic mistakes.

'So she didn't care?'

'I wouldn't say that exactly,' Evie said. 'What I would say is that she cared a great deal about the life she eventually made so that losing that chance only hurt a little. Only sometimes and only a little, Zoe.'

Only sometimes. Only a little. Like all things, places, people you once considered you couldn't live without, that you lose or leave behind. That man. Brian, Bruce, David, Sam. You once loved him so intensely he was in your head. In your dreams. You slept, ate, lived, drank him. When he left you felt as if your heart was sliced from your body. And now you don't know where he is. Couldn't care. You rarely think about him at all and if you do it's with a shrug, a grin or grimace of fondness, cynicism, distaste. That person you knew gave you life.

But I didn't understand that then. Didn't see how something you desire with all your heart can give way to something different. I didn't see how a man, a child and a home could in any way compensate for fortune and fame. And I didn't understand that Hannah's loss wasn't fortune and fame so much as the chance to test herself and that gift she had. To push and haul her body up a hill covered by dense tearing bush to stand momentarily in the light and scan a spread of glittering ocean.

But today I must haul myself from bed and make certain of making the most of this last day. And so I shower, eat some fruit, look out on this ocean and coastline, now so familiar, and phone Ben.

'Hello? Ben here.'

My son has an American accent which makes me smile. This newly acquired accent reminds me that when we had a visitor from Scotland, Ben developed a decided brogue, that when he had a new best friend from Gore he began to roll his r's.

'How are y'all?'

He laughs and the accent disappears, 'Mum. I'm not in Alabama for God's sake. How are you?'

'Fine. More important how are you? How are you surviving over there?'

'Okay.' He recites, 'I'm eating well and having enough sleep and I'm looking after my money. And not walking down dark alleys late at night.'

I grin. 'Good. You're doing what your mother tells you, then.'

He talks about his work, what composers he's studying, papers he's writing, what he's playing. I tell him about the articles I should be working on.

'Where are you?' he asks. 'I phoned you at home but I got Tom. He said you were away for a few weeks. What are you doing?'

'I'm in the Hokianga. Then I'm going down to Evie's for a while.'

'Having a holiday?'

'Kind of.'

His voice is not so light, 'Why didn't Tom go? How is he? Is there something wrong?'

'He couldn't get away. He's got a lot of work on right now. He's fine. Truly, darling, nothing's wrong. I just needed a break and it wasn't the right time for Tom to take one as well.'

My son likes to think his mother is being cared for by another male while he's away. Likes to think of me safely engaged in middle-aged security and stability while he roams the world. And, despite his initial suspicion of any man who dared to approach his mother, he's grown to love Tom.

'Where did you say you are? What are you doing there?'

'The Hokianga. Nostalgia probably. I came here with Evie years ago.'

'You never took me. What's it like?'

'Beautiful. I'll send photographs. But it's not exciting. There aren't any rollercoasters. Not even a picture theatre. You always wanted to go to places you thought were exciting, Ben.'

'Not always. I would've gone. Why didn't you take me?'

I think about it and this time I'm honest, 'I suppose it wasn't important then but now it is. Don't ask me why because it'll cost a fortune on tolls if I try to explain. I'll write to you. And I think it was also because I thought it might be too painful.'

'Because you went there with Evie?'

'Yes, partially that anyway.'

'Will you go with me when I get back?'

I smile at that, think of walking with my tall, beautiful son along the beach, watching the clouds group and change, watching the sea and the sky.

'I'd like that.'

'I miss you Mum.'

He is my small child again looking appealingly up from his bed afraid to be left alone with the light switched off. I want him home where I can see and touch him, be irritated by him, know I can keep him safe.

'I miss you my darling. Take care.'

'I love you Mum.'

I put the phone down, tears in my eyes. Oh God I miss Ben. But at least this is something I've done well. I can't count raising my son among my failures. God knows I've come close to it at times. I could have done it better. But I see his spirit, know that somehow, love mixed with endurance, stubbornness perhaps, we've got through.

'You're what? What did you say?'
'I'm pregnant. I said I'm pregnant.'
'Christ. I thought you said you'd gone onto the pill.'
'I did. But it made me sick and so I went off it for a while. I didn't think a few days would make any difference.'
'How do you know? Are you sure?'
'I went to the doctor.'
'Jesus.'
We gaze, appalled at each other. I begin to cry.
'I'll have an abortion if you like.'
I start to cry louder at that idea. Begin to ferociously sob as I imagine searing pain and blood seeping from my body in some grimy back street abortionist's. Or having to fly alone to Australia to be prodded and torn by punitive nurses and doctors. I'd thought I would quite like a baby. Hadn't really meant to begin one but I thought babies were soft and sweet and smelled nice and they made you feel safe and real, gave you something to do with your life. But I'm suddenly petrified. All this comes sharply into focus, becomes an actuality.
'They're illegal aren't they?'
'Yes.' I sob loudly. 'But if you don't want it, I'll just have to do it.'
He stares at me then his face changes. He becomes the man his father expects him to be. Courageous, loyal and true-blue. The kind of gentleman ladies may depend on.
'I couldn't let you do that. I'll look after you. We'll just have to get married.'
I'd anticipated a more romantic proposal. A silk dress brushing against my ankles, a garden. Roses. Somebody on his knees imploring and adoring.
'But you don't want to.'
'Of course I do. I love you. Anyway there's no other choice.'
'You're only saying you love me because you think you have to.'
He says it as if it's something sticky and awkward he has mistakenly put into his mouth.
'Don't be silly. I do love you and I do want to marry you.'

He smiles at me, comes over and dabs at my eyes with the handkerchief his mother washed and pressed.

He has seen film stars do this at the pictures. Men wipe away women's tears and stand by them even though they are undeserving of such loyalty. It is how men behave. Women are silly and difficult to manage. They get pregnant and cry and bleed and sulk. They aren't really like ordinary people so you can't possibly take them seriously at all. Despite that, men are obliged to humour and look after them. There really isn't any choice. Its the way of the world.

But despite the inauspicious start Ben and I made it. I always wanted him. Misguided and naïve with hopelessly romantic notions of mothering, I pictured myself as a whimsical Madonna, although of course sexier.

I was unfit for motherhood. But I always wanted you, my Benjamin. I've been fickle with my men but not, thank God, with you.

I buy fruit from the shop, walk slowly along the shelves, stop and look at the postcards, listen to the voices — *wanna hear a Maori joke? good band the other night eh? where you get that dress, you look like a filmstar eh? you goin tonight, see ya there* — the gust and rush of laughter. I hear a phone, look around, realise I've left my cellphone on after my call to Ben and it's there in my bag. There's a woman taking milk from the refrigerator beside me and she looks up, grins.

'Don' think that's for me,' she says and everyone is laughing.

My face is red but I laugh too. I take the phone out, switch it off, then buy my fruit, walk along the beach for this last day. I choose shells and stones to take with me. A flat smooth-edged stone with milky-white veins running through, one etched with greenish ridges, a silky piece of driftwood shaped like a miniature canoe, purple shells, pink shells, one spiked like a porcupine.

Yes, I've been fickle. Disloyal with my men.

I have done those things I ought not to have done.

My own history. The Zoe stories which indicate that the loyalty, self-effacement and integrity evident in my grandmothers had been supplanted by an unwillingness to make a lifelong commitment to anything, anyone other than Ben.

Some time after I left my husband I believed I'd fallen in love. The object of my devotion was married but since I believed myself to be in love that seemed a minor misfortune, an irrelevance in the context of great passion.

Viewed from my present detachment, this passion represents the usual dreary cliché. Mid-life-crisis-menopausal-male forms an attachment with younger-vulnerable-recently-separated woman. Who just happens to be a student in his journalism class. Flattered younger woman is swept away by his intellect, sophistication, mature attractiveness. Tempted older man is diverted by her undeveloped — certainly he can help with that — but sound intelligence, her quaint enthusiasm for her studies, her newness, freshness. Moreover her obvious awe of his superiority so perfectly mirrors his own opinion. As well as that she's quite good-looking.

But when I was living my infatuation I was enmeshed by obsession for my lover. If he didn't phone, if he couldn't see me, if he couldn't stay, if he didn't convincingly say he loved me, if he was preoccupied, brusque or cool my stomach knotted and my heart stopped. If he phoned and I heard his Chardonnay-and-brie voice telling me he only wanted to hear my own, if he brought me flowers (from the supermarket) wine (ditto and most often on special), if he complimented me on my appearance, my cleverness and, glory of glories, if he could manage to evade his wife and bestow his presence upon me for an entire night it was as if I were visited by angels.

A pathetic tale. I went to journalism school because I needed the qualifications, wanted to get better at writing the stories I wanted to tell, because I needed to earn money to support Ben and myself. I wanted to spend my life doing something I loved and doing it competently. And I spent a great deal of my time there wondering if and why this man was looking at me or was I hallucinating? Then attempting to stun him with my attractiveness, my informed intelligence and spending extraordinary time and energy wondering what he was doing or thinking. Then getting rid of him.

So often it's what women do. What I've done. You start with an agenda of clear and defined ideals and goals and then some man comes along and you allow him to intrude, to change your own story.

I believed my married lover to be so dauntingly clever, irresistibly attractive and erudite. His hair elegantly greyed around the edges, his body sun-lamped, kept taut from the hours he spent at the gym and his eyes were slightly slanted, as brown and gleaming as a clever little monkey's. I gazed at him rather than textbooks and articles and when that wasn't possible, into the mirror at myself. Since my intellect wasn't up to much, my own face and naked body were the only weapons I owned to procure his enslavement, but the flaws and imperfections I saw were alarming. I observed the little bits of extra flesh around my waist and thighs, the less perky breasts than society deems desirable. The skin on my face was not so youthful as I'd thought and horror of horrors I had stretchmarks on my belly. How could he possibly love me?

When I observed at a staff and student dinner that his wife had a large wide body, her hips padded with thick solid flesh, I was comforted enough to parade my nakedness around the room during our next encounter. When he said his wife was less than enthusiastic during lovemaking and rarely orgasmic I responded with the hottest, most energetic screwing I could manufacture complete with wildly thrashing, shrieking orgasms. I felt affirmed when he said I was sexy.

Our passion ran the usual course. The initial stage of obsessive attraction — my heart made suitable flurries when I saw him — a heightened, all encompassing passion when we would entwine and press our bodies and our mouths together as our hands reached and stroked and we staggered towards the nearest horizontal surface. Hours in bed touching, stroking each inch of body, each inch of mind and memory. *I love you.* And then the predictable tears. The agony of drawn out silences. The reproaches. Because of course he couldn't leave his wife and his mortgage. Of course people were beginning to talk. Of course I became difficult.

When I thought I loved him I considered death a more attractive option than living without him, couldn't imagine a world so bleak it could be devoid of his presence. But, as Evie said, stories have a way of changing, perhaps not in a way you would choose but in the end you simply have to continue. There isn't any other choice. Hannah losing her chance, me losing my lover, Eliza losing her home. It's as Evie told me, like gardens. Each time you begin a new garden you must begin the digging and building and planting all over again but each new start is easier since you may take the cuttings and the seedlings along with you.

In the end it was me who called an end to the pattern of love-making, intense talk, tears and drawn out farewells. There was no courage in it, no martyrdom because in the end I became sickened by my need and tears, his explanations and promises. It was as if one day I was entrapped by it and the next I found myself out of love and uninvolved watching two pathetic creatures immersed in a paralysing and comical self-indulgence.

I saved myself. It's what I always do. I can weep and wail with the best of them but in the end I always step aside, extricate myself. Perhaps it's self-preservation, perhaps hardness, but I don't have my grandmothers' capacity for self-effacement. I used my words, brutal, waspish words and drily, rationally dissected our alliance. Cut out the belly and the heart and laid it bare and mutilated before us as he sat, head bowed, hands clasped. I used my words better than in any class or assignment when I'd tried so eagerly to impress. Used them more skilfully than when I'd spoken of love, entreated him to stay with me. And when he stayed silent I said how strange, how rare for him, usually so eloquent and quick to penetrate and analyse. So surprising he was suddenly without words. He said quietly he didn't want to lose me and I shrugged, said he divided love into mean little parts, one little bit for me, a fraction for her, a teeny bit left over for the kids, he wasn't capable of loving, he was a wimp and I opened the door and stood beside it averting my face as he bent to kiss my cheek.

Strength is one thing, Zoe, hardness another.

I was bitter and unbending because I also accused myself. In the end I didn't love him enough. Not enough to surrender myself.

Out beyond the bar the clouds are blackening, hunching low over the sea. I feel the first splattering rain on my head and bare arms as I walk back to the hotel.

Since it's my last evening I venture into the bar. I tell myself I shouldn't leave without going in, finding out for myself the other truth of the place. There's the beauty of Hokianga but also the ugliness of the shouting and tussles in the car park, the revving bikes and cars. I may write about it in the end and the bar is important, central.

But I'm nervous, feeling my difference, my whiteness. In Asia I've felt like a pale giant, gross, ungainly, an unnatural colour. But I've never felt that way before, not here in this country I think of as my own.

I buy a beer and sit in a corner. I watch without directly gazing. Entertain myself by wondering if perhaps some cousins of mine are here. All those children from Luke's marriage. Perhaps there were children from William's liaisons. The bar begins to fill. Leather jackets, long hair, dreadlocks, tattooed arms. I imagine a future dinner party where I describe my sojourn into this bar, the scandalised, amused, disapproving responses — 'Zoe, you did what? Weren't you afraid? God, you could've been mugged. Or raped.'

But I'm not afraid. Because the atmosphere here, at present anyway, is just people having a gossip and a laugh, having a good time. And gradually I'm also drawn in. I look up into black singlets, topped by tattooed chests and arms. And all they want is to know where I'm from, then there they all are sitting around my table *we seen you round, eh, how long you staying, what you think of round here?* I'm drinking another beer courteously handed to me and laughing, suddenly laughing amidst these women looking me up and down appraising my haircut, grey shirt, navy jeans (boring eh?), these men who laugh and tease *what you come here for, too boring for youse townies.* And I see when two older women come into the bar the younger men go to them, welcome them with courtesy and respect, *you sit over here, Aunty.* The women nod to me and smile.

I ask about the Hokianga, about growing up here. *Schools weren't too good, teachers kept changing, some schools closed down, too far to go eh... No jobs round here.* Most of them left, went to the city, now have come back. I tell them I understand that. I understand little but I understand returning to this place. Then I thank them and they're surprised when I say I must leave — *you not staying? Stay and have another beer, party on later, up the road, you're welcome.* I shake my head. They shake my hand.

I go back to my room. Sit on the bed. I'd gone into the bar with the intention to expose the place and people with slick words. I'm ashamed. I knew nothing.

I make coffee. Look out on the Hokianga. I feel alone, lonely. I want Tom, want Ben to be home, want the familiarity and comfort of people I know, things I understand. I want to cook with Tom, drink wine with him, go to bed and feel his body beside me and hear his breathing. I want to give all this up, go back and resume my other easier story.

I walk down in the dark to the sea. Take off my shoes and paddle in the shallow water, feel the stones under my feet. I look across the smoke and silver harbour. I take off my shirt, then my jeans and I'm running with icy waves leaping around my body, plunging into water so cold it takes my breath away, numbs my body. Lie outstretched on my back held and buoyed by the lapping, muttering sea, gaze into blackness streaked with moonlight, lit by a multitude of stars.

10

In the morning the clouds which threatened yesterday are pelting a slow steady rain. After a late breakfast, I wait for the bus that finally lurches into the carpark. I give Annette the key to my room — yes I'll be back, of course I'll be back — and find a seat near the front. Easier to leave today since last night I said goodbye to the sea, earth, sky.

We drive along the harbour, then begin the slow rise to the top of the hill through bush. I look back, grey glass today with clouds hovering close. Then a flash of sunlight sprinkles the water with light.

The driver looks back at me. 'Turning out better.'

We leave the sea behind and spiral through acres of solid bush, past churches with a huddle of weatherboard houses nearby. We see a group of boys on horses and the driver waves at them. 'How they all used to get about not so long ago. Kids still ride their horses to school round here.' Past the marae the driver points out, across flat, green country, through minuscule towns — a grocery shop, garage, a pub, another church — then bush again, cabbage trees, flax, karaka and pine. I rest my head against the seat feeling the motion of the bus, the twist and wind of the road.

Paihia is civilisation. Hotels and motels crowd the beach frontage with signs offering deals. There is a style to suit all tastes. Colonial with dormers, Spanish haciendas, black-and-white Elizabethan with tiny latticed windows. '70s ranchsliders and concrete balconies; tinted windows and gleaming blockwork of the '80s, the glossy pink-tiled stairs rising to pastel stucco '90s. You may have a spa pool, an outside or inside pool or both, a spa bath, a sauna, an in-house video and Sky. You may have cooking, bar, barbecue, restaurant facilities and waterbeds.

I find the nearest shabby motel to the bus terminal. The walls of the office are covered by posters offering *experiences* of Cape Reinga, sailing ships, four wheel drives, horses, dolphins, fast boats. The people in the posters are obviously enjoying *experiences*. Young, golden, blonde, with astounding blue eyes they are dressed in tight bright swimming suits and poised against blue-blue sky and water. Their hair, blown casually back from their faces by light cooling breezes, exposes tanned faces with luminescent, large-toothed grins. They are healthy, carefree, uncomplicated. They have long tapered legs.

The woman who books me in offers me a super off-season package deal, a fast boat ride including snorkelling and dolphin viewing and a bus trip to

Cape Reinga including a visit to the marae, picnic lunch and sand surfing. A combination of culture and fun.

I explain to her I'm only staying one night and intend leaving early in the morning.

'Sand surfing is great,' she says. 'Everyone goes for sand surfing. You tried it?'

'No, I haven't.'

'You've gotta try it,' she says. 'You on holiday? Where've you come from?'

'A kind of holiday. I've been staying over at Hokianga.'

'Nothing much doing over there. You should've been over here. Just had the Country and Western music festival. Been pretty busy.'

I put my bag in the room and stand at the window looking out. Beside the entrance is a tree hung with miniature bunches of green bananas. I think about Evie's orchard behind her house. The grapes should be ready.

I pull on my jacket and walk off up the street. There's a strong wind whipping up off the sea and the sky is darkening. Up along the small narrow streets making up the mall there are a multitude of shops and restaurants where you can eat Chinese, Japanese, Turkish, European, hamburgers, fish and chips and choose from a selection of crafts. There are brown or white dolls correspondingly outfitted in Maori or colonial costumes, bowls and toys crafted from polished kauri, woolly sheep, plastic kiwis and dolphins, pot-pourri, dried flowers, lace-trimmed pillows stuffed with lavender. There's an array of paua and greenstone brooches, carvings, earrings, rings, bracelets, pendants and necklaces. The streets teem with people. I find a chemist, buy what I want and put it in my bag.

Beside the obvious effects of civilisation the landscape's different over here. Gentler. More amiable, malleable but it doesn't have the wild grandeur left behind me. I walk away from the shopping centre, along the road past Henry Williams' wonderful grey stone church then across to the beach. I take the ferry over to Russell, hunching the collar of my jacket up over my neck and my ears, watching the water, dull today, thick, green and dull...

Along the waterfront with the other tourists I gaze into cottages — 'so cu-ute' an American woman says, peering over a fence at a man cutting a lettuce from his vegetable garden.

Christ. What'd that be like? Life as a tourist attraction. I'm tempted to ask for an interview. *Charlie and Jeanie Godsbury in their cosy, lovingly restored Russell cottage, laughingly say they don't mind tourists at all. Certainly a head — of any nationality at all — may appear at a window at any time of the day or night but, as Charlie says, they're only admiring the place.*

'It makes me feel a bit of a filmstar,' Jeanie says proudly.

I like Russell, it's charming, and has somehow stayed itself. I walk up the rise to the church. The cross-beamed ceiling, the tiny paned windows set high into stained wood walls. There at the front, the raised pulpit and plain cross. There is such simplicity, such dignity. I walk behind the church and look at the graves. Children who died too young. Women who died in childbirth. Men drowned.

I find Nene's grave and commemoration plaque. Nene, the great chief. Seen by some as traitorous since he left the Hokianga, built a pa at Okaihau allying himself with the Europeans against Heke. He never returned but lived here in his self-imposed exile until his death. Nene, who befriended and protected William and Eliza.

You will remember me mentioning Tamati Waka Nene, the old chief. Well, he and his wife have adopted James and have brought to us a big pig as food for their child. On one occasion Tamati's wife carried him all the way from the Bay of Islands to Hokianga on her back, two days journey.

I lay the palm of my hand against the stone. Feel the wind beat against my face.

Stories of love, death and betrayal which tell us what we have been, make us as we are.

In the evening I watch the news, acclimatise myself again to the dreariness of violent crime and political wrangles. When I first became a journalist I watched the news with my phone beside me, notebook and pen ready. I was fired up, ready to expose, to fight injustice. I believed something could be done. Even if nothing changed, people should know. Now I observe it all with a cynical detachment that frightens me. I watch the politicians bicker about expensive taxi rides and underpants, listen to the glib answers to questions about unemployment, education, benefits, hospitals. I'm sickened but unaroused.

I think about an article I wrote. A schizophrenic woman was living on the streets. She ate and drank and smoked what she could find, smelt of the shit and piss she lay in. The authorities said it was her right to live like that. It was her personal choice. I interviewed her parents. They wanted her taken into a hospital and looked after. They'd sat in a car watching her on the streets foraging for food and lighting cigarette butts. The father nodded as the mother explained that they'd taken their daughter home many times and washed her, given her clothes and food, watched over her as she slept in the bed she'd slept in when she was a child. But she always left. In the end she raged and wailed and smashed things and left.

The father says they don't know what to do, he can't understand it, she was a lovely little girl. Always chattering to them, wanting a cuddle. Beautiful. And clever. Never anything wrong with her brain, was there Marg? Never. First in her class one year, wasn't she? Was it them? Did they do something wrong? He thinks and thinks about it, trying to work it out. Something that could've happened. Something they could've done different. He thinks about her all night, can't sleep.

'She's not right,' the mother explains. 'She's just not right. She won't take her pills and the doctors say they can't make her.'

I ask if she feels like giving up and her eyes fill with tears.

'That's my daughter you're talking about. That's my daughter out there. It's my blood, my guts sleeping out there filthy in the gutters. How could I give her up? What sort of person would it be that gave up their daughter?'

I cared then. I was angry. Angry but powerless though I didn't see that.

But time to attend to my own narrative. I take the package out of my bag and read the instructions. So easy. I unwrap this white plastic disk with the power of clairvoyance since it will indicate if not the course of my life at least what the months ahead have in store. I take it into the bathroom, pee into a paper cup, pour some into the plastic tube provided, then place a few fat drops on the indicated circle. Simple. All I have to do now is wait. I put the disk on top of the bathroom cabinet.

I make coffee and despite the ease with which this task is accomplished my mouth is dry and my hands shake.

'Why won't you go to the doctor?'

'I'm not ready to go yet.'

'Shouldn't you go? What if you are? You'll have to do something about it reasonably soon won't you?'

'Tom. I'm not ready to see a doctor. I don't know what I'll do.'

He looks at me as if I am an imbecilic child. 'You wouldn't go through with it, Zoe? Not really would you? Not now. Christ, it could be dangerous. Darling, you're going to have to do something. It's almost four weeks isn't it?'

I say it's just that I truly don't know what to do.

'Go to the doctor, Zoe. For God's sake go to the doctor. At least then you'll know.'

And now I know as, of course, I've known all along. The middle circle is splendidly pink and marked clearly with a darker pink plus sign and I'm shaking so much I have to sit down on the orange sofa, Christ this place really is '70s, never redecorated, Christ all this orange and brown decor and oh God whatever am I going to do? I sit on the bed. Press my hands against my belly.

'Ben, my darling, you're going to have a new baby brother or sister.'
I laugh out loud at the thought, then moan.
'Mum why haven't we got a brother?'
Ben is six and the other kids have them but unlike an Action Man or Star Wars character a brother cannot easily be procured.
'I'm not sure, darling. We've just never happened to get one.'
Coward.
I lack the moral fortitude to take this ideal opportunity to illuminate my child regarding the facts of procreation. As well as the sad circumstances of our own personal lack of a stable fathering implement.
'Well I want one.'
I murmur something vague about perhaps one day and we must just wait and see then swiftly divert his attention with freshly-made, iridescent green playdough. At least I follow some of the instructions I anxiously and compulsively read in my library of manuals on child development. This mothering is a serious business. But for now the crisis is averted.

But what to do about this one? I turn up and down the TV, change channels, make more coffee, tell myself there is nothing I can do about it at present, promise myself I'll attend to it next week, then weaken and reach for the phone.
'Hello,' I say as brightly as I can manage, 'It's me.'
'Zoe.'
He's angry and he's pleased. Relieved as well. I hear all that in his voice and remember how well I know him.
'Where are you? Why haven't you phoned?'
'I don't know.' I laugh, but weakly. 'Just got caught up in Hokianga lethargy probably.'
'How was it? Did you get my phone calls? God, Zoe, I've been worried about you. I nearly phoned the police to make sure you'd got there, that you were safe.'
'Tom, I've been most of the way around the world and nothing's ever happened to me. You've never got the police out after me before.'

'This is different.'

His voice is flat but there is a question in it that I evade.

'Not at all,' I say lightly.

He is silent then carefully asks how I'd enjoyed the Hokianga.

'Oh. Beautiful. Amazing.'

I tell him about what I did and saw and found. I know he's listening. It's something I love about Tom. The way he listens silently with intense absorption. He doesn't talk or ask questions, just listens.

And he tells me about the case he's working on and it's been colder in Christchurch over the past week, so cold he got firewood in. And the dog's missing me, she's sulking.

'And I am too.'

He says it quietly and I wonder why I'm miles and miles away from him at the other end of this country and not reading the morning paper in bed with him, not sitting in front of the fire trying out a new wine he's discovered and triumphantly produced. Not listening to music, watching a video, making love. I'm angry. Angry at this alien thing that's invaded my body, these alien tales and thoughts which've invaded my mind causing me such disquiet, such unrest.

He says tentatively, 'How are you, Zoe? How are you really?'

And I almost cry, laugh almost, since this is one of our jokes. That hackneyed pseudo-counselling, pseudo-psychology technique we find so amusing — how are you? But how are you, how are you ree-ee-ly? we enquire of each other and laugh. But not now.

'Oh,' I say. 'Oh. The same.'

'You're pregnant aren't you?'

'Yes.'

God that word. I hate it. I feel trapped by it.

'Christ, Zoe.'

'You haven't thought about it? Changed your mind?'

He sighs, 'Zoe don't ask. It's untenable.'

Untenable. Does he think he's talking to one of his clients?

'Not necessarily,' I say coldly.

'What I can't understand is how it happened in the first place. I thought all that was taken care of.'

'It's the woman's responsibility and duty to take care of all those unpleasant things so that the man can just enjoy himself, is that what you're saying?'

He sighs. Zoe doing her outraged feminist stuff again.

'It's not what I mean and you know it.'

'What happened is that my — my, since obviously all that is my responsibility — my contraceptive method failed and I've got myself pregnant.'

That's another joke which is no longer funny. *She got herself pregnant.* How? We ask ourselves. By artificial insemination? By divine intervention? How does anyone get themselves pregnant?

I say, 'Look we've been through all this. How it happened and whose fault really isn't relevant.'

'Zoe, come home. Get the next plane. We have to talk. We've got to do something about this. Come home. I love you.'

'I'm not ready to come home.'

'You can't come home. You can't go to a doctor. Because you're not ready? For God's sake, Zoe, you can't just hang about like this, this is irresponsible. We've got to start making some decisions. How long do you think you can wait?'

'Long enough to go to Evie's,' I say. 'I'm going to Evie's.'

I'm crying. Because I want to come home, of course I do, but I can't, I can't yet, I don't know why but I have to go now because I can't talk, you know what I'm like when I start crying. I hardly ever cry. But when I do I can't stop it.

His voice is clipped. He asks me to phone when I get there.

I put the phone down and rock and cry, my hands pressed on this ridiculous belly. No I won't go home. I want to go to Evie's. I'm going to Evie's.

Because Evie will gather me in her strong thin arms hushing, soothing, stroking my hair. Evie will press a cool, fragrant flannel to my forehead, place lavender beneath a white cool pillow to help me sleep. Everything will be calmed. Everything will be all right again.

I have to go to Evie's.

I drink the last of the brandy. Dream about Tom, about Ben, about plane crashes, missing a train, rowing a boat through thick black water. I wake too hot, sweating. Make tea, switch on the bedside lamp and read until morning.

I pick up the rental from the garage, drive along the waterfront looking out towards Russell, across to Waitangi and then I'm gliding in this shiny car away from the sea, curving through bush, concentrating on the unfamiliar road.

There's hardly any traffic and I relax, push my foot down on the gas and the car soars forward like a galloper allowed its head so that I gasp, ease back. Slot in a tape. Enjoy the driving, the curve of road, light sifting through bush. The wooden churches, rusted roofs, the paint turned to bleached streaks, some with hay spilling through broken doors.

In Whangarei I find a car park and call in for my appointment with the benefit service. I want some facts for an article I've started. Statistics relating to unemployment. The percentage of beneficiaries in the Northland population.

I wait in the queue at the reception counter. The receptionist manages a smile and makes a phone call after she finds the time to look me up and down, judge me respectable and ascertain I don't want a benefit. I sit on a chair and wait.

The room is crammed with people. Women with babies in their laps, children playing on the floor, men staring down at their feet, young kids in groups whispering, occasionally laughing out loud, old women, slumped, quiet. People are frowning over forms grasped in their hands.

Then there are those being attended to at the desks. As soon as one is processed another name is called. I see an old woman struggling, almost weeping as she tries to explain the circumstances of her life to the woman who asks questions then ticks the boxes on the form. I hear a woman with a child sleeping on her shoulder tell the man in front of her she had to pay her bills and now she hasn't got any money left to buy the kids some food, could she have some food vouchers? I hear him telling her all advances are redeemable, does she understand any money they advance will have to be paid back? I see an old man leaning over the counter. His skin is grey and he looks ill and shocked. He explains this is the third time he's come here, she is the third person he has talked to. His money has been cut. Why has this happened? He hasn't got enough now, he doesn't understand why this happened.

It's a sad place, this overheated room crammed with people whose need and powerlessness and anger and confusion are exposed to public scrutiny. But privacy is a luxury exclusive to those who help themselves. Phones ring, forms are filled, names loudly mispronounced, computers beep. A woman behind her desk shifts impatiently, raises her eyebrows and sighs as she explains again the criteria for a hardship grant to the man who sits, head bowed, in front of her.

What fine stately men these Maoris are and their tattooed faces seem to add to their dignity.

I'm ushered into an office and shake hands, smile brightly, sit, arms loose, leaning forward, an intelligent expression on my face, insightful questions, perceptive comments at the ready. I procure my facts, scribble notes, smile again as I thank this suit in front of me. He nods to the room outside his office as I'm going through the door, 'Too bloody many of them.' I escape through the desks and queues.

'Too bloody many of them.'

I didn't pause, didn't even attempt to prick his complacency by explaining icily that once I was one of those people. Once it was me sitting there waiting. Filling out a form and waiting until the woman in the navy suit and white shirt called me over and handed me a paper. I looked at the figure written in front of me, *your entitlement*, did a swift calculation, mortgage, electricity, phone, what was left over for everything else? God it couldn't be only that much, how can they expect anyone to live on that, how could we survive?

Except I was never them. Not entirely. I had Evie to help us, ways of getting out. They can't ever get out. That fire in a shack up north last month. Kids dying because they can't get them to a doctor. Too bloody many of them. Jesus. My nice smiles and questions. Jesus.

I drive through the city. Find the turn-off. Tears running down my cheeks. Rage.

At this ruined country. At myself. Quintessential bleeding-heart do-good do-nothing liberal. Jesus.

'What are you crying for? You're always crying.'

My husband, this man I hardly know, is gazing at me. I see he's curious. Curious and exasperated. Maybe guilty as well that he may have upset me in some inexplicable way. I can't scream I hate the awkwardness of this loathsome, misshapen body. Scream that I hate lying never able to sleep beside his hot clumsy snoring body. Hate the cloying atmosphere of those antenatal classes, being one of those complacent moon-faced balloon-bellied women the nurse calls 'ladies.' Hate the speculative way people stare at my belly, glance upwards at my hand for a wedding ring. I hate my navy pinafore dress.

I hate the crochet-edged napkins, hand-knitted singlets, that cutesy stupid stuffed Donald Duck, the recipes your mother gives us. I hate being talked to as if I'm an oversized imbecile who must constantly be warned about her fragility, feeling like an egg about to burst. I want my body back. I want my life back. I want you to disappear, to just piss off, and for me to wake up out of this nightmare. I can't say it. I want you to piss off. I want you to just fuck off. I want my own self, my own flat-bellied self back.

Don't say it.

I smile. 'I think it's just that I'm pregnant.'

And start to cry again.

He frowns, 'Does it go on like this right through?'

'I don't know. It said in that leaflet from the doctor's it's the hormonal changes. They make you emotional.'

'But you're always crying. You never stop. It's not normal.'

What do you know about normality? You've been pregnant have you? You know all about it do you? The sore back and bursting breasts and this kicking and prodding under your ribs when you want to sleep and the red marks all over your previously pristine belly and thighs and breasts. Those marks screaming to you that your skin is stretching tighter tighter tighter and even if you don't explode you'll be hideous forever.

'I think it is normal. Anyway I can't help it.'

I sob again. As alarmingly and irritatingly as I can possibly manage and he draws me into his arms, pretending to comfort me although I know very well that in the end he'll want sex. Comforting me is his version of foreplay. I allow the hands around my body that begin to creep and slide inside my clothes, the mouth that presses against my hot wet face. I want to slap and scream and shout and kick but I allow it because I need him.

And inside me now is this other uninvited thing, which, if allowed to continue, will cause similar chaos to my body and mind. Probably worse. Better to abort, to simply, cleanly have it vacuumed out of my body and continue as before. I could fly back tomorrow. Have it over in a week. Go back to Evie's with Tom and have a slow easy celebratory holiday.

I wonder if Eliza, when she discovered she was pregnant again at the grand old age of forty entirely welcomed the news. I wonder if she was filled with hope and joy at the expectation of another child or if beneath her seeming acceptance of God's will and stoicism she wept and raged. She was already worn out by hard physical work, a disappointing husband, pregnancies, grief for the babies who didn't survive. All those long months of pregnancy and the suffering of childbirth may merely have resulted in yet another dead child. Her own life could've been lost and her sons left motherless. It was unjust. Perhaps she secretly contemplated the possibility that she might lose this child early in pregnancy. But instead she was rewarded with the gift that was Hannah, her daughter.

I think also about that.

11

From time to time Evie used to remark that the men in our family either go missing or die.

Certainly this was so with Hannah's Alexandre.

The marriage began in grand style. Alexandre's brother, who'd come to advise him on the purchase of family land was best man and his friend, Antoine, was groomsman. Hannah's gown was made from icy-white figured silk brought over from Sydney and around her neck she wore a pearl choker which had been in Alexandre's family for generations and brought out of France during the revolution. Although Eliza insisted the marriage took place in the small Wesleyan chapel where she and Hannah worshipped each Sunday rather than the Anglican church which was Alexandre's preference, the chapel was grandly decorated with sprays of white roses displayed against a foliage of fern. One hundred and twenty-two guests were invited and the building was crammed. The women were elegant, hair elaborately coiled beneath feathered hats and dressed in opulent silks, velvets and furs. The men were equally splendid with moustaches waxed and best tailcoats trimmed with heavy watch-chains and gleaming collars. Alice wrote to her mother *it was quite a marriage in high life, for Alexandre was reported to be worth fifty-six thousand pounds, and it seemed it was no small thing to be Madame Guinard.*

After the sumptuous reception Hannah changed her bridal gown for a high-necked dress and matching satin shoes and with the pearl necklace encircling her neck, the thick golden ring encircling her wedding finger, left with Alexandre and Antoine for the wedding tour which would take them across the world to Cuba where she would make the acquaintance of the Guinard family.

They returned after six months. Hannah was pale and thin, but not, as Eliza initially suspected, pregnant. Alexandre placed her in the care of her mother and, with Antoine, immediately set off to inspect progress on the house he was having built on his property. After greeting her mother and assuring her that she was not ill but simply tired from a long journey, Hannah went directly to the bedroom she left on her wedding morning. She took her violin from where it had nestled during her absence, rested her fingers on the polished amber surface, then took it up and tucked it beneath her chin. She tuned it, then glided the bow over a series of scales. She played a little Bach, Vivaldi's 'Winter' from *Four Seasons*, then was silent and still. She stood for a time with her eyes closed, cradling her violin in her arms then began to play a Beethoven sonata, her music singing again through the house with such sweetness, such sadness, soaring, piercing, weeping like mountain water pulsing over rock.

This is what I think of as I make this journey down the coast, inland then again crossing the island. I think about Hannah playing her violin in the bedroom she left as a bride on her wedding morning. Of Eliza sitting in the small parlour which looked out into the street. I think of her laying down the crochet she was working at, resting her head against the back of the chair, listening to her daughter's sweet sad music. I think of Eliza and Hannah carefully packing the old china from England, the new wedding china from France, the crystal, the silver. Folding and placing the lace-edged linen in chests as they waited for Alexandre to return and take them to their new home.

Alexandre did not consult with his wife over the design and building of the new house. Indeed, until Hannah and Eliza made the journey with Alexandre to his property they had little idea of where they would live. But Alexandre had chosen well in the purchase of the thousands of acres of rich, fertile coastal land. Although the builders complained about access and the inadvisability of building in a position so exposed to coastal wind, he insisted that the house be built at the top of a cluster of hills with a clear view over the wide blue expanse of the Tasman on one side and an outlook into kauri forest on the other.

Alexandre was largely absent for the twelve month period following his and Hannah's return to New Zealand. He remained mainly at his property with Antoine who he described as his helper and adviser, living in a temporarily built shack and supervising the burning off and clearing of his land and the building of barns, stables and the house.

The child which normally closely followed the return of a young couple from the marriage tour was not forthcoming. Eliza and Hannah resumed the customary pattern of their lives. Hannah helped her mother attend to domestic affairs in the mornings and during the afternoons practised her violin while Eliza made her visits to the prison and the hospital. On Sundays they attended the morning service at the Wesleyan chapel, ate the midday meal prepared the day before since no work could be done on the Sabbath, and read aloud to each other from the Bible in the afternoons. Apart from Alexandre's occasional visits and preparations made for the removal to their new home it was as if the marriage had never taken place.

I'm climbing through bush and scrub-covered hill, glancing down from time to time at the map. Somewhere near here I have to turn off the main road, head up through Kirikopuni, through Tangiwahine, turn off again at Maropio, onto the coast road to Mamaranui. And home.

These names. These names, so magical, so splendid. Kiri-kopuni. Tangi-wahine. Ma-ro-pio. Ma-ma-ra-nui. I say them aloud as Evie said them to me, slipping my tongue over the consonants, drawing out the soft vowels.

Names of magic and splendour.

When Evie and I first came here you could take the train all the way up from Auckland. My new Aunt Alice cooked bacon and eggs for us and because the early morning was so warm, and Evie and Alice believed children should benefit from fresh air whenever possible and especially when a long journey was imminent, we ate breakfast at a folding table on the verandah. Everything was new, everything an adventure. The breathless Auckland air. The bellbird calling from the garden. The bacon was salty-sweet, edged with a crisp rind, and the egg had a bright yellow centre so soft that when I punctured it with my fork the yolk ran, savoury and delicious, across my plate and I scooped it up with white, soft, thickly-buttered bread.

We saw the black taxi stop outside. Evie kissed Alice, picked up the suitcase and walked down the path. Alice bent down and kissed my forehead and, for a moment, rested her powdery old-ladies' cheek against mine. Then she looked directly into my face and I saw her eyes were bright and keen.

'You're going home at last, Zoe,' she said.

Going home. Tangiwahine, Maropio, Mamaranui, Kirikopuni. Evie said the names and the train repeated them. Ma-ma-ra-nui. Kiri-kopuni. Going home.

It was a day's journey then. We stopped at Dargaville for lunch, ate pies from paper bags, steaming hot, salty gravy streaming from the edges of the pastry. Evie had tea in a thick white china cup. It was too hot she said and when the station master rang a warning bell she poured it into the saucer so it would cool quickly then tipped it down her throat.

'Inelegant,' she said looking down at me over the edge of the saucer. 'Dreadfully inelegant, Zoe, but needs must.' She laughed, scooped me up into the carriage and told me we hadn't much further to go.

I'm past the turn-off and the car is skimming now, skimming, soaring around the corners, speeding across the wide empty stretches of road, through Kirikopuni past the shop, the pub, the church, past where the little cottage was once over there on the corner. I almost stop to touch the briar rose that used to wind around the fence, to pick a fragment of honeysuckle. But I'm there, almost there now, through Tangi, through Waihue, Maropio and then off onto the side road winding upward and over the brow of the hill, down through Mamaranui, onto the gravel road. The home road, my road home.

The train grunted, wheezed, creaked then finally stopped with a flurry of soot and smoke at each station where I peered out through the tiny blurred window and asked if this was the one, are we getting out here? And at last Evie said, here we are, and we stood up and the train shuddered and we were out on a smooth concrete platform flanked by a weatherboard building with red doors labelled by decoratively figured bronze plaques — Ticket Office — Restrooms — Luggage — Refreshments.

There was a tall man standing by *Exit* and Evie said 'Samuel, this is Zoe.' He shook my hand, gazed down at me and said I was my grandmother over again, that was for sure and he picked up Evie's suitcase and we followed him. Through swinging glass doors, over the green tiled floor, past crimson leather seats — *Waiting Room* — down the steps to an immense silver-blue car of a rounded hunched shape, so polished that the body and the chrome trimmings gleamed in the sunlight. He undid a catch beneath the back window and a door sprang back revealing an expanse of empty and scrupulously clean boot-space. He lifted our suitcase, carefully placed it inside, then opened the back door for me and I slipped in, smelling the leather seats, feeling the cushioned firmness at the back of my knees. Samuel inserted the key into the ignition, turned it and the car purred. He pushed the clutch in firmly, coaxed it into first gear and we turned with stately grace out onto the road.

Once Samuel was in the driver's seat he would not speak. His concentration was firmly focused on manoeuvring his beauty through the perils of potholes, puddles, loose stones and mud patches so that she would arrive unsullied at her destination. That journey home over the gravel road. It was part of the pattern, part of the passage. Evie on the wharf. The palm of her hand resting on my face. The long train ride with the acrid soot smell in my mouth. Aunt Alice's house in Ponsonby and Annie Laurie and bacon and eggs. The train again, then Samuel and that beautiful beast-car that was his joy and his pride. And all the time waiting. Oh yes, loving it all, every minute and inch of it, but still waiting. Waiting for that moment when Samuel stopped the car, unfastened and hauled back the heavy iron gates and we glided through the entrance and up up the long tree-edged drive, through Evie's orchard, through the stone-walled edges of her garden and home.

That smell and feel of leather. Samuel's concentration. Watching late sun filter through bush, listening for the sea. The long slow climb up the hill, that final part and the car shuddering, complaining a little as Samuel changed down to second and then first. Seeing the tensing muscles begin to stand out, the redness flood across the back of his neck if it had rained and he couldn't avoid splatterings of mud. At the end he would sigh, a prolonged sigh which mingled with the slow pumping of brakes as we slid to a standstill. He would leap from the car, take the suitcase into the house and return with a bucket brimming with warm soapy water, his chamois, his polish, the anticipative expression on his face. At the end of every journey I ever made with him he said exactly the same thing.

'Better get her cleaned up quick before she rusts.'

I wonder what Samuel would make of this car. Oh certainly sleek and shiny but it's a throwaway car without ambience. A car of dubious character. I can imagine him walking around it frowning, prodding the body built to impress with its shapeliness and trimmings but, as he would soon ascertain, shoddy and insubstantial. I imagine he'd remain unseduced, his fidelity intact. This car is a dollybird, a little bit of fluff built for lightweights. Samuel's car was a dowager, to be approached with obeisance.

When Hannah and Eliza made the journey from Auckland by coach they were forced to remain two nights at Topuni because of flooding. Alexandre rode on ahead before the rain became heavy, and was unable to return across the river which swelled and spilled over the bank. The women were alone apart from the coach driver, and, with no inn in sight and the rain streaming down, were unsure what to do. However, a farmer passing on his horse stopped, spoke to the driver and offered the use of his cottage until the weather cleared. They were grateful but it was a cold, cheerless place. They lit a fire and huddled over it until their clothing dried, then the driver stretched out in the chair while Hannah and Eliza slept pressed together in a narrow single bed beneath a draughty window.

Still, they remained optimistic.

'Mother, what an adventure.'

When the driver decided they could continue Hannah was feverish but insisted they go on. She sat trembling, huddled in a rug on the hard seat as the coach slid on mud, lurched and shuddered over rocks exposed by rain.

They didn't approach the house until late afternoon but as they climbed Eliza glimpsed, through the bush, tawny roof tiles glowing in the sun. The driver stopped to water and rest the horses before the last stretch. At last Hannah had fallen into restless sleep and Eliza did not want to wake her.

But as the coach crawled and tipped its way uphill Hannah woke and stared blankly out into the scrub edging the track. She didn't speak but watched as the bush gave way to cleared land. She saw the barns and the stables and there looming at the top of the rise was her house.

I wonder if she did as I did when I was that child who came here with Evie. When I first saw and absorbed my view of that glorious house. I wonder if she too threw out her arms as if embracing it, shouting out her surprise and delight.

The house was perched in a bare brown paddock of mud before Eliza and Hannah and Evie worked their wonderment with flowers and bushes, but was still both elegant and extraordinary. Evie said it had good bones. Now its hard edges are softened and made more beautiful by the gardens and the vines and roses which wind around the verandah and balconies.

When I was older Alice told me Alexandre was a weak and conceited man but his life was redeemed because of two major creative activities, begetting Evangeline and building the house. *Heaven only knows how he managed either of them but he did and then thank the Lord, took himself away and left the bringing up of the child to her mother.*

Alexandre had an eye for beauty, perhaps afflicted with the family propensity towards extravagance, the need to possess and surround oneself with superior objects — *the Guinard family houses are adorned with the best and most ornate. Their women are always most elegantly turned out, beautiful, spirited and witty.* His own preference must have been in the acquisition and only occasional admiration of these beautiful ornaments since he was rarely in his house or with his wife.

The house is decidedly French, high and quite narrow but still perfectly proportioned. The roof, made from terracotta tiles, tilts high then slopes steeply down overlapping the walls which are plastered both inside and out. Inside they are painted a stark, glistening white. Outside they are washed with the pale blush-pink and apricot colour of sunset. The windows are shuttered and both the shutters and frames which edge and divide the glass into small square panes of light are painted grey like the sea at night. The outer sides of the sills are deep enough to hold the large clay pots filled with yellow nasturtiums and pink and red geraniums. Inside the house they are deep enough to sit in and feel the sun warm your body through the glass and look out on garden, bush and ocean. Arched, small-paned French doors lead out onto the wide verandah which spans the front and two sides of the house. Upstairs shuttered doors open onto balconies enclosed in delicately curved wrought iron.

The rooms are shaded and peaceful. An enclosed dark-wooden staircase runs to the upper floors from the entrance. There is a grand room with a glossy polished floor, a chandelier and a vast marble fireplace. But it is the kitchen I most love. That and the upstairs bedroom which was Evie's when she was a child, then Grace's and became my own.

When I first went there Evie took me up the stairs. She showed me the room and said it was to be mine, my own room whenever I came. Nobody else would be allowed to stay in it and if I wanted to I could keep my own things there and any pictures or toys or ornaments I may like that were now in other parts of the house. She took my clothes and shoes from her suitcase then opened the empty wardrobe and the drawers of the empty chest I could use to store them in.

Then she bent down to me and held me in her arms close against her body, 'I want you to be happy here, Zoe,' she said. 'Take your time to explore. Remember this house is also yours.'

She left me there and I went to the window which was also a door you could climb out of onto a little balcony. Beyond me was bright ocean edged by white-trimmed waves. I turned myself around and sat in the window with the sun on my back looking into my room.

It's still exactly as it was. The walls are the colour and texture of smooth vanilla icecream, the ceiling high and crisscrossed with knotted, light wooden beams and the floor polished wood covered partially with a thick knotted-rag rug. The narrow bed has high black iron ends and is covered by a thick ivory linen spread. The curtains are fine cream silk. Beside the bed is a scrubbed oak table, and a massive chest of drawers in the corner of the opposite wall. There's a bookcase filled with books from Evie's, Grace's and my own childhood. On the wall opposite the window is a vivid painting of a Paris boulevard with high buildings on each side of the cobbled stone street and tables topped with striped umbrellas. Above the bed is a small oil-painted portrait of a youthful Eliza, completed in England shortly before her departure to New Zealand and sent to her after her mother's death.

I sat on the window ledge looking into the room. Walked along the landing pushing open doors. Gazed in at each bedroom. The black and white tiled bathroom with the bath so large a child could swim in it, and the high wash stand. The small square sitting room at the end of the passage.

Down the stairs I found grander sitting and dining rooms, a vast bedroom with a small dressing area at the side, a room brimming with as many books as a library, with a fireplace and studded leather chairs. I heard Evie's voice call out, opened a door and found the kitchen.

I'd never seen a kitchen like that before. Our own kitchen in Christchurch was, like most of the so-called kitchenettes in my friends' homes, narrow with a small window. It was tacked onto the main part of the house, a purely utilitarian room for doomed women to scuttle into and manage as swiftly as possible, the unavoidable family cooking followed by the dreary wipe-down and wash-up. A place to be shunned.

But this room was huge and filled with light from French doors opening into a stone-walled garden filled with the mingling scents of mints, thyme, basil, rosemary and coriander I always associate with Evie's kitchen. And like my bedroom and all the other rooms of this perfect house it has remained the same.

The floor is tiled with granite faded to a dull grey sheen. Filling almost all of one side of the room is a fireplace raised to waist height above the floor with a series of shelves beneath built from the same rough red bricks and holding wooden boards, cast-iron grills, iron and clay pots and an enormous Dutch oven. On the mantelpiece above there are black iron cooking utensils, the strangely shaped forks and ladles and trivets. Strands of garlic hang from the knotted beams spanning the ceiling. There's a wide, solid, scrubbed table in the centre of the room where the marble mortar, the wooden pestle always remain, a marble bench with shelves above it filled with baskets, bottles of wine vinegars, jars filled with jams and pickles and chutneys and preserves.

Besides his eye for beauty Alexandre also had a taste for good food. As well as the marble, granite, roofing tiles and the chandelier, he had a chef imported from France. Evie learned about gardening from her mother but learned her cooking from Philippe.

I loved to be with Evie in the kitchen. I loved the unfamiliar smells of garlic and herbs, of fresh baked bread, of salt pork and beef shanks mixed with garlic, herbs, broth, wine, best olive oil and tomatoes and fat black olives simmered for hours in the *daubiere* in which countless daubs had simmered for countless hours. I loved the new words I found and spat out with my mouth pursed as if I was sucking sour gooseberries, *pot-au-feu, gratin, tian, saucisson, pistou*. I loved the way Evie assumed a French accent and waved her hands about imitating the way Philippe directed the one docile, blank-eyed kitchenhand he had as if ordering a kitchen crammed with budding cooks *Now you must listen to me. Are you paying attention? This is how we must commence. Pour a rasade of olive oil into the poelon ...*

'Ritual in the kitchen is at the heart of good cooking,' Evie would say. And smack a garlic clove hard with the heel of her hand, take the loosened hull from the ruptured clove, toss the garlic into the mortar, take up a pinch of coarse sea salt, throw it in then pound them together to create a silken, liquid paste.

'Good cooking can never be complete without a bed of wood for grilling the food,' she'd say as she laid pieces of bread, rubbed with garlic and dribbled with olive oil on a heavy wire grill over the embers. She baked long loaves of bread, crisped hard on the outside, the centre meltingly soft. She cooked my favourites, the gratins and omelettes, frail and pale-gold filled with sweet white onions, peppers, scarlet-fleshed tomatoes.

I'm through the gates now. Turning. Through the orchard, past the low stone fences enclosing the courtyards and gardens. I stop outside the house and stare up into the windows. My bedroom. The kitchen window. The grandest bedroom on the lower floor where Evie and Grace were born.

When the house came to me I didn't know how I could keep it. Although of course I knew I must. The acres bought by Alexandre had long been sold off for farm land. When I first came here Evie had sold the last block to a neighbouring farmer leaving the five acres of orchard and garden now with the house. But despite the quantity of land being manageable my work didn't allow for me to live here permanently. Ben was still at school. And there was Tom to consider and how could I have lived here without Evie? I knew the land needed attention and the house needed people to live in it. I couldn't bear to think of it empty, abandoned here at the top of this hill.

Somebody told me about Lucy.

Lucy was an artist who wanted a retreat, an isolated place, cheap, certainly cheap — but it had to be beautiful. A place where she could live and paint. It seemed a solution but I was nervous about it. I couldn't have someone who didn't love Evie's house living here. But I was told she was a gardener and in the end I phoned and we arranged to meet for coffee and a talk.

Lucy is well named. Her hair swings and crackles with light. Her eyes and voice spark. Her clothes are electric, blue-purple, orange, saffron yellow. Copper and silver and gold. I immediately said that of course she could have the house and she threw her arms around me, moved in the next day. She paints and cares for the house and garden. Most of the time she's alone but sometimes her man, Clem, is here as well and prunes trees, paints walls, fixes things. They live here and I have my house well cared for.

She's there at the window and I wave, watch her running through the door onto the verandah, down the steps, hurtling at me as I get out of the car.

'Zoe. Zoe, why didn't you tell me you were coming?' She hugs me hard, pats my hair, is talking talking talking. I must see her painting, her new one, it's the best thing she's done ever, truly but can you believe this day, isn't it gorgeous? You're looking so well Zoe, oh won't you just look down there at that sea. And, oh, she nearly forgot. She did think I might turn up because Tom phoned. Twice. Or it might have been three times.

We drink coffee on the verandah, talk about her painting, my writing, Ben, Tom, Clem, then walk through the garden — Zoe, just look at the roses, they've been so wonderful this year — to the old stables, now her studio with the flat above, and look at paintings, vibrant, glowing with Lucy's own light.

I take my bag from the car, wander about through all the rooms as I always do when I come back then lastly to my own room. Leave my bag on the floor, open up the doors. I'm lying on my bed, looking out over the sea, closing my eyes, placing my hands over my belly, pressing down. Testing. Still flat. I stretch. Think about babies. About the bedroom below me, the room facing onto the verandah where Evie was born, Grace was born.

Evie told me her husband Joe would not budge from the chair he sat in on the verandah right beside the bedroom doors, even though the midwife told him men weren't wanted at these times and he'd be no use to his wife later on if he was too tired to help. He sat there all throughout the long labour and Evie said knowing he was there helped with the pain, helped her to know she'd come through, both her and the child. After he heard Evie's last cry followed by a silence, a faint mewing cry, he came in through the doors, kissed Evie and looked down at her with tears standing out in his eyes.

And while Evie slept he took his daughter from the shocked, protesting midwife, wrapped her in a blanket and took her out into the night *to give my darling girl her first sight of this glorious earth given us by God.*

The black sky alight with stars, the pinpoints of jasmine shining out of the shadowed garden, the pewter sea below. He stood with his daughter propped against his chest, his big hands holding her tiny body, her head lolled against his shoulder and he cried for joy.

My mother. Grace. I feel the prick and sting of tears, the tightness in my throat.

12

When Evie's house came to me I did consider the possibility of living here for at least a part of the year. For a few months I'd retire from the world, bake bread, set up my computer in the library. I'd write differently here. I could be a poet, writing profound musings as I gazed out of the window. Maybe I'd write like Lawrence sometimes did, sling a hammock between two trees and be inspired by nature. I thought I'd be a romantic figure. A hermit, if there are female hermits, retiring from the materialistic world, retreating from men, television, traffic, all those nasty noisy demanding things. I'd while away my time tending to my garden, writing soulful poetry, and wafting about.

But I've always needed an audience for my various personae. Tom grinned mildly and rejected the position of estate gardener. When I suggested Ben might like to spend half his year in retreat from the world he looked outraged and delivered his typical response to my excesses, 'You wanna do *what?* Mum, get a life.'

Anyway my selected persona then was the tough, vocal crusader rather than the gentle recluse I envisaged as my metamorphosis. I was embroiled in my course perhaps not to save the entire world but to at least inform a small portion of it of injustice, scandal and fraud with my lucid, probing exposés. I had to do my bread-and-butter stuff, articles on midlife crises, and how this or that one got through some or other trauma by self-actualisation, meditation or eating natural yoghurt. And never looked back

The woman/man/combination-of-both-plus-offspring who lived/sailed around/climbed in Afghanistan/Borneo/Antarctica/The Andes Mountains/The Falkland Islands and are much better people for it now. Working Girls, reconstituted families, clairvoyants — I had my hand, cards, chakras, aura done in the name of research and for a short time toyed with the idea that a young dark musician would saunter into my path and my letter box would fill with money. I did anorexia, bulimia, women who'd lost thirty kilos and were subsequently living fulfilling lives going to aerobics and wearing glamorous clothes — *I used to slink into shops and hide behind the racks, even the largest sizes were too tight, and now I'm size twelve, I can wear anything, even the little strappy evening dress I bought for our tenth wedding anniversary, my husband loves me again.* I did school reunions, alternative education, vegetarianism, the breakdown of the nuclear family, communes, TA and TM and workshops to discover the goddess in you.

I did write stories I'm still proud of. About children with cancer, about old age, the Vietnamese refugees, violent death, poverty in Auckland, women's refuges. The stories which made me humbled by courage I felt fortunate to observe. The ten year old who knew she would die and wanted to stay but accepted it. The Vietnamese woman. I'll never forget her. I went to the house and she came to the door carrying a black-eyed baby on her hip. She was slight, fragile, exquisite. She beamed and nodded as I explained slowly who I was and she took me into her kitchen, ushered me to a chair set in front of the two bar heater beside the chipped formica table — all their furniture was donated, was a combination of old sofas, cabinets, shelves and beds, nothing matched and everything was very worn — carefully made me a cup of tea, triumphantly smiling as she managed the new words — *you take milk, please?*

And for the afternoon I sat and with a combination of the English she was learning at polytech classes — *very help, very lucky* — and waving arms, nodding and pointing and laughing over the drawings we sketched quickly to help clarify the words, I learned about her life. The son and daughter dead from typhoid in the refugee camps. The illnesses, hunger, worry about her family — she still didn't know whether her parents had survived. She and her husband made the long, difficult trek to the overfilled, disease-ridden camp in Thailand. Waited for news. For death. Then finally they were put on the plane which brought them to New Zealand. *New Zealand very good place, very kind people. Husband have job, small son very strong.*

When I think about some work I've done I recall the language, remember probing for clear, hard words, labouring for the glib phrase, the witty, cutting comment. Brittle, hard-edged, glossy scraps. But with other stories it's not my words I recall but the people I wrote about, the spirit which shone bright in their eyes, the tears they sometimes couldn't hold back. I also remember their laughter. The people I most remember could laugh at themselves and at the world. I interviewed a Jewish woman, an artist who'd survived a concentration camp. I was nervous about the interview, wary of the questions which might result in unbearable recollections of cruelty and suffering. I asked about her painting, her life in New Zealand, finally, tentatively, about her life before she came here.

'Ah,' she said. 'You will know I was in the camps. Four years in the camps. My mother and my father and my brother, all dead there. You want to hear about the camps? So terrible. Children torn from their mothers, wives from their husbands. I watched a woman try to feed her child from her breasts but there was no food to make her milk and in the end he died. She held that child in her arms three days until we took him from her. So cruel. So bad. But I'll tell you something about those camps. Never have I laughed so much, never in my life since that time. Never laughed so much. Never had so much sex. It was what kept me alive. Laughing and sex.'

The people I remember. Brave, kind people. People who laugh. I burned with my need to discover, understand, to write with words as good as I could make them because I believed in the importance of the stories.

But I'm starting to see that now's the time to consider my own history and the legends which have made and shaped me.

Perhaps I'm now old enough, tired enough to live quietly here. Perhaps I'd still choose to write poetry but not those jangling, strident strings of words I'd have written then. Now that I'm less certain of the ground I stand on I'd observe more kindly, question more tentatively.

'My God, Zoe, you're becoming mellow in your old age.'

Tom's laughing at me. Because I have mildly and sympathetically forgiven one of the new backbenchers a pathetically stupid television interview, *It's ignorance rather than malice, he can't know what he's saying. Surely.*

They know not what they do.

Or do they?

I'm not sure any more.

That prickly post-divorce, post-married-lover woman, chopped-off spiky hair, no nonsense jeans and gymmies and chewed down fingernails would've known. Because she knew everything. For example she knew that all the misery of this entire miserable fucking world was caused by men, the bastards. She bristled, almost spat if a man stood aside for her at a doorway, called her a lady, said she was looking nice today. Said fuck so regularly it was tiresome. Was filled by rage, bitterness and pain.

Was softened, probably saved, by her son. By her lover as well?

Maybe. Not that she would have thanked you for your opinion.

Morning is the best time in Evie's garden. Oh certainly you have to admire it at midday when the flowers are brazenly on show, fully open and florid. But it's the early mornings and evenings when the plants gleam and the scents are sharpest I love it most. I make thick black coffee in the kitchen then sit on the wooden bench placed here on the stone Alexandre had taken from the hills then pounded and sliced into rough, irregular paving.

The garden is divided by low stone fences. There are the herbs and behind them the house vegetable garden which was once prolific with green, yellow and red peppers, tomatoes and beans, baby marrows, squash and yams, sweet and plain potatoes, garlic and onions, both red and white, and shallots, all spilling over the thick black soil. Now Lucy grows small amounts of what she most likes.

Then there are the flowers. In the spring following Eliza and Hannah's arrival Luke came with a cart filled with seedlings, cuttings and seeds from the Hokianga garden. By that time the soil had been prepared. Alexandre had his farmhands dig up an acre of ground beyond the house into long wide beds then dig in compost from the kitchen, and manure. He planned the garden carefully — the walls, courtyards, orchard and the vineyard — creating a sense of constraint yet irrepressible abandonment. The walls contain the growth but are covered by vines, and softened by foliage and the hanging branches of trees planted close by. The formal stone sitting area beyond the house is edged by climbing roses and the steps lead directly down into the orchard. Flowers, trees, vines spill, climb and intertwine in a multitude of colours and sweet, balmy fragrances.

On the morning following my first arrival, Evie took me out into her garden. I take my coffee and follow where we walked. Across the paving, through the stone archway, across the damp lawn. Through the lavish profusion of late-blooming poppies and daisies and larkspur, granny's bonnets, foxgloves, lavender, past the rose beds. The colour pours across this part of the garden like a pallet filled with oils, singing yellows, reds, greens, all the shades of blue from dusky mauve to violet. An orange like the sun when it's a bright fireball, the pink and grey lavenders, white and lemon daisies shaped like stars. I walk past the rose beds to the grapevines. Each year a local wine maker takes the grapes and we both are repaid by the wine we share which is golden and fills your mouth with a delicious richness. Finally the orchard, the old apples, pears and apricots — my wine maker takes these too and turns them into thick, decadent liqueurs. I look up into the dark-leafed towering fig tree, nurtured from a seedling which grew beneath that other fig tree in the Hokianga.

This is where we stopped that first day. We sat under this tree, rested our heads against the broad trunk and Evie told me how the garden was built, that it was where she played as a child, that my mother played here. And she told me about Hannah and Eliza.

After Eliza and Hannah came to live here the china, linen, crystal, glassware and silver was unpacked and placed in the cabinets, clothing hung in the wardrobes and underwear and nightwear folded and placed in the chests with lavender bags. When the servants had been appointed and their duties arranged — there was a housekeeper, manservant, housemaid, kitchenmaid, a gardener and of course Alexandre's French chef — the furniture placed and the curtains hung, Eliza and Hannah turned their attentions to this garden. Hannah rarely sought to have influence over anything related to her husband. She made no comments about his business dealings and was content for him to build his house and furnish it however he wished.

But the garden was different. Like Eliza, she loved the freedom of digging and plunging her hands into the rich dark earth and the creativity of planting, waiting and watching for some fragile, flimsy scrap of green to grow. Alexandre believed the occupations of digging, hoeing and raking were degrading to his wife and fit only for the *hoi polloi*. He was repulsed by the sight of Hannah with her hair loose, pinafore splattered with mud and up to her elbows in wet soil but in the end he was forced to agree.

'I do not ask for anything else, Alexandre,' she said, 'and you must, of course, pattern and arrange the garden as you wish. But Mother and I wish to plant and tend it.'

The house was frequently visited by Alexandre's brother and when Alexandre was there his friend Antoine always accompanied him. Acquaintances visited and stayed weeks at a time as did James and Alice and their children, William, Anne-Jane and John. Luke visited less frequently and always without Ruth and their constantly expanding family. During those times the house was busy. The guests had to be provided with food, clean linen, company and entertainment. There were daily picnics, games, coach drives and riding and in the evenings the great mahogany table in the dining room was covered by a cream damask cloth then set with the best dinner service, crystal and heavy silver cutlery. For the remainder of the time Eliza and Hannah tended the garden, dealt with the domestic affairs of the household. In the late afternoon Eliza wrote letters and Hannah practised her violin.

There was no child. Alexandre was most often absent, staying in the town house in Auckland and attending to business affairs, or on one of his frequent voyages. Hannah never accompanied her husband and his companion on their journeys. If she was disappointed by this or by the absences, or the absence of a child she did not speak of it.

During these years Hannah was often silent. She'd been a lively and articulate child. Now she glided through the rooms of Alexandre's house, a moving ornamentation, slim, upright, graceful, her fair hair coiled and catching the light from the windows, fanning out from her small uptilted head. She did not speak of her marriage. She didn't speak of love or happiness or her French husband's charming nature. Whenever he was home they walked together through the garden in the evenings. She smiled whenever he came looking for her.

Hannah is in her garden. She carefully clips the dead heads from the roses, the dry, browning, overblown flowers which fall apart in her hands. She pauses, then turns to look beyond the beds of flowers, the stone walls, the slim labelled saplings recently planted in the orchard, to the sea. There is a ship, sails filled, winging towards the horizon. She watches until it tips across and disappears over the distant grey-blue line. She turns back and continues to cut away the decaying growth.

Hannah takes up her violin, places it beneath her chin, tunes it. The guest who is about to play the piano and has suggested she accompanies him, strikes a few notes to encourage her. He selects the pieces, then launches into *Come Into The Garden Maude, Pomp And Circumstance* then *Rule Britannia* with such loud enthusiasm, such a rousing tenor that the missed notes and poor phrasing are almost disguised. The sound of Hannah's violin hovers softly, curls discreetly about the vigorous pounding bass.

She stands beside the open window in an upstairs bedroom, breathes in the sea salt she can smell even from this distance, watches the waves cluster and break along the coastline. She turns. Smooths the white linen cover on the small iron bed.

Midway through the last year of the century Alexandre returned unexpectedly from Auckland. He was shortly to set out again on a further journey to Europe. He was alone — Antoine had engagements which required his presence in town. During his short stay he was silent and morose.

After he left Hannah was at last pregnant.

She expects the bleeding at her usual time of the month and when it does not happen dismisses the change as trivial, perhaps it will start next week. But when it doesn't happen the next week or the one after that or indeed during the whole following month she's surprised, anxious, excited. She observes with intense concentration, the changes taking place in her body. The swelling, tingling breasts, nausea, the feelings of overwhelming sleepiness that occur in the afternoon.

A child. With child. I am with child. Unto thee a child is born.

But she will wait for the third month before she makes her announcement. She may after all be mistaken. But she vomits, triumphantly vomits in the mornings and her nipples change to a dark brownish-pink. The sound of her violin peals and trills and purrs.

'Mother. Mother, we're going to have a child in the house.'

Despite Hannah's slim, frail body and the narrow hips Eliza fretted over, Evangeline Alexandra Eliza was delivered without fuss or anxiety on the first day of the new year. The confinement was brief, the pain minuscule. The baby simply poured into the world.

'*A new child for a new century,*' Eliza said of this tiny girl, her own granddaughter. She carefully washed and dressed her in fine flannel and lawn, wrapped her in the soft knitted shawl then settled her in Hannah's arms.

Alexandre did not return in time for his daughter's birth. Hannah wrote to his anticipated destination to tell him the news of their expected child. She thought he would return towards the end of the old year but in the past his business dealings had often kept him in places longer than he calculated and ships were frequently delayed.

They anticipated Alexandre's return, looking forward to showing off his baby daughter, this black-eyed charmer, to him. While they waited, the baby Evie — she was always Evie — was the focus of their mutual joy and attention.

Alice told me Evie was a beautiful child. She inherited Alexandre's dark good looks but was like Hannah in her good-natured temperament.

'Although not always,' Alice chuckled. 'Evie had a devil in her. A temper. You hardly ever saw it, mostly she was a good, kind child. Like her mother. She was all sweetness with her cousins most of the time, play any game, give them any toy they wanted. Almost. But not quite. There were some things she wouldn't do and some things she wouldn't share, wouldn't even let anyone touch and if she was crossed or pushed too far about those things, well woe betide the rest of us. She could scream blue murder and she'd hit out at anything in her way. Anything and anyone. She knocked William over once. He was twice her size. She frightened him. Her mouth was wide open screaming and her legs and arms were going. Kicking and slapping. She could be a terror, that's for sure. Hannah and Eliza'd come running and both of them would have to hold onto her until she stopped. Then she would sob, the poor wee mite, just sob and sob. She'd have to spend the rest of the day on her bed with a cold flannel on her head, she was so overwrought and sorry. You hardly ever saw it but if you did it was something you didn't forget in a hurry. Of course she's patient now, so patient. But your grandmother wasn't always so. That wise, patient woman you and I see now is who she's grown into but it didn't always come easily. That temper. It was the darkness in her.'

I couldn't imagine my Evie who was never angry caught up in a rage.

'Did it go away when she grew up?'

'It wasn't so much that it went away as she learned to control it. I've seen her turn red then bite her lip and walk out of a house to stride off down the road. Just turn herself around and push herself out through the door with her hands clenched up into fists. When she was younger, mind. Never now, not for a long time. Not since…'

She glanced down at me as if she suddenly noticed who I was and her eyes changed from that dreamy remembering way they looked when she was telling me her stories. She shook her head slightly and stared at the clock, 'Glory be is that the time, well isn't it time now for that cake I've got at the back of the cupboard and we've still got a bit of that orange drink left that you like and would you like to find your grandmother now, Zoe, and tell her I'm making a pot of tea.'

Evie was exactly the daughter to entrance her father for she had his black eyes fringed by the same curling thick eyelashes topped by slanting black wings of eyebrows. Her face was full and round, her skin silken, mouth generous and perfectly formed — exactly like a rosebud, Hannah said, gazing down at this perfect little creature. And she beamed and crowed and chuckled and waved her small fists and kicked out with her small plump legs. The world was in love with her and she with the world. She was a beauty, the perfect baby daughter to beguile her father.

Except Alexandre never returned to see and celebrate his child. Hannah waited for him, for a letter at least, and when it was midway through the new year and still she'd received no word she wrote to his family and to officials so that ship records could be checked. But her letters were unanswered and there was no information forthcoming from official channels. It seemed he and his family had disappeared without trace.

When Evie was two years old and there'd been no Alexandre and no communication, Hannah sought legal advice. Fortunately Alexandre had appointed a capable and trustworthy foreman to oversee the work and business of his farm. But there were affairs which had to be settled and Hannah was at a loss as to how to deal with a huge property and a mislaid husband. She was advised that she must wait seven years. After that time it would be assumed that Alexandre was dead and if there were no other claimants she and Evie as next of kin would subsequently inherit his estate.

And so they waited. And while they waited Hannah was given good advice by the farm manager and became increasingly caught up in the affairs of the property. She began to speak out as well as to listen during consultations — Alice said she found her voice again — and to make decisions of her own. The farm, which eventually became hers, flourished.

As did Evie in the care of her doting mother and grandmother. Evie said she had the kind of childhood she would wish for all children. She was loved, so very much loved. 'And lived in the midst of all this,' she said throwing out her arms towards the garden.

In the evenings Eliza and Hannah and Evie sat on the verandah. Evie sat on a stool in front of Eliza's chair with her head resting against her grandmother's knees. Eliza brushed her hair. Hannah read aloud, sometimes played for them. At other times Eliza told the stories about England and about coming in the ship to New Zealand. And then there were the Hokianga stories.

'We were in the middle of Heke's war, Evie, and everyone was so afraid. The *Osprey* — it was a man-of-war — was sent to protect us, or take people back to Auckland for safety if they wished to go. I was rather frightened and almost wished we should but William said our place was there and how could we remain as missionaries for God if we did not keep our trust in Him? One night, there was such a noise outside. William said we must remain calm and I must not be afraid but I was and I knelt beside our bed praying with all my heart but with my head lowered so that I was almost hidden. My heart was thudding so hard, Evie, I believed those outside would hear it. William took his Bible in his hand, a candle in the other, opened our door wide and stood in the doorway. He spoke with the group outside our house for some time. I could hear the voices rising and muttering, my Maori language was not good enough then to understand what was being said but the voices sounded so angry and unhappy I was wishing myself safe back to England. But then I heard William call out. A good night to you all. Go in peace. He came smiling through the doorway and said they meant us no harm and we must give thanks to our Deliverer and believe me Evie, my prayers were heartfelt that evening.'

They sit in the evening dusk. Evie sits close to Eliza as she brushes then plaits her thick dark hair and their voices murmur and hover in the stillness, the air fragrant with scents rising from the garden.

It's the way I like to think of them. On the verandah in the evening. Eliza brushing Evie's hair as Evie brushed mine. Telling the same stories Evie told to me. The stories she told Grace.

That's what I think of as I sit in the garden looking up to the verandah. The women, the myths, the much-loved child. Evie was right. Love, beauty and stories are essential ingredients to make up the journey that is childhood.

If I were the good fairy at the baptismal feast, they're the gifts I would bestow. The gifts I had and remain most grateful for since they gave me my resilience. I can wail and weep when I feel hard done by but in the end I always pick myself up and get on with it. Stories led me to understand, prompted me to look harder and further. Love made me strong, made me the survivor I am.

'Certainly, Zoe, the capacity to love is a gift we're born with. But it has to be learned as well and cared about, not taken for granted. Sometimes it's when you're most complacent about love you find you know nothing at all.'

I hear her voice. Feel the brush tug then slide through my hair. Yes Evie. The love, stories, lessons. Your words are a stored richness, an everlasting wealth tucked beneath my heart.

13

More than ever I'm missing Tom. I miss his firm, wide back I like to creep against in the night when I'm cold. I miss his thigh curling around my own, miss putting my arms around his body feeling that scrap of un-firm roundness about his belly he can't remember to tuck in while he's sleeping. I miss his voice, his quick funny comments, raspy laugh, his arm around me as we drink tea in bed and listen companionably to Morning Report Shit, now would you just listen to that? before we drive off into our days.

I tell him on the phone I've found out I didn't go away because I wanted to leave him.

He says drily he's delighted to hear it.

'And I miss you. I wasn't sure that I would.'

'I'm pleased to hear that as well. In fact this is becoming a most satisfactory conversation.'

'I love you. I've found that out too.'

'Oh joy. Was there much doubt?'

'Not much. Probably not too much.'

'My cup runneth over,' he says.

I did not know about missing. That hungry aching void missing can manufacture inside your body just below the centre of your ribs. Not until that first time I left Evie standing on the wharf in Wellington and went back on the ferry to my mother and Christchurch. I didn't know about missing because, up until that time, there'd been nobody and nothing for me to miss.

But now there was Evie and Alice and Sam Samuels and Mrs Samuels and sometimes their son and his wife and their grandchildren. And Hannah and Eliza, Luke, James, William and Alexandre. The garden, the beach, the orchard, the house and the verandah.

'Yes, Zoe. When you love something or someone, as well as the happiness you have the risk of loss and change and the pain that goes with it. But that experience of loving, that first bright joy, is what you remember later, when the loss is not so hard.'

I'm fourteen, on my bed crying about the boy I met on the beach. The boy I'll love forever. Rodney. Rodney the remarkable. Almost every day I've wordlessly patrolled the shoreline with him, holding hands and gazing shyly and soulfully into his eyes. On the few evenings Evie allowed me out 'for a walk' I kissed and kissed him until my mouth was swollen and numbed. I'm addicted to the tingling that takes over my body when his hand brushes my bare shoulder, when his warm full mouth plants itself firmly on my own. But in the morning he's returning to Auckland. His holiday is over. As is my life.

During the last week before I was to return to Christchurch Evie and I did not speak so much. My mind was busy thinking about my mother. I remembered the blood, the heaving vomiting in the night, my mother lying unmoving in her bed. I remembered the men from the ambulance manoeuvring the stretcher down the stairs and into the back of the ambulance, closing the doors on my mother covered by the red blanket, her eyes closed, her body still and her face yellow. I remembered the neighbours whispering. Prosecution, prosecution if she's not lucky.

Evie had a letter from her. I knew because she handed me a sheet of paper from the back of it which said my mother was much better and I could come home soon and she hoped I was enjoying my holiday. Evie's letter was much longer and she sat for some time, frowning over it then sighed and took her glasses off and went to stand beside the window. I saw she was wiping her eyes. Then she said, 'I think a walk along the beach. Come on Zoe.'

I was afraid to ask what was in the letter. To ask about prosecution. Had that happened to my mother? Would it happen? What'd she done? I was afraid to ask when I had to go home but most of all to ask if I would be able to come back again.

I felt a deep black anger and guilt. Anger with my mother who allowed me to believe we were orphans. Guilty that I did not want to go back. Guilty that sometimes in the night I woke and listened to the sea sounds and wind, smelt the salt and the scents from the garden, saw through my open window the blue-black, star-scattered sky and I wanted my mother prosecuted. I wanted her to go to prison and remain there a very long time so I could stay with Evie.

We took the train back to Auckland, stayed with Alice, made the long, slow journey down to Wellington and Evie put me on the ferry. She took me to my cabin, asked a steward to look after me since I was travelling alone, and then sat beside me on the narrow bottom bunk bed I was to sleep in.

'Well, now, Zoe.' She took my hand and squeezed it tightly.

I looked down at our hands. Mine was small, tanned pale golden. Hers was wide and splotched with dark freckles, the fingers very long, the knuckles knobbly, standing out, and I could feel the calluses from gardening on her palm. I looked down at those hands I'd become so accustomed to, watching them digging, cutting back the roses, feeling them stroke my forehead, brush my hair, reach and hold me. I'd kept back my tears until then but now they poured from me, out of my eyes and my nose so I could scarcely breathe.

'I don't want to go. I don't want to go home. I want to stay with you. Let me stay with you.'

'Ah, Zoe, you think that for now but you need your mother and she needs you as well.'

She tucked my head against her shoulder and said she loved me very much and I must be brave. I held my tears back again until she left.

She didn't say I could come back. I thought about it all through the night feeling the sea beneath me, hearing the creaking and the waves and the wind, *She didn't say I could come back.*

My mother was waiting on the wharf. She was huddled against the wind in her black coat and a red hat. She put her arms around me. That was always an awkward matter, her embracing me. Her lips darting against my cheek, arms awkwardly reaching for me seemed more of a social etiquette — what was expected of her — than tenderness or love. She put her arms around me and my body turned rigid. I thought she felt thin and insubstantial. I looked up into her oval, powdered, red-lipped face and was overcome with an aching wave of need for Evie.

'You look well. You're very tanned,' she said.

'It's hotter up there.' I said.

'Yes I remember.'

She carried my bag onto the train. She asked if I was hungry and I shook my head. She said she didn't have to go to work today and we would go shopping for some school things. School on Monday, she reminded me.

If you can remember it's hotter up there, if you remember about school on Monday why couldn't you remember to tell me about other things? About my grandmother, about my Aunt Alice, about the garden and the beach and the house? Why didn't you tell me? Why don't we live in Evie's house, in the sun with the garden and the sea? Why do we have to live in this dark, damp place in a half-house? Why didn't you tell me about my grandmother?

I stared out of the window at the houses, flat, damp paddocks, the dark of the tunnel, the dark concrete platform of the station.

My mother bought heavy school shoes, warm vests and knickers and long-sleeved shirts and I returned to school. If she noticed I was quiet she didn't mention it. She didn't ask about my 'holiday' and I didn't speak about it. Neither did she speak about her illness and there was no mention of any prosecutions. Whatever she'd done was hidden away to be forgotten. I began to doubt myself. Perhaps I had misheard the neighbours or dreamt their conversation.

We resumed our lives. Each morning we had breakfast together. The radio was always switched on and we ate hardly speaking. I returned from school, peeled the potatoes and did my homework up in my room. When my mother came home she took off her coat and cooked our meal which we ate just after six o'clock. In the evenings we listened to the radio. Sometimes my mother asked me about school or played a board game with me. There were no men visiting any more in the weekends. I never again went into her room and burrowed into her bed.

But although the habits of our ordinary lives resumed, although I attempted to fulfil the requirements of school and home duties, it was as if somehow it was not me at all. I watched myself go through these activities as if I was watching some child away in the distance. At school I'd suddenly become aware that other children were listening to or writing or reading something I'd missed. Sometimes I'd look closely at my mother and realise her delicate beauty and recall how I'd loved her. At night I would wake up listening for the sea.

Each Saturday a letter arrived for me from Evie. My mother silently handed it to me and I ripped it open and read about what had happened through the week, about Sam and his family, about the work, the weather and the garden. At the end she always said she loved me. I'd tear through the letter looking for the words saying I could come back. When I couldn't find them I'd return to the beginning and search more slowly.

My mother did not like to be questioned. She had a way of drawing back from you, raising her eyebrows slightly then turning away. I didn't ask about her illness and what had caused it. I didn't ask all those questions churning inside me. Why don't you ever see Evie? Why don't you ever talk about her? Why don't you talk about the house and about growing up there and about the Hokianga? Why do you make us live here? But I asked another question, one I couldn't hold back.

'Can I go back? Can I? When can I go back? When am I going?'

At first she didn't answer but when I was persistent she said she didn't know, perhaps some time, she wasn't sure. When I asked every day, she shouted, I was to stop.

'You must stop this, Zoe. Stop it right now. If I'd known how this would turn out I'd have left you with the neighbours.'

During the year before my mother's illness I read *Heidi*. Now I understood about her loss, her missing. I understood her yearning for the mountains and the clear glacial air and the alpine house and her grandfather. Because I had my own loss of sea and garden and house and grandmother and that yearning clawed inside me.

My mother thought to create diversions to cheer me up. She said I looked pale, peaky and needed fresh air and some outings. She took me to the Botanical Gardens, to the pictures, to the museum. I trailed miserably behind her. She gave me a tonic to drink before I went to bed, took me on the bus out to Sumner Beach. I followed her along grimy sand, looked at grey water. Everything was dirty. Everything was dirty and dull and cold.

I didn't sleepwalk but like Heidi I acquired a condition which eventually created alarm. I discarded my appetite. I threw away my school lunches and ate little of anything else. Then I stopped sleeping. I lay awake in the nights with my eyes wide open, hearing the clock, occasional footsteps or a car outside, the milkman, the early morning factory whistles.

But in my half-consciousness I listened for the hum and throb of the sea and the wind whirring against roof tiles. I searched for a house the colour of pale sunset, for vines and flowers and trees tumbling over low stone walls, for a stretch of seamless sea and sky in all the colours that blue can be, for white walls, and a narrow bed with black iron ends and a cool linen cover.

My mother began to receive phone calls from my teacher and then the school principal, *Whatever is the matter with Zoe? Well, no, it isn't her behaviour. Zoe's behaviour could never be faulted in any way. But has she been unwell? She is so quiet, yes of course, she always has been a quiet child but, well, you could always get a smile out of her, she has a delightful sense of humour, you will know that yourself, of course. But she is so quiet, I would say, almost, well, withdrawn and I hate to say this but a teeny bit sullen, hardly speaks to the other children, very unresponsive in class, she seems half asleep most of the time. And her work is suffering. Her work definitely is suffering and Zoe was always one of our more able students. And have you noticed? She's so thin.*

My mother gritted her teeth and sat through more Saturday afternoon matinees. We went on a day's excursion, a train trip to Little River. She tried another tonic and bought icecream, small cakes decorated with cream and chocolate and jelly pieces, grapes and mandarin oranges, to tempt me. At first she tried to patiently reason with me, 'Zoe, this is silly, now come on, you must start eating properly again and you look so tired, what about if I take the radio up to your bedroom and you pop into bed and listen to your programmes and have an early night?' Then she used anger, 'If you don't pull yourself together, young woman, you will make yourself properly ill.'

When I heard my mother crying in the bathroom I was almost sorry for her. She didn't usually cry.

But I was glad as well. That hard, cold part of me. I can generously and compliantly give and give. But I'm no martyr. I won't give all of myself. I'd loved my mother, she'd been the centre of my life. But I believed she'd betrayed my trust and love for her and I was filled with rage. She'd denied me Evie and now she was keeping me from her.

Never would I forgive my mother. My ribs stuck out and my clothes hung on my body. My face was sucked in and translucent and my eyes stared into the mirror out of grey-purple hollows. I examined myself with satisfaction. I would hold out. I would win. I would not forgive her. I would die first. Unless she let me have my way.

I felt hot and achy one morning, and my throat was sore. My mother took my temperature and said it was a little high and I should stay home from school and rest, she would try to get home early from work. She said, looking closely at my face, trying to sound optimistically bright, I would be perfectly well again tomorrow.

For a while I listened to the radio. I was not very sick. Days away from school were a luxury. I lay snugly in bed with a newly-filled hot water bottle and the house quiet, the morning sun at the window and listened to the radio serials.

My head felt hot and it began to hurt and the pain in my throat was worse. I thought I'd probably be sick the next day as well and lay back on the pillow drifting in and out of sleep with the radio a blurry, background haze.

The lunchtime factory whistle woke me. I felt agonising pain in my head and neck. I was sweating, my body smothered by sweltering heat. I began retching. I got out of bed, my body weak, my legs wobbly as if they couldn't hold me up properly. I had to lean on the walls, then I was kneeling over, clinging to the sides of the toilet and heaving up dark-yellow, sour bile.

I lay on the bathroom floor resting. Vomited again and again and again until the stuff I was bringing up looked like black blood. I crawled back to bed and lay freezing and shivering, my head ablaze with pain and my neck so stiff and sore I could hardly move.

I slept, vomited, slept again. The pain pounded so I couldn't move. I retched and retched into my bed. I was going to die. I'd made myself so ill I would die. I sobbed with pain and fear. Closed my eyes tightly against the agony of light coming in the window. Sobbed and retched and slept slipping in and out of pain and cold and heat which pulsed in waves through my body. Slept and woke. Heard breathing. Was it from me, that rough rasping filling the room?

I heard noises, tried to call out but my mouth wouldn't open, my voice wouldn't work. Heard my mother's voice call out she was home. Was I feeling better? Heard her on the stairs.

Her face hovering above me, her voice was saying, 'Zoe. Zoe? Dear God. Zoe.' Somebody was shouting. Screaming downstairs on the phone. Something cool pressed on my forehead, wet and cool, pressing and dabbing, taking away some of the fire, something pressing coldness on my face, *Hold on, hold on Zoe, oh Zoe, my God, please, darling, the doctor, they're coming, Jesus where are they, oh please, Zoe, come on darling, wake up, oh please God don't let my baby die.*

Hands lifting.

Ready. Now. Careful does it. Taking, holding, jolting the body. Somebody is screaming. Is screaming. The pain is so bad, her head is filled with heat, hard hurting white light, it will burst. Somebody has her hand, tight, somebody, *hold on Zoe, hold on, hold on, nearly there.* A noise like the screaming in the air above the girl on the flat hard bed in the back of the truck, going so fast.

I wake. White walls.

Evie. Evie?

I wake and see white walls, feel heat, pain, something is jabbing into my arm, hurting, can't move to pull it out, the lights are too bright, hurt my eyes, something sharp digs. You are hurting my arm.

I wake and listen. Turn her over. Ready. Now. Sharp pain floods the middle of my spine. Keep your eyes closed.

Somebody calls out.

No no no no, not you. Evie. I want Evie.

Somebody's legs are kicking, kicking out hard and somebody holds them firmly with strong hands and says ssh ssh it's all right, it's all right Zoe love. Rest now.

Evie? Evie?

Hands lift me, sheets are taken away, new ones tucked beneath me. I feel warm damp towels gently pressed against my body, hear voices. I'll do her face now. Better cut her fingernails. I feel pillows settled under my head, covers tight around me. And the needles. Sometimes they push up my eyelids. I see flickering light.

I wake and sleep, wake and sleep. What are the dreams and what is real? There is the sea and the ship, the verandah, somebody is brushing the girl's hair. Evie. Evie? There are the men and the ladies in the white coats and my mother is holding onto my hand. I hear a word I don't know. Hear it over and over. Meningitis. Meningitis. Will she be all right, she's going to be all right isn't she? This child is so thin, she is malnourished, nothing to fight with, what on earth has been going on? Somebody shouts, somebody crying. She refused to eat. She wouldn't eat I tell you. She said she wasn't hungry.

I woke. Felt the afternoon sun streaming through the curtains on my face. I opened my eyes and saw the high black end of the bed.

I'm home. Home at Evie's.

I saw the high sides.

Dreaming. I'm in a baby's bed. A baby's crib.

I called out and a woman in a white coat and hat leaned over me and said quietly, 'You're with us again, my dear. You're in the hospital, you've been asleep for quite a while. Grandma has just popped out for a cup of tea but she'll be back presently.'

This was too much information all at one time. Hospital? Asleep for a while? Who is Grandma? I began to sob. She lifted my head, tilted a glass with a plastic spout at the end of it into my mouth, told me to take a little sip then pressed a bell on the wall above the bed and a doctor came. He shone a light into my eyes and asked slow, gentle questions, tell me your name, how old are you, where do you live, what school do you go to, do you remember what happened? Later my mother explained that the doctors were afraid the illness may have affected my brain but it was as if I'd fallen into a nightmare. I'd gone to sleep in my own house, in my own bed and woken locked up in a baby's bed in a strange, frightening place with a woman feeding me from a baby's cup and a man dressed in a white coat asking absurd questions.

But then I saw Evie was behind him. Evie was there standing in the doorway. I was dreaming again but this time I didn't want the dream to stop. She bent over me and rested the palm of her hand on my forehead, 'Here you are now, Zoe.' I began to cry again and she sat on the chair beside my bed and took my hand, 'Rest now, Zoe, and I'll sit with you.'

Sometimes when I woke my mother was there and sometimes Evie. I did not ask how this came about, but simply woke and smiled and murmured at one or other of them, drank something, was fed something from a spoon held by either of them. I felt the injections in my arm or my bottom, my blood was siphoned into tubes, medicine poured into my mouth and I slept again.

My mother told me I'd been in hospital almost a month. Her voice was husky and tears stood out in her eyes. She said she'd believed she would lose me. That's when I forgave her and when I understood that she loved me after all. I saw she didn't want to lose me.

After that I understood her fear of our separation and that she may lose me because I knew how afraid I'd been that I might lose Evie. Because of my mother I almost lost Evie. But I almost made myself die. She almost lost me. We were even. We could begin again.

That's when the truce was settled. When I was almost well I woke to find Evie and my mother sitting on opposite sides of my bed. My mother explained they'd talked. She said she'd come to understand I needed my grandmother. She quietly explained she had been very wrong, she'd been jealous, 'After all, Zoe, you're all I have.'

And so they'd come up with a solution they hoped would make all of us happy. During the year I would remain with my mother in Christchurch. At the beginning of December, just after school was finished, I would go to Evie and stay with her until the end of January. And perhaps some other school holidays. We would see. But definitely each summer I would be with Evie.

Before she left Evie gave me a diary with the day I would go on the ferry across to her in Wellington marked by a red circle. It was a large diary, with a heavy navy cover and gold lettering.

'And this is for you to write your own stories in, Zoe,' she said. 'We all have stories and it's important we keep them. Perhaps when you come you may want to read some of them to me.'

That's when I began to write. There were years in my life when I wrote nothing, but always I have come back to the recording of stories, coming back to the memory of Evie giving me that first diary and telling me the importance of remembering and storing.

I wrote in my diary and counted the days until the red circled Monday near the end. My teacher wrote on my school report that *Zoe has again become a conscientious and actively contributing member of our classroom.* I began to fill out my clothes and my mother said happily she believed I would need some new and bigger dresses for the summer.

I began to love her again, although never with that anxious yearning idolatry I'd felt for her before. Each morning we walked together to the school gates. Each morning I stood and waited as she crossed the street to the bus stop then turned and waved.

She was like those mannequins we watched parading the clothes you could buy in the big shops in town with her smooth, powdered face, her black high heels which made her slim legs appear longer, the little suit which curved snugly around her body, the small, black-feathered hat which sat close to her head. I saw her beauty, the red lips which smiled back at me and the dark blue eyes which sparkled. But I no longer idolised that pretty perfection. I'd heard her say she was wrong, heard her admit to fear and jealousy. I had heard her cry uncontrollably and scream. I still admired her beauty but she'd revealed her flaws, her vulnerability. I learned to love her again for that.

14

On the afternoon of the last day of the school year, my mother and I went shopping. We'd select shorts, tops, a bathing suit, a summer dress or two and sandals for me to wear while I was with Evie. These clothes were always more important for me than any others. I'd look out for clear, bright colours, ask my mother anxiously if she thought they might fade, rub the material between my fingers to make sure it was light and cool. Once I found a polished cotton sun-dress the sheen and shade of ripe lemons. It was my most loved dress for the two summers I fitted into it. After choosing the clothes we'd have sandwiches and cakes at Beaths. Then we separated to find each other's Christmas presents. I carefully searched for exactly the right thing for my mother. I wanted something to make her happy while I was away. I would search for small things for her, little china ballet shoes joined with a narrow pink ribbon, a crystal mouse, perfume in a tiny blue glass bottle. Later we'd meet and she'd help me choose presents for Evie and Alice and we'd buy a double-layered box of chocolates for Mrs Samuels and Sam.

On Sunday we celebrated an early Christmas with a tree and a special lunch. We took our tea to the Botanic Gardens and ate it on the river bank while we watched the rowing boats and threw scraps to the ducks. Back home, we exchanged our gifts in the evening. My mother would admire her own present in a way which convinced me she was truly pleased. First of all she would look closely at the picture I'd stuck or drawn on the card, then open it and read the message aloud. She would carefully unwrap the parcel and hold the gift in her hand, lifting it up to the light, marvelling at its perfection, its intricacy. Then she would search about for the right place for it to be displayed. She always gave me presents that I loved. A round glass fishbowl with two fat, popeyed goldfish. A book with pages edged with gold and delicately tinted pictures and a silver box with a dancer who popped up and twirled around to music when you lifted up the lid.

The early Christmas celebrations I had with my mother were never overshadowed by the expectation of the one I would share with Evie, or by a longing to leave. This was a special time for us, made poignant by the fact I would soon go. I felt sorry my mother would miss me and be alone.

But it was all part of the agreement, the truce. So long as I could have my summers with Evie I could be a loving and co-operative daughter during the year with my mother. It was an arrangement that taught me invaluable lessons. It taught me about loyalty, because, despite the rift between them neither Evie or my mother criticised the other, nor attempted to win me exclusively. I learned also about endurance. I endured those cold fogs, the grey dankness, the air which caught in your throat and the loneliness of returning daily to an empty house because I held inside me that feeling of sun on my body and a house filled with light. I learned also that life is rarely perfect. I learned the importance of compromise where you momentarily remove emotion and look for an arrangement which creates the most positive outcome at the least cost.

And so we shared our early Christmas. I said goodbye to my mother at Lyttelton Harbour and the next day dived into Evie's arms and began that long winding journey through bush and hill and coastline up the island. That journey which ended with me sitting drunk with joy and heat and the smell of leather on the edge of the back seat of Sam's beloved car watching for my ocean and my house and my garden.

We arrived in late afternoon. We always had tea on the verandah, a walk through the garden, a talk and a story and an early bedtime — *You look tired, Zoe, off to bed now my darling and in the morning we'll go down to the beach.* I lay in bed in the room I'd thought about every day of the year and looked through the open window into the dusky evening, at the first stars, listened to the sea, smelt the warm salty night wind.

The beach is much the same as it was then. You walk through the orchard, down a track edged with flax and toetoe and across hot powdery sandhills to endless waves breaking on a stretch of amber sand. There are rock pools where I used to try to catch cockabullies, holding a jam jar under the water in the hope they would swim inside. Where I used to find sea anemones and hold my finger in the centre to feel it enclosed in soft, insidious tentacles. There are bright clusters of iridescent shells, a rim of foam left where the sea laps inwards.

Cottages are scattered on the hills behind the sandhills. Most of them are much as they were when I first came here, shacks thrown together from recycled timber, bricks and iron, unmatching windows and doors picked up in demolition sites. But some, I see have been refurbished, painted or reclad, rooms and decks added, curtains covering aluminium windows. I suppose eventually the place will change — we are too close to Auckland to remain untainted — and the hills will be terraced with houses occupied in the summer by a smart beach set equipped with four-wheel drives and yachts, kayaks and boogie boards.

Now there is nobody here. I walk down to the sea past fresh horse tracks in the sand, take off my shoes and run along the edge in the shallow waves. I feel like the child I was. Have to stop myself from turning to wave at Evie settling herself on a rug stretched beneath a sandhill.

The straw hat is pulled down over her eyes, her cotton sundress tucked around her bare ankles, her long brown toes dig into the sand. She raises her arm and waves back.

We always came here on the first morning. I'd run down over the sand feeling it hot then cooler beneath my feet, feeling wind and heat on my body, running, hurtling, pelting my body forward with all my energy and strength. Through the shallow water and out into the waves. Hurling myself against them. Feeling the power of the ocean pelt against me, feeling my ocean hold and rock me as I lay on my back out beyond the waves, buoyed and lulled and comforted, drinking in the sky. *I'm back, hey I've come back.* I lay there hardly moving feeling the waves lift and drift, feeling the heat on my face, intensely concentrated on all the sensations. It was here I shed my winter skin.

Other times I came alone. I became a capable swimmer down here, churning out past the breakers, ploughing my way back into the shore. If I could add up all the hours I've spent on this beach it would stretch into months maybe years. Below the sandhills is where Evie and I lay on rugs reading, talking. Sometimes we fell asleep. I first kissed a boy on this beach. I've walked miles along the curve of ocean, sand and rock. I walked here with Evie, with my husband, with Ben and with Tom. I've laughed and played and shouted and wept here. I always come back to it. In the middle of winter when I'm walking in the city with wind and rain whipping against my body this is where I place myself. I remove my hat and scarf, my raincoat, my woollen skirt and jersey, my boots and my tights and position myself on a rug in the sun beneath the sandhill. I feel sun burning my back, dig into hot sand with my fingers and bare toes and deliciously wriggle.

Evie said the ocean is the place for thinking. You lie in the sea and feel that great, vast power around you, walk along the shoreline and see it stretch a million miles beyond. She said the sea makes you feel small and limited in your human-ness, it makes you regard the things filling your head as insignificant and petty. But it also makes you aware of the greatness of the human spirit, the capacity to perceive beauty.

When I was here the days overlapped, each stretched seamlessly into another, the garden, the beach, the house, the verandah; a world of stories and slow soft talk. On Christmas Day sometimes it was just Evie and me,

Mrs Samuels and Sam and sometimes their children with their babies. Sometimes Evie's cousins came with their children and grandchildren. Cousin Anne-Jane, William and John materialised, not as the children I imagined from Evie's stories, but as tall men with salt and pepper suits and grey hair and a small round woman with Alice's blue eyes and a fluff of tight, light curls above a pouched face. Alice never came for Christmas any more. She was well into her nineties and Evie said travelling made her too tired now.

I was almost fourteen when Alice died. We'd stayed a night with her on the way as we always did, and she'd smiled and talked and laughed with us, walked us around her garden, holding out the stick she used to help her walking to point to the clump of Christmas lilies which had come out early, the honeysuckle which must be cut back. Before we left she held me against her frail, small body as she always did and said I must remember her to my mother. Just after Christmas Anne-Jane phoned to say Alice had died suddenly. Her heart had simply given up early that morning.

She was the first person to die that I'd loved. I raged over the injustice — *It's not fair, why did Aunt Alice have to die? she wasn't even sick* — and cried bitterly over it. Evie didn't say it was for the best, she was old and becoming frail, better it was so sudden, she always had good health, she had a happy life, better she went quickly rather than suffered. She didn't say it because I knew all that, I'd worked it out for myself but it didn't make my grief for the loss of the Aunt Alice I'd only just found any easier. Evie stroked my hair, tucked me into bed, sat with me, held my hand, rubbed my shoulders, rested her hand across my forehead. She didn't talk but made soothing sounds as she held me. I was too caught up in my own grief to think of hers. She'd known Alice all her life. Her prettiest Aunt, her pretty Aunt Alice.

Evie went to Auckland alone for the funeral, dressed in an unfamiliar suit, hat and gloves. I stayed with the Samuels; children did not attend funerals in those days. We came down here in the evening following her return.

We did not say much at first. It had been an overcast day, so humid that you felt at any time the sky would open up and pelt down a torrent of rain. I felt unhappy and sticky with the heat. Evie had been away the previous night and I hadn't slept well. I couldn't believe I'd never see Alice again, never go to her house and sleep in the bed with wooden slatted ends in the bedroom looking out into the garden. I was hot and I was angry. Why did being with Evie mean being away from my mother? Why did people die just when you were starting to know them? Why couldn't everything be better organised so there was not always sadness mixed up with happiness? It was like tasting something you expected to be sweet and good then biting into it to discover something so sharp and sour it made you shudder.

We walked unspeaking. The tide was on its way out and we walked close to the sea edge on cool hard sand. Then the wind blew up, cooling the air.

We went among the rock pools and Evie climbed over the rocks towards the sea. She called out for me to come, she thought she'd seen fins further out and I went and stood beside her. We waited, staring out towards the horizon and then we saw them. A whole pod of dolphins playing out there just beyond us, flipping and soaring up from the waves, lithe and gleaming, moving with swift grace.

'Ah, Zoe,' Evie said, 'aren't they grand?'

Eliza died shortly after Hannah's thirty-fourth birthday. In the evening she felt flushed and a little dizzy. She left Hannah and Evie on the verandah and went into the coolness of the house. She walked up the stairs to her bedroom and stood beside the open window looking out at the sea. It was ashy and swelling up into high buffeting waves, much as it was in those five days she and William waited in the ocean beyond the Bay of Islands before they could come in towards land, towards their new home. She looked out over the ocean as she always had since coming here as a young girl, thinking about England and her mother and father and her brothers. Her parents of course, were long dead and her brothers now grandfathers but still she thought always of them as she last saw them.

Her mother with gentle eyes and hands, her father who towered above her, her brothers with straight lean bodies and dazzling eyes. This is how she likes to think of them. Her mother is dressed in her best liquorice-green dress, her father and her handsome brothers in their suits and they are seated, heads bowed, at the large mahogany table laid with the best silver and pink and white china for Sunday dinner. It is a never-changing tableau. Something perfect and static in this imperfect, ever-changing life she'd had with all its joy, its bitter disappointments. It is a picture in her mind which remains unchanged.

Although, of course, William is dead and she no longer is that girl she once was, in love with William. Or perhaps she was in love with the idea of him as the heroic deliverer of pagans. In love perhaps, with that idea of herself as helpmeet to a great, grand cause. That cause more important than self.

O may my life, my all, be spent
In telling pagans Thou was sent
To save their souls from sin and hell
That they might in Thy presence dwell

She thinks of the poem she penned with such zeal following her first meeting with William. He stood so tall and admirable in the pulpit, his voice booming out, vehement and noble, telling of his mission.

I have entered on a new scene — left the parental roof, and the friends and guides of my youth, to become a wife — forsaken my native land and embarked for a distant barbarous clime as the partner of a Christian missionary.

She smiles a little, remembering, then sits on the chair beside the window and takes up her needlework — she is smocking the bodice of that new dress for Evie. Feels the shooting pain in her side, the numbness which swells from her shoulder down her arm.

Hannah was inconsolable. Apart from those months away from New Zealand during her wedding tour with Alexandre, she had never been without her mother. Eliza's body was taken to Auckland — it had been her wish that she would be buried beside William in the Symonds Street cemetery — in a coach driven by Luke who rode down the island from Hokianga directly after being sent news of his mother's death. Hannah and Evie followed in the coach behind. Evie said her mother came down the stairs dressed in a black dress and black hat and tied a black satin ribbon around the sleeve of Evie's dress. She said she was afraid. Hannah sat, for all that long jolting journey to Auckland, mute, rigid with a handkerchief pressed against her lips.

They stayed with Alice and James. On the afternoon of the funeral the children were supervised by the governess. When the adults returned Evie watched Hannah come into the vestibule and then go directly to the bedroom they were sharing. Evie followed and stood outside the closed door with her fingers on the handle. She wanted her mother. But as she turned the door handle she heard a sound so disturbing, so frightening she couldn't move. Her fingers locked around the handle. *The sound of such grief, Zoe. Such searing, wracking, agonised grief.* When Hannah came out of the bedroom her face was pale and her eyes red but she smiled at Evie, took her up on her knee and sat among them again.

Eliza's death was marked by a handsome obituary notice which commented on her occupation with many religious and charitable causes and her calling, at an early age, to mission work in New Zealand. The obituary was unusual since few women in those days were accorded public notice; although she was referred to, of course, as Mrs William White. The funeral service in the Pitt Street Methodist Church was well attended and the minister spoke movingly about the woman who had remained his respected friend for the fifty-five years since he first met her. The young gentle girl who'd made her garden in the Hokianga.

Alice returned with Hannah and Evie to stay until Hannah's grief subsided. On the afternoon following their return Hannah planted a new tree, an oak sapling in a corner of the garden. She called to Evie and Alice to walk with her down to the sea. It was where she and Eliza had walked each morning and evening.

She calls for Evie and Alice then walks swiftly off down the track. Evie runs to keep up and catches at her mother's hand. She wants to ask where is her grandmother Eliza? She cannot understand how her grandmother who was here only last week, here talking and telling stories and brushing her hair, telling her milk is good for you — Evie, come on my lamb you must drink it up — placing a gentle hand on her shoulder, holding up her face for the goodnight kiss and sewing with her mother, this grandmother is no longer here but grey and not moving, buried under the earth in a wooden box. She wants to cry, to loudly cry and shout she wants her grandmother to come back but she can't because of her mother's stiff, sad face. And so she scuttles along behind Aunt Alice and her mother who walk too quickly, not talking at all, up along the track in front of her.

They walked on the beach, then climbed as we did, over the rocks. The dolphins were there. Hannah and Alice and Evie stood on the rocks and saw the fins, the ebullient leap and flight of silken bodies.

Hannah watched silently then took Evie's hand.

'Mother watched them those five days while they waited out there in the ocean. Dolphins followed the ship for part of the way when she and Father finally could come in. Mother always looked out for dolphins when we were at home in the Hokianga and when we came here. Dolphins were divine creatures, she said, closest to us, but without our loss of innocence, without our cruelty and deceit.'

Evie said Eliza was her first death and like me she was overwhelmed by loss, anger and fear. 'Because, Zoe, I thought if my grandmother who seemed so strong could die, then everybody else may begin to die as well.

'But death and sadness as well as birth and happiness are the business of a family. Of life as well, Zoe. I've had many deaths to bear since Eliza's. Too many, I sometimes think. Every time someone you love dies it's so hard. Death isn't something you become immune or accustomed to. But you do have the loving and knowing to remember as well as loss.'

The business of a family. The business of a life. The losses and the knowing and the loving.

In the months before I went away it was loss I was obsessed with. I forgot the knowing and the loving and the joy and was caught up with what Eliza saw as our loss of innocence.

I do not have my great-great grandmother's *zeal in well-doing, steadfastness, catholicity of spirit* the Minister had referred to in his eulogy. Neither do I have her faith in a Master.

But when I wrote my exposés on the injustices and cruelties I observed all about me, oh then I had her sense of rightness in a cause. I was brim-filled with a righteous, raging will to set things right. To set things in their proper places.

And I heard a great voice out of the temples saying, Go your ways, and pour the vials of the wrath of God upon the earth.

Oh I had it then. A heady mixture: her determination, crusader's zeal combined with my own spirit. And my own talent for assembling and shaping my words into bright, blistering missiles. And unlike Eliza I wasn't denied my right to give voice to my passions, not obliged merely to *almost wish it were common and proper for women to preach*. I had my language and my voice.

I had words but I lost them. Because after the stories about women and children whose bodies and minds were maimed by battering, about the old woman who was raped and beaten and no longer could leave her house, about the drinking and the abuse and the stabbing and the violence, it all just went right on. On and on and on. In spite of all the words and tears it just goes on. That small, scared boy, raped by whoever fancies him is the man who climbs into your window tomorrow in the dark and holds the knife against your throat whispering his savage, desperate words as he violates your body.

I interviewed a family. The magazine I was doing some work for wanted an article on sexual abuse. The twelve-year-old girl had been removed from the house. A boy sat passively in front of the TV. The father was in prison, the abortion arranged. The mother never knew anything — well how could she, working night shifts? The house was meticulously clean with framed photographs of children above the fireplace and on top of the wall unit.

'That's her,' the mother pointed at one of them. 'That's Michelle. That's the latest one. Just took last year.'

She crosses the room, picks up the photograph and holds it out to me. 'She was a pretty girl.'

She speaks as if her daughter is dead, has accidentally been taken from her by some event she cannot comprehend. Some misfortune which has also spirited away her husband.

'We were always close, Shell and me. Always. Really close. She could tell me anything. Close to her dad and me, close to Ross, there, as well.'

She stares at the photo in her hand. The boy scowls at the telly. I wondered where it happened. When. Did he go to her room when the boy was dead asleep and heard nothing? Weren't there any signs? Jesus, how can a child be raped in her home and nobody hear anything, nobody know anything?

When I left I drove swearing and crying to the beach, lurched along the sand and then vomited. I wept out the taintedness I felt. Christ. Why do people do these filthy things? Christ. What drives them?

At the time I was filled with misery and loathing and self-disgust. Tom poured me a large brandy, made me toss it down, then put me into a warm bed and gave me another. He said he knew he was saying what I already knew but I should try to remain detached, I mustn't become so involved. I said, 'Damn you Tom.' Then cried and said it was the photo. She was a kid. Just a pretty kid in a school uniform.

Tom felt sorry for me and I felt sorry for myself. But then, at least, I felt. Something. I felt something. At least I could feel anger and sorrow and pity, even helplessness. In the end during those last months I felt nothing. I picked up newspapers, turned on television news programmes, saw more rapes, more beatings, more violence, more deaths. And violence, corrupt politicians, judges, lawyers, accountants, poverty had turned into everyday occurrences, nothing could be done and it was senseless to try. All that unpleasantness was just the stuff of life. I cried for no apparent reason, feeling nothing but perplexity for the fact of some tears running down my cheeks.

Life's a bitch and then we die.

I saw it on the T-shirts. I wanted to congratulate the wearers on their insightfulness.

Ben left for the States and I waved him goodbye, telling him he was wonderful and would do well. I waved at the plane and wondered if I would ever see him again. The plane would crash. He would be mugged. Kidnapped by Moonies. He'd contract some dreadful disease. It happened all around us. Nothing could be done.

In the week after Ben left I had to phone Income Support for information for an article. A recorded voice instructed that the operators were busy but to save time I should have my customer number ready and to please hold. I held and the muzak came on, an orchestral rendering of 'Pomp and Circumstance.' The recorded voice returned and informed me about Income Support's busiest times, about the hours when Income Support operators were available. I was instructed to continue to hold. The muzak ringing in my head.

Land of ho-ope and glory,
Mother o-of the free.
No operators are available. Continue to hold the line.
How shall we-e extol thee?
Who are born of thee!
My inquiry will shortly take precedence. Continue to hold.
God who ma-ade thee mighty,
Make thee mightier yet.
God who made thee might — eee
Make thee might-i-er yet.

And I am shouting, suddenly shrieking into the phone like some crazy person. I object to this bloody music. Because there is no hope, there is no glory any more in this country. It's an insult. I shout *It's a fucking insult* and crash down the receiver. Stand unmoving. Shocked. Staring at the phone.

I am mad. I've gone mad.

I tell myself I'm fortunate. I'm loved by a gentle, intelligent, articulate man. I love him. My son who is successful, charming and well-adjusted also loves me. I have friends. I have a career. I have more than enough money.

And I cannot shift, cannot shrug off this creeping, insidious feeling of malaise, dis-ease.

I miss a period and believe it's hormonal. Pre-menopausal. Or stress. That lovely, comforting, well-used word which can stretch to an explanation of any kind of disagreeable sensation from headaches to heartburn to feeling you've been pitched into an icy void.

I begin to cry and snap at Tom and retreat into silence. I say I must get away. I must go away. I make plans.

I have to go to the Hokianga.

And I want to go to Evie's.

'Why now Zoe? Why can't you wait until I can come as well? It's what we both need. To get away by ourselves. Away from work and the phone, have

a bit of time together. If you wait another month I'll be able to come.'
'I don't want you to come. I want to go on my own.'

15

The evenings remain warm and light. After dinner I sit drinking wine with Lucy on the verandah and watch the sunsets blazing crimson above the sea, sliding into gilt-edged smoke and violet dusk.

I fill Lucy's glass. We survey the gleaming sky, the garden blurred by shadows. I tell her I'm pregnant.

'Oh,' she says. 'I thought there might be something going on. Do you want to be?'

'It certainly wasn't planned if that's what you mean.'

'No it's not entirely what I meant. Do you want to be now you've found out you are?'

'Probably not. I don't know. I don't want to think about it. Or deal with it. I'd like it to just never have happened and go away.'

Lucy says drily that it's what some people might call denial.

'Probably it is. Except pregnancy's something you can't entirely deny. It becomes alarmingly evident. Shit, it's there all the time, at the back of my head. This voice in my head asking what am I going to do about it? It never goes away. Except I can't seem to do anything. I can't make up my mind about anything at all. Days and days are going past and I know I should just get on the next plane to Christchurch and get it fixed. It could be all sorted out in a day or two. But it's like I'm immobilised. I know what I have to do but I can't.'

'An abortion's not so bad,' Lucy says. 'I've had one. If it's what you want to do.'

'I'm sure it's what I should do. I'm forty for Christ's sake. Who wants to be having babies when they're forty? And can you imagine me going into an interview with a baby in a backpack? God knows what Tom's kids and Ben would think. Probably disown us. I just wish it wasn't happening.'

'But it is, Zoe,' Lucy begins to laugh. 'Sorry. I shouldn't laugh but you always seem so, oh, directed. Directed and controlled. I always feel as if my life is so utterly unmanaged and haphazard in comparison. When I'm with you I feel as if I'm a complete flibbertigibbet.'

I stare at her then laugh as well, 'Directed and controlled? Hell. I sound like a sergeant major.'

'Not at all,' she says. 'You just don't seem to be the type who'd accidentally get pregnant when she was forty.'

We both laugh. My dilemma seems suddenly very funny. We laugh and laugh and I say breathlessly, hysterically, imagine telling Tom's kids — we've got something very important to tell you. Christ, imagine Tom's face, his kids'd have to know we actually do it, turning up to interviews nine months pregnant, imagine me trotting along the footpath with a baby buggy. Shit. Kindergarten committees and cake stalls, breast-feeding, nappies, oh my God.

We laugh and drink wine. This is disgraceful, a pregnant woman getting drunk — oh God an accidentally pregnant forty-year-old woman getting drunk. She should know better. On both counts. Drunk and pregnant. Disgusting. I'm laughing more than I have in months. So much my stomach is aching. Everything is absurd and in the middle of it Tom phones and I splutter down the phone I've just told Lucy I'm pregnant.

He says, 'Oh Christ, I suppose it is funny in a nightmarish way.'

I agree happily with him.

'But what are we going to do about it?'

It's that suffocating weight again. I say I don't know, well probably yes, of course I know, but I can't, not yet, I can't leave, can't leave just yet, it's not the time. Tom sighs and I sigh and we laugh gently together at the whole mess of this and I say goodbye, go up the stairs and lie on my bed with the room and my head swimming with wine and babies. What if? What if I did? My eyes and Tom's mouth? His gentle temperament, Evie's wisdom, how could I possibly?

And what if it's deformed, damaged in some way? What if it cries all the time and I'm trapped. What if Tom starts hating it, hating me?

There is an absence of men in our family. The men in our family go missing.

In the doctors' rooms. Years ago when I was having Ben — that slogan on the poster advocating responsible parenting. *Every Child A Wanted Child.*

I must get on a plane tomorrow. I must make up my mind to get on the plane probably tomorrow and take control again of my life. Absurd to even consider having a child at my stage of life. *If you won't consider yourself and Tom for God's sake think of a child in the midst of all the turmoil and activity of your life, you only managed Ben by the skin of your teeth mainly because he's an almost perfect human being, you can't think you'd be that lucky again.*

In the morning I phone the airport, enquire about timetables — no, I won't make any reservations at present, thank you — before I take coffee out into the garden and sit on a bench in front of one of Alexandre's walls. I lie my head back, feel warm stones pressed against my back.

I could be in Auckland, easily by early afternoon, then catch a late plane.

Or then again, I could spend another day here, pack tonight, leave in the morning, get on a plane and be back in Christchurch by two o'clock. I could phone my doctor, make an appointment for tomorrow afternoon or first thing the next morning. I'll finish my coffee, go inside, make the necessary phone calls then phone Tom, tell him I've decided and everything will be back as it was. A middle-aged, middle-class life. Civilised.

Certainly I will be a little unwell, a bit sore and groggy for the weekend but Tom would look after me. He'd be pleased to. He's good at it too. He'd make tea, buy grapes and treats for me from the delicatessen, give me brandy and lemon to help me sleep. I could be back at my desk by Monday and no harm done, just a temporary aberration from my usual control and directedness.

Everything back as it was.

I rub my back up the knobbled wall, feeling the warmth then stretch and close my eyes. The weather is so balmy, the sun so genial today. The sun, this smell of roses, this warm wall, they are the reasons I can't get up just yet and make necessary arrangements. The radiance of light seeping through the windows and the doors of this house, the sound of sea, the garden, these all prevent me from putting the things I must attend to into motion. I'm reluctant to resume a winter life of grey drizzle settling about grey streets, fog and frosts and smog. Glancing up from the pile of work on my desk out onto dripping trees and a listless sky. I can't move, can't make up my mind because I can't leave this sun.

I believe Ben survived my mothering and thrived to become the funny, gentle young man he is because he managed to somehow evade his father's genes and mine and is made up of a careful selection of ancestral qualities. Evie's forbearance and patience. Hannah's gentleness. Eliza's stoicism. Perhaps his stubbornness comes from William. He has Alexandre's charm and dash. Certainly he has Hannah's musical talent.

Ben carefully removes the flute from the plush lining of the new black case. He runs his fingers gently along the stretch of glittering silver, holds it to his mouth, blows and gazes up at me wonderingly.

I wake to that trill and ebb and flow of chilling sweetness. Listen for it as I come in from work and during the hour between homework and going to bed.

I hear Ben usher the girl down the passage to the front door. They're both thirteen and have been working on a shared school science project. I hear them pause, hear Ben solemnly and courteously explain his rejection of her offered kiss. While he would very much like to kiss her he can't. He has to practise his flute so much you see his lips have become very dry and cracked. He hopes she doesn't mind.

I press a tea-towel to my mouth to suppress my laughter. My Benjamin. My eyes are full of tears. Tears of laughter for his awkward solemnity. And love. Overwhelming.

I wonder if another child would be so blessed. Another child might be awkward as I was. I always wondered at Ben's beauty. I was plain. People would glance down at me and then back to my glamorous mother with obvious surprise. As I got older I became tall like Evie. My feet and hands far too large for a child and my face too sharp, my eyes too dark and knowing. When I was twelve I stood for some minutes staring up at the portrait of Hannah above Evie's mantelpiece. I looked at her hair, that pale sheen around her small head, at her dainty folded hands, the tight bodice of her dress which curved over narrow ribs to the pinched-in waist. I wished I was like her.

'Why couldn't I be like Hannah? Pretty with blonde hair. And little. I'm so big. I'm huge, Evie. I'm the tallest in the class now and that includes the boys as well. I look stupid. And my skin's so brown. Everyone says I look like I'm Maori.'

Evie observes mildly that surely would not be the worst thing in the world.

'But I'm not am I? If I was I wouldn't care. But it's dumb, looking like a Maori when you're not even one. How come I've got brown skin and black hair?'

Evie explains the French are often quite dark, Alexandre certainly was, she also has his dark skin. And she believes my hair which is a shade or two darker than hers ever was, must come from my grandfather's side, Joe's family, who, as she told me, was Irish. Joe was quite fair, she says, as you can see from the photographs, but she believes his sister had very beautiful dark hair. Hair like a stretch of black silk, Joe always said.

'Well mine's not beautiful,' I say. 'And neither am I. I've just ended up with the worst bits of everyone. I'm too big and nothing fits together properly and my hair's horrible. I look terrible.'

Evie says when she was thirteen she thought she was so ugly that nobody would ever want to marry her and having somebody to marry her — 'Well now, Zoe, that seemed a rather important concern when I was thirteen. I'd look around at all the other girls with their curls and blue eyes. I used to feel a wave of embarrassment creeping over me. I was a whole head taller than all of them and my hair was straight and my eyes were black and my feet were so big Mother had to have my shoes especially made. But then I grew into myself. I was never pretty like the other girls but I was myself. When I met your grandfather he loved me for that, for my own skin and my own eyes and my own big feet, and you will grow into yourself, Zoe, just as I did.'

But I didn't want to grow into myself. I was already much more than a self should be. Rather, I wanted a diminishment of self, to be like Alice, reduced down and down and down and reappear as a dainty, waif-like creature, fair and curled, featureless and fitting in.

My personality did little to relieve my lack of beauty. I wasn't 'bubbly' or 'sunny-natured.' I rarely made anyone laugh or even smile apart from Evie and occasionally, other adults. If I was commented on at all, adults labelled me quaint or old-fashioned. Other children said I was shy or boring or brainy. Apart from when I was with Evie or during those rare close moments with my mother, my inner world was more important than the exterior.

At school the only way I earned any renown at all was through my ability to regularly gain the highest marks in tests, to always have my composition read out as the best in class and to faintly irritate and perplex teachers since I was able to add up, subtract, divide and multiply long lines of numbers in my head. The teacher would write up a list of figures on the blackboard, at least a half-hour's occupation for the class, and my hand would instantly shoot up to call out the answers. I got into trouble for not writing the problems down, not setting them out correctly, nor would I explain how I did it. In primary school it was my one rebellion. I was never chosen until almost last to be in sports teams. In mathematical quizzes I was always chosen first.

Adding up, multiplying the numbers and calling out the answers. Perhaps it was the beginning of subversion, since through that I got a taste for the satisfying tingling that fills your body, making you want to slyly grin, laugh out loud. Beating the teachers. Catching them out. Being quick and cleverer than them. And devious. Covering it up by a virtuous, self-deprecatory denial of any intended effrontery.

Please Sir, what should you do when you've finished?
Please Sir, but the answer for number nine is incorrect.
Please Sir, but I've finished.
Please Sir, I've finished that as well.
Please Sir but I've finished, can I tidy the nature table, please Sir?

Could you check number twelve, please Sir? I've triple checked it and my answer's different to yours.

It was the only time I was noticed, the only time I made anyone my own age laugh. I enjoyed that brief moment, the stab of power.

It was those times when I briefly overturned the controlling power which led to my later full-scale rebellion against any authority which limited or confined. But when I was waging those later battles I was lonely. I had no warming satisfaction, no encouraging laughter. I felt alien, bitter and angry.

Perhaps my mother, because of her own grim experiences with men, wanted my adolescence to be as far as possible, boy-free. Or perhaps her veins carried some of Eliza's refinement and an over-large share of Alexandre's snobbishness. But whatever her reasons, she was fixed on sending me across town to a small private girls' school for my secondary education.

I wanted to go on with the other children to the large co-ed school but she would not give way. She said, flattering me, that my teachers said I was highly intelligent and she was determined I should be given the best education she could manage. I would benefit, she said, from classes made up of small numbers, superior teachers, the better library and equipment this school offered. She said I would not have to endure the distraction or dominating presence of boys in the classroom. She said going there would open up possibilities in later life. She said I would mix with a nicer type of girl.

The school was enclosed in a high ivy-covered fence. I walked through the arched gate at the beginning of February, the time of the year when Christchurch is smothered in a series of thirty degree nor'westers. I was enveloped in a heavy gym frock which clung around my legs and knocked against my calves as I walked, an over-large Panama hat, gloves, stockings, a stiff-collared shirt, a tie and a blazer which sagged around my fingers and reached almost to my knees. I was growing too quickly to risk buying anything expensive that I may grow out of and this particular uniform was almost twice the cost of the others.

I knew nobody and was nobody. I lived in the wrong house in the wrong suburb and had the wrong name. I did not ski or play tennis, my vowel sounds were not sufficiently full or compelling. Daddy wasn't a doctor. I was surrounded by Angelas, Priscillas and Mirandas. I was not even disliked. I was merely beyond notice.

I complained to my mother that I hated the school and nobody liked me. She sighed and said I would get used to it in no time, it would be good for me, I would realise that looking back. She said I looked beautifully smart in my uniform. She said for heaven's sake, Zoe, try to remember how difficult it was for me to get you in and how expensive it is for me to keep you there, and be grateful.

My mother must have lied to get me in. Perhaps she invented a gentleman husband, a devotion to Anglicanism, a string of female relations as past pupils, an entirely new address and an attendance or two at garden parties for the Governor General. Perhaps she seduced the bishop or described, during the interview with the headmistress, some fantasy daughter with well-rounded vowels, a sporty disposition and ballet-lessons' posture who could manage any social occasion with aplomb.

Whatever my mother did, she was misguided. The school propagated and thrived on a dulling smugness. Complacency in its own superior traditions — *the First Girls' School in 'Chraistchurch'* — and its girls — superior since they issued from the loins of the superior ladies and gentlemen of Canterbury. The mission of the school was not, as my mother hoped, to deliver strong, sharp-minded young women into the law, science and humanities divisions of universities but to distribute socially adept ladies who could set a fine table and sew a fine seam among suitably connected young men intending marriage. The female issue of which would automatically have their names put down for future entrance into The School.

I didn't fit. Not because of the unwillingness of such a school to accept or even acknowledge a pupil such as myself but because I wouldn't be part of something I saw as dishonest.

Every morning my mother went to work and every evening she came home and cooked the tea and did the housework — oh certainly I helped — but she did most of it on her own. Some mornings she looked exhausted even before she left for work.

My mother and I had enough food, new clothes occasionally, some bits of furniture, somewhere to live and a radio. We didn't have a car but we had enough money to get by. We weren't rich but we weren't totally poor. We lived in town near the park. On the other side of Christchurch near the factories there were rows and rows of little wooden houses all nearly the same, where people lived who were poor. My mother said they didn't earn nearly enough money to live on. They worked but they didn't get enough money.

My mother worked at the newspaper and my grandmother worked in her garden, in the orchard, on the farm and doing the paperwork with

Sam. I expected to work myself.

But at this school I learned there were people who didn't and never had. The girls' mothers didn't work. Most of them had women who came to their houses to do their housework and cooking. The girls did not expect they would work either.

I'm going overseas when I leave school. When I get back I'll probably get married. Of course I wouldn't have children straight away, I'd want to be madly social for a year or two before all that.

I was outraged by the injustice. I'd always believed the adult world was managed with a strong sense of fairness. But here was the evidence in front of me that this was not so. There were people living in this city who worked but didn't have enough money. There were people like my mother, who worked hard but were never rich. But the hard-working people were inferior to those who didn't work, who somehow had much more money. The girls at school whose fathers had the most money, even though they were the most insipid, weak-minded, girls there, were the most fawned over and sought after.

I told my mother about these injustices expecting she would be so shocked and fully in sympathy with my moral outrage she would immediately whisk me from the school after some hard-hitting words to the headmistress. I burnt with outrage. I passionately explained my theories on false superiority and work ethics in our society and my voice rang loudly through the room.

My mother watched me over the top of her typewriter. When I was finished she smiled.

'Oh, Zoe. You're your grandfather's girl and wouldn't himself be filled with pride, to be sure.'

She said it with a soft Irish burr and laughed. I didn't understand her. I wanted to be angry but I saw tears stand out in her eyes.

'But it's not fair,' I said.

'Things rarely are. Things rarely are, Zoe.' She bent her head again over her typing.

I see now she was right. I can smile at my naivëte.

For the first year I was silent in class. I kept my grades at a level slightly above the average. My pride could not allow me to sink lower than that — no deadheads are beating me! — although I was tempted to force my mother to remove me from the school by failing everything. But neither would my pride allow me to enter into serious competition with girls I disliked at a school for which I had no respect. If asked a question I would simply lower my head and remain silent. If requested to read aloud I'd oblige in a monotone.

At home I skimmed indiscriminately and haphazardly through *Rebecca*, through *Gone With The Wind*, through every Dickens, Brontë, Hardy and Austin I could get my hands on. I read and wept for two whole nights and half a wet Saturday over *Anna Karenina*.

I begged Evie to intervene. The school was terrible, I said, I hated it, I wasn't learning anything. She said she wouldn't interfere. I said I would run away and come and live with her, go on the bus to the high school at Dargaville and if she wouldn't let me stay I would run away somewhere else.

'You can't do that, Zoe. It would hurt your mother terribly.'

I said my mother couldn't love me. How could it hurt her so terribly? How could she possibly love me and send me to a school she knew I hated?

Evie said my mother loved me, of course she did and she wouldn't send me to the school if she didn't believe it was right for me.

I said that's the problem with people in authority, they make up their minds about what's right for everyone else and even when they're wrong they keep on thinking they're right.

Evie turned away but I saw she was smiling. Then she told me about Gandhi and passive resistance. She told me about the blacks in South Africa and America, the Jewish people and the camps, and the Jewish resettlement in their own homeland. She told me the hardest times in her own life were when she learned the most. She told me about Hannah's death and about Joe.

I heard the words she said but I didn't understand or absorb them. She had an adult's patience and control. I was a child, forced to return every day to a place I hated, surrounded by girls and teachers I thought hated me.

But I heard her words about resistance. I thought if I have to stay in that place I will make my mark. I won't be so easily ignored, will no longer be some faceless nobody from nowhere.

I hoisted my uniform above my knees. I brushed mascara onto my eyelashes in the bus on the way to school. I chewed gum in class, lost my hat, didn't wear gloves, forgot or misplaced homework. My marks soared one week and plummeted the next. I found a used condom in the park, carefully picked it up with a stick, dropped it into a plastic bag and popped it into Marjorie Harcourt's desk. I sent anonymous notes spreading various scandals around the school. I wrote a letter using a pseudonym, to the newspaper complaining about the disgustingly impolite behaviour of girls from the school, on the city buses. It was so successful that the headmistress called a special assembly — *I believed girls with such obvious advantages in life would behave in an exemplary fashion. At all times. This, sadly has not been the case...* I taught myself methods to diminish superior people to a size I could more happily deal with — the groaning, gaping yawn suddenly emanating which you quickly hide behind your hand with a look of amazement, the slightly raised eyebrows, the grimace which fixes on a spot or least attractive feature — protruding ears and noses and saggy breasts worked well — the expression of resignation you finally deign to bestow on someone who dares to address you.

I was noticed but the attention did not make me happier and the subversion, well it gave me some sense of power and control but it was a futile game and I knew it. I remembered what Evie said but I couldn't think what such a school could teach me.

It utterly failed to provide me with the advantages Grace hoped for. The facilities, the teachers, mixing with a nicer type of girl, all that was lost on me. Still, it taught me about questioning and about the value of free thought. It taught me about corrupt values and how you can never give into them. I could have rounded my vowels and talked about Mummy and going to my Grandmother's farm, I could have watched and mirrored and fitted in eventually, but I didn't and I'm pleased with myself for that. I was angry and rude but retained a sense of self.

I began to grow into myself as Evie said I would. And however awkward and belligerent and socially gauche, that self was my own.

16

If Evie loved me any less — that lumpy, angry adolescent I became during those years at school — it was never apparent. When she put her arms around me and drew me against her body the top of my head now rested against her own. She said I was her beautiful girl, her tall, strong, beautiful Zoe.

My breasts became a source of shame. I was horrified I had them, horrified they were — to me anyway — so immense. My body, like me, rebelled — in an arrogant battle against its owner. Spots made surprise appearances on my forehead and chin. I grew hair on my body in embarrassing places. I was enraged by the mess of monthly bleeding. I was spotty and smelly and hairy and disgusting. There were paddings of flesh around my hips and at the tops of my thighs. I couldn't run without my breasts jiggling. Sometimes I woke in the night thinking about my body, and my spine and arms and legs became rigid with distaste and rage at its disloyalty. I showered twice, sometimes three times in a day, standing under water as hot as I could bear, scrubbing ferociously at my face and body. I would be clean, at least I'd keep myself clean.

It was not that I wanted to be a boy. From my scanty knowledge of male anatomy I understood that boys were also afflicted by body parts lacking in restraint. I did not want the encumbrance of a penis. I merely wanted my own skinny, straight, uncomplicated body back. I didn't want to be a woman.

I wanted to remain a girl unburdened by breasts, unsullied by blood. I had no intention of ever experiencing that grossness, *sexual intercourse*, and consequently would not require breasts. For me having breasts was entirely without a purpose since I would never be feeding any babies. I was overwhelmed by repugnance at the thought of the animalistic activities described in the book my mother gave me *Now You Are A Woman*. Imagine exposing your body in that way, imagine allowing somebody to do *that* to you. Imagine a baby coming out of *that* part of you, the indignity of people actually seeing it. Imagine publicly exposing your breasts and your nipples, having a baby actually suck milk out of your body. My face burned with disgust. I was relieved that I disliked males. From my sparse experience I'd found men to be alarming and boys erratic. I envisaged any dealings I had with any of them would be motivated entirely by necessity and cut as short as possible. I doubted I would ever voluntarily seek male company. Or that any male would voluntarily seek out mine. I would never be called on to permit *sexual intercourse*.

I was miserable with my body. It seemed inevitable I'd become an adult and a female one at that, and the adult world suddenly was fraught with complications I'd never suspected or anticipated.

The hardest times are often when you learn the most.

But what could I learn, tormented as I was by an ugly, uncontrollable body, by having to remain at a school I hated, by the realisation that the doom which was adulthood was imminent?

At the end of my fourth form year I walked for hours alone on the beach and on the hills. I wore voluminous shirts to hide my body and I strode and swam endlessly. I would shake and pummel away the paddings on my thighs and my hips. I'd cover up my woman's body with thick, tough muscle. I was Diana, virgin goddess of the forest.

I told myself Evie had had it easy, so safely cocooned here. She was taught to read and to write and do whatever was necessary with numbers by Eliza and Hannah and the odd governess. She never had to leave apart from a year or two at the local school. And that was different: she never had to spend her days locked in a classroom with people she despised. When her body was wreaking havoc she didn't have to experience the daily humiliation of displaying new spots, fat thighs and sprouting breasts to the world.

I'm in bed with Tom. His knee is hooked round my thigh, my head is burrowed between his shoulder and neck.

'Do you think I'm huge?'

He laughs softly, removes his hand from my head and prods my ribs.

'Nothing extra here.'

'My hands and feet, though. Don't you think they're enormous?'

He finds my hand, holds it up above us and we consider it.

'Looks perfectly all right to me.'

'My breasts are too big.'

He's laughing, burrowing beneath the blankets measuring my feet and my breasts with his hands by a process of tickling and squeezing. I'm laughing, squealing, squirming. He comes up for air and kisses me hard on the mouth.

'Exactly the right size.'

'But wouldn't you like me to be, you know, smaller, more compact. I'm too spread out. I'm too long.'

'I like you, Zoe. I love you.'

And I think happily, that having grown into myself I am loved for it. For my own self, my own long-boned legs, my own long narrow feet and hands and for my rounded hips and breasts. For my skin which is faded and dull in the winter but turns shiny and tawny in summer. For my straight black hair, for my black eyes and full bottom lip, for the smell of my own skin.

My mother said of course I would stop growing eventually and the other girls would catch up with me and I would be no larger, no different to anyone else. She said probably I was going through a growth spurt. She said my breasts weren't particularly large and anyway, large breasts are often envied. She said the bleeding was just something I'd have to get used to. She said some women called it the curse. She said sometimes it was more of a curse if it didn't happen and she raised her eyebrows at me, inviting me to share in this grown-up women's little joke. I narrowed my eyes back at her. Directly, sharply back at her with her disgusting, tasteless comment about a disgusting and tasteless subject, and flounced off to my room.

Evie said being a woman may seem difficult, even perhaps, unpleasant. But it does have compensations.

I said I hated it and if I could have my way I would have an operation which would change me into a neuter.

The girls at my school cultivated long fingernails which they filed during the hour lunch-break. They painted their fingernails with layers of clear polish to make them shine and protect against breakage. They pressed back the cuticles to expose the pale, glossy ovals adorning their fingertips.

They sat every lunchtime on the concrete in front of the classrooms with their gym frocks pulled up above their knees exposing their legs to the sun. They pressed smoothly shaved, smoothly oiled bare legs against those of the girls beside them to compare tans. Sometimes they said ooh but they'd forgotten to shave their legs and don't they look repulsive?

The girls at my school ironed their hair and sellotaped their fringes to their foreheads every night and plucked their eyebrows and shaved their armpits and legs and learned speech and dancing. They began to go to parties where they consorted with boys from Christ's ('Chraist's'), or if less fortunate, from St Andrew's. Some of the girls pashed with the boys. One of the girls in the sixth form was already secretly engaged. Everyone said the engagement would be announced after her deb ball.

I didn't go to parties. I was above such frivolities. Neither, of course, was I invited. Sometimes when the radio was on, my mother, hearing a piece of music and remembering that dancing is a social obligation, would persuade me into a lesson. She'd be the man. She would place one of my hands on her shoulder, place one of hers around my waist, then take my other with her free hand and propel me gently about our small room telling me to listen to the music but at the same time pay attention to instructions concerning my feet. When I was smaller than her it wasn't so bad, we'd begin to move and then whirl around together before I began to laugh too much to properly concentrate. When I was older and going through my growth spurt my head loomed above my mother's and my feet lumbered about like boats caught up hopelessly in turbulent water. I was enormous. I told my mother I did not see dancing as a social obligation which had any relevance to me. I did not want to learn how to dance because I had no intention of ever dancing with boys. Or doing anything else with them either. My mother smiled and said she believed I may eventually change my mind.

I sit on the verandah smiling at that gauche, frightened self. Think about Evie who told me stories she hoped would help me make sense of my own.

'Ah, Zoe, now when I was a girl I didn't much like boys myself. I thought they were nasty, loud, pushy creatures. They frightened me a little, I have to admit to that. I didn't see too many of them. I was like you in that way. I saw them at church and I'd see them out in the fields working with their fathers. But I didn't talk to them unless I had to. I thought that was the way I preferred it, the way it'd always be. Just me and mother. Sometimes there were mother's brothers and their boys, sometimes married couples came and of course the manager and the workers were always about. But mostly it was just Mother and me and Grandmother Eliza, of course, before she died and Alice and Anne-Jane often were here. Just women and girls. No fuss and not too much noise. Just gentle and quiet and companionable.'

When Evie was twelve Hannah decided she would learn more than she could teach her herself if she went to the local school at Mamaranui. She was assured by the women in the district that the new teacher, Mr Joshua Wright, had high morals, kept good discipline and was an excellent teacher. The older children already had a little Latin and could recite two French poems from memory. Hannah believed also, that Evie would benefit from the company of other children.

It was arranged that one of the farm workers would ride part of the way with Evie each morning until she met up with other children from the surrounding farms who also went to school. It was a good distance, Evie said, but they cut across paddocks and then down the hills into Mamaranui with the churches and the store and the butchery and the drapery, the few cottages and the school house.

The school was a single room in the middle of a paddock edged with pine trees. As Evie rode up each morning she'd hear the school-bell begin to clang. She said the sound of a bell ringing still gave her the shivers.

The school room — *it was only a very small room, Zoe, I realised later* — seemed dauntingly vast with row after row of double desks placed so there was an aisle down the middle along which Mr Wright strode up and down rapping his stick to keep the recitation of the times-tables in unison. There were sixty children in the room ranging from the little six-year-olds to the big children who were thirteen or even fourteen. Mr Wright had appointed two older girls as teaching pupils — *I was afraid of them, Zoe, I thought they were so bossy and mean.* They were his pride and joy and he supported them in all their decisions. He hoped they may eventually go to Auckland for further teacher training.

There were few books. The process for much of the learning was through memorising, rote-learning, with the children repeating tables, the spelling of words, poetry and geographical and historical facts after Mr Wright. They also practised on slates the careful replication of the slants, curves, lines and ovals that was writing. Sometimes in the afternoons Mr Wright would read to them and they shivered and laughed and cried over Huck Finn and Tom Sawyer and Oliver Twist and David Copperfield.

Evie felt buried in this immense room with the striding teacher with his pounding stick and booming voice, *Twice five is TEN, thrice five is FIFTEEN.* The room was dim, barely lit by the high windows you could not see out of, and smelled of chalk and sweat. She found the noise of the squeaking slate pens, the drone of the reciting voices overwhelming.

But playtimes and lunchtimes were worse. The other children would push and race from the classroom to gather up balls and hoops and skipping ropes and the paddock surrounding the school became filled with frenetic activity. Evie said she didn't know how to break into all that. She said she'd visit her pony, rub his nose and place her head against his mane for her own comfort, then sit and wait for the sound of the bell. But even though she repeated over and over to herself that she did not want to be a part of all that rough, loud playing, she longed to jump over the rope with the other girls and join their chanting. Longed to chase and catch, to feel a hoop, smoothed and shined by other hands, in her own.

Evie. Her long legs and black eyes and her straight hair like my own. She sits in a patch of sun beneath a pine tree. She wears thick black stockings and boots which button over her ankles and a checked dress partially covered by a starched white petticoat. She sits perfectly still with her hands folded in her lap and her thick dark plaits lying flat on her shoulders. Her face is prim and impervious as she watches the children playing.

Evie said when she was at school she always looked up to the windows so she could see the sky. The same sky, she said, that would be above her as she rode home, as she sat in the garden or on the verandah. Above her when she looked out of her window into the dusk. That always made her feel better, she said, knowing about the sky always being there.

Hannah would not allow Evie to stop attending the school and remain at home. She said she needed to experience the company of other children her own age. Evie said she came to understand she could not stay the remainder of her life sitting quietly alone with her hands folded in her lap. She knew, she said, that she was more an observer than a participant in life, who preferred to watch and think before becoming involved whereas other people may behave with more spontaneity — 'And, Zoe, there is plenty of room in this world for all types of people and none is better than the other.'

But while she understood that about herself she also learned that however hard it is, sometimes you must simply stand up and walk over to someone and hold out your hand. Up until school everyone had always come to her. Everyone had loved her and made a fuss of her because she was Hannah's child and Eliza's granddaughter, the only child in the house. At school she had to make her own mark. Or not make it. It was up to her.

She learned about risk — oh it is risky to go alone up to a group and say you want to play too, because what if they laugh at you or chase you away? But if you go up to a group you start to see the faces, Zoe. You see that group you were so afraid of is just made up of faces, all different, but still a little like your own.

It's something I wouldn't learn then, *Those girls are stupid. I have no interest in joining in with stupid girls.* But it's a lesson that remained with me. Like Evie, my natural bent is to observe, to think rather than act. But I've learned to drink a glass of wine rather too quickly then force myself into a group of chattering people. And yes, you see the faces and sometimes there is a face you would like to see more often. Occasionally, more closely. It's how I met Tom. And it's a lesson which I tried to draw on, when I wrote my stories on the street kids and gangs.

Me in my navy suit. Ms Middle-Class-Rich-Bitch. For Christ's sake why didn't I think about what I looked like? It's turned into me against them. The black leather and the chains and the long hair and the dangling dreadlocks and the tats. The dogs. They look at me and they're grinning. Rich bitch. My heart's pounding and my mouth is dry. I'm so terrified.

Jesus, I can smell the sweat reeking from my body. Can they? Can they smell my fear?

The groups were ferocious in their collectiveness, the long hair and the acrid fearsome stink and the leather and the bikes and the glue and the bags and the bottles and the syringes. I forced myself closer. Saw the faces. Saw the human-ness. Began hearing the stories.

Then I was disdainful of her advice about approaching the other girls. Still, sky watching was a problem-solving device I took home with me. My school's classrooms also had windows set close to the ceilings. The tiny panes made seeing out more difficult still. But I gazed for hours at those panes, and the girls and the rounded-vowelled voices and the bored, groomed teachers faded into a remote froth. I stared through thick panes of glass into an occasional faint blue wash, most often into smoggy cloud.

But I thought about the sky at Evie's. The intensity of blue, the luminosity of light, my skin bared to the heat of a burning sun. About a crimson, golden, purple spread of sunset. About the glimmering evenings.

I still watch the sky. Retreat into it. All the worst times. When I was pinned to the bed by my attachment to the drip which was *settling you nicely into labour*. Wracked by pain and loneliness and fear I watched the sky. When my lovers left, when I left my lovers, when I was sick, when my husband shouted, when editors sent back my stories, when Ben turned into a child monster, when the car broke down, when the plumbing went, when Grace and Evie died. I watched the sky. I watched the sky and it became Evie's sky, that grand expanse which spreads above this house and garden, which spreads and spreads until it becomes sea.

Tom and I have learned to settle our agreements in an entirely adult way. Negotiated and agreed upon. We rarely argue. When we do it is an important issue. We do not raise our voices, call each other names, malign our respective friends and family or attack the other for past offences. We listen carefully and speak rationally.

Despite my measured tones, I brim with rage. When confronted, the ploys I've used in the past to win are those which I now forbid myself, but most desperately miss. In the past I shouted, swore, slandered and allowed irreparably damaging utterances to emerge from my mouth. Now I only have rationality available I stutter my opinions and seethe. But I have to behave. I won't allow that flushed, dangerous child to intrude upon this adult world we inhabit. Tom is so gently reasoning, so sweetly persuasive, so calm and so bloody right.

Following these occasions, I take myself off into the bricked and flower-sprinkled pocket-sized handkerchief which is our back garden. I sit on a garden seat. I seethe and stare at the sky. Usually Tom comes to find me. And I'm warmed by sun, lulled by the light and colours of Evie's sky. I'm not upset, not sulking, I'm simply watching the sky.

As I watch today.

It's a haze of grey. Occasionally there is an underlayer of faded blue and fine threads of bleached-out yellow.

Watching the sky.

It's an activity psychiatrists would probably label denial, an unwillingness to enter into discourse with the difficulties which disrupt our lives. But watching the sky soothes and smooths out anger and sadness and fear and although you may continue to be oppressed and plagued by errant husbands, leaking radiators and unplanned pregnancies you emerge from sky-watching buffered and somehow reassured.

Evie continued to attend the village school until she was fourteen. It was always hard for her, she said, that sense of being closed in, kept from the sea and the garden. Never easy being among the other children. They were so unpredictable. She'd not known people could be unpredictable. At any moment any of them may shout or cry or become angry.

Ah, Zoe, there are some things which are too hard. Things which watching the sky makes no easier to bear.

When Evie left school Hannah was not entirely sure what was to be done with her. 'Mother was a strong advocate of education, Zoe, she said she would not have her daughter ignorant of the arts, of science and literature, the worlds of possibilities and beauty and ideas education explored.' She considered sending her to a girls' boarding school in Auckland but Evie was so unhappy with the idea she didn't pursue it. In the end she decided she would engage a tutor to teach Evie French, Latin, science and mathematics and to oversee her reading. The position was advertised in the local and Auckland newspapers and Miss Georgina Simpson duly presented herself and was appointed.

'It was so funny. She just turned up at the door. This squat barrel of a person, no hat and her hair cut off quite scandalously short. And so oddly dressed. She was enveloped in an enormous grey tweed coat and with these huge black boots. Mother couldn't take her eyes off her. We couldn't think how she got there, she seemed to have simply materialised on the doorstep, but she said she'd seen the advertisement in the Auckland newspaper, got on a coach and walked the remainder of the way from Mamaranui. She stuck her hand out, said we should call her George, handed Mother her references, rattled off all the schools she'd taught at and asked when she should start.

'I was quite afraid of her. She had a booming, authoritative English voice. But she was the only applicant we had and Mother was determined I should continue my education. George was a bit of a mystery. She told me, much later, she'd left England because she didn't approve either of its archaic society or her family. She said she wanted to see if a new country would manage things better. She taught in a Wellington girls' school and then in Auckland but she had differences of opinion with both headmistresses and they erupted into such bad feelings that she left. *Because I got cross and told them they were teaching a load of rot. Cooking and sewing and etiquette. Total rot...* She said she would never again teach in a school which promoted female domestic servitude.

'But George was a wonderful teacher. She loved books and ideas, loved teaching and learning. Before she came I read with my heart. George taught me to read with my head as well, to see how the words fitted together to create precision and clarity and power. She'd be reading aloud and then something, a phrase, a sentence, would strike her in some way and she'd pause and glance up at me and there'd be such admiration in her eyes, such awe and respect for those words.'

In the mornings they read together. In the afternoons they went out onto the farm. George had lived all of her thirty-seven years in cities and large towns. She learned with Evie, about plants and trees, about walking on sand with the sea beyond you and the wind pressing against your body.

When Evie was almost seventeen George left. She said although it was hard to leave, Evie could manage her education quite adequately without her and it was time she took a look at the rest of the country. They wrote to each other for years. George set up a small school for girls in Nelson. She said educating girls to use their minds properly might ensure men didn't make such a mess of this country as they had of all the others.

'But when George left, it was almost like a death, Zoe. She'd become such a good friend. I'd be reading the books I'd read with her or working in the garden and I'd hear her voice.'

She missed George and Hannah saw that and mistook Evie's sense of loss for loneliness. She decided Evie needed young people about her, she must put her own feelings aside for a time and consider her daughter's needs and they must leave their home to enter the little bit of society which Auckland offered. Evie needed friends, new company and while she did not want to lose her daughter, what other than marriage could life offer a girl? Evie would never meet a suitable candidate for marriage shut away, as she was, on a farm.

And so they left the farm in the capable hands of their manager and departed for Auckland to remain during the season with James and Alice. Evie would mix with a convivial group of young men and women. She would Come Out. She might hopefully, meet and marry a suitable young man.

'It wasn't that Mother wanted rid of me, Zoe, and of course she did not want me unhappy. But she wanted to see me secure, married to a nice young man from a good family. She said it was no life for a young girl, being tucked away at the end of beyond.'

During the first fortnight of their stay Evie was fitted by a dressmaker for day-frocks and evening gowns. She was draped in silks and muslins in fashionable pastel shades. Alice and Hannah purchased an assortment of parasols, fans, gloves and hats which matched her new dresses.

'The first social occasion Mother and I were asked to attend, Zoe, was a garden party. I wore a pink and white shot-silk dress with a glorious ostrich-feathered hat, neither of which suited me in the least. You know how I walk, Zoe? I stride — it comes from walking over the paddocks wearing boots. Well, I strode. While the other girls minced along with their dainty little steps I strode. I didn't know how to flirt with boys, to blink and bat my eyelashes at them and giggle behind my hand and I didn't know it was expected that I appear meek and delicate. I ate heartily and I talked loudly and directly. I talked about cows and gardens and books. I was entirely without grace or proper conversation, Zoe. By the middle of the season I found myself festooned in my silks and lace and Mother's jewellery, sitting on my own on velvet seats at one ball, one soirée after another. Sometimes my cousins took pity on me and asked me to dance but I was miserable and bored. I missed the farm and knew I could never really leave. It was my place. My home. I would not give it up. Even if the impossible happened and I was pursued by one of those smart young Auckland men, even if one of them flung himself at my feet and begged me to marry him and live in a smart Auckland house I wouldn't do it.'

Evie's eyes gleam and she wryly smiles. 'On the other hand, Mother received an enormous amount of attention. She had never danced as much in her life. Every widower in Auckland was mad about her.'

'In the end I refused to go anywhere. I packed up all my finery and said I would never wear it and Anne-Jane must take it all, the frocks could be cut down to fit her. She was much more a hat and parasol person than I. I told Mother I would go home; I'd never marry. No self-respecting man could possibly want an opinionated and unmannerly woman such as myself and we'd have to make the best of it. It was better that I went back to the farm and learned as much as I could about how to manage it than sitting about on fancy chairs looking silly. Because the farm and the garden would be my life. It may have been thought of as no life for a young girl but it was what I wanted and I had better get on with it.'

Hannah smiled her relief. She said goodbye to her widowers and they went home.

'The sky, Zoe. In Auckland I watched the sky and wanted to be home. Wanted to be here on the verandah, see my sky and feel it around me.'

They returned home and Evie learned about the farm. Whereas before Hannah had consulted alone with the farm manager, the bank manager and with James who acted as the farm's accountant, now Evie was included. For some time she silently listened. She walked for miles across paddocks, began getting up to watch the milking, read books on agriculture she ordered from Auckland. Then she extended the orchard and planted berry-fruit and vines.

'It was a happy time, Zoe. I was so busy learning everything and working hard. I was never meant to be a lady. Mother laughed at me when I came in and said I was like a Russian peasant returning from the fields. But she was pleased with me. I saw that in her face.'

There was no need to look at the sky then, except with gratitude and with awe.

'But then, Zoe, there was no time to watch the sky. Neither was there any comfort in it while Mother was ill.'

17

When I think of the 1920s I imagine glamour and envisage gleaming cars with leather seats and picnic hampers strapped to the back, crammed with chicken and champagne. I see elegant, cigar-smoking young men with swept-back hair, loose-fitting suits and black and white shoes. The women have fine dresses, thistledown and gossamer skim over narrow, boyish bodies. They have neat little hats hugged snugly to sleek, clipped bobs. They have long beads to the waist and wave stiletto cigarette-holders. Everybody does a frenetic jitterbug and is called darling.

Oh dah-ling.

When I was fifteen I fell in love with Scott Fitzgerald. I had scarce admiration for Zelda although I envied her dainty body, her face with the large, guileless eyes and bow-shaped mouth and her blonde curls. But all that charm had little appeal to me because, I concluded, she had failed to understand Scott. She did not fully appreciate Scott's — in my head I always called him Scott, sometimes in moments of affection, Scotty — great talent. She was neither truly appreciative of, nor sensitive to his genius.

I, on the other hand, understood after reading his novels, short stories and biographies, that he was a superior being, possibly the greatest writer of all time. Indeed, had he been better blessed by a woman who shielded and encouraged his gifts, this would be recognised without doubt. I wept and smiled over his perceptive insight into character, sighed over his lucid and penetrative analysis, gloated over his tight arrangement of perfectly selected words.

Poignant was his favoured word and so it became mine as well. My school essays were splattered by *poignants* and *poignancies* — a character in a play, a story, a novel, an historical figure, even entire countries were rendered *poignant*.

Francis Scott Fitzgerald is the greatest author of our century — I was cautious in claiming greater accolades although I believed him far superior to Dickens, Fielding or Trollope — *and yet his life was marred by poignancy*

And, although I had decided on a life of celibacy, I knew that had I had the opportunity to meet Francis Scott Fitzgerald I may well have been persuaded to marry, nurture and protect him from a world which failed to appreciate the genius in its midst. I may even have been coerced into *sexual intercourse* had he so desired.

It was truly poignant that the only man I could ever love was dead.

And so for a time the '20s became for me, a gorgeously romantic era I sighed over and yearned to have back again. I asked Evie if she'd found the 1920s a wonderfully exciting time. What sort of clothes did she wear? Did she dance the Charleston and did she know any flappers? And, oh joy, could she have been, was she ever herself a flapper?

Evie smiles at me, 'Certainly it was an exciting time. The war had ended and the world was determined to be happy again, to forget about fear and killing and perhaps while all that glamour and gaiety appeared brittle, it was for an important purpose. It was to help forget the horror, to cover it over and live again, live for the day. We read about it in the newspaper. The parties and the dancing, the new-style clothes. It seemed quite shocking that women were cutting off their hair and drinking alcohol and smoking like men. And women — well we had always been cosseted, looked after and protected. I suppose you could say we were restricted in what we could do. But now women seemed to be having enormous freedom. We read about young women going, unaccompanied and unsupervised, to parties and driving about in cars.

'But that was on the other side of the world, Zoe. Oh certainly it was beginning to happen in New Zealand but only in the larger cities, Auckland and Christchurch and Wellington. But New Zealand was conservative then. We were puritans, suspicious of frivolity and fun, and strong drink as they called it, well in many places in New Zealand it was illegal. If you wanted to be accepted you had to conform, you had to wear the same clothes and do and think as everybody else. If you were a young man you found work and probably you would stay in that same work for the rest of your life. If you were a woman your work was your marriage and your home and your children and perhaps the church. Before she married, the main occupation for a young woman was to prepare her trousseau. To embroider bits of linen and silk and collect china for future dinner tables. Everyone knew their place, Zoe, and woe betide anyone who stepped much beyond it. No, I was never a flapper but I was a farmer and that was quite shocking enough.'

This was not the world of the '20s that I envisaged. Certainly it was not the world of Scott and Zelda's all-night champagne parties, careering about Europe in fast cars with silk scarves flying behind them in the wind, nor of ferocious arguments and emotional reconciliations and love and passion and madness.

Evie watches me, smiles at my obvious disappointment.

'I was not a flapper, Zoe, neither did I know anyone who was. But even so, I became the focus of a certain amount of curiosity and suspicion. It was quite unheard of for a single young woman to occupy herself in farm business and turn up at auctions and stride about inspecting the livestock and then bid. As it was quite unheard of for a young woman to make it known she had no interest in marrying. When we returned from Auckland, I suppose the news got out that I'd not managed to procure a husband for myself. I doubt I was seen as a highly desirable property, Zoe, but the farm, well that was an entirely different matter. I was constantly being bothered by young men on their knees in our parlour pleading protestations of great love. In the end I let it be known to some of the young women around the area I'd had a secret lover killed in France during the war and I'd vowed to remain faithful to his memory. I swore them to secrecy of course, and of course the story was all around within a week. After that I was left alone to my grief. I'm sorry to disappoint you Zoe, but in the '20s I was out on the farm in strong boots and the large aprons Mother made out of calico to cover up my clothes. A flapper on the farm, well it would never do at all. But I consider I was a bit of a rebel in another way.'

I was disappointed because I considered this farming life to be rather passionless and I rather fancied the idea of passion although I would not, of course, choose it for myself. But strong emotion came eventually into Evie's life, although emotion related not to love but to sadness and fear. Hannah became ill.

'There are times in your life, Zoe, when you can't understand or find an explanation for the things you hear about or see. They're so hard and painful you can't think why God could allow it, so bad you can't believe there is a God to allow suffering like that. I thought it in the war. Young men living in those trenches surrounded by mud and death and unspeakable horror. Good young men slaughtered or coming back so maimed in their bodies and minds they could not re-make their lives. But I was removed from it. I was fortunate because nobody I'd been close to had died. God knows I felt horror and compassion at the suffering but I had no faces to lose or to remember. The men from around the district, most were exempt since they were needed for farm work or they were too old. Those who did go were lucky and came safely back home. My cousins were in the army, but they were officers, they were accountants involved with figures and paperwork, they were never near the front.

'When Mother became ill, suffering and fear and loss were no longer remote.'

Initially they thought it was a cold. Severe, but still just a cold. Hannah had sat out on the verandah long into the late autumn evenings. Perhaps she'd been chilled without realising it or perhaps the change from the cool of the verandah to the house warmed — maybe overwarmed — by the fires, had brought on an infection.

Evie persuaded her to remain in bed for a day or two until she regained her health. The cook made up soothing drinks mixed from oranges and lemons from the orchard and honey made on the property.

The two days extended into a week. Although Hannah said she was simply feeling weak and there was no need to bother the doctor, Evie became concerned. She could not remember her mother ever remaining ill in bed before this.

At the end of the week she got up from her bed and dressed herself. Evie saw from her loose clothes she was thinner than she'd ever been and as she walked from room to room she'd pause, regaining her breath and place her hand against a wall as if for support.

Evie said they must send word to the local doctor to call — perhaps he could provide a tonic — but Hannah said all the tonic she needed was fresh air and sunlight and gentle walks in the garden. She would feel much better when her appetite returned. She said she was not pale, she'd seen in the mirror that morning her colour was good which was a certain indication of her improving health.

Evie was forced to agree. Her mother's face glowed and her eyes were bright and if it were not for her physical weakness and the frailty of her body she would appear to be in perfect health.

She had a chaise-longue set out on the verandah. Hannah would recuperate there in the fresh air close to the garden. Each morning Evie took her arm and helped her through the doors and tucked pillows behind her head. The cook made broths and eggnogs and poached fish to tempt her appetite.

But she remained tired and listless and weak. The infection had left her with a cough, a relentless wracking cough which shook her body and prevented her from sleeping.

Evie called for the doctor who said there was a slight weakness in the chest but nothing to cause real concern. He prescribed a tonic and a cough elixir and said she must rest, avoid exertion and must not risk a draught or chilled air until she was well again.

The cough abated. She was healthy again. Still weak — she began to use a stick to rest against whenever she walked out into the garden and she remained on the chaise-longue for most of the afternoons. But better. Until the cough returned and Evie found her mother collapsed beside the verandah steps.

The doctor returned, noted the feverishness, listened to the list of symptoms; the chest pains, weakness and the cough which clattered about the house through the days and nights. This time he looked grave and offered pleurisy as an explanation. He told Evie her mother must remain in bed until she had made a full recovery as, with the help of God, he expected she would do. He left medicine and instructions and promised to return within the week.

The small weakness of the chest, the pleurisy, was finally diagnosed by a specialist in Auckland as pulmonary tuberculosis.

'As you will understand,' he said, 'the disease is serious. However, it is not of long standing and the prognosis is not entirely hopeless.'

Hannah could enter a sanatorium or be nursed at home. Evie would not consider a sanatorium, she'd take her mother home to be cared for. They would remain in close contact with their own doctor, employ a nurse if need be and return to Auckland for treatments whenever necessary.

'I don't know if I was right, Zoe. I still wake in the night thinking about it. Would Mother have been cured in the sanatorium? I knew she'd be unhappy away from her home. She may have been unhappy and lonely and got no better. At least she was where she was happiest.'

Evie hired a happy, gentle girl, Rewa, who had home-nursed around the district. Evie would come in from the farm and see them sitting together on the verandah. Rewa was so healthy with her glossy skin and eyes and hair. Hannah, in the chair beside her, wrapped in a shawl with a rug tucked around her legs, was like a porcelain doll. She was waif-like, her hands waxen.

During the three following years they never gave up hope. Hannah would recover. Sometimes she grew stronger for a time and walked in the garden and the orchard. At other times she'd smile and say she wasn't able to walk straight today and so she supposed she must just remain where she was. She said she was in good company; Keats had tuberculosis. She did not say he had died from it.

Then there was bright red blood from the coughing. And the difficulty of breathing. The pain in her chest like terrible burning. Evie saw her sitting with her arm held above her head. She said it gave her relief. Sometimes she was excitable, irritable and easily exasperated with Rewa, with Evie, with the doctor, the cook, anyone who was in the house. The days were too hot, she could not possibly exert herself in such heat or she was too cold to move from her room.

But for most of that time, Evie said, she remained patient and hopeful and loving. She protected everyone by denying her pain, by pretending that fearsome bright blood which sometimes appeared when she coughed was of no importance. She knew the disease was most often fatal. She settled her affairs, was insistent that Evie knew the details of her will, of all the business of property and finances. 'Now my dear,' she would say, 'I know this is difficult and probably unnecessary but, just in case, I want you to know.'

She had always played her violin, even in her later years, but now she was too weak. That was the only thing, Evie said, she ever became truly angry about. I wouldn't care so much about everything else, she'd say, if I could only play a little.

She knew she was dying. She sat for hours on the verandah, her hands folded in the rug looking out on the sky and the garden and the sea. In the letter she left for Evie she wrote that she had been blessed during her life by her friends, by a dear mother and by a small gift for music — all these she was grateful for. But the greatest blessing of her life was the company of a loving daughter.

In the spring following a winter which had seemed harsher than most, Hannah was well again. She began to walk in the garden in the mornings before it became too warm. One evening was particularly mild and she longed to go out into it. The garden was becoming beautiful again after the cold. She wanted to be out in it.

Evie took her arm.

'She was radiant,' she said. 'Excited. It was as if she had shed her illness, her eyes were bright and her skin glowed, her beauty somehow had come back to her.'

Evie took her arm and they went down the verandah steps into the garden. They walked among the flowers and the trees, past the stone fences and into the orchard. The trees were covered with blossom.

Hannah had not walked so far for some time. She looked over into the corner for Eliza's oak tree.

She let go of Evie's arm and walked slowly on alone, then seemed to forget all caution and was almost running across the orchard to the tree. She placed her hands against the trunk, turned and called back to Evie.

'I can't believe how much it's grown. Oh, Evie, just look at Mother's tree.'

Her face was filled with joy.

She staggered and began to cough. Evie ran to her and held her up in her arms. The blood came, spurting and gushing from her mouth.

That's when I knew there could be no God because how could a God allow this? My Evie, covered in her mother's blood, carrying that beloved, frail body back to their house.

Hannah was buried as she had wished, in the small churchyard behind the chapel at Mamaranui. After the ceremony Evie walked down to the sea and waited for the dolphins.

'That year following Mother's death was the only time I've experienced loneliness. I've been alone here often, but loneliness is different from being alone. I was filled with fear. I ached with loss. It seemed as if I was being smothered. I dreamt so often about Mother and woke in the mornings with the sun coming in at the window expecting to hear her voice. I couldn't accept her death. I wouldn't let her go. I blamed myself, for not looking after her better, for not taking her to the sanatorium, for not seeking another, perhaps more modern, medical opinion. Perhaps I should have taken her to specialists in Sydney or London. I should never have allowed her to walk so far into the garden that evening. I would wake in the night listening for her cough and remember she was dead.

'I didn't think I could ever recover. I didn't think I'd ever laugh again.'

But that's when Evie became most aware that Hannah had been right in sending her to school in Mamaranui. Because after her mother's death those children in the area who were now the young adults came, first to pay their respects, then to ensure she was not without company.

Evie sighs but she is smiling, 'They wouldn't leave me alone. Oh, they knew I had plenty to busy myself with during the day and they would not intrude on my work. But hardly an evening went by without someone or other calling by. They were so kind, Zoe, although I did not think so at the time. I believed them to be interfering and invasive. I thought they were patronising me, pitying the poor lonely spinster. I was filled with bitterness and self-pity, Zoe. I didn't behave well. I was unwelcoming and usually we sat mainly in silence. But they always came back.

'Perhaps it was because they loved Mother and wanted to look after me as a way of thanks. Mother sometimes appeared remote but she was gentle and kind. She visited families whenever there was illness and helped wherever she could. And they loved her for her music. She played at the special services in the church and people would sit transfixed, spellbound by her playing.

'I refused their invitations but I continued to receive them, well I had no choice, but as the months went by they became more insistent. In the end I was simply too worn down to refuse and I began to go to picnics and musical evenings and to teas and dinners and parties. And despite myself I began to enjoy them.'

Evie laughs. The corners of her eyes crinkle. 'It's the closest I ever was to being a flapper.'

Towards the end of the year after Hannah died, Joseph Francis Liam Connolly left his mother, father, three sisters and younger brother behind in Belfast and journeyed to New Zealand. His journey was by steamer and, although he shared a small cabin with a fellow passenger, a comfortable one.

More comfortable than that of his Great Uncle Liam, seventy years before by sailing ship. Every evening at seven he was locked into a cramped berth which was not unlocked until ten the following morning. He shared a narrow bunk with two other boys from Belfast and felt every pitch and tremor and toss of the ocean since the cabins for the lowest-paying passengers were situated in the bottom of the ship.

But Uncle Liam did well for himself. In 1861 he was in Otago scratching together a living through casual work. When the news came through about gold someone had found, he decided to try his luck. He was there close behind the first miners.

He worked hard and prospered, though there were tough times. He lost his gold and almost his life to the river. He had a thieving bastard of a partner he had to chase and beat to find where his money was. But he saved his money for the land. Rich green lush land. As much as he could buy. It had been his dream in Ireland but there he'd had to put it out of his head. No matter. It was a dream he'd realise, no matter what, in this new country.

When it seemed the gold had dried up he took his profits and travelled around the country searching for his land. He did not care for the dampness of coastal Otago or the dry arid inland, nor for the English snobbery of the settlers he encountered in Canterbury. He decided to try the other island.

Perhaps he was foolish, perhaps it was a fanciful notion he had in his head about this land. But he knew he'd know it when he saw it. He'd worked hard for it, working beside the river in temperatures so cold a man would have to be mad or driven to bear it. Well now, but he was a driven man, driven for his land.

He found it at Maropio, cleared the bush, built a homestead and married a local girl.

Their son, the only surviving child of the marriage, also married a local girl but there were no children. The farm required an heir. Liam wrote to his niece in Ireland requesting that her eldest son come. There would be no promises but the lad could have a chance at a new and better life.

And so Sean had gone. He wrote to his family this was a glorious country and he was as welcome in his mother's family as if he was their son. Eventually he wrote to tell them the farm was willed to him should he survive his uncle and his cousin and that he wished for his brother Joseph to join him on the farm. He wanted to share his good fortune with his own blood.

Evie met Joe at a picnic to celebrate the new year.

'I looked up and there he was. Beauty is not often a word associated with men, but Joe was beautiful. He was tall and straight and lean and his black hair curled back off his forehead and his face was slim, the skin stretched tight across his cheekbones. And his eyes, they were your mother's eyes, royal blue fringed with those thick inky eyelashes. He was over by the river talking to his brother. He wore a white shirt and brown tweed trousers with braces and he had his hands in his pockets. I blushed all over my face and all over my body and me almost thirty. My heart began to beat so hard and fast I thought everybody would hear it. It was just like in those dreadful romantic books and all those thoughts about never marrying, well I never thought them again.'

Evie married Joe in the Easter of the following year. Alice came a month early to supervise arrangements for the wedding and possibly to safeguard her niece's virtue — this unpredictable niece of hers who was throwing all caution to the wind and marrying a wild Irishman. She brought with her the gown she'd had made for Evie. It was creamy satin, the bodice beaded with small pearls, the sleeves long and close-fitting and the skirt falling in soft, lustrous folds.

'I never cared for clothes but I cared about this dress. I wanted to be beautiful, and this dress Zoe! The satin was so light and cool and smooth. The colour like beaten butter.'

They were married in the small chapel at Mamaranui. Before they returned to the house for the wedding reception, Evie kissed Joe then walked around to the back of the chapel and placed the wedding bouquet which she had made from the late white roses and small gold chrysanthemums in her garden, on Hannah's grave.

18

I hear Evie's voice. Feel the brush tug then slide through my hair. The stories are a richness tucked beneath my heart. Death and birth and love. The business of a family.

But I wonder about the sense of this. Instead of taking a plane back to Christchurch to resolve this story of my own I'm shivering in the coolness of late evening on the steps of Evie's verandah with her stories winding and weaving about me.

She said Joe made her laugh. 'Certainly, Zoe, he was a handsome man but as well as that he had a lovely way with him. He looked for the good in the world, and for the beauty. He would see something, something most people would pass over and he'd stop and look at it, really look at it and make me stop too — *ah Evie wouldn't ye look at that now*. I still hear his voice. He was gentle and had a wonderful charm. That soft singing Irish accent was lovely in itself. Alice used to laugh and tell him he could charm the very devil if he wished. He had a wry quick humour and a remarkable way of putting words together.'

Sean sent for the youngest brother to share his good fortune. Evie and Joe had a brief honeymoon in the Bay of Islands then returned to the farm. During the days they worked sometimes separately and sometimes together. Evie would look up from her garden and see him close by, watching her and smiling. He told her about Ireland and his sisters and his mother and father. She told him about the Hokianga, about Eliza and William and about Hannah. They walked through the garden and the orchard, sat together on the verandah in the evenings. During the days she thought about his long lean body, his hands, his voice whispering to her in the dark and her skin sang. In the nights they slept close, her body curled against him, his arm around her waist.

In my fifth form year I put in enough effort to ensure I'd pass School Certificate. I continued to hurl myself into novels although I took great care my English teacher did not suspect me of reading anything other than the bare requirements which would enable me to pass my examinations by the skin of my teeth.

But through the novels I developed an interest in the potential of love. My reading suggested perhaps falling in love was unavoidable and passion may be a profound human experience. I began to experience a crisis of faith. Up until then I'd believed myself to be embarked upon a life of solitude and celibacy. But how could I refute the possibility of the life-enriching experience that passion with a smouldering Rochester or Heathcliff look-alike could provide? What if an F. Scott Fitzgerald sauntered across my path?

I began to re-evaluate my scorn and repugnance for sexual intercourse. Some writers seemed to recommend it. Some writers suggested that contrary to my own opinion of the practice — I winced at the mere thought of it — it could, between impassioned participants, be a heightened experience of a spiritual nature or at least pleasurable.

I made a new discovery, DH Lawrence. *Aaron's Rod. The Plumed Serpent.* All those symbolic penises leaping out at you from steamy passages — *so that around the low dark shrubs of crouching women stood a forest of erect, upthrusting men, powerful and tense with inexplicable passion.*

Well, I told myself, Lawrence certainly recommended the phallus as an instrument of enlightenment. But then again he would, being a man. It seemed that was all men wanted to do. Stick their penises into the nearest aperture. But what if I arrived at the end of my life having missed the chance of a profound human experience? What if just because of mere queasiness I remained unawakened to my true feminine power?

I began to observe males with more interest than before. Not that there was much chance of satisfying my new curiosity. There were four male teachers at the school, all in science and maths. They were ancient, at least forty, all with sparsely distributed, fading hair and double chins. They wore tweed jackets with leather patches at the elbows, greying shirts which had seen better days. One smoked a pipe. I yawned and fidgeted through their classes. I could not envisage any of them immersed in heady passion, nor in the violent throes of copulation.

After my mother was ill we rarely had visitors to our flat but eventually she resumed a social life of a sort. People occasionally called and she infrequently went out in the evenings. If men stayed overnight I was unaware of it. But they did occasionally visit.

These men were clearly superior to the maths and science teachers. For one thing they looked much better. Their clothes fitted properly and their hair was trimly cut, in fact they were quite stylish considering that they were old. Besides that they laughed a lot and talked about films and plays and books and music. Clearly they were interested in things other than photosynthesis, triangles and logarithms.

I made a habit of staying up late when my mother expected visitors to watch for any signs of passion or lust. I wanted to observe it before I tried it for myself, to have some glimmer of understanding of how an innate repugnance for such an embarrassing and messy business as sexual intercourse could be swept away by desire.

But if there were any signs I didn't see them. I began to look more closely at the Christ's and Boys' High boys who lingered around the corners a block away from the school. I couldn't imagine them as suitable objects of passion and, anyway, they rarely glanced back at me, tall and lanky, my hat jammed down on my head.

I began to regard my body more attentively. I stood naked in front of the mirror, saw that my breasts though hideously large, slanted upwards, that my legs were long and quite pleasantly shaped, that the flesh around my ribcage was tight, that my waist curved nicely inwards. My nipples became erect and turned a darker pink if I stroked my fingers across them and my body tingled, but not so much as when I put my hand down between my legs. Once when I was standing in a crowded bus a man lightly brushed his hand across my buttocks. I moved away but my face burned with heat from the terrifying pleasure which bolted through me.

At the end of the year I went up to Evie's and spent much of my time swimming, lying on the beach, reading one book after another and taking long walks along the beach at dusk. I was a solitary figure. I'd come to a decision. Of course I would not actively seek it, but, should profound passion present itself I would not deny it. But I would never, never squander myself on anyone I did not consider remarkable in some way.

It was the year I met Rodney. His parents had recently purchased one of the holiday cottages. During the days his father hammered and sawed and painted and his mother sewed and cleaned and cooked and baked. Rodney was forced to escape these irritants by retreating to the beach.

Rodney was remarkable because he had long brown legs and blonde hair and blue eyes. He was remarkable because he was a boy and spoke to me although not terribly often and certainly not for very long. His speech was succinct and to the point:

What's ya name?
Wanna swim?
Wanna walk?
Wanna icecream?

Although Rodney and I were in each other's company for almost every waking moment during an entire three weeks, I learnt little about his life in Auckland and nothing at all of the rich inner life and creative thoughts I was certain he regularly experienced. Still, my patience with his taciturnity was amply rewarded. We lay for hours on the beach, unspeaking, gazing into each other's eyes, occasionally sighing and often kissing. His arm rested across my body leaving a white imprint on my tanned back which I treasured and preserved by lying only with my stomach facing the sun after he had returned to Auckland. I stood peering over my shoulder into the mirror at it, pensively weeping, for days after he left.

Evie was tolerant. She simply smiled at my excited bursts of energy and wild, untuneful singing and allowed me to return each day to the beach and occasionally, take evening strolls provided I was back before ten o'clock. She did not caution or warn me but remarked often on my good common sense.

I retained my good common sense during our evening strolls despite his untrustworthy hands and muffled pleas.

Come on. Just there.
I love you. Do you love me?
If you loved me you'd let me.

We kissed and kissed and kissed. We kissed until my mouth was sore and swollen and my body tingled and my head swam. During the third week I allowed him to unhook my bra and put his hand on my breasts. He squeezed my nipple between his thumb and finger. My body shook and I nearly fainted from rapture. Repulsion disappeared but fortunately was swiftly replaced by fear. Fear of pain, fear of discovery, fear of pregnancy. And so I continued with my kissing and my no's and my wrestling.

One evening he said quite casually they were off next morning. I was unsure how to behave in such circumstances — *my lover is abandoning me* — so I took my cue from him.

'Oh.' I was as calm as I could manage.

He said he'd write to me if I liked. We resumed kissing.

I returned broken-hearted to Evie's, lay face down on my bed and sobbed into the pillow. My life was over. Love was denied me. First I'd fallen in love with a dead person and now I'd been abandoned by Rodney.

Evie brought me strawberries and cream for breakfast and cooled my face with a damp cloth. She found me books to read and coaxed me down to the beach for a swim. She didn't tell me my heart would mend quickly or that there would be other Rodneys.

But by the time his desultory mis-spelled letter arrived, mostly news of his elevation at the beginning of the year to the First XI and descriptions of subsequent matches, other Rodneys had begun to appear. I returned to school to find a sixth form extended by three new pupils. Three unruly girls who'd achieved badly in School Certificate and had been sent there by parents as a last resort to instil some discipline and good manners into their daughters.

Ruth, Jo and Lindy. We recognised each other instantly. We were immediate friends, united against snobbery, conventionality and conservatism. We sat together in class, drawled out our opinions with arrogant shrugs of our shoulders and mockingly raised eyebrows. And in the weekends we Did Things together.

My new friends had other friends who had parties. Doing Things in the weekends meant going to parties and smoking and drinking as much alcohol as we dared. It also meant meeting boys.

I did not forget my original pledge. All my Rodneys were remarkable. For their blue or brown eyes. For their prowess in tennis or cricket. One of them water-skied, another surfed, one could play the guitar. I was enraptured by them all. I kissed and kissed and kissed, allowed my breasts to be stroked and squeezed, sometimes kissed. Wrestled away hands which veered off in forbidden directions.

My mother wondered what I would do when I left school. She'd hoped the school would hone and sharpen my intellectual capacities so that by the end of the upper sixth form I would automatically continue my studies at university. She told me once, that she herself had been at university in Auckland and although she didn't finish her degree she'd been happy there.

'The ideas,' she said. 'The ideas and the talking. So many clever people. Other ways of seeing and thinking. Writers I'd not known about. It was wonderful to be even a small part of it.'

Her eyes looked wistfully back to that time. I asked why she'd given it up but she didn't answer.

My school certificate marks were exceptional in their accuracy. I got it absolutely right. I'd studied enough to avoid the humiliation of failure but not so much as to suggest to my teachers they'd made any particular progress with this dross inhabiting their classrooms.

'Zoe is not university material,' my form-teacher informed my mother. 'Perhaps if she would consider applying herself we may get her into dental-nursing. Or teaching. Kindergarten of course.'

What to do with a girl who'd shame the school by failing miserably at university? Who refused to do Home Science? Who could never marry well?

But in the sixth form I flourished. I gave up science subjects and maths. I was blessed with a new English teacher and new friends. I wrote blistering essays and joined the debating club.

We were to discuss the question of the English monarchy. The debate was for the school assembly. Jo, Ruth and I were opposing with me as first speaker. Our team was meticulously prepared, we had the historical, financial and moral evidence at our fingertips. We pointed out the injustice and possible corruption of privilege based on birth.

I knew we would win. The affirmative's arguments were unprepared and flimsy, *the queen is always busy opening things like parliament, who else would do that? we have to respect the royal family* and so on and so on. They giggled, hadn't memorised their notes. Their voices were weak and unconvincing.

The judging was by popular vote. There was an uneasy silence when they called for votes for the affirmative team. I held my breath. They were the more popular girls with the more popular viewpoint but everyone knew their performance had been pitiful.

I watched the headmistress. I saw her run her eyes over us and the assembled girls then gather her black gown around her and slowly stand. She turned towards her champions and began to clap and the whole school followed her.

I watched her and was filled with rage. And then I left. I stood up, walked down the stairs, off the stage, down the centre aisle. I kept my head up, kept walking although the headmistress called out my name over her microphone and commanded me to stop. I heard her say something about a bad loser and I turned around and smiled at her before I went through the double doors and down the corridors. I took my bag from my locker and walked out into the fresh bright air. I had, from habit, put on my hat and my blazer and my gloves but I flung them off, tossed them into the rose bushes and walked home, all the way, bareheaded and in my shirtsleeves, breathing in the air and pausing to stare into gardens. All those days, those long monochrome days and now my world had burst suddenly into technicolor.

I would not go back. I absolutely would not go back. My mother said, 'Zoe, darling, it was only a school debate, surely you're not going to allow something like that stop you from at least finishing your sixth form year. Your marks have improved so much. Please Zoe, won't you at least try?'

But it was much more than that. I could never win at such a place among such people. I didn't mind a battle but the terms had to be just and equal. It was only a school debate but the memory of it still makes my face hot and wrenches my gut. Injustice, misuse of power, they turn my stomach. But it taught me to retreat from a confrontation where there is no hope of winning. Retreat and survive. Try something different.

My mother suggested I should finish school at the closest co-ed but I told her I'd had enough of authority. She suggested I should apply for teaching or nursing but I happily told her I wouldn't have a hope of getting in. I spent my days blissfully sleeping in, reading until whenever then setting out on long meandering walks. In the evenings I read more or visited Jo and Lindy and Ruth and listened to records, went to more parties.

My mother said I would have to find something to do. I wanted, even then, to be a journalist, a writer, but I couldn't tell her that. Such an admission would result in a lecture about my poor marks and school reports, the lack, even, of a school's letter of recommendation. She'd tell me I must return to school and try to redeem myself. I must finish at least the sixth form, improve my marks and then we would see. And she would end by saying she had tried to tell me, she had told me over and over that unless my school performance improved I would not be able to do the kind of work I would enjoy and obviously was capable of. She would say, 'I told you, Zoe, but you would not listen.'

I would do it my way. I was unsure what that way would be but I was certain I would succeed. But I would live fully first, fill my life with experience, then write.

My mother sighed loudly, raised her eyes to the heavens and said I must find something to do. I must at least get a job.

Jobs were plentiful. Anyone looking for a job was spoiled for choice. There were positions for factory workers, tearoom assistants, shop assistants, receptionists, waitresses, office workers, anything you liked.

I became a biscuit-sorter at Aulsebrooks, then assisted shoe purchasers for a short time at Dowsons. I carried pots of tea and plates laden with sandwiches, lamingtons and cream puffs to ladies in Beaths, was on the toy counter at Woolworths, advised on the suitability of cosmetics for madam's skin at Hays, sold sweets, flowers and lingerie. Sometimes they said I'd not worked out. Usually I became bored and moved on.

After a year of this I went up to Evie's. I'd not worked out in china. I'd broken a figurine and appeared interested in neither the product nor the customers. I'd not learned about the brands and value of china as was expected when they offered me the position. My mother said while I was away perhaps I may give a little thought as to how I anticipated squandering the remainder of my life.

It was autumn as it is now. The evenings were darkening, becoming cool and there was that same catch of air in your throat if you went out early in the mornings. But the days were glorious and the garden blooming, glowing and humming with colour.

I worked with Evie in the garden cleaning up before the winter. We picked grapes and apples in the orchard.

I told her about my aborted careers. She listened, smiled, laughed sometimes at my stories of dissatisfied customers.

'I could've gone for a job in Ballantynes tearooms,' I said. 'It was in the paper just before I came up here. I had experience for that. From Beaths. But then I thought I'd probably end up serving afternoon tea to the girls from school and their mothers and I might be tempted to sprinkle them with hot tea and so I thought I'd better not.'

'Very wise,' Evie smiled.

I told her my mother was disappointed I hadn't got good marks and gone to university. That she thought I was a failure.

Evie said she was sure that was not so. And although my mother's opinion of me was important, it was not so important as the question of whether I felt satisfied with myself.

I said of course I wasn't satisfied with myself. But it wasn't my fault. I'd been made to go to the wrong school. How could I do well when I was at the wrong school? And now I had to take terrible jobs because I couldn't do anything else, because I didn't have the right marks and qualifications but that wasn't my fault.

Evie was silent. Then she said the apples seemed better this year.

'You think it is, don't you?'

Evie sighed and smiled, 'Does that matter, Zoe?' Your fault? Grace's fault? My fault, perhaps? In the end does it matter about others' disappointment if you're doing something you find satisfying? I don't believe it matters so much what you do as long as it's something you want, something you choose to do rather than just anything you happen to fall into.'

'I don't know what I want. I have ideas but I don't think I can do what I'd want. I've been useless at all of my jobs.'

Evie chuckled, 'I can't see you selling china, Zoe. Or serving afternoon teas to ladies.'

'Yes but if I can't do that, well, what can I do?'

'You have ideas, Zoe. The main thing is not to let them go.'

I said my mother left university, why did she do that if she loved it so much? It seemed to me that she wanted me to live her ideas instead of leaving me to have my own.

'It was what Grace wanted. She wanted it very much, Zoe. I believe she may have wanted it for you because it was a life she saw as rich and valuable which she thought would make you happy.'

'Why did she leave it then? If she was so happy there why did she give it all up?'

'That's Grace's story. That's hers to tell. But I will tell you something, Zoe. Your mother would not impose her wishes on you at the expense of your own. Personal freedom, now that was always very important to Grace. Perhaps more important than anything else.'

I asked her to tell me about my mother. Nothing that would intrude on her privacy. But I wanted to know at least something of her childhood. I wanted to know the child she'd been, to make some sense of the complex woman she was. That cool and intensely private, clever and elegant woman who would draw herself away from me, withdraw her body and her mind, but also, on occasion, impulsively pull me, laughing, into her arms.

Evie took some time before beginning. She was silent, gathering together the stories. And she warned me she would only tell so much.

The rest, Zoe, is for Grace to tell.

Grace was born the year after they married. When Evie told Joe she was pregnant he took her in his arms and whirled her about shouting out his joy. His Evie, this rich, lush land and now a child. He had not expected such blessings. When she felt ill he sponged her face, crooned little songs into her ear and made her smile. He took enormous pleasure in her swelling belly, rubbed her body with sweet oils, lay his head against her to listen to his child's heart beating and feel his child moving.

The midwife would not allow him in the room while Evie was in labour so he sat outside waiting. When he'd heard Evie's last triumphant shrieking wail, listened in the silence for the mewing whimper signalling life and heard Evie's cry to him it was a girl, he came in through the door, stayed with Evie till she slept, then wrapped his child up and took her out into the night.

They were unsure of a name. Evie wanted her named for Hannah of course, and he wanted his own mother remembered but they wanted also, a name which was just her own.

'She was so beautiful,' Evie said. 'Always. Small, delicate features, a perfectly shaped little head and body. Beautiful and so alert. From the start she watched us with her dark blue eyes as if she knew all about us and about the world.'

They wondered over the perfection of this miraculous little creature. There seemed no name quite fit for her.

One afternoon they watched her as she lay on a blanket in the garden. She lay quite still, looking up into the trees, then languorously moved one arm, held it above her head, kicked up her legs and smiled.

They both laughed.

'She's going to be a dancer,' Joe said. 'She's graceful even now.'

And so she was Grace. Grace Bridget Hannah.

She was her father's girl. She loved her mother but if she had the choice it was her Da she went to.

'To see them together was a sight that always made me smile. They were so pleased with each other. They'd be walking along together, Joe holding onto her hand as if she was the most precious object in all the world and her looking up at him as if he were a lord.'

He called her Gracie. Gracie Bridie. He taught her to ride and swim and row and told her about the family he'd left behind him in Ireland, her Irish grandmother and grandfather and her aunties. He told her the stories of Ireland, its heroes and its legends. In the evenings they sat together on the verandah, Grace on her father's knee, him telling the stories, his singing Irish voice husky in the dusk.

Then they came to a large island and they saw in that island a large and high fortress, a stronghold by the sea, and a great adorned house therein. Seventeen girls with golden crowns upon their heads were there, preparing a bath. And they landed on that island and set themselves on a hillock at the entrance of the fort.

Mael Duin said this, 'I am sure that yonder bath is being prepared for us.'

Now at mid-afternoon they beheld a rider on a magnificent horse coming towards the fortress. There was an adorned horsecloth beneath her. She wore a blue hood, and a bordered purple mantle. Her gloves were embroidered with gold and her sandals were golden too. As she alighted one of the girls took the horse and then came out to them.

'Welcome,' she said. 'Come into the fort: the Queen invites you.'

So they entered the fort and all bathed. They were given fine clothing to wear. They were taken into a room which was richly furnished. And the Queen sat on one side of a table with the seventeen girls and Mael Duin sat on the other with his seventeen men about him. Silver platters laden with food were set down in front of them and precious crystal vessels filled with rose-red wine.

When they had eaten and drunk their fill the queen spoke thus to Mael Duin.

'Stay here, and age will not fall on you, but the age you have attained. You will have everlasting life: and riches will come to you without labour. You will

have happiness always and be no longer wandering from island to island in the ocean.'

'She loved those words,' Evie said. 'She would have her father repeat them over and over again.'

You will have happiness always and be no longer wandering from island to island in the ocean.

I think of them now. My lanky grandfather with Grace on his knee, her small head against his shoulder, her arm around his neck. Evie close beside them. I hear the voices hum and sing through the dusk.

You will have happiness always and be no longer wandering from island to island in the ocean.

19

I returned to Christchurch determined I would find something to do, something worthwhile to stick with at least for a time. My mother suggested reception work. Maybe I could go to night classes, learn typing and eventually move to secretarial work.

I was scornful — can you imagine me, Mother, with lacquered hair and manicured nails sitting at a desk answering phones? Me, as a nondescript pink-fluffy-twin-setted clone among the rows and rows of pink-fluffy-twin-setted young women clones in a typing pool? I said I'd rather perish than be a secretary.

'Well I give up. But I'm warning you, Zoe. You must have something by the end of the month.'

One of the salons in town was advertising for a hairdressing apprentice — *apply in person*. I pulled on clothes, combed my hair, strode into town and presented myself.

The salon was dazzlingly, dauntingly glamorous. One wall was mirrored, the ceiling and other walls were glistening emerald. Plants with polished leaves cascaded out of brass planters; the seats and driers and fixtures were black; there was a thrumming, trilling sound of guitar music. The room was populated by Gods and Goddesses who cut, combed and smeared mixtures onto hair and gazed blankly into the mirrors. Gods and Goddesses with hair so perfect, so precisely cut, with trousers so flared and skirts so short it made you gasp.

I edged back to the door to flee but one of them had spied me.

'Yeah? You wanting an appointment?'

'Um. Uh, I came about the job.'

She turned her expressionless face away from me.

'Gavin. She's come about the job.'

Gavin was delicious. It's the only way to describe him. He wore a brilliant multicoloured shirt and purple trousers, tight across his thighs then flaring voluminously out over patent-leather boots with silver heels. He had Paul McCartney eyes and lustrous hair which flopped casually about his thin, pale face.

He briefly scrutinised my too-long skirt, my shapeless shirt and jersey and hair. I saw his dismay.

'You're interested in hairdressing?'

'Mmm, I think so.'

'Why?'

'I thought it might be, uh, creative.'

Perhaps the possibility of playing Pygmalion appealed to Gavin or it may have been there were simply no other applicants but he said he'd give me a try.

'All right then darl, we'll give it a whirl.'

I told my mother I was to be a hairdresser and she raised her eyebrows.

For the first few weeks I swept hair up from the floor. During the next few weeks I swept hair up from the floor and did shampoos. After that I was allowed to apply perms, rinses and tints with something that looked like a paintbrush, so long as somebody else mixed the solutions. I stood for hours watching cutting techniques, how to set different styles, how to frost and streak and back-brush.

I loved it — the slim deities, their clothes, hair, their drawling, lazy voices. The way their fingers moved, cutting and brushing and coiling hair, concocting such miracles of tint and shape. The smells of perfume mixed with ammonia mixed with hairspray, the quiet, awed clients, the green-green shining walls, the glimmering lights, the music, the magazines brimming with gloss and glitter, the long painted fingernails, the black rimmed eyes, the yawning stares.

I wanted to be transformed but I wasn't sure how I could manage it. The other girls were neither friendly nor unfriendly. They were simply far too superior and aloof to approach.

I spoke most to Gavin since he was instructing me and so, in the end, when we were cleaning up at the end of the day I asked him.

'Uh, I thought I might do something about my hair.'

'Oh, great, sweetheart. Good.'

'Uh, I thought you might, uh, give me some advice.'

He sat me down, held my hair up, dropped it, pursed his lips, combed tendrils around my face, pulled them back, gathered my hair in a lump behind my ears, frowning all the time into the mirror.

'Good strong hair,' he said.

One of the girls had hair crimped into tight tiny curls coloured gloriously red. I hesitantly mentioned I might suit something like that.

He threw his hands up in horror. 'No, absolutely not. I forbid it.'

I became an experiment. Everybody was told they must stay behind after work next evening. I was placed on a stool. Gavin asked for assessment. They prowled about me, fingering my hair, peering at me.

'Yeah? Suggestions?' Gavin asked.

'Long curly. High on the crown?'

'Oh darling, with that face?'

They conferred. My fate was decided. Gavin sliced off the full length of my hair and began snipping. I felt the scissors so close to the nape of my neck I shuddered and closed my eyes. He put a rubber cap over my head, fished out strands of hair and brushed on a solution that reeked of ammonia.

My hair was cropped into my neck and cut on a sharp, precise angle a quarter-inch below my cheekbones. I had a thick straight fringe. I had streaks in my hair the colour of mahogany, glowing like glossy chestnuts. My eyes were large and shiny and shaped like almonds. My cheekbones were high and defined. I had a pointed chin, a slim face and little ears close against my head.

I had purple boots which laced up to my knees. Skirts six inches above my knees. I had hipster jeans which displayed my navel, skinny-rib jerseys and tights patterned with silver clocks. A Mary Quant dress, platform shoes and a silky fun-fur coat the gleaming shade of pale lilacs. I was gorgeous. I was glamorous. I gloated into my mirror in the mornings. I had panda eyes and white lips and I stared as blankly as the others as I snipped and curled and brushed up. My heart sang.

My mother continued to raise her eyebrows but I caught her sometimes smiling to herself as I flew out the door to the bus stop.

My new glamour earned me attention. Men gazed at my legs. Women glared at my legs. When I went to parties boys stared at me. And I pranced about revelling in it.

And then I fell in love. The usual story. I went to a party, got a bit drunk and there he was. My long lean brown-eyed boy. Jeremy. My Jem.

He was in his first year at university doing science. If he did well enough he'd go to Otago the following year to Med School. His parents lived in Cashmere on the hill. His father was a doctor. I loved him for his brown eyes, wicked smile, his long-fingered hand on my shoulder, his mouth, the hair which curled on his neck, his flat brown belly. He loved me because I was a dizzy, glittering dollybird. He loved me because I didn't muffle myself up in duffle coats and talk about Eliot, Beckett and Freud. Because I was seemingly unperturbed by the meaning of life. Because I kissed and kissed and kissed him with my mouth open and my arms around his neck throughout an entire LP at the party.

The first time. Despite everything which followed I still smile over the memory.

I'm at Jeremy's flat. I've gone there to have lunch but of course we've ended up on his bed. His shirt is undone and his jeans unzipped. My jersey is pulled up to my neck, his hand is inside my knickers. I have this rigid, oversized worm butting into my stomach and thighs. I'm weak, dizzy, sodden with desire. And Jeremy's groaning.

Jesus, Jesus, Zoe. Come on.

I sit upright pressing my knees against my chest. He rubs his hands over my legs and back and I'm shivering, murmuring.

Oh God, I want to. I want to. What if I get pregnant?

But he has a condom his mate gave him. I say yes, all right then and lie back with my eyes tightly closed.

Jesus, is that going to go inside me?

He kneels between my legs and labours over unwrapping this ugly, plastic thing, unrolling, carefully, unrolling it. I hear it snap and crackle over him. I would giggle if it wasn't so disgusting. My body has clenched up.

I don't want to do this any more.

He lies on me, starts pressing and pushing. This is as absurd and awful as I'd always expected. So awkward and embarrassing and silly my body tightens. I will not let him in. I'm going to sit up, push him off, tell him to stop. I feel his face, wet, pressing against my neck.

Zoe, God, Zoe I can't.

I open my eyes. He looks like he could cry. I open to him, my body arches up to him. I feel him inside me — so strange, that probing harsh rawness. His hands grip my shoulders and I feel him shudder, hear him gasp, his body melts against me — *lovely* — and his arms curl around me, his mouth is on my breast.

Zoe. I love you, Zoe.

I love you.

Oh my Jeremy.

Rather than conversing about the mysteries and profundities of life, we had sex. Sex standing, sitting, lying in all sorts of positions, at all sorts of angles at any odd time of the day and night. We had sex, giggling, licking, biting, groaning, screaming, crying. We were obsessed. Jeremy found the Kinsey Report in the Science Library and it became what we termed our bedtime reading. We worked through it slowly and methodically together since this was our special research project and we had to perform experiments related to any new discoveries. I laughed helplessly until my throat hurt and my stomach ached while we tried to ascertain how long it took for me, and then for Jeremy to orgasm. How many orgasms can a female have during a two-hour period? How long can you remain motionless with an erect penis inside you?

Now stop that Zoe, this is serious. Zoe, concentrate.

We read *Lady Chatterley's Lover* and we said, *oh my love thou do fuck well* as we rolled giggling around the bed. We fucked in cars, on floors, on chairs, on couches, in the bath, in the shower, in the Nursing Mother's Room of the railway station. We fucked thoughtfully in front of carefully positioned mirrors. I examined his body. I allowed him to prod and probe and scrutinise mine. I was sacrificing myself to further his future career, I said, giggling. Always giggling.

Oh I loved him. I loved him in that intense, absorbed way that's only possible when you're eighteen. I loved him in that pure, perfect way when love is uncontaminated by awareness of the frailties, the human-ness of the love object.

Yes. I loved him. His body moving on mine, his thighs hard against my own, my hands twisted in his hair. I'd look up into his face and be dizzy and faint with love. The knowledge of his eyes, his mouth with its full bottom lip, that square, tense chin.

Perhaps such love is narcissistic. It may be that having emerged a butterfly from the dark, ugly enclosure of the chrysalis, I fell in love for a time with my own beauty, projecting that new-found perfection on Jem since he happened to be close by. Perhaps I was in love only with myself. But whatever the psychology, he filled my mind — my body too, whenever and wherever possible. I snipped and curled, applied solutions and brushed up with glassy-eyed aplomb while my blood rushed and sang through my body as I relived our latest encounter. I'd recall that long straight stretch of his body and my eyes would water and my face flush.

We recited 'I love you' like a litany. Yes. Of course we loved each other, we would love each other forever. Of course we would get married, spontaneously, naturally, somewhere on a beach or a mountain — and have four children (two boys, two girls) and a dog (we both preferred spaniels) and a cottage in the country after living in Paris for at least two years.

I smile now, but for years I called him the love of my life and the cynicism with which I said it, (raised eyebrows and a little laugh) were a pretence. When I finally made it to Paris and drove through the dark flurry of streets at midnight in the back of a taxi half-dead from hours in a plane, I felt suddenly that cold stone beneath my heart I recognise as missing and loss. I remembered him sadly. My Jeremy. My boy lover.

When I met him all those years later and saw that his charm and brown eyes had become weapons through which he got his way, I felt that loss again. At first the meeting-up-so-unexpectedly-again and the subsequent dinners and flowers were wondrously exciting. So romantic. But then my thirty-something cynicism saw it for the sham it was. His third marriage had failed. As had all the in-between and at-the-same-time affairs. He'd never finished medical school. He'd sold pharmaceutical supplies, had businesses, lost businesses, owned and sold property. He had that unhappiness and disappointment around his mouth and eyes common to middle-aged men once reliant on the disarming power of youthful charm.

Loss for the charming, disarming boy he was. Loss for my trusting girl-self.

'I should have stayed with you, Zoe. Everything went wrong after you.'

I smile, raising my eyebrows and gazing directly into his eyes. 'And you think if you'd stayed with me everything would have turned out perfect?'

He looks helplessly at me. 'I should never have left you.'

I laugh. Despite myself I'm flattered. I've waited years to hear this. Revenge is always sweet, even when it is somewhat petty.

'Why did you leave me then?'

'I don't know. I'll never know that.'

'If you'd stayed with me you'd be saying exactly the same things to some other woman. You'd be saying you married the wrong woman and everything would have turned out better if you'd met her first.'

But I say it with a smile. A flirtatious one at that.

'It's just I never realised. Never realised your potential. Just look at you. You're successful in a way I'd never have imagined. You were a pretty girl then. Fun. God, the sex. I've never forgotten it. Never forgotten that bedroom at the flat. Come on, you must remember. I knew you had a great body, Zoe and you were fun to have around. I never knew you had a brain as well.'

I smile sweetly at him. I say we both were obviously mistaken then. I was firmly convinced he had one.

I had my victory. But also my loss. Because I was no longer that girl in love with a glittering bubble. Now I saw it clearly. My grown-up-woman's fingers seized and held it close up against the light with a careful and dispassionate scrutiny. Saw it for the poor insubstantial froth it was. For the miserable lurch through rows, tears and infidelities towards the inevitable divorce it would have been.

But that perfect, shimmering bubble was not the only loss.

When he had established himself in Dunedin in his new flat and was courting his new, blonde girlfriend, the pregnancy I suspected was confirmed by the next missed period, by my tingling breasts and morning nausea.

I'd been careless. We sometimes used condoms but they were so obscenely ugly and ruined most of the pleasure anyway and half the time they wouldn't go on properly or came off inside me. And there were those awful, hot, fizzy pills you stuck up first, and had to wait until they dissolved. Christ, who wants to plan penetration to a stopwatch? I'd thought I might go on the pill sometime but everyone said it made you fat and at that time not many doctors looked kindly on unmarried young girls who wanted to have sex. Most of the time I relied on the supposedly safe times of my cycle although I wasn't entirely certain when they were. But if there was an accident, Jeremy loved me, he'd marry me, we could put off Paris for another time.

He didn't answer my letters. When I phoned, the girl who answered giggled and said he was out.

I was lucky. During the third month I was delivered by sudden wracking pain, by a slow seep of blood which was sliding down my legs by the time I'd excused myself from my perm and staggered to the flat Lindy and Jo shared around the corner. I squatted over the toilet bent double with spasms of pain until it was over.

Yes. I was lucky if you can erase the memory of fear and helpless crying for that charming, oblivious boy who so easily abandoned me. I was lucky I was no longer pregnant. Lucky that unwanted thing had been swept away in those sudden benevolent spasms of pain and blood. It was nothing, nothing but an ugly mass of blood-soaked flesh. An ugly mistake rectified. Better to prise it quickly from your mind and count your blessings.

I didn't think of it until years later when Ben was born and I held his perfectly-formed, utterly complete body and I remembered and recognised my loss. And, as he grew, sometimes it was as if there was a shadowy ghost-child hovering — was it a girl or a boy, this child I never loved or wanted, who would it have looked like, what would it have been like now? When I lifted Ben, squealing above my head, when I scrupulously inspected, washed and bandaged a tiny red scratch on his brown firm flesh, perhaps when I watched him sleeping, reluctant to leave him in the dark, there was my shadow child.

And will this other bloody scrap of mistakenly united cells emerge occasionally from that room where I've tucked it into shadows and tiptoed away, firmly shutting the door behind me? This time I've not been so fortunate. I've not been rescued.

But there's still time. Anything up to fourteen weeks without too much trouble and even later with good reason. I can luxuriate in my decision-making a little longer. The sun is on my shoulders, the smell of apples in the air about me. I won't think of it now.

I'm in the garden sweeping up leaves with Lucy. I'm hot, dripping with sweat. I straighten up my back and groan.

Lucy looks over and laughs. Oh she's certainly iridescent today. Smug. Post-orgasmic, I think sourly. Last night Clem turned up from Auckland. We drank late harvest wine on the verandah. I went to bed, heard them giggling in the orchard and smelt the sweet acrid burning of the joint they were sharing.

'What are you thinking about?' she calls to me. 'You look very serious, Zoe.'

'Men. I'm dwelling on past errors.'

She laughs again. 'Men,' she says comfortably. 'So hopeless and so nice.'

'So nasty as well. Not at all nice when you fall in love with one of the nasty kinds.'

Falling in love again
da da da da can't-remember
What am I to do?
I can't help it

Lucy sings, laughing at me, tossing leaves at me. I laugh despite myself.

'Love's supposed to be fun, Zoe. Love should be happy and nice and fun.'

'Oh yeah? What about when it all falls to pieces, where's the fun in that?'

'Plenty more apples on the trees,' she says lightly. 'Who wants to be miserable?'

It's easy to dismiss adolescent love when you're a self-contained, worldly-wise forty-year-old woman suspicious of full blown abandonment. You forget the loss. Memories of that pit you were once engulfed in blur. As does the joy, that initial response to passion.

When I first encountered Tom I'd made my mind up I'd never fall in love again. Life was more manageable without all that. I'd had enough of men, enough of relationships. Obviously I was no good at them. My mother-in-law remarked once as I was indulging myself with a petty and desultory bicker with my husband over the dinner-table that poor Zoe doesn't really know how to deal with men since she had no brothers. At the time I was outraged but I came later to a point where I not only recognised this was probably so but was pleased by the realisation. Yes. I didn't know how to deal with men and their vagaries and conceits. Nor did I wish, any longer, to attempt to do so. Behind me trailed a dreary series of failed relationships and a feeble marriage. Love was a sham and as for sex, well at least with masturbation you didn't have to dress up and diet and try to think up entertaining conversation for afters.

But Tom made me grin. He made me laugh. Evie said that was the best kind of man there is — oh handsome is all very well, Zoe, but a woman may easily become bored spending her life gazing at a handsome object.

Another cliché. Cynical thirty-something-year-old goes off to a party to find her heart erratically thumping because some man happens to glance once or twice in her direction. I told myself it was nothing other than a post-menstrual hormonal aberration, went home and dosed myself with a stiffish brandy or two.

And then I found, from time to time, I'd notice him. See him cross a street, get into a car, eating lunch close to the window of a bar. He always smiled, always raised his hand and my heart always thumped. Jesus. It was pathetic.

I went to another party. Made myself wangle my way into the group he was standing in.

'Tom.'

'Zoe.'

He was a barrister. Oh. I was thinking about doing this article on violent crime. I wonder if he'd be able to help me? Yes. Yes he would. Could I phone? He handed me his card. Over lunch, perhaps?

We were very pleased with each other. We'd arranged the meeting we both wanted but with carefully defined motives and adult restraint. If we found no pleasure in the meeting, well then it was for strictly professional reasons anyway, no harm done. I said coolly I would contact him the following week if that was convenient and he replied coolly that it was.

I went home and succumbed again to the brandy and fantasised about his hands and his wondrous grey eyes and agonised over whether he was married. A house in Fendalton, I thought. Oh surely. A Great Dane. Private school kids. A wife with pearls and a smooth blonde bob.

That's what I told him when we finally sighed, accepted the inevitable and fell into bed. And after I came grudgingly to the recognition that brandy is no substitute for a murmuring, moaning, yawning, laughing, snoring body made up of hands and legs and a fuzzy chest and a slightly rounded stomach and all manner of interesting bits warming up at least half of a double bed. And after he was coaxed to the recognition that the buzz aroused while entwined with a good woman was at least equal to that resulting from the release of endorphins during a 12km run.

He said I was perfectly correct except for the Great Dane although there had been a Pekinese. That was before Angela (a bob, certainly, and blonde, yes, but streaks) went off with her dentist.

I didn't fall in love with Tom with the abandonment only possible for the very young or maybe the very stupid. The heart thumping and sparks were held at bay and carefully examined. The grey-blue eyes and the heart-stopping smile and the charm, wit and endearing laugh, all were there to be enjoyed and admired. Undoubtedly a less suspicious woman would adore him. But I was no longer unsuspecting. I'd been tricked before by charm and bright eyes. I came to love him when I saw his charm came with patience, kindness, a trusting vulnerability.

After Jeremy I chose men for their dispensability. I chose men I could love but not quite so much that I would lose myself in them. Not so with Tom, although his indispensability crept up and overtook me before I was entirely aware. He's so indispensable that when I became caught up in that blackness, that aridity of soul, I retreated rather than risk losing him.

'Zoe, Zoe for God's sake what is wrong with you?'

'I don't know. I don't know.'

Evie strokes my hair. 'Sometimes, Zoe, standing your ground isn't the best way to manage things. Sometimes it's better to let things go for a time, let yourself retreat and keep a hold on the things you have.'

After the fear and bleeding and pain. After I finally acknowledged it was true, Jeremy really had left me, I trailed along to party after party. I drank too much and screwed whoever asked me. I closed my eyes, let the bodies move on me. Closed my eyes, felt the tears seep down my cheeks. Closed my eyes, imagined it was Jeremy.

My mother was sympathetic then became exasperated — *No boy is worth all this, Zoe.* I answered her queries with shrugs, grunts, sometimes tears.

I went to a party. I drank vodka and when that ran out, cider mixed with gin. I woke early in the morning, wet and shaking and covered in vomit in Hagley Park.

I left work and went to Evie's. I told her I was a failure. I'd never be good at anything. And the worst was I didn't even have the guts to face it. I didn't even have the guts to stay.

That's when she told me there are times you must retreat, when you must simply save whatever you have left. 'Sometimes certainly you must stand your ground and fight it out but you have to be strong enough and you must be sure it's the best way. Never, never say you're a failure. Some things we don't manage so well as others, but nothing's lost, not when there's been love. Nothing's ever entirely lost.'

I stayed with her through the autumn. We picked apples and raked leaves. I returned to Christchurch. I was strong again and if not happy, at least resigned. I didn't return to my hairdressing career. I'd had my sojourn into the world of glamour. I took an office job. Filing and receptionist duties for Williams, Cooper & Sutton, Barristers and Solicitors.

20

And so I re-invented myself. An office girl for a legal firm. Sensible and efficient, competent and correct. I threw away my false eyelashes and bought a camelhair coat with leather buttons and a kick-pleat, a tweed skirt and grey mohair jersey to blend among the pin-striped suits, woollen coats and twinsets. I filed, answered the phone, arranged biscuits on plates and made coffee, tea and appointments. In the evenings I watched television with my mother. My life was wholesome, manageable and regulated.

That's when Grace and I were most comfortable together. Our relationship had been uneasy all my life. When I was young I'd suffered that wistful, passionate longing for her. Later I felt rage and resentment that she kept me from Evie and unjustly kept me at a school I despised. Then the angry shame at her disappointment in me. All these emotions were so strong, so encompassing and added to that intensity of feeling was frustration for the questions she would never answer. Who was my father? What possibly could have happened to so irrevocably separate her from Evie? How did it happen that she and I came to be living in a little half-house in Christchurch? She wouldn't tell me. Once when she was at work I went through her drawers looking for letters and papers and photographs. Nothing. There was nothing. When I secretly sent for a copy of my birth certificate there was no name, simply *unknown* written into the space beside *Father*.

But during my years at Williams, Cooper & Sutton all that emotion, that mixture of love, rage and resentment dissipated. If we were disappointed in each other we did not speak of it. Maybe we'd come at last to an acceptance. Certainly as a mother, as a daughter we were both sadly lacking. I was not the brilliant and accomplished daughter who could have made the fact of myself bearable and worthwhile. Neither was she the patient and communicative mother I would have preferred.

But we muddled along well enough. In the mornings we walked to work together, we cooked and ate our evening meal and sometimes went to films or concerts. We began to talk about books. My mother listened attentively and politely to my opinions whereas before she'd narrowed her eyes and smiled sardonically at my excesses. We began to like each other in a quiet way. My mother was still beautiful, but less dauntingly so. I felt less the ugly duckling waddling awkwardly among the shadows with those silver, beating wings stopping up my bit of sky.

Sometimes she talked about her childhood. Little things. About school, about a friend she once had, about her own pet calf and her own pony, about swimming down at the sea early in the summer mornings before anyone else was up. Sometimes she mentioned her father but always as an aside — *and then Daddy took hold of the bridle. Daddy said I should always take care to...* She spoke, then, with her eyes bright with pain, looking back into a distant time of simplicity and easy joy.

There were no more boys, no more men. We didn't speak of that either of course, but we both sniffed and retreated to our bedrooms and our books rather than face up to grand passion on the television screen. Did Grace look all those years for a prince who would catch her up in his arms, set her behind the silken mane of his haughty charger and whisk her off to his palace? I don't know. I never asked. I knew my own prince, the-only-man-I-could-ever-love had abandoned me.

And so I inhabited an orderly world. I enjoyed the grim figure reflected each morning in my mirror. The clean blouse, the straight skirt at a sensible length above mid-brown tights and brown shoes topped with hair of a nondescript style and length and an unadorned face. Perfect. The outwardly sensible, yet inwardly suffering, heroine. Probably I would work forever answering the phone and boiling the zip at Williams, Cooper & Sutton *a most reliable staff member, with us now for almost forty years I believe.* Probably I would remain a spinster. My youthful bloom would fade suddenly away and be supplanted by premature grey streaks in my hair and severe facial lines. Probably I'd remain a spinster and look after my mother into her old age, nursing her until death, until she also left me. I was again a tragic figure. There was no doubt about that. But at least I'd enjoyed, although only for one brief, precious moment, a perfect love.

After I had been with Williams, Cooper & Sutton for eighteen months and acquitted myself as well as a girl can be expected to, I was entrusted with the weekly banking. On Friday afternoons I was to go to Mr Blackwell's office, knock on the door, wait until it was convenient and then enter. Whereupon he would open the safe with the key he kept on his own personal key ring, count the takings, list the coins, notes and cheques, then place it all in a grey cloth bag, all the time glaring and repeating I must take great care. Then I'd carry the bag along the two blocks to the bank and hand it to the teller who would count the contents and check for any discrepancies.

There was a young man at the bank who'd sometimes serve at the counter but mostly be in the offices at the back. I noticed him there, because whenever I came in he glanced up at me through the glass partitions. After

I'd been a regular Friday visitor for some weeks, he would smile before lowering his gaze again to the important rows of numbers covering the stacked sheets of papers on his desk. The stacks of papers were arranged into tidy, regular-sized piles which he seemed to be methodically working through. I admired his stoicism.

I smiled demurely back before averting my eyes. After all Williams, Cooper & Sutton insisted on the amiability, at all times, of their employees in dealings with the public.

After three months of smiles I was treated to the odd wave, albeit a rather brief and slightly limp raising of one hand. But then, it seemed he began waiting for my arrival because whenever I arrived tightly clutching the grey fabric bag, the evidence of the responsibility bestowed on me by Williams, Cooper & Sutton, he'd jump up abandoning his regulated stacks and open up an entirely new place at the counter just for me.

'Have to look after our regular customers,' he said every week.

I wondered about this young man. Probably he felt sorry for me having to queue every week and Friday afternoons were generally busy. He felt sorry for me and he was being helpful and friendly. Anyway All That was in my past.

But then he began to chat a little. How did I like working for Williams? He'd heard they were good to work for. I lied and said I found it very interesting. And wasn't it a nice/cold/wet/windy day? Yes it was. I took up my skirts — just a little bit — and had my hair cut and reinstated my eye shadow. But discreetly.

And then one momentous Friday he talked more animatedly than usual about the weather, cleared his throat once or twice then enquired whether I had a busy weekend coming up.

'Not particularly.'

After another clearing of the throat he confided that he didn't either. But he thought he may go to *The Godfather* on Saturday night, he'd heard it was good, had I seen it?

'No, not yet.'

And so the inevitable happened. We went to *The Godfather*. He bought me an icecream. Vanilla, chocolate-dipped with nuts. During the torrid sex scene wherein the bridegroom energetically fucks one of the bridesmaids against a door with accompanying loud wailings and rhythmical thumpings, Robert removed his shoulder from where it was almost touching mine, rummaged about in his pocket, covered his face with a handkerchief and firmly blew his nose.

We had coffee. We went to the bank parties and the end of year bank cabaret. We went to Sunday dinner at his parents' house and I sat on the edge of the lazy-boy chair, sipped the small glass of pre-dinner sherry (dry) and answered their questions. They nodded happily when I told them which school I'd been to. I don't believe they approved of my name. His mother commented that Zoe was rather an exotic name wasn't it? There was also the question of my fatherlessness but my school, camelhair coat and Williams, Cooper & Sutton almost made up for that. He met my mother. She raised her eyebrows and said he seemed a rather dependable young man.

My dependable young man was named Robert. Never Bob — that was his father. My dependable young man and I continued to go to films, parties, cabarets and Sunday dinners. On Saturday nights we drove up to The Sign of the Takahe so that he could kiss me and press the top half of his body against mine. After a month or two of that I allowed his hands to press against and fondle my breasts but only on the outside of my blouse. He said he loved me. I let him stroke my thighs. His hand shook.

I was flattered by his attentiveness. If I loved him at all it was for the security of knowing he would phone each evening at seven, that we would go to a film on Wednesday and that my weekends were filled without any effort on my part. At first I endured the wet-mouthed, amateurish kisses but then the probing tongue in my mouth, the fumbling, the desperate rasping breathing against my ear became somehow pleasurable. I enjoyed the shaking hand on my thighs. I enjoyed the power I felt.

We began to transfer to the back seat of the car for our affectionate exchanges. It was more comfortable, we could spread ourselves out more. We began to press our bodies agonisingly together. We began to remove clothing. I heard my own breathing begin to rasp. In the end we drank more than was usual at a party and lay locked together on the back seat. He reached down, scrabbled about, then pushed into me. I began to cry.

He thought it was because he hurt me. I was crying for Jeremy, crying because I'd given in and accepted the ordinary, the commonplace. I thought I'd never again feel that elation, that soaring rush of love.

He apologised. He believed it was my first time. I didn't tell him otherwise. It became incorporated into our routine. We went to a film on Wednesdays, a party on Friday night, on Saturday night we had sex. I wouldn't call it making love. It was always a furtive, joyless, fumbling affair in the back seat of his car. I went on the pill but I was careless about it. And, in due course I became pregnant.

He stoically accepted his role. He would stand by this woman who, without the moral fortitude to fend off his attentions, had got herself pregnant. His father looked at me with greater interest — whether he saw me as a previously unsuspected sexpot or as a breeding device I'm unsure. His mother was shocked but then cried and forgave me since she understood we were 'very much in love.' I heard her on the phone to her friends. Robert's getting married, a wee bit of a shock, I'm afraid there's a baby on the way — oh dear — but they're very much in love. My mother met his parents. She raised her eyebrows again and asked if I was sure I knew what I was doing.

I was convinced. After that final crying over Jeremy, after my tears when I discovered I was to be punished for my lapses of self-control up on the hill beneath The Sign of the Takahe and my carelessness in safeguarding my body against the consequences, I became absorbed in my new role. I told Mr Williams I was to be married and snuffled a little as I admitted to my dreadful mistake, the pregnancy which was now forcing me to regretfully resign from my position with Williams, Cooper & Sutton. He patted my shoulder and said such things happened even to the nicest of young people and I was a valued employee and could certainly stay until I, um, began to, um, my condition became apparent.

We announced our engagement in the newspaper and bought a small solitaire diamond ring. I looked after my nails. From time to time I extended my left hand to regard, with comfortable satisfaction, my ring glittering demurely there on my third finger. Robert said we should buy a house rather than rent since anything spent on rent was dead money.

I had an image of bank notes flopping over onto their backs like dead fish but I didn't laugh. Marriage was a serious business. Robert explained to me we were in an almost perfect position since he was entitled to a very attractive loan from the bank. If I had continued to work we could have counted on being mortgage-free in a matter of a few years. Robert said mortgage-free in a way which sounded as if it was the most blessed state anyone could be in. I attempted to appear suitably penitent since I was the one preventing that from happening.

We were married in St Cuthbert's Anglican Church before an audience of sixty people. We had a reception afterwards, but not a dance. Robert's mother said in these circumstances there shouldn't be too much fuss but even so Robert should be allowed his little send-off. She invited her friends and arranged the *luncheon*. We had champagne. I was allowed one glass only for the toasts because I had to think of the baby. Robert's mother cried. She wore a green and pink Thai-silk suit, black shoes and gloves and a black straw hat.

My mother wore a navy suit. She left as soon as she could without socially disgracing herself, and, by implication, me as well. Before she left she came to me, held my shoulders, and looked into my face, as if she could not entirely believe what she saw, pressed my shoulders so hard with her fingers I thought she would begin to shake me and left.

Evie wrote and said she would not come, *but I wish you every happiness, my dear.* She sent Eliza's china teaset.

I wore a cream dress with a pin-tucked bodice creating a soft and full effect about my waist and lower body. Robert's mother did not think a veil was appropriate. I wore a cream picture hat decorated with daisies.

By that time we had a Queen Anne bedroom suite and a Colonial three-piece lounge suite with a matching, extending, formica-topped table and four chairs which we could add to when required. Robert had chosen a section in a suburb he believed would go ahead. He had a builder and plans for a split-block, three-bedroomed bungalow with aluminium windows and a ranch-slider leading from the lounge onto a concrete patio.

Surprisingly I was happy. I'd stopped vomiting each morning. Perhaps my hormones had settled me down. I was content — in fact, bovine. I continued at work until Messrs Williams, Cooper & Sutton began casting distressed glances towards my condition. After I gave up work I went to antenatal classes and sewing classes to learn how to make curtains. Robert bought me a sewing machine for my birthday. In the weekends we drove to the section to inspect progress on our house.

Robert and I got along well enough. I began to think there was nothing at all to marriage. I gave him his breakfast, sent him off to work with a packed lunch to save money, cooked chops, potatoes, peas and pumpkin for his tea and learned to make puddings. It was easy. You could marry almost anyone at all and provided you both behaved nicely to each other it would be certain to work out. In the afternoons I ironed Robert's shirts and watched the soapies on our new twenty-three inch television screen. I watched the weeping and the dramas and the failures in communication and the sultry, desperate kisses, relieved that I had grown far beyond all that tawdry nonsense into my sensible, matronly twenty-two year-old self. I owned a husband who wore suits, shirts, polished shoes and tasteful ties to work. I owned half of a house and two-thirds of a baby. Apart from the occasional crying jags and waves of hatred towards my husband and his family I was content. My life stretched safely ahead.

When Ben was born I fell in love again. In love with a ferocious all-encompassing passion for my child. I wrote to Evie, rhapsodising over his perfect features, his physical strength, his obviously superior intelligence — *he is very alert and I'm sure he smiles at me although the Plunket nurse says it's still just wind. He is very handsome, I think his eyes will stay blue but remain quite dark. He can almost roll right over and is beginning to sleep through the night.*

Robert's mother cried and fussed. His father was pleased it was a boy. Robert also was pleased it was a boy. So much pleased with me for producing this evidence of his manhood that he allowed me to name him. Benjamin — *favoured son*. And Joseph. Robert tacked on the end as a concession.

Only a concession. Because he was my baby. Mine alone. I longed for the times when Robert left in the mornings and we could begin our day together. I fed Ben and bathed him and took him in his pram to the park. I clucked and crooned and rocked and sang to him. We sat on the new grass behind our new bungalow and he batted at it with his fat hands, crowed and smiled and dribbled.

He was a beautiful baby. Even my mother was pleased with him. He sat on her lap, beamed beatifically into her face and wound his hands in her beads. He rolled over, crawled, grew teeth and walked and talked, all with benevolent aplomb. His eyes were dark Irish blue and his hair straight and silken, the colour of pale sand.

At the same time, Robert was doing well. He easily passed the exams for the papers in accountancy and management he studied each year by correspondence. He was regularly promoted. It seemed he would easily achieve his life's ambition to become the manager of a bank before he was forty.

We furnished our house. We put up curtains, erected and painted fences and hung prints we'd selected to blend with the decor. Robert and his father built concrete paths, dug up a section of soil and planted a vegetable garden. We had ornamental shrubs surrounded with pebbles in the front. I had a little garden at the side of the house to plant the seeds and cuttings Evie sent to me.

If we argued it was because I'd forgotten to iron a particular shirt or some article of clothing had somehow been damaged by my haphazard means of laundering or I'd not provided him with something he desired, that day, to eat. I always cried. He always said he was sorry. I listened to his stories about the dazzling cut-and-thrust world of commerce in which, each day, he was embroiled. I learned to hurry through my own descriptions of my baby's cleverness and bravery, my trip to the supermarket and the inflated price of groceries so we'd be in time to watch the news. We made love, if that's what you can call a few kisses, a stroke or two and a quick roll on then off, every two, then every three or four days. But I was perfectly satisfied with it. We both were far too tired, far too responsible and grown-up to attempt anything more experimental.

Sometimes I heard sounds of misery from the outside. Those sounds from the surrounding suburbs sifted through the windows and doors of my house intruding into my cocoon. Anger and pain and disappointment — *You bastard, you promised, bitch, bitch.* I shivered, turned up the television or the radio or buried my head beneath my pillow. Robert and I would never speak like that, never in that unguarded, uncivilised way. We would never inflict the damage of an unhappy family background onto our child. We were married. We were happy. We loved each other. Of course.

We sold our house and built another in a better location. Then we sold and bought and sold and bought another and another and another. In the end we bought and sold our way into paradise. We lived in a tree-edged street close to the city and the park. We had a double garage, four bedrooms and a family room as well as a formal dining room and what we had come to call the lounge-room. No discordant sounds filtered into our house from this neighbourhood. There were no sounds at all, other than the muted hum of smooth cars rolling out of garages in the mornings and rolling back in during the evenings.

Yes. We had bought and sold our way into paradise. We didn't have curtains any more, but professionally made drapes, heavy, expensive coverings which pulled across our windows to shut out the dark and the cold night air. We had sun filters which remained across the windows during the days to provide privacy and to protect expensive furniture and expensive carpets against the light. We had a scattering of original art works. We had help and direction with our decor. I had a pile of *House and Garden* strewn casually on our family-room wicker-and-glass coffee table. I had nice clothes. I could smile as ingratiatingly, dress as decoratively, give as good a dinner party as any other wife.

I learned to drive. I was on the kindergarten committee. I met my mother-in-law for lunch and shopping. She told her friends we'd done well. I visited my mother. I polished up our house, arranged flowers and went to Cordon Bleu cooking classes. I played with Ben, read to him and selected educational toys. I read books on child-rearing practices, *How to Raise a Gifted Child.* My life was packed with purpose.

I visited Evie each spring. Ben and I flew to Auckland then took the bus the rest of the way. But Evie and I were less comfortable with each other and because of that our interest and attention became focused on Ben. We watched him totter round the garden, dig scoops of sand into his bucket at the beach, listened carefully to his new words, picked him up and clucked when he fell over. In the evenings when he was finally coaxed to bed we sat together on the verandah. Between the silences I chattered about Robert's plans for whatever house we had, about his amazing progress in the banking world. Evie did not ask *But what about you, Zoe, what about your own ideas, your plans, what about yourself?*

But I saw those questions in her eyes whenever she looked at me. I'd sold out, lost myself. I could forget all that — not think of it at all when I was in Christchurch titivating myself and my houses. But I couldn't deny it when I walked around Evie's garden, when I looked from the windows out into the ocean, when I lay unsleeping in my bed. I felt angry. What else could I have done, Evie? What else could I have been? What else was I prepared for? And whatever is wrong with being a happily married woman with a well-adjusted child and a few nice things and a nice house for God's sake?

After our removal to paradise Robert decided that my proposal to have another child was at last feasible. We were financially well set up, almost mortgage-free. Another child would be less disruptive now he had completed his studies. Our new section was safely fenced. Ben would start school soon and I would be left with time on my hands. I went off the pill and waited for my daughter.

Except that the signs and symptoms I confidently anticipated each month did not eventuate. At first I was unconcerned, of course it would happen. Then I began to look for reasons and to initiate more regular sex, maybe we weren't doing it at the right times. I began to cry each month when I felt the cramps at the bottom of my stomach. It wasn't fair. I'd become pregnant twice by accident and now that I wanted to be, it wouldn't happen. I felt guilt — I was being punished for my failure of honesty to my husband. I'd not told him about Jeremy and what had happened. He remained oblivious of my sordid past. I went to the doctor and he gave me a chart and told me to take my temperature each morning before I got up and record it and ensure I had intercourse with my husband whenever it seemed to be heading up above normal. I sat each morning in bed with a thermometer in my mouth wailing that I felt like a battery hen.

Ben started school and I flopped listlessly about the house. Eventually

Robert found all the lamenting and temperature-taking tiresome. If I had something else to think about, he announced tersely, if I had something else to do and was less obsessed and stopped complaining about it all the time it would happen naturally. A job was out of the question but why didn't I take up charity work? After all his mother was kept very busy and satisfied with Meals on Wheels. I could help with that. Or hospital visiting. Normally I was quite a bright and cheerful person and seeing people a lot worse off than myself would do me some good. Or then again I could do a course. Other chaps in the bank had wives who did courses. Perhaps there was something I could do by correspondence? Was there anything I was interested in?

Although I didn't fancy Meals on Wheels I thought there may be something in what he said. Perhaps I'd become so nervous and tense waiting that I was preventing it from happening. And I did need something to fill up this interim time before my daughter arrived. I sent for brochures. I narrowed the selections down to Art Appreciation, Interior Decoration or Freelance Journalism.

Robert's preference was Interior Decoration. It would save money with the next house and, you never know, in the future I may turn what I learned into a little business venture. He could manage the finances. He was disdainful of Art Appreciation. Too airy-fairy. As for journalism, well he wasn't sure about that, did I really believe I could cope with it?

Perhaps it was the tone of his voice *It's not really as if you're very bright, Zoe, is it? after all you've never exactly achieved anything very much have you?* which made me decide. I said firmly I would try journalism. Perhaps it wasn't so useful as learning about interior design but if it didn't turn out I could always go on to that in the future. I'd always liked writing. And after all wasn't it best that I tried something I already liked? I wanted to give it a go.

He said kindly it was my decision and he only wanted me to be happy. He would support me in whatever I decided, he said. He brought me home a surplus electric typewriter from the bank with a basic word-processing package added to it. He paid the fees for my course and I nervously awaited the arrival of the first package.

21

At first I was so afraid of failure that my heart raced and my mouth turned dry before I could bring myself to open the brown paper packages. The course comprised a series of instructions, readings and assignments, beginning with writing paragraphs and moving to simple articles and finally longer features requiring research and interviews.

I came to love it. I'd sit reading through the lessons with my highlighter poised. I'd gaze up at the ceiling, drift through the motions of making coffee, absorbed in the ideas, thinking them carefully through. My head was brimming with images, abuzz with phrases. I laboured over the first assignments, leafing through the dictionary and my newly bought thesaurus — my magical saviour — searching for the exactly right word.

I learned to edit, but with regret. Scrubbing out that wonderful language, the glorious string of adjectives and adverbs, the paragraph I was so proud of but which had nothing to do with the topic. It was such a cruelty, during that first phase of writing when I fell so completely in love with those beautiful words rushing about my head, that I had to capture and scrutinise these wriggling, brightly coloured, exotic things.

My assignments were marked then returned. Certainly there were criticisms — *this needs to be cut — unclear — what has this to do with the topic? — imprecise — not much logic to this — not really the right word is it? — over-emotive — try to be concise.* But as well as the criticism there were occasional positive comments I gloated over, and sometimes high praise indeed.

You have an obvious gift with words.
I laughed out loud here.
Crisp, persuasive, riveting. A tightly constructed argument.
Well done.
Very well done.
Very well done indeed.

At the end of the year I had my first article taken by a women's magazine. It was a silly little thing which humorously lamented the horrors of pregnancy. I followed it up with frivolous pieces about the rivalry mothers must undergo for children's birthday parties, about family Christmases and holidays. They were little bits of nothing but I managed a wry tone editors liked.

I couldn't wait for my mornings to begin. Robert, Ben and I ate breakfast together, I flew through making the beds, cleaning up the kitchen and delivered Ben plus lunch to the school gates. The day's washing in the machine, and I could begin.

Me and my typewriter and the sun coming in the window. Me and my stories. Bliss.

Robert became less perfectly blissful. At first he was relieved I was no longer hunched wailing in bed with a thermometer hanging out of my mouth. He was quite pleased too, that his wife could not only manage to find her way around technology but turn out something reasonably creditable as well. He didn't appear quite so elated as I was with my first acceptance of an article but that was perfectly understandable. He was busy and he had his own successes, and after all, it was only a women's magazine.

Then I had something taken by radio and by *The Press* and then a travel magazine, then National Radio wrote and asked if I had anything more. People asked Robert if it really was his wife who wrote those articles.

Puffed up as I was with my new success I began to state my opinions with more vehemence than before. I disagreed with him, corrected him when he got his political facts wrong — after all I was the one who was most closely following the issues of the day. And when there was any kind of heated discussion at a dinner party I was right there in the middle of it. Boots and all.

He said I'd changed. I shrugged my shoulders. Isn't that what people do? Develop, mature, evolve? Isn't change inevitable?

'Not necessarily and this kind of change isn't for the better.'

The purpose of my taking a course was, it turned out, to fill some of my time, not take it to the point where my home and husband and child were suffering from neglect.

I could not believe my ears. 'What neglect?'

'It's all around you, if you would only take the time to look.'

Our home was neither clean nor tidy any more. The laundry particularly was disgraceful. I had to admit that. Nor was the garden properly cared for — when was the last time, for instance, I'd dead-headed the roses? And the meals, they had become makeshift, thrown-together affairs. His mother had noticed. His mother was worried. And it'd been weeks since I'd bothered to clean my car.

I was unused to Robert criticising me. He was either mildly pleased by my efforts or, more often, seemed oblivious of them. My eyes stung with tears at the injustice of all this. I was working so hard. Didn't he want me to do well? Didn't he want me happy, doing something I loved?

'It seems to me,' he said ponderously, 'that your first priority must be your home.'

'That is my first priority,' I said stiffly, 'but surely I'm entitled to something for myself as well. I've never complained about you studying at night. Or about you going away for work or going to golf.'

'That's different. All my efforts are for the family.'

And so the dreary battle commenced. The bathroom was not properly cleaned. We were out of dental floss — how can a well-managed home run out of the bare necessities? His shirt wasn't ironed properly. Did we have to have chops every day of the week? The stove and the fridge were so grubby it was surprising none of us had come down with typhoid.

I could ignore most of it, absorbed as I was in my new world of words. And I tried so hard. I ran around at the end of the day in a frenzy of cleaning, wiping, picking up. I tried out new recipes for our evening meals. We had puddings and real coffee. I'd become used to pleasing him.

But now it seemed I could no longer do so. I began to announce any successes tentatively, to slide them in as an aside or at the end of a conversation. When I was asked to do a weekly column, a flippant account of the everyday matters of domesticity for a weekly magazine, and when *The Press* phoned and asked if I'd be interested in trying something for them, he was enraged. He said I was exploiting our family and our friends. I was using them for my material. He said my articles weren't even funny. He said I was using my child. Using him and neglecting him, he shouted.

That was the worst part of it. He said I'd become an unfit mother, all my energies went into this nonsense and Ben was suffering. Of course it wasn't so but Ben was my Achilles heel and he knew it. I agitated each day as I left him at the school gates — he looked far too frail to deal with a world inhabited by ferocious-looking children, difficult teachers and the dangerous play-paraphernalia spread about the playground. I sped with him to the doctor at each cough or sniff. I wanted him happy and well and loved. I wanted him more cherished and safe than I'd felt.

It may be that we'd have survived it. Perhaps Robert would have eventually recognised that his wife had an incomprehensible penchant for turning out frivolous little bits of nothing whenever the muse overtook her, and regarded it with amusement. Or perhaps I would have finally become pregnant with our other child and let it go in all the flurry of excitement and activity involved in birth and babies.

But Grace became ill.

Robert did not much like my mother. He tolerated her infrequent presence in our house. He found her coolness, her level gazes, her way of raising her eyebrows instead of answering his questions, disconcerting. As well as that he believed it was disgraceful I was unaware of who'd fathered me. He also believed Grace's methods of bringing me up, fatherless, frequently unattended — a working mother, for God's sake — verged on negligence. In the early days of our marriage my occasional misdemeanours — incompetence in housework, failure to remember certain required articles, a tendency towards overly-spicy food — were benevolently excused because of the haphazard nature of the household from which I'd emerged.

'After all it's no fault of your own,' he remarked kindly and frequently.

Grace made no comments at all about Robert. She listened, in that quizzical way of hers I found provoking, to my account of his superior intelligence, proven by his ability to get on in the bank. She preferred me to visit rather than to come to us.

She loved Ben. *He is like my father. The same lean face. The same lankiness and slow smile, the surprisingly blue eyes.*

She rarely phoned and always for a reason which she would immediately announce then deal with in a few brisk sentences. My mother was never garrulous.

And so when she phoned and talked for some moments of the weather, *So much warmer now, it's nearly spring, some blossom out already and it's already lighter in the mornings don't you think?* I was surprised. She asked about Ben and if I was writing anything interesting and her voice trailed off and she was silent for a moment or two. I waited, wondering what she was about to say and she told me she would be away for a night or two. She had to go into the hospital for some tests. She said briskly it was nothing at all and I wasn't to worry, there was no need to visit, she would be perfectly all right.

Of course she wouldn't say what the tests were for. She said only that she'd been tired, the doctor was fussing over nothing at all and she was merely letting me know in case I called in.

She didn't tell me about the weight loss, or the purple bruises which had appeared on her body. I discovered those for myself when I visited her next evening, taking grapes, flowers and a book. I expected to find her sitting up in her hospital bed with her hair and make-up immaculate, wearing her usual elegant dressing gown, bored and restless and disdainful of other women in the ward.

Instead she was in a room on her own and sleeping. The ward sister whispered she needed rest but I could sit with her if I liked, she might wake. She looked solemn and I felt a sudden unease.

Grace was dressed in a hospital gown and the skin on her neck and face looked grey against the white cotton. I'd thought lately she was thinner than usual but I'd been so caught up in my own concerns I hadn't given it much attention. She was always slim and fine but I realised looking down at her that her body had become frail, as frail and slight as a small girl's. One of her arms lay on the pillow, looped around her head and I saw bruising on the grey-white flesh. I saw, also, the purple shadows beneath her eyes. I felt such a rush of fear my heart began to thud.

Mummy. Mummy.

Don't die, don't die, don't die.

She woke finally. She felt tired. It was amazing she had any blood left, she said smiling weakly at me. They thought she may be anaemic.

I felt reassured. Anaemia was certainly curable. Probably just a few weeks of proper rest. I imagined she would take iron tablets and everything would right itself. Living on her own she probably wasn't taking proper care of herself, or eating properly. I decided when she was out of hospital I'd insist she had some meals with us. I would phone more, keep a closer watch over her, meet her for lunch at least once a week. She was getting older. God, she looked old. She'd never looked old before.

She slept again and I called at the nurses' office to talk to the sister. Would my mother go home tomorrow? She wasn't sure. Did my mother have anaemia and was that at all serious?

She wouldn't look at me. She said they were waiting for the test results. She said she really couldn't comment. She said I could make an appointment to see my mother's doctor.

That's when the dreary, desultory battle became a bitter and destructive war. When I got home Robert was waiting beside his car. Had I forgotten he had a meeting this evening? Had I forgotten he could only look after Ben until seven-thirty? I'd promised to be home and just look at the time. Almost eight o'clock. It was absolutely typical of me to be so selfish and unthinking.

I began to cry, 'Grace is sick, Robert. I think she's really sick. Please stay home.'

He stared at me, moved as if to come closer, put his arms around me, but he turned away and opened the door of his car.

'I can't possibly stay at home,' he said. 'I'm sure your mother will be perfectly all right. Anyway I don't know why you've got yourself into such a state over her. I'm sure she's never thought much about you.'

I stared at him. Then I shouted. I shouted I'd known for some time he was a stupid, insensitive bastard but now I realised he was even more limited, more stupid than I'd given him credit for. I went into the house and slammed the door so hard that the pseudo-stained glass panels rattled. I heard him drive off.

Grace's doctor told me she had leukaemia. She'd almost told me the truth. I phoned Evie and told her. She said she'd come whenever I needed her. If Grace wanted her. Over the next few months Grace had countless blood transfusions, radiotherapy, chemotherapy. She lost her hair. She'd brush it and it'd come out in great clumps. Sometimes she was well enough to be home but then she would be ill again and back in hospital.

The doctor said the prognosis was not at all positive. When I managed to steady my voice enough to ask if there was any hope that my mother would live, he looked compassionately at me for a moment and then held out his hands, palms upwards.

'What can I say? I could talk about miracles but you're an intelligent woman. I wouldn't insult you in that way. We can hope for a remission which sometimes can run into years. Your mother is a healthy woman and I imagine she's a fighter. Whatever happens we'll do whatever we possibly can.'

When Grace was well I went each day to her flat. Sometimes when she seemed weaker than usual I'd pick Ben up from school and we stayed with her during the night. When she was in hospital I sat with her in the afternoons and evenings until she slept. I learned about blood counts and the effect radiotherapy and chemotherapy have on the body, their potential to cure or at least prolong life. I learned also the devastation of the vomiting afterwards, the cruel pain and the tremors and exhaustion.

I tried to write in between the havoc but in the end gave up. The editor of the magazine wrote and tactfully suggested a pause. My articles lacked their original freshness and vivacity, she said.

I wept over that letter. I couldn't write and my mother was dying and my marriage disintegrating. Nothing could be saved.

Robert accused me of putting my mother before my own husband and child. He insisted I employ a babysitter rather than rely on him to look after Ben when I went to the hospital in the evenings. The house was in such disarray perhaps I needed a housekeeper and did I expect him to pay for that as well as everything else? I didn't support him as a wife should; his parents had lost respect for me and his friends thought I was odd and unfriendly. I was a bad mother, an even worse wife. I was unresponsive in bed and when was the last time I'd bothered to change the sheets?

I said he paid little enough attention to his son. His mother had no backbone and nothing at all between her ears and I didn't give a toss about her respect, or about his friends either. It was difficult to feel passion for a man who didn't have interests other than money and an obsession with cleaning. If he didn't feel able to change his own sheets I was sure his mother would do it for him.

And so on and so on.

In between the shouting and the accusations were the long cold silences. I went back on the pill. I would never have another child with such a man. I gritted my teeth whenever he touched me, this man I had almost imagined I'd come to love. This man turned monster.

Grace became increasingly ill. In the end she was permanently in the hospital. She wanted to stay at home but she was too weak to move about or do anything for herself. In the end all they could do was keep her comfortable and clean, and try to control the pain.

She slept most of the time. Sometimes when she woke she was perfectly clear about what was happening and where she was. Other times she didn't know me. The pain was most intense when her mind was clear. I saw in her eyes the sharpness of her seeing but also the agony. It became a relief when she didn't know me, when her voice and eyes were blurred and dull and I knew she couldn't feel that pain.

Then she was back with Evie and Joe on the farm. Back beside the sea. There in the garden. She called for Joe to tell her the stories, for Evie to watch her ride. She called out it was too dark in the bedroom, her daddy must come and turn on the light. Sometimes she talked about people I hadn't heard of. Sometimes she talked about me. Zoe. Zoe. The baby.

Each day I expected she would die. I wanted her to die. I couldn't bear to see her pain or the humiliation severe illness brings when the rotting smell of your body is stronger than the disinfectant. When you're covered in sores and you can't pee or wash yourself or wipe away your own shit. I couldn't understand why the lungs and heart in her shrunken, ruined body would continue to breathe and beat. But I held her hand and talked to her when she wanted that and listened for her breathing.

Her doctor, David, became a friend. I'd go to his office and rage and cry.

'It's so cruel. Why can't you do something? God, if she was an animal you'd put her out of her pain. This is barbaric. Please, David.'

'Just hold on, Zoe. You're strong enough. You're like your mother. A brave woman.'

One evening he found me crying silently beside Grace's bed.

She was sleeping. He took my arm and led me, sobbing out of the hospital, across the park to his flat. He took me inside and made me drink brandy and took my hands, held them tightly in his and said it wouldn't be much longer, a week, two at the most. And whatever I thought to the contrary, I was helping Grace, she did know I was there and that was a comfort to her. She loved me very much. She was enormously proud of me.

'No. No, I'm her disappointment. I always have been. Just a bloody awful disappointment and a mistake. Having me, it wrecked her life, must have, and now she's dying.'

He was silent, then he pulled me closer and gripped my shoulders, 'That's not true, Zoe. It's not what I've seen.'

'It is true. It is. I ruined her life and I couldn't even be what she wanted.'

I was sobbing, out of control. He rocked me in his arms. He kissed me and then we made love. I don't know how that happened. Perhaps it was a combination of his pity for me and my need to be held and stroked and touched with affection rather than with the angry, resentful need in which Robert had begun to use my body. But whatever the reasons we kissed and stroked and touched and made love on the floor, then gazed at each other with astonishment.

'I didn't expect that to happen,' he said. 'I don't know what to say.'

'Don't say anything. Don't feel sorry about it either. It's the best thing that's happened to me in months.'

I hadn't expected it either but while I might have felt shame, instead I felt nothing other than a pure, soaring release. I had been touched and held with care. I felt strangely in control again as if I'd been given back the sense of my own self. I'd go home, deal with the next few weeks, whatever they brought, then set about salvaging what was left of Robert and me. Be a better mother to Ben. Scrub the house till it shone and cook thick warming soups and make bread.

I drove home. I was late but Robert and I had come to a truce about looking after Ben in the evenings. He would stay with him until the babysitter arrived.

But the house was dark and when I unlocked the door I heard Ben screaming. I ran up the stairs and turned on the light and he threw himself against me. Daddy had put him to bed but then when he woke up nobody was there.

I held and rocked him and murmured comforting words, it was a terrible mistake, it would never happen again, mummy and daddy just got mixed up, it was all right, love, all right now.

Ben slept and Robert came home. I shouted at him he had no sense of responsibility, leaving a five-year-old child alone in a house.

He said a five-year-old child is a mother's responsibility.

I said did he have no feelings, no care for Ben to leave him on his own in a dark house?

He said did I have no feelings, no sense of responsibility leaving my child every night?

I said for God's sake my mother is dying.

He said I always put anyone and everything before him and that was why he was having an affair, that was why he was in love with somebody else.

I hit him and said I wished Ben wasn't his.

In the morning I packed a suitcase and took Ben to Grace's flat. I said we would have a holiday at Grandma's house. I phoned Evie and said she must come. Please. She must come.

22

Tom phoned last night and I was crying. He said, Zoe, I don't like to hear you cry, why don't you just come home? I told him it was good for me. I'd not taken the time for remembering or for crying for too long. I told him Evie said the past was as important as the present, you must pay attention to the past.

He said quietly, Evie was a wise woman.

He's no longer angry with me, but sounds only worried. Perhaps he's resigned to my errant behaviour. I lost my husband because of my absence and preoccupation with people and things other than him. I don't like to think I could also lose Tom.

I say lightly I hope he's not beginning to forget me. I hope he's not starting to take notice of the dozen or so attractive women who fawn all over him at the office.

He laughs. 'How much energy do you think I have, Zoe? I don't seem to be able to manage you. How could I manage another woman as well?'

I say I'm perfectly aware of his limitations and I meant instead of. Not as well as.

He laughs again. 'Never instead of, Zoe. Never as well as either. I'm too worn down by you to even contemplate another woman.'

Robert has married the woman he was obliged, by my negligence, to fall in love with. Her name is Joanna. Robert and Joanna and Tom and I have smiled very sweetly at each other and talked of this and that at school prize-givings, sports meetings and graduations over the years. They have a daughter who, Ben tells me, is really amazing at maths. I learned from Robert that you cannot, after all, marry just anyone.

Evie came. There was no ferry any more between Wellington and Christchurch and so she said she would take her life in her hands and fly. Ben and I met her at the airport. I watched her walk from the plane down the steps. Her hair was almost completely white but she held her body straight, upright and walked as surely as ever. We ran to her and she held us both tightly in her arms.

We were careful with our conversation, careful not to talk too openly with Ben listening and so we talked a little about Grace, more about the farm. But after we had called in briefly at the hospital, found Grace sleeping — *no change* — and eaten dinner and watched over Ben's bedtime rituals, Evie looked into my face more closely and openly than she had in years.

'How strong you've become, my Zoe.'

My eyes filled with tears. 'Not so strong.'

'Not so strong?' Evie smiled into my eyes. 'Not so strong that you don't cry? Is that strength?'

'I'm strong in all the wrong ways. If you could even call it strength. I've been strong enough to leave Robert but that's not strength. Not really. It's just self-preservation, just pure bloody-minded selfishness really. If I were really strong I'd've thought about Ben, put him first and stuck it out.'

'And what would that have given Ben?'

'Security. Stability. A home and a father, for God's sake. Kids need all that. I've taken it away. Robert is right. I've behaved badly. I've been selfish and now I've lost him and probably ruined Ben's life as well.'

She touched my cheek with the palm of her hand. 'You're tired, Zoe. Too tired to see things clearly.'

'But I've ruined everything. It was the one thing I could do properly, the only thing I ever succeeded at. And now I've spoiled that too. There's no other way of seeing it.'

'I see it another way, and in time you may as well. But I see you love Ben and at least you know that and he knows it too. He knows he can depend on you, Zoe, he trusts you absolutely and even though it may be the only certainty in your life just now, believe me, it's more important than anything else.'

'But how can I do it on my own? I've made a bad enough job of looking after myself. However am I going to manage to look after Ben properly?'

'I don't believe you've made such a bad job of yourself. When you can take time to catch your breath you'll start to see that. You're not a finished product yet, my darling, not even close to it. You're growing into yourself and this is a hard time for you, as hard as anything could ever be. But the hardest things, it's like when you run as hard and as long as you can down our hill and along our beach and you want to stop because your body hurts so much but when you've done it you can take your breath again and know you've pushed yourself harder than you ever thought you could and you haven't given in. The things that are hardest and hurt most, they're also a gift because they make you strong and help you to see clearly and truly. You never look at anything in quite the same way again.'

'I don't want to be strong. I want an easy life. I want to be easily happy.'

'You're telling me, Zoe, you'd deny what you are? You would deny your intelligence and your spirit? That kind of life may make you comfortable. I doubt it ever could make you content.'

Evie cosseted me. Her child was dying and she cared for me. It was always her way. To love me selflessly.

In between the hours at the hospital sitting with Grace, I slept. For weeks I'd been unable to, lying for hours through the nights. Knowing Evie was in the house made me feel safe enough to sleep again. I'd wake and know she was below in the kitchen or sleeping in the bedroom across the passage. She cooked, tempting me with delicately flavoured soups and souffles and omelettes. She met Ben after school and took him to the park. If I was resting when Robert phoned for another one of our business talks she put him off politely and firmly. 'Zoe is sleeping. She's too tired to talk just now.'

Grace held on. We sat with her, talked to her and held her hand. We listened to the shallow, rasping breathing, saw the flickers of pain on her face as she woke. Sometimes I looked across the bed at Evie. She sat, sometimes with her eyes closed, her face tranquil and calm as she held Grace's hand loosely in her own. I was so grateful for her presence, her courage and her gentle spirit. Her ability to look directly into the face of death and know and accept it. She made me less afraid.

I would like to think Grace and Evie came to a reconciliation. I would like to be able to say that Grace clearly saw and lucidly welcomed her mother and that during those last days they talked and understood and forgave each other. But Grace was in a dreaming place, that halfway place between living and death. When she was awake she was her child-self, back on the farm, in the orchard, down beside the ocean. If she recognised Evie it was only as the mother she'd been.

Perhaps it was a kind of reconciliation. Perhaps the best there could be. Grace travelled back into her child's world and that allowed them to briefly draw closer again as they relived a time they were happiest.

She was more alert one afternoon. We found her sleeping but she woke, drew herself up on the pillows and gazed around her room and at us. She looked at Evie as if she'd not seen her for some time. 'Oh,' she whispered, 'Mother?' She asked how I was, she'd been wondering how I was. She asked about Ben.

'He's the dearest little boy. Zoe, you must take great care of him.'

We left her sleeping. My brave, elegant, little mother. The hospital phoned at two next morning and said she was slipping away. By the time I got there she had died. The nurse said she went peacefully as she slept. I took her small cold hand and sat with her.

And you will have happiness always and be no longer wandering from island to island in the ocean.

Grace left me a small amount of money and her belongings. Evie and I sorted through them. She had never bought or kept much. There were her few bits of jewellery, the tiny pearl earrings she usually wore, a silver bracelet, a gold and a silver neck chain, an amethyst ring and her watch, some fine china and her books. I smiled over her narrow shoes and stroked the smooth leather with my fingers. I held her clothing against my face, breathing in her perfume as I'd done when I was a child.

I had the things I wanted stored along with chattels and furniture — my share of the marital settlement. Robert and I came to some swift and, I believe, fair decisions about our mutually owned property. He would keep the house, buy out my share. I would keep Ben. He would have fair and reasonable access, whatever that meant. We divided everything else up. We didn't argue. We spoke dispassionately and in the presence of solicitors. It was easy. There was no anger, no emotion. We'd had enough of each other.

Then Ben and I went north with Evie. I went to Evie's to catch my breath. To draw it hard in and look over the past years and see what was left and where there was to go.

Ben went to the local school. The bus collected and delivered him every day to the gate at the end of the drive. He said his new school was cool, his teacher was kind and pretty and the other kids were nice to him. He brought his friends home and they tried to play rugby like the big boys they watched every day, on the grass beyond the house. My tough blond boy. *C'mon boy, tackle him, use yer boot.*

I thought about staying. I thought I could stay there for the rest of my life. Ben was happy. It was the place where I'd always felt happiest and most at peace with myself. I could stay and help Evie with the garden and the orchard. Although she'd sold most of the land there was still a good-sized piece to look after. Certainly she managed perfectly well — she still had Sam and Mrs Samuels, and their son was with them as well now — but there was always work, there'd always be something for me to do. I didn't want to go back to Christchurch. And if I went back what could I do? What sort of satisfying work could I possibly find without any training or qualifications or experience to speak of? What kind of life would it be for Ben, living as I had, in a little flat with a mother who hurried off to work every day?

Better to stay. I talked about it once or twice with Evie and she said she'd always wanted me to think of this place as my home. I saw the uncertainty in her eyes and understood she doubted it was right for me.

I walked for hours along the beach feeling the wind pull and surge, looking across the expanse of sand out into the ocean. I went to bed early and fell asleep hearing the sea. I swam feeling the coolness of the water, felt the heat of sun again on my body. I'd felt numb, displaced, my mind somehow separate from my body. But that cold wash of water and rain and wind, the warming of sun began to drive me back into my skin.

Whatever was I to do?

Evie and I were together on the verandah in the evenings. We sat unspeaking for much of the time. She understood my need for silence. But she started to tell the stories. In the early evenings Ben sat with us and she told them to him as she'd told me.

Listening in the half-dark to the words, those soft murmuring words filling the warm evenings. Listening while the sky turns crimson and gold and lilac and pewter and the stories roll back and forth and the night is filled with pictures.

'Ah, now my Ben, did you know that your great — how many greats would it be now, Zoe? — yes three, your three times great-grandmother Eliza and grandfather William sailed across the ocean from England — think of it Ben, all that way from the other side of the world in a frail ship propelled by nothing other than wind. It took them five months and then they had to wait five days out there beyond the Bay of Islands because a great wind blew up. Yes certainly it was very dangerous, I would imagine their lives were in great peril — peril, Ben? Enormous danger. Your grandmother Eliza was really not much more than a young girl, not quite nineteen and never away before from home. And when the ship sailed into the harbour, canoes filled with Maori came out to meet them, Maori warriors tattooed all over their faces, women with moko on their lips and chins — yes, I daresay she was afraid. Afraid and tired and homesick but she made the best of it. She had to Ben, there was no going back. She and William had come to teach the Maori about Christianity. And while that may seem presumptuous nowadays when we have more respect for other people's beliefs, well I certainly hope we do, they believed in what they were doing and they were sure in that belief. I believe, whatever the rights and wrongs of it, we must admire her strength and courage. And Ben, when they finally set their feet on land — and when you've been a long time at sea and your feet have got used to the motion of the ship on the ocean, you feel wobbly and dizzy when you're on land again. I would think they needed to walk around and to rest as well. When they had set their feet on shore and had rested, then they had to set out for the mission station in the Hokianga, way across those hills covered with bush and no roads of course, just narrow mud tracks.'

The stories.

About William and Eliza who came across the hills through bush so dense it was as if they were travelling in twilight and eventually wound their way down to the edge of the bush where Eliza first caught sight of that wide stretch of gleaming ocean which is the Hokianga Harbour. The darkness of bush on one side, the stretch of tawny gold on the other and, despite her exhaustion and fears, she caught her breath at the beauty of it. About the little raupo house in the Hokianga where they first lived. The children who died. Eliza's garden. The land wars. The children. James and Luke, and finally the daughter, Hannah. How Hannah took up her first violin as if it were the missing part to her body she had found. How she could play more sweetly than any sound Evie ever heard. How it was that she and Eliza came here, how this house was built, how the garden has in it the seeds of plants from Eliza's garden in the Hokianga. Why we call that huge old oak tree in the corner of the garden Eliza's tree. And then Evie. And Joe. And grandmother Grace.

'And your own mother, Ben my darling, and now of course, you.'

The stories unravelling, weaving through the night. I hear them still, Evie's voice telling them, hear Ben's child's voice asking the questions, listen to those murmuring voices, the laughter and the sadness of those stories are here now. The words and pictures twine about me this night on Evie's verandah with the darkness closing in. I breathe the scent of musky apples and roses, that scent of sharp-sweet lavender which rushes at me, piercing unbearably to my soul. Evie's scent. I see Evie curved into that cane chair. See Ben on her knee, his arm around her neck, his cheek resting on her bare brown shoulder. I feel Ben's heavy child's body, breathe in the smell of him as I lift and carry his hot, heavy, sleeping body up the stairs to his bed. I cover him with a sheet only, it's so hot. I stand over his bed smiling over my small blond boy. His eyelashes are wonderfully thick and long and his mouth is pink and shaped like a perfect little flower and, oh God I miss him. I miss them both. Oh God I miss Evie.

It was a night like this. Hushed and balmy and dark. I took Ben up to bed and went back downstairs to the verandah. Evie and I were drinking wine, a sweet late harvest wine from the previous year.

'He's already asleep,' I said.

We sipped our wine and listened to the night sounds. We talked about what there was to do the following day. That afternoon I'd cut back and hauled out a mass of overgrown mint and lemon balm from the herb garden and I smelt the scent of it on my skin and clothes. My body felt strong, sharp and hard at the edges, and I knew that my skin was glossy brown. Tomorrow I'd dig out bulbs, put them in trays and store them in the shed for the winter.

I felt tranquil and in control. My life was turned around with these ordered, regulated days — the early morning walks down the track to the beach and along the sand, the work in the garden and the orchard in the afternoons, these evenings filled with stories. I told Evie I was happy. I said Grace should have done the same as I had. When her life began to crumple about her she should have come back, brought us both back here. We could've been happy, I said.

'It wasn't the right way for Grace. This wasn't the right place for her to be.'

'She wasn't happy where she was,' I said. 'What did she ever achieve? Writing up court cases and meetings and doing recipes and fashion for women's pages. She worked for that newspaper doing the same things over and over for more than twenty years, and most of those years she earned hardly more than a pittance. What kind of life is that? She would have been better off here with you. We both would have been better off.'

Evie smiled. 'It's always so much easier knowing what's best for other people. What's most difficult is seeing what's best for yourself.'

'She should've come back.'

I wanted Evie to agree with me. Wanted her to say I was right and she should have come back and stayed where she was loved, where it was safe, where you both could have been happy. I longed for her to say she should have come back as you have, Zoe. She should have come back with her child and stayed with me.

'She could have come back,' Evie said. 'I like to think she knew she always could and considered it from time to time. But I knew in my heart she wouldn't come, not ever. She always had such a strong, strong will. Even when she was a little girl, if she said she'd do something she would do it even though she might have to wait and work on it for days or even weeks, Zoe. We had an old bike out in the shed. Joe used to ride it. Well Grace wasn't very old, not much more than six and it was far too big and heavy for her but ride it she would. She'd not listen to anyone telling her she couldn't do it until she was older. Every morning, first thing, she had it out there on the lawn trying to get her feet up on the pedals and keep her balance. It took her three weeks. She fell off it a hundred times and hurt herself as well but she wouldn't give it up. Wouldn't take any help either.

Joe went out there when we could see she wouldn't forget about it and wanted her to let him hold the back of the bike to help get her balance and she wouldn't let him near it. But when she finally had it going it was like the sun came out. There she was riding that huge awkward bike with a wonderful beaming smile. As for her work, Zoe, you must not think of that as a failure. It wasn't what she hoped for, or could have achieved had things turned out differently, but she was a writer — of sorts anyway. She always wanted that.'

'Grace wanted to be a writer?'

'Oh yes. She wanted to do many things. To study French and English literature at university. To travel overseas and see the places she'd read about. To live in a large, beautiful city and write poetry in an upstairs room which looked out across a green park. That's what she always said, Zoe.'

'Why didn't she want to stay here? Didn't she like it? Why wasn't she happy here?' I couldn't see how anyone could be unhappy here. Why anyone, having lived here, could want to leave and never come back.

'She was happy here,' Evie said slowly. 'She loved it once as much as you've come to love it, Zoe. Whenever she said she wanted to do all those things she always ended by saying, but I'll always come home, this is always my home, Mum. She said this would always be her own Hokianga, her own returning place.'

We were silent. I didn't ask questions. Evie had told me before Grace's story was her own and she would not tell it. I stared into the dark and thought about Grace. About her beauty and elegance and her quick sharp intelligence. How she could draw me so closely to her, how she drew so quickly back, drifted so distantly away.

'It was as if she moved away into a different country.'

I said it aloud.

Evie looked quickly up at me.

'I know it was sometimes hard for you. I know yours wasn't an easy childhood. But Grace did love you, Zoe. When she drew back from you, I believe she'd have been afraid.'

'Afraid?' I felt angry. Filled with bitterness and hurt. 'How could she be afraid of me? I was only a little girl.'

'Afraid of loving you too much. Afraid she may become dependent on you. Afraid she may lose you. It's hard to say, Zoe. But I tell you now, it wouldn't have been that she didn't love you. Never that. More likely she'd be frightened of loving too much. I know she had friends, Zoe. And men, of course. We both know that. But think about it — did she ever become close to her friends, did she ever allow those men to stay longer than a few months? If she'd wanted to she could have so easily married, she was bright and so beautiful. But she chose not to. She chose not to allow those men to come close to her, chose not to have other children. She had been too much hurt, Zoe. She was too afraid.'

'But she spoiled my life.' I was suddenly shouting it. 'She spoiled my life. She was my mother and I could never please her. She was my mother and she wouldn't even talk to me.'

And I sobbed. Great gushing sobs of wanting my mother, of losing her. And Evie sat silently waiting, allowing me my grief and when it was over she drew her chair closely to me and took my hand.

'Hush now, my Zoe. There is a story I must tell you now. It's a story I hoped would be told to you by somebody else because it's a hard story for me to tell and not entirely mine, of course. But it's too late for that now and so I hope you will have patience with me as I tell it.'

Grace was an utter gift of a child. Bright and quick and clever, beautiful and good, kind and loving. It was as if all the good fairies had bestowed their blessings on this child at her baptismal feast. Evie and Joe wanted more children, but Evie miscarried a second child then there weren't any more. Still, Grace made up for the children they didn't have. More than made up for them. They only had to look at her to count their blessings.

She loved Evie of course, but loved her father more. And he doted on her. The mornings were their time. They'd be up out of their beds and down in the kitchen drinking tea before anybody else was up. It was not a time to intrude. They sat at the table, Grace with her cup filled with sweet milky tea, Joe with his own strong brew. They discussed the business of the day then were out the door and off for a leisurely patrol around their property.

Evie told her stories. She taught her about plants and trees and showed her how to save seeds and bulbs for the next year's planting. Joe told her about Ireland, told the Irish stories, sang the Irish songs. He taught her to ride and row and drive a tractor. She went to the local school and then to the district high and the teachers said she was clever, exceptionally clever. She got the prize each year for first in class. Joe and Evie wondered if she was getting the education she deserved and if they should send her to a boarding school in the city. But she didn't want to leave the farm and they really couldn't bear to let her go. Joe said they would have to let her go soon enough.

'It was a happy time, Zoe. All those years were so good and happy. There was the war but that did not affect us although we grieved of course, for the men who went and were hurt and lost. For all that needless destruction and outrageous cruelty. But Joe didn't go, he was needed on the farm and exempted from duty because of it. And you know how things are here. You lose sight of the rest of the world, perhaps that's selfish and unseeing but it's how it is. I love this place. It's in my bones, Zoe, I am soulless away from it. I was happy, had that body-filling contentment you discover during parts of your life. I had my place and my child and my man and I loved them all.

'I loved Joe. He was a good man with a wonderful spirit, a wonderful sense of fun. We were always laughing, Joe and I. Laughing and kissing, Grace said once. She was quite small and she said it as if she were accusing us, as if she might be envious. Joe took her up into his arms and kissed her all over her face — c'mon now, come on Gracie Bridie give your old Da a kiss — and she laughed as hard as we did.'

Who was Grace? What was she like, this young-girl-Grace? What did she most like to do, what did she most want? I tried to make up pictures in my mind of the girl I was hearing about. This girl who was so pretty, so good at everything she did, who grew up here loving her mother but her father most of all, loving this place as I did. She read. She read all the time. She had her own pony. She rode him most mornings and every evening. She grew up and in her sixth form year she had a boyfriend. She'd known him all her life. They went to the dances at the church hall together. Joe teased her about him. But she said all that wasn't for her. She said she'd live at least one year of her life in Paris.

'She did well in her sixth form year. She worked hard and she was tired at the end of it. But she had her holidays mapped out. She'd spend some of the time helping around the farm, some of it reading and some days she'd go down on the beach with her friends. One morning she stayed late in bed instead of getting up early for the tea-drinking ritual with her father. When she got up she filled up a thermos and made bacon-and-fried-egg sandwiches — they were his favourites — and took them out across the paddocks for their morning tea.

'I heard her screaming. Screaming. She came running across the paddocks screaming something over and over. I couldn't understand what she was saying. I ran and grabbed her and held her still. When I understood what she was telling me I started to run.

'He was unconscious under the tractor. His body was crushed. By the time the doctor got here his heart had stopped beating. It had been raining the night before and the tractor slipped and overturned in the mud.

'After that she hated the place. She wouldn't go out beyond the garden and she wouldn't ride her pony. She believed this place had killed her father, it had taken away the person she most loved. She wouldn't cry. She wouldn't talk about it. The day it happened, she screamed and shook and cried but after that she tried to push it all away. Push me away. She said she wanted to go to school in Auckland for her last year. She was absolutely calm, absolutely rational. It would be better preparation for university, she said. I didn't know how I would manage. I'd lost Joe and now it seemed I was also losing Grace. But I thought it best to let her go. I hoped if I let her go willingly she'd come back.

'She continued to do well at school. She came home for some of the holidays but stayed for the most part, with the new friends she made in Auckland.

'She was so distant. So quiet. Perhaps, in her mind, I was too caught up with her father for her to see me separately. Perhaps being here with me made her loss too painful, too raw.

'When she was at home she was most often with her boyfriend. Peter, he was called. She drew closer to him. I worried about that. He was a nice boy. Solid and kind. And he loved Grace. You could see that in his eyes and hear it in his voice.'

Physically he was much like Joe — tall, dark and blue-eyed. He came from similar Irish forebears. That was what most concerned Evie. Not Grace's closeness to him. She welcomed any happiness Grace could find. Not that, but the reasons behind it.

'And he was a farmer. To his bones and soul he was a farmer. He was destined for the farm but Grace's destiny, well that lay elsewhere. Grace didn't talk much about him, or anything else for that matter, any more to Evie. But she came home early one night from a dance she'd gone to with Peter. She was restless. She stalked about the room, then flopped into a chair. She'd broken with Peter, she said. She wanted him to come to Auckland, to come with her to university. To at least try it for a year. He was bright enough, he'd do well if he gave it a chance. But he wouldn't. He said he wouldn't leave. His father depended on him to take over the farm and anyway it was what he wanted for himself.'

'Let him stay,' she said. 'Let him stay and be a hick nobody from nowhere. What do I care?'

'Grace went to university. Peter stayed on the farm. He started to be seen about with a local girl. Evie saw their engagement announced in the local paper.

'Grace came home after finals. She sat in her room reading. There was nothing to do here, she said. She came back from seeing friends one afternoon and her face was flushed and her eyes red as if she had been crying. Evie thought she would have heard about Peter.

'She went to the New Year's dance. She wore a cherry-red dress and high black sandals. She coiled her hair on top of her head and her lips were the same colour as her dress. She came out onto the verandah and held her arms out and spun around. Her skirt whirled around her.

'How do I look, Mother?' she said.

Evie looked up at her, 'Lovely,' she said. 'Grace, take care.'

'She danced with all the boys and as she laughed and slid closer up against their bodies she knew Peter was watching. She danced with him, and again more closely and took his hand and tugged him out into the dark.

'She waited for him next day and when he didn't come she went back to Auckland. At the end of February she came back. She was pregnant, she said, her eyes glittering. Well, she'd just have to make the most of it and be a farmer's wife after all. She loved Peter, she'd tried hard not to but she did and that was all there was about it. She didn't want to go to Paris so much after all. She'd just get married. She and Peter would get married. That was all, really, that she wanted, to be married and be happy like you, Mother, like you and Dad and have a child. They would just have a tiny quick wedding and be together. There was a farm cottage they probably could live in, well who cares about details? It all would turn out perfectly well.'

She kissed Evie and said it would be all right and she must be happy for her.

'Just think, Mother,' she said. 'We'll be just across the hill, me and Peter and we'll probably have dozens of babies. Peter always said he wanted children, well now he'll have them and you'll have your grandchildren and everyone will be perfectly happy after all.'

'He wouldn't marry her. He'd given his word, he said. He loved Grace, of course he loved her, but she had left him and he'd given his word and he could not go back on that. The wedding was less than a month away. How could he go back, now, on his word?

'She came back. I heard the car in the drive. I waited and she didn't come in and I knew.

'Finally she came inside. She looked at me and said the bastard won't marry me.

'I went over to put my arms around her. I felt such pity, such love. She'd lost her father and now this boy. She was my child, my little girl and somehow in all that hurt and upheaval we'd become distant from each other. I wanted to hold and protect her, let her cry and make everything better.'

She said, 'Leave me alone, Mother. This is something you can't fix up. You can't tell me what to do about it. You've always been so bloody safe here haven't you? So bloody right. Well this is happening to me, Mother. To me and I'll do what I want.'

'She moved away and turned her back to me. I asked what it was she wanted and she turned around and faced me. She was alien to me, this angry young woman who was my daughter.'

'Well.' Her voice was hard and very loud. 'I'll just have to get rid of it.'

'That's when I hit her. I hit her and when she cried out and flinched away from me, I hit her again. I screamed at her that she was a disgrace to me and to her father. I hit her as hard as I could.

'She stared at me with blood running down her face. She said, oh you too, I can't even trust you. And she went up the stairs and came back down with her bag. She said she hated this place, hated me as well and she'd never come back.'

23

We sat unspeaking in the dark. I was cold, shivering, but I couldn't move. I couldn't go through that motion of standing and walking through the doors to find something warm to cover me up. Knowledge is power, they say. Well, it's also pain. And regret and anger and pity.

'I lost control of myself. I had a temper when I was a child. Terrible. This surge of pure emotion, hate and rage that took me over and terrified me. I battled with it. I believed I'd tamed it. But that night I lost control of myself and I lost my daughter. I've lived with it and regretted it the rest of my life.'

I breathed in hard. I'd not seen Evie vulnerable before, not glimpsed any frailties.

I said it's perfectly human to sometimes lose control.

'Ah, yes,' she said. 'But this was too much. Grace was hurt and angry. Everyone she'd counted on was lost to her. I was the only one left and she found she couldn't trust me either.'

She didn't know where Grace had gone. The car she took was left at the railway station. Evie presumed she'd gone back to Auckland. She wrote and tried to phone but there was no contact. Alice called around to Grace's flat but the girls said she'd gone. She hadn't left an address.

'I was frantic. I had no idea what had happened to her. I imagined her dead, Zoe. I imagined backstreet abortionists, her being hurt and ill somewhere and too stubborn to ask for help. That night she left, well, I thought her capable of anything. I heard nothing for a year. Then Alice had a letter. Grace was living in Christchurch. She was perfectly well. She had work. The baby — a girl — was doing well. Alice was to tell me but I was not to contact her.

'I don't know how she came to be living in Christchurch. I worried over what sort of place she was in, who was caring for you while she was at work. I wrote immediately and asked her to come home and live here, at least until you were older. I sent money. She wrote back saying only she would not come home. She sent back the money.

'I said I would respect her wishes but hoped she would consider this place as a home she could return to. She must remember that if she needed me I would always come to her. I wished her well for her life and her child.'

Evie looked closely at me. 'Zoe, you're so cold, you're trembling.'

She poured more wine into my glass, then went through the doors and came back with a blanket and tucked it around me.

'I've thought about it all these years. Over and over. I've wondered if I was right to allow Grace to go away for that last year to school. If it may not have been better to keep her here so she would have had to remember her father, be forced to face what had happened. Perhaps I should have been stronger with her or perhaps softer and more loving. I don't know. But I made a mistake, one I've paid for all my life.

'All her life, up to that terrible time, was blessed. She'd been so loved, so protected — oh I don't mean that Joe and I set out to do that, to keep her from the world, nothing like that. But she was our only child. She never had to compete as other children might, for her parents' attention, she always had it. By right. And she was so small, so delicate and beautiful with her dark hair and creamy skin and those wonderful eyes. Like dark pansies, I always thought. Everybody loved her, everybody doted on Grace.

'I'm sometimes reminded of that folk-tale when I think of her. Princess Aurora Rose, who was given all those wonderful gifts — beauty and cleverness, and those special talents by the good fairies. Except she also was cursed. And that was how it was for Grace. Not long after her sixteenth birthday she was pierced by pain so deep and sharp she never recovered from it. But unlike Princess Aurora Rose there was no awakening. Grace wouldn't allow anybody close enough to tear down the brambles and the branches. That curse which turned into the blessing of enlightenment for the princess always remained a curse for Grace. A dark, debilitating curse.

'Joe and I tried to make Grace's childhood as perfect as we could. That wasn't difficult. We were happy together living here in this place we loved. Nothing much ever disturbed us. We thought with only one child we must give her everything that was possible, every advantage, her childhood must be blessed. I believe now the most valuable kind of childhood is one where you also face up to some difficulties because how can you endure difficulties without any experience of them? Whenever anything was difficult for Grace we stepped in; anything she truly wanted we gave her, and when things went so terribly wrong it was a blow she never recovered from. She saw it as an injustice and drew her bitterness around her. I'm not saying her life was wasted, mind, she had you and she achieved some of the other things she wanted. But it could have been better, so vastly better.'

'She had me? How's that an achievement? I wasn't even wanted. She wanted to get rid of me.'

'But she didn't. And however she came to that decision I believe, absolutely believe, she would have made a firm decision to keep you. It's not something that would have happened because she was too afraid or simply left it too long. She had money and, Zoe, remember her determination? If Grace'd wanted an abortion she would have had it. And after you were born she could easily have given you up for adoption. But she didn't do that either. You must believe, Zoe, that in the end she wanted you. She wanted you and she loved you and she would not give you up.'

'What about my... what about Peter?'

'He married the girl. He stayed on the farm, of course. They had three sons. I believe he's quite active in Rotary.'

Evie shrugged. We couldn't help but grin at each other.

'Perhaps I should visit.'

My romantic nature took over.

I am at the farmhouse door declaiming I'm the long lost daughter. I'm taken into the arms of a red-faced farmer while sons, barking sheepdogs, an aproned wife and whisky-gulping Rotarian associates look incredulously on.

I giggled and shook my head. Too late for me to have a father. It'd be rather like bringing on an unexpected and largely irrelevant character five minutes before the end of the final act. A third-act clown put there to confuse and obscure the major plot.

'I think I'll stick with what I have. I think this family is quite enough for anyone.'

Evie smiled. 'I've told you all this, Zoe, for two reasons. The first is obvious. It's your right to know what happened. To make sense of it all. The other reason is something I hope you'll think about.'

'After Joe died and Grace left, apart from the people we had working on the place, I was on my own. I'd had a husband I loved dearly and a child. In just a few months all that was gone and I was left quite alone.

'I felt a terrible loss. Fear for Grace and such pain and anger that this had happened to us all. I felt alone, terribly alone. But never lonely. Never that. Never that apartness, that displacement, true loneliness makes you feel. Over the next few years the work here and this place itself, well it healed me, Zoe. I still had the farm to manage. I never forgot what had happened, I never stopped missing Grace and Joe. I did my grieving for what I'd lost, what I'd hoped for. I had all these images, these pictures in my head. The sorts of things you see in family photographs. Me and Joe with Grace in her graduate gown, in her wedding gown, her holding a child with us beside her. We all do it. We all imagine things as we desire them to be. But despite the loss it was possible for me finally to be content again.

'That's because I was in the right place. The right place for me. I am a gardener, Zoe and I was doing the work I was best at. If you believe this is the right place for you, that this is your work, nothing would make me happier than that you should stay. But darling Zoe, you must think about this carefully. You must not stay here for me or even for Ben. It must be for yourself. You mustn't stay here because you've been bruised and hurt and have lost faith in yourself and other people. You mustn't stay because this is safest.'

She left me alone, then, on the verandah. She tucked the blanket closer around me, poured the rest of the wine into my glass and rested her hand against my cheek. I sat there until after midnight thinking about Grace, about Evie and Joe, about myself.

When I was a child and Grace told me that story I loved most, the story of the voyage of Mael Duin she always ended it with Mael and his seventeen men remaining on the island with the queen and her seventeen beautiful maidens. She always ended it with those words which have remained so strongly within me.

And age will not fall on you, but the age that you have attained. And you shall have lasting life always; and what came to you this day shall come to you every day without labour. And be no longer wandering from island to island in the ocean.

Years later I recalled the story and went looking for it in the library. I discovered in fact, that Mael Duin's journey did not end there on the island. He chose instead, to continue his quest despite the complaints of his men and despite his own temptation to accept the offered gift of immortality and to remain in paradise with his beautiful queen.

I cannot judge Grace harshly. It's not surprising she retreated, turned in on herself. She was propelled too harshly and swiftly out of paradise and had no time to choose her own way, her own quest.

There was nothing else for it. I had to go back and get on with it.

We stayed until the end of the year. That was the best time with Evie. I was no longer a lost child or angry adolescent, nor was I any longer that socially-invented, complacent young matron so defensively boastful about her life and husband. We'd become equal adult women who knew each other well. Knew the best and the worst of each other. We talked and worked together, laughed more than we ever had.

And now that I knew, now she'd told the last story, she could talk freely about Grace and I could see her as she'd been, the little girl who beguiled her father. I heard about the first ride on the first small pony, about the Christmas doll ordered from England, about the best friends, the birthday parties, the visits to Alice, the dress she wore to the first dance — so pretty, Zoe. Alice sent it from Auckland, she always was so clever with clothes, a very full skirt, polished cotton, a soft creamy-lemon patterned with tiny violets. Matching her eyes.

I began to know my mother better.

And there was something else I discovered. Out of all the stories Evie told her, Grace's favourites were those about Eliza. She listened closely to those stories, always asked for them and it was always Eliza's portrait she'd gaze at most intently.

Evie remembered there was a box up in the attic where Grace had stored away letters and photographs and treasures. She said I could look through them. 'No harm, now,' she said.

There wasn't much. A half-kept diary or two. Some letters from Alice and Anne-Jane. Some school exercise books filled with entries about her ponies. There were two letters tied together by a ribbon. I carefully opened up the fine, yellowed paper covered in faded spidery writing.

Dearest Zoe, they began. *My dearest Zoe*.

I took them down to Evie.

'Look at these, Evie. Whose letters are these?'

She looked at them, frowning. 'Oh Zoe. Have I never remembered to tell you? They're to Eliza from her brother. Zoe was his pet name for her. He was quite a bit younger than she was and I believe it's how he first pronounced her name. All these years and I've never thought to tell you.'

I had thought Grace chose my name haphazardly from some book or other. Because it was a little different, maybe exotic. Because she would not have a name associated with her family.

But I was named for Eliza. Her favourite grandmother. I was named with care.

All the things we talked about in those last months. I believe Joe and Grace hovered around us in those evenings on the verandah, drew close and listened as we talked.

Evie talked also, about seasons, about gardening. About storing the dry golden seed husks through the winter to plant them again in the spring for the harvest in summer. She talked about the patience needed in the waiting. About winter when the earth remains cold and damp and you cannot imagine that anything will grow in this inhospitable place. And the work you must do then, the feeding, the hoeing and the digging to keep the earth breathing and alive. She talked about loss and grief and celebration and joy.

'The glorious things, the best things we have, most often emerge from what seems hard and cruel and ugly. You see it all the time in nature. You see it in our greatest art. You see or hear that sublime beauty but know also the tortured lives of many of the creators.'

She talked about losing a husband and a daughter then finding, years later, a small, silent, white-faced girl she'd thought also lost to her. About waiting on a wharf, waiting for the ferry and finally looking up to see that newly-found, so dearly loved girl standing there on the highest deck, her hair blowing out behind her in the wind, laughing down to her, waving down to her with both her hands.

'That little girl. Such potential. So quiet, so observant. Her eyes always watching closely, making her own sense of things. I see it still there, Zoe. Still to be realised.'

I lay awake in my bed, walked along the beach, sat for hours staring into the night. What to do? Oh God, what should I do?

Endlessly I talked about it with Evie. It always came back to her leaning towards me and smiling. 'But, Zoe, what do you want to do?'

I wanted to write. To be a journalist. But it was too difficult. I'd done a little bit of learning and writing. Not nearly enough to feel I knew what I was doing, neither had I ever thought of it as a proper job. I'd been lucky. For a short time I'd churned out a few insubstantial articles which had somehow hit a mark. But how could I make a living out of something so precarious? I didn't know enough.

Evie suggested perhaps there may be longer and more advanced courses to take — Zoe, think about all the written material surrounding us, now they need writers for that don't they? I wrote letters, waited for letters back, made applications, waited again and in the end it was decided. I'd return to Christchurch and begin a two-year journalism diploma course in February. I was afraid, excited.

Before I left Evie's she wrote out a cheque and handed it to me. It was a substantial amount and I looked down at it and shook my head. But she said I must take it, do whatever I wanted with it; anything she had would come to me eventually — why not have something now when it's needed? And so with Grace's money and my marriage settlement and Evie's cheque I was a woman of means. Enough anyway to buy Ben and me a house, albeit modest.

Those two exhilarating, testing years. I bought a sharp, scarlet treasure of a Japanese car then found out it must be fed from time to time with petrol, oil and water. I waitressed, cleaned motels and weeded gardens to subsidise a meagre separated-person-with-one-child benefit. I made new friends. Had my first affair. I studied and wrote. Wrote and studied and wrote. I bought a house.

I had looked at practical places, brick boxes close to town — *aluminium joinery, walking distance to schools, shops and kindergarten*. I looked at townhouses — *no maintenance, no lawns, a golfer's dream*. I looked endlessly at the type of place I knew I should buy and the agents trailed patiently behind me and Ben trailed impatiently behind them while I surveyed the new paintwork, the tiled roof I would never have to replace, the formica kitchen with the melteca-finished completely-wipeable surfaces, the strategically placed fan-heaters — *fully electric*.

But Ben and I discovered our own house, our much-loved and totally impractical little house. We went out to Sumner for a jaunt in our shiny Japanese treasure. I was in despair over my inability to make up my mind and simply buy any one of dozens of perfectly adequate houses.

It was a warm early evening and we walked over wet sand at the edge of the sea. We ran through the cave, climbed over rocks and peered into rock pools. We took off our shoes and walked up to our knees in the sea.

'This is the best place. We should live here, Mum.'

I said it was too far out of the city and where would he go to school? Anyway, I had to go to town every day for my own school and it would use up a lot of time and petrol driving in and out every day. We had to be very sensible about where we lived.

Still, the treasure took us off on a slow journey around the streets before we turned back to town and our temporary flat. We wound our way around, just idly looking about until we stopped outside a fence with a *For Sale* notice on the front.

It was a white-painted weatherboard house with an iron roof and a row of small windows along the front. There was a dishevelled garden with a large tree in the centre, a swing made from rope and a plank of wood hanging from it. Ben said in a loud and satisfied voice that this was the house we wanted and that was his swing. I drove swiftly back to the city explaining why we could not possibly buy a house so far out of town and why it was silly to buy an old house with peeling painted walls and probably a rusty roof as well. We went to look through it at nine o'clock the next morning and had signed up for it by lunch time.

I bought it because I intuitively knew that a house not only provides physical shelter but also shelters souls. I knew I had to live in a house I could love. Behind all those windows making up the front wall was the sun-porch which became my writing room. There was a large bedroom and a smaller one beside it, a living room with a stone fireplace along one wall which sometimes smoked but which also pelted out heat in winter. There was a tiny kitchen without enough cupboards or benches but with a leadlight window and a dining room beside it you stepped down into which had windows looking out into the garden. There was a wonderful falling-down shed which smelled of dried apples and onions. There was a lemon tree.

You couldn't see the sea but you could hear it and smell salt if the wind was blowing the right way. I painted the walls creamy-pink and lilac and lemon, sunset colours. I made curtains and planted the seeds and slivers of cuttings Evie sent. Eliza's foxgloves and lavender and cornflowers and larkspur grew up around us. Ben played in the garden. We walked along the beach and swam in the stinging cold sea. We settled into a routine. Each morning we took our lunches and went to our separate schools. We ate together and did our homework in the evenings. Ben went to Robert's every second weekend.

I cried over my failures, felt sweeping elation for my triumphs. I studied and read and wrote. I passed my tests and my assignments and I thrived and Ben, thank God, thrived as well. It's the house where I cried because my married lover would not leave his wife, cried because the power bill and the phone bill and the car bill were all due on the same day and the tap in the bathroom leaked and the washing machine had given up the ghost. But it's a house I could retreat to, creep into and pull those pink and lilac and lemon walls around my body like a great warm rug. It's the house where I lit fires in the evenings that Ben and I huddled around as I read to him and told him stories. In the night I listened to the sea.

I am sitting at my desk. Sun pouring through all those little panes of glass, drenching this room in such a hazy, fuggy heat I'm sleepy, unable to work on this interview I have to finish by tomorrow. I stare out into the garden thinking the hedge must be trimmed and the grass cut again and I see Ben, home from school, stop beside the gate. He stands talking to his new friends and glances shyly up at me. It is uncool to acknowledge your mum when you're with your mates. I lower my eyes to spare his embarrassment and pretend to read my notes.

I hear the gate click. Look up and see his grin.

24

I've not seen very much of Lucy for a day or two. She's been mainly in her studio. Probably mostly in bed, since Clem's been here. But he's gone back to Auckland and she appears at the door with a bottle of wine.

It's warm enough to be outside this evening although I've lit the fire in the living room and sat close beside it during the past few nights. Lucy teases that I'm positively blooming with health, this interesting condition I'm in so obviously suits me but should I be still knocking back alcohol?

I open the bottle and throw the cork at her and say I'm continuing to ignore what she so coyly refers to as my condition. I would be very grateful if she would not draw my attention to it.

'Huh. Still in denial. A kind of reversed phantom pregnancy.'

'I've still got plenty of time. I'm having a holiday. I haven't had a proper holiday in ages. Not a long resting holiday. Not in years.'

Tom and I have holidays together but they're brisk, carefully planned affairs, structured to fit in as much as possible between the time we get off the plane and the time we get back on. We walk endlessly and take buses and boats and trains to destinations, all the time looking, looking, in case there's something important we may miss along the way. And I've loved those times, pouncing on new places, devouring the different foods and sitting at tables outside bars drinking wine, surrounded by crowds of people. But although I've loved all that buzzing movement, all that noise, all that talking and discovery we do, there's been no time for rest. For restoration.

'Do you miss Tom?'

'Actually quite a lot. I know it's nearly time for me to go back. Not quite yet, but soon.'

'I'm always pleased when Clem comes,' Lucy says. 'He always seems to appear about the time I think I might start missing him. But when he's ready to go, my God, I'm ready for that as well. I'm no good at living with a man. I don't like having to think about another person all the time. What they want to do, what they want to eat. If they want to talk or have sex. All that's quite exhausting after a while.'

'I don't have to consider Tom much. He's reasonably self-sufficient.'

'Well Clem's not,' Lucy says. 'I love him dearly of course, but he's quite hopeless. God knows how he ever manages on his own in Auckland. He can hardly peel a potato without talking about the best way of doing it and what size he should choose and what he should do with it when he's finished.

And he gets hurt if I don't want to chatter on endlessly. And if I don't want to have sex, God he's stricken to the heart and thinks I don't love him any more. You know men never really grow up properly.'

And so we laugh and complain and compare our observations about men. All the varieties we've personally noted and sampled. Their common weaknesses and faults. The pleasures they bestow which make them so undeniably necessary. And I'm thinking all the time about Tom. How gentle and funny and careful of me he is. How he doesn't really fit into those male norms Lucy and I are presently lamenting. I suddenly miss him so much I want to run to the phone and shout down it that I love him, I'm coming home immediately.

Lucy's telling me about meeting up with a former discarded lover outside an Auckland restaurant and how affected she was by how crushed he looked when he saw her. So much so that when she was passing an hour later and spied him still sitting, his back turned to her, his head bowed, she was moved to dash in, clasp her arms around his waist, rest her head affectionately against his shoulder and whisper *Hello tiger* as seductively as she could manage into his neck. Except it turned out not to be him at all and the wife Lucy hadn't noticed was both unamused by the antics and unconvinced by the husband's and Lucy's protestations — punctuated by Lucy's bursts of hysteria — that they were in fact complete strangers and it was all a dreadful mistake.

I laugh and tell one of my own amusing little anecdotes — how I came to meet my dear friend Jane. There we were sitting together at a school concert, dutiful mothers watching our children perform. We began talking of this and that and discovered we were both single. And of course as always happened in those heady single days the conversation turned to the topic of men. The unavailability of the better ones — (married or gay) and the limitations of previous and present candidates. We subsequently discovered to our mutual surprise and outrage, that rather than as we initially thought our present men coincidentally shared the same Christian name we were, in fact, shared by the same man.

I watch Lucy laugh. Her eyes shine in the darkness. Women friends. They were my salvation in those years after my marriage. Newly-single women. We gathered each other up at polytech courses and school concerts and the Newly Single and Finding Yourself workshops we'd turn up to out of desperation. Propped each other up, looked after each other's kids, wailed down the phones to each other and listened and listened and listened as we drank on-special wine from the supermarket.

We talked about men. What we wanted, what we valued most, who we fancied, if in fact, they truly were necessary at all. We all said we were far too busy for them and anyway all the vaguely reasonable ones are taken. We all said we'd never get involved with anyone who was married. And we all did — *Well at least he's not a reject nobody wants, at least he knows how to relate to women.* We all slandered and belittled their wives. We all rhapsodised about our one's intelligence, sensitivity and sexual prowess. We all hoped and laughed and waited and cried. Realised eventually, the futility of that particular path and extricated ourselves. Emerged harder and brighter.

Those years. Those difficult, funny, exhilarating years when I pushed myself hardest.

It's my first day at polytech. Far worse than my first day at school. I hoped to be inconspicuous in my carefully selected navy skirt and striped shirt but I rather stand out among these T-shirts and jeans, *Christ, I look exactly as if I'm Robert's wife let out for an hour or two from Fendalton.* I gather up copious course outlines and details of assessment and notes and directions for further reading and lists of books to be bought, *Whatever have I got myself into? How ever will I manage all this?* I follow the group from room to office to room. These people who are laughing, talking and asking questions, they are obviously so much more articulate and clever than I am. So confident, so competent. I want to cry, toss my growing piles of paper into the Avon and take myself with all haste back to Evie and throw myself into her arms.

My first human interest assignment. I interview my neighbour from three houses down. She's worked in the toll exchange all her life except now she's being made redundant. She's renting out the house she's lived in since she was a child and using the redundancy money to go to Israel.

'I've never been anywhere. Never even had a passport. Dad got me the job in the exchange, he was in the Post Office, he said, Phyllis it's a safe job and it'll do until you get yourself a bloke, well that's a laugh, you know, about it being a safe job. And about the bloke. I never did, see, not Mr Right anyway. But I always wanted to go there. Israel. I seen the pictures in the back of the Children's Bible at the Sunday School and it looked nice, all that sand and the sea and the blue sky and so I thought well Phyllis girl you've got the money so here's your chance.'

And it comes back to me marked with a big scarlet A. I marvel over how satisfyingly symmetrical and beautiful that letter is. Ben and I celebrate with strawberries and icecream.

I buy myself a dinky little recorder and set off to interview a visiting South African poet. This is such a coup I've managed to set up. The rest of the class will be so bloody envious, my lecturer so impressed. I ask the careful, cleverly constructed questions I've agonised over for days. Which reflects of course, my thorough research, my own sensitive reading of his work. Then it's over. His plane is due out in three hours time. I shake his hand, thank him profusely and fly across the park to my car — oh I really am so clever and good at this. When I'm at home I push the tape into the player. I want to gloat immediately over my brilliance. There is nothing. I turn it over. It must be on the other side. But nothing again. Bloody nothing. I rap on it, fast forward, rewind. I can't have turned the thing on properly. Nothing and not even any notes. I wail and scream and throw the tape onto the floor and jump on it and Ben comes in to stare at me and I tell him and cry. And laugh. I'm holding onto Ben and laughing hysterically.

I burst into my house and lean against the wall. I've just made love for the first time with my sophisticated and erudite married man. I've just made love and drunk champagne — well, a reasonable NZ sparkling. Oh. Oh. God. My first fuck in over a year and my pulse is racing, my body so deliciously tingling. I should never have driven home like this, I'm dizzy, my head is pounding, but oh God, I'd forgotten how truly marvellous sex is. Except I must pull myself into a sensible mother shape before Ben arrives home and shit, I promised to feed the neighbour's dog over the weekend, he must be ravenous by now. I run next door and rummage hopelessly around in the cupboards while the dog looks doubtfully on. And because I can't find a can-opener and can't bear any creature to be so cursed in the midst of my own favours and blessings I give him the large wedge of pate from the fridge.

   At the end of each year we went up to Evie's. For much of the time Evie took charge of Ben. I sat in the garden reading, took a rug down to the sea and lay there doing nothing other than feel the sun on my back, turning over to warm my face and shoulders. I talked to her about what I was learning, what I hoped to do. I saw her watching Ben and me. She smiled, touched my face, said I was looking so well.

   'Zoe, I hope you know how wonderfully you are doing.'

   At the end of the two years, when my tests, assignments and exams were at last completed and marked, my diploma came to me through the mail. Within a month I was a cadet journalist, a junior newspaper reporter earning a pittance and writing reports: council meetings, minor court cases, the

Lion's latest charity project. I was allowed to take the official newspaper van — bright-white with a dashing red logo on the side — whenever I was out hunting down my trailblazing news releases.

Henry Marcus Smithdon (25), deckhand of Lyttelton, was convicted, sentenced to 30 hours community service and ordered to pay court costs $75, when he admitted driving while disqualified on Lichfield St, at 9.30 pm on Monday, November 14.

Market stalls will be set up on the village green in Lincoln for a special fund raising event on Saturday. For collectors and bargain hunters the highlight of the day will be the auction which is to be held in the hall. Local WDFF member Annabel Greenslade said that among the more unusual items for sale was a Victorian nursing chair, a chaise-longue and an elegantly framed watercolour of two elephants drinking from a waterhole.

I loved it. Careering about in the van, my note-pad, my recorder at the ready. Loved it when I started getting the slightly — very slightly — more newsworthy stories to write up.

Preliminary plans for Maitland's new swimming-pool complex include waterfalls, interactive play features, a raindrop unit and the re-siting of the present dolphin-shaped water fountain.

Eventually I was promoted to a little feature work and naturally to *Fashion & Decor*. I drummed up recipes, did the interviews for the new restaurants opening, all that stuff which women supposedly prioritise. But what the hell. I had a job and I loved it.

I was good at it. They said my articles were sharp, sometimes witty, that I had a fresh approach. I've always loved doing interviews. So-called ordinary people who do extraordinary things, find themselves in extraordinary situations. I love finding out about them, digging in deep, getting them to tell me their stories. People who were well-known, people who've been interviewed at least a dozen times and have it down to a fine art telling the same things in the same way and giving away nothing. I try to get them to tell something more, to give away a little bit more of themselves. Truth. That's what I always looked for. And not just the factual details but the real truth, something other than the glib patter. What I dug for was the inner truth. Sometimes you hear an uncertainty in a voice, see vulnerability in eyes. Just for a moment. But you know it.

It's why I write. It's why despite loving my years at the newspaper, loving the people I worked with, all the teasing and the jokey-ness, the Friday night pub sessions, despite all that and the security of the fortnightly pay cheque, in the end I left. I left to write the articles that were important to me, that I thought needed telling. Make no mistake, there are stories not told by newspapers for all sorts of political and personal reasons. But working freelance meant there was no censorship. Sometimes no market and money either but that was the risk I took.

Had to take. Because of Evie. As I grew through those years I came to recognise that her presence, her tranquillity and wisdom and peace weren't trophies instantaneously handed out to everyone entering old age but hard-earned. Gifts that come with integrity. Integrity of the spirit. Evie said to me once that while she was unsure about the existence of a God she believed in an order to things, she believed living was for the journey of the soul — it's all that's left of my faith, Zoe. Out of that great vast sweep of Wesleyanism, that grand faith that brought William and Eliza here, nothing left but this scrap of debris. Well it's all I believe now, Zoe, all I'm certain of and it will just have to do.

The journey of the soul. I came to see it was a journey to be made with care. When I wanted to leave work to write the stories I believed were important, I phoned Evie.

'I want to leave my job, Evie. I like it well enough, but it's all so predictable, you can look around for interesting stuff, but only to a certain point and there are stories they won't do. They don't want to upset the people they think are important. There are kids living in the streets here but no-one wants to know about it. Christchurch is too nice a city. God, Evie I'll go insane if I have to do another fashion supplement. But what if I go freelance and nobody takes my articles? What if there's no money coming in? Ben and I — well we've just started to get a bit more comfortable.'

Evie listened without speaking as I listed all the reasons I should keep my job. Ben's flute lessons, his rugby boots, new spouting for the front of the house. Maybe a better car at the end of the year. And what if I failed? It would be terrible if I failed.

I sensed her smiling at the end of the phone. She answered as she knew I'd expected her to.

'Yes, well, all those things are important, and of course, as you say failure would be terrible. But would it be more terrible, Zoe, than always wondering if you should've taken a risk?'

There was no new car that year and the spouting along the front of the house continued to leak. But Ben had his flute lessons and his rugby boots and we didn't starve. I set up a weekly and then two monthly columns and that paid for our bread if not always our butter. I learned to take creditable pictures with a second-hand camera. I wrote and sent out my articles and had some of them taken, most of them returned. But finally I had a little bit of luck. I got some commissions. The work started coming in. And, thank God, the cheques.

Ben grew up in his own incongruous way. He practised his flute, went to rugby practise. Came home caked in mud from Saturday games and off out again looking like an angel to play in the youth orchestra concerts. In the weekends the house was filled with boys and noise. Then girls.

How do you know when you're in love, Mum? Really?
Don't ask me that one, Ben. Just let me know if you ever find out.

Friday evening, late-ish. I'm in bed reading. I hear Ben come in, hear him hover for a moment outside my door. He goes away and returns handing me a milky cup of tea. Sits looking pensive on the end of my bed loudly slurping his. I sip dutifully wondering why he can never remember to leave the teabag in for more than half a second. Realising, too, that something is up. Ben has made me a cup of tea entirely voluntarily.

He slurps thoughtfully. I ask if he enjoyed the film.

'Mm. Not bad.'

I ask if he would recommend it, I thought I might go sometime as well.

'Oh. Yeah. You might like it.'

I drink. He drinks. I tactfully enquire about school, his friends, his music, his present financial situation, what time he has to be at rugby the next day and does he need to use the car? He answers with nods and grunts and monosyllables and gazes vacantly towards the curtains.

In the end he says, 'Mum?'

'Ye-es?'

'I went to the movies with Sally. I walked home with her, I put my arm round her, you know, and then we stopped at her place, we were talking outside and then she stopped talking, she was kind of staring at me. You know. Then I said I'd better get going home and I said see you and took off and when I looked back she was standing outside her gate staring at me.'

I'm trying very hard not to smile.

'She must think I'm a dork.'

I say that personally I'd rather go out with a dork than a sleaze.

He looks hopefully at me, 'Do you think so, Mum?'

'Absolutely.'

We drink our tea and he asks if it's all right to borrow the car tomorrow and we negotiate. He takes the cups down the passage. I hear him whistling in the kitchen. I pick up my book and stare down at it. I'm laughing quietly but my eyes are filled with tears. Oh my Ben.

Ben's girls. My men. My married lover. The widower who only wanted to talk about his wife, the newly qualified social worker who only wanted to analyse me, the accountant, the odd interviewee, the American academic on a year's sabbatical, the photographer and the dentist. Some lasted a month or two, some almost a year. We had dinners and lunches and beddings — most more to do with performance and agility than with affection and intimacy.

How do you know when you're in love, Mum? Really?

I did not know.

Finally after yet another desultory dinner — this time the newly encountered object of possible desire had set alight the menu by holding it too close to a candle then asked searching questions about my 'ex' — I told my women friends I was giving up on men. I said I simply could not bear one more dinner. I could not bear the whole miserable process of having to get dressed up and desperately trying to think of something to talk about with this utter stranger who is certainly expecting some sort of intimacy before the end of the evening. I said I'd had enough of sitting across tables wishing I was at home eating baked beans on toast with a good book beside me on the table. From then on that's exactly what I intended doing. I'd stay at home in the evenings and be slovenly and comfortable and reclusive. Anyway I'd rather remain celibate than continue to risk my ligaments in sexual gymnastics.

Then I met Tom and for months we grimly scrutinised and interrogated each other over carefully spaced-apart lunches, dinners, films, concerts and drinks.

We told each other it was pleasant to have a friendship like this without involvement or expectation. We complained to each other that other people — our friends and business associates — asked where this was going, was it going anywhere? We complacently agreed with each other that a relationship — *sorry, friendship* — did not in fact need to be going anywhere at all. A friendship did not require any kind of destination. We sat through the films, plays and concerts then discussed their strengths and weaknesses over wine and espresso coffee. We visited galleries on wet Sunday afternoons. We didn't touch each other unless by accident.

We did not touch each other until the evening when, after the carefully selected Chardonnay was sampled, commented upon and drunk and after the film we'd seen earlier was dissected and the new CD listened to, Tom leaned towards me and kissed my cheek. He kissed my cheek with a moderate warmth — an action, he later explained excusing himself, which was intended merely as a communication of his pleasure and gratitude for the evening and an announcement of his intention to leave my house. Our arms wound around each other and we lurched entwined into the bedroom and fell into bed.

All those months I'd so yearned to reach out and cup the palm of my hand around the nape of his brown warm neck, to trace his face slowly with my fingers, knowing him, to burrow close in against his body. We murmured and clung and held and slept curled together and woke and laughed.

You seduced me.

No it was you.

I thought you said you didn't want any involvements.

I thought you said you wanted to keep this entirely platonic.

I sit on Evie's verandah smiling into the dark, remembering that sweet, gentle time, falling into bed and into love. I walk into the house, pick up the phone, dial our number and wait. Then listen to the answerphone message — *Tom and Zoe are not able to come to the phone right now, please leave a message …*

He's probably working late, probably has a meeting. But still I'm disappointed. I want to talk. I tell the machine it's me and I'll try again in the morning. I go to bed but I can't sleep. The wind's strong and I'm restless, listening to the sea, looking out into the dark.

25

In the morning the sky is dull and the wind so bitter and vigorous I almost give up on my morning walk. But I tighten the cord on my anorak, push my hands into the pockets then force myself down the track. I trudge through sand, look out onto a swollen sea. The cold had to come eventually, I suppose, but today I feel heavy and tired. Somehow I'm out of sorts. I walk slowly back up the hill, light the fire and make coffee.

I try our number, get the answer-machine again. I'm disappointed. Above all irritated he hasn't phoned back. Though that's irrational and unfair. He's probably busy at work, maybe away overnight. Still. It's days since we talked.

What if he left me? What if he actually did succumb to one of those doting office women who obviously find him oh-so-cute? What if I've been away too long? Been too difficult? Too self-obsessed? Any one of those women would pounce on him, dote on every word that sprang from his lips.

Okay, that's absurd. But Jesus Zoe, time to put your life back into order.

I phone Ben instead and he's great, really great, Mum, been invited to be the soloist in a concert coming up. Mozart's Flute Concerto in D Major. He's met someone. Katherine. She's beautiful, but quietly beautiful, Mum. You know. And nice. You'll love her, Mum. She's a painter. She paints wonderfully, like an angel.

But today — oh God what is wrong with me? Today I feel less pleasure than usual, less empathy for his enthusiasms. I pump some warmth and effusiveness into my voice. She sounds lovely, good news about the concert. Of course I want to come over. As soon as I possibly can. Yes everything is absolutely fine. Yes Tom's well. I'm still at Evie's. But I'm going home soon.

I phone Tom again and slam the phone sharply down on the machine. Pick it up again, dial through to his direct line at work — *Tom Ashton is unavailable at present, please leave your number...* Christ sometimes I hate technology. These machines telling you absolutely nothing. Tom, where are you?

I pile logs onto the fire, sit close to it and drink my coffee. A caffeine fix perhaps may inject some levity into my lumpish disposition. Another one, this time with slurps of cream and sugar. And toast with melting globs of butter and honey. So long as I'm bad-tempered and miserable I may as well be fat as well.

The sky clears and I go out again to walk off this heaviness in my stomach and my mind. Think about Ben. Wonder about Katherine, *she paints like an angel, Mum.* What she's like, what she paints. I'm reminded that for years I've vowed to start reading about art or take an appreciation course so at least I'd know something, wouldn't have to stand peering in front of a painting trying to make sense of the shapes and shades and breathing some nonsense about it being interesting. I fell into music because of a natural inclination and because of Ben, and books were always there. But visual art. I've been lazy about that. Not entirely unappreciative but lazy.

I walk about the garden telling myself sternly that I must become more informed about the art world. And about philosophy and religion. And I'm completely lost if anything untoward happens with my computer. Besides that I have absolutely no idea how faxes work, imagine all those words somehow squashing together and squeezing themselves down a tiny narrow wire. I don't know how they split atoms up and would anyone else on this planet not actually know how electricity works or about systems analysis or exactly where Afghanistan is? I'm totally uninformed, so unforgivably ignorant.

All the time the sun is beginning to simmer and there's a scrap of radiance above the odd broken cloud. The apple smell is growing stronger as the day warms and the wind is now only a tuggy breeze. In the end I put myself down in the grass, wriggle my head and spine into a tough, knotty tree trunk. Close my eyes and breathe in the fragrance of warming air and listen to the silence.

She paints like an angel, Mum.

He has stolen Evie's words, *Ben, my darling, you play like an angel.* Such delight in her eyes, such pleased response in his. And she is right.

This is how Ben plays his flute. He takes the pieces from the case and as he assembles the parts a look of inscrutability, of intense preoccupation comes over his face and he will not speak. He blows, frowning, through the mouthpiece to warm it, adjusts the sections, plays an exercise descending softly in semitones to a resonant B flat. Tries a scale or two, soft chirrups and trills of sound, all the time fiercely listening. He seems no longer my son.

And then he plays. Bird-song. Ripples of joy. Low notes. Liquid dark. Such clarity and precision. Curving trills and flinty sparks and bubbles. Sweet ice trickling up and down my spine. Painful and exquisite.

He finishes and grins.

See, Mum. Told you I could do it.

And now the last story. The final one. After the nail-biting rugby matches and the first formal and the driving lessons and the exams. After Ben finished school and went to Canterbury for his music degree. After he tentatively said perhaps he should go flatting next year. After I prodded him to go, telling myself that children must eventually separate from their mothers to achieve psychological wellbeing, that he needed his independence. After he left and I told everyone I was enjoying the silence and peace, a clean, uncluttered house, the opportunity to listen, after all these years, to my choice of music, to be actually allowed to hold a remote control. After I prowled miserably about my house in that first month of his absence, unable to settle to anything much, unable to arouse enough motivation to cook or work or find any pleasure in my garden.

Tom's children and I first negotiated a truce then fell into genuine affection. I took Tom to Evie's and they immediately liked each other so much I felt superfluous.

Tom and I decided it was rather ridiculous to live separately in largely uninhabited houses and drive miles across town to visit each other. Then decided that two houses may after all be the more satisfactory arrangement — *What if we get bored? disagree? what if we take each other for granted? What if we stopped loving each other and it turned into just another one of those god-awful messes?* After our talkings and waverings and silences, our small eruptions of fear and distrust and suspicion. After we decided, finally, that all this indecision was faintly out of control and we were after all, intelligent adults who knew each other well and could make compromises, would make it work.

We chose our house in town with wide windows to let in the sun and see over the stretch of park clear across to the willow trees edging the river. I cried as I packed up and left my house.

'Zoe, whatever's wrong? I thought this was what you wanted.'

'I thought you wanted it too.'

'I do. Of course I do.'

'Well why did you say you thought it was what I wanted?'

'I meant myself as well. You know that.'

'Why didn't you say it then?'

'Zoe, for God's sake, darling, it's what we both want. We've talked and talked about it. It's been settled for months.'

'I know it has. I know it has. But I hate leaving my house. And I'm just so afraid.'

I throw myself against him and bury my head into his neck.

'What if we fail?'

'We fail,' he says. 'In Lady Macbeth's immortal words.'

'Well everyone knows what happened to the Macbeths,' I say.

He grins mildly at me, tells me nothing so grizzly will happen to us, turns my body around and directs it towards a packing case and opens up another drawer.

'But what if we do?' I say. 'Fail, I mean.'

'Well then, we'll have a divorce and hate each other just like every other normal couple. Now then, Zoe, just moving on to a question of even more importance. Could you possibly bear to part with some of these antique teatowels? Bearing in mind we will have a dishwasher? Mmm? What do you think, my darling?'

Sometimes I love Tom.

After my books, *Saints, Sirens and Tragedy Queens: Myths of New Zealand Women* and *My Mothers' Gardens* were published. After I'd been overseas. After I'd dressed myself up in suits and white shirts to interview prima donnas and politicians. After all that.

All that. Exactly at a time when I felt as complacent as a cat in the sun. Like an Italian mama happy to grow round and solid and sit in quiet repose in the sun, head resting on the back of a chair, broad bare feet set solid on the earth. Watching the abundance of life. Watching children and gardens growing in the light.

I could not believe my blessings. This man I loved, this talented boy, the house with light pouring in the windows, the exciting work. And always Evie. Evie at the other end of the phone or at the end of the drive from Auckland. Always solid and real after the glitz and ritz and gloss, the Chardonnays and the cappuccinos, the language of ownership and excess.

I leave Auckland around five, get away as soon as I can after the meetings. I crawl out through the huddles of cars and buses then I'm out onto the motorway, negotiating that mad flashing, rushing flurry of peak-hour traffic, the horns and the hoons, the late model Holdens, the diving, dashing Alfa Romeos. I'm a wimpish driver staying mainly in the slow lane, but I believe there are more dignified ways of dying than mangled in a crumpled Japanese rental car underneath a truck.

Once I'm further up the road my heart stops racing and the muscles in my arms and legs and neck and spine are less rigidly clenched. I can slow down and begin to breathe properly again rather than in tight puffing bubbles.

I drive slowly up the coast, glancing out to the sea, blue-glazed and dappled by the gold of late evening sun, the dark ferns and cabbage trees, the flash of the pale feather-fronds of toetoe edging the road. Dargaville then Kirikopuni, Tangiwahine, Maropio, Mamaranui, the magic of those names I learned when I was a child. Those names I chant in my head. The names she taught me. Taking me now to Evie.

Up the coast and change down for that final climb up the drive. I stop the car, get out and stretch and she's there striding towards me with her arms held out and her voice calling to me in the dark. There's the rose and honeysuckle and apple smell of the garden. There's wine and peaches and cheese and crusty bread and garlicky soup. The sound of the purring, tumbling ocean beneath us. Me and Evie in the dark. In our garden. Our hushed verandah world.

She often spoke about death. Not in some inflated, new-agey way — death, our greatest adventure. She had little patience for the type of nonsense which offers instant enlightenment. But she spoke of death as she saw it, an inevitable, integral part of our lives.

'Perhaps in a way death is at the centre of our living. Perhaps if we considered death and placed more importance on our mortality our choices would be more carefully made. The people you've loved, who have loved you, what you've seen. Beauty and ugliness. Those things which have been the most difficult to accept along with the joys. Those are the things you think of, Zoe, as you approach death. Nothing's entirely lost to you, nothing that's been of substance in your life.'

I didn't want to talk about death. Like a child, I wanted her to live forever. Why ever could that not be so? She was as tall and almost as straight as ever. She was in her eighties but was still herself, that strong brown-skinned woman with the marvellous flashing smile and the dark deep eyes who'd taken me into her arms all those years before. Her mind was as clear, her laughter as swift. I believed her memory better than mine.

Probably I failed her. I said I wouldn't have her becoming morbid, I wanted to speak of living not death. I told her we could not be without her. I said she'd certainly live to be a hundred. I said we would have an enormous party with the official letter from the Queen framed in gold hanging on the wall. I said I could not possibly manage without her.

She told me she had her name down at an Auckland nursing home. If she was ever to start to lose her mind that was where I must take her. She said it wouldn't matter, her heart and soul would remain here anyway. She would not be a nuisance. I told her I didn't want to listen to such stuff. I would never put her in such a place. I would come here and nurse her myself before I allowed that. I told her that her mind was far too stubborn and entrenched to ever become lost.

I asked the Samuels to contact me immediately if she was unwell. They said she'd most likely outlive them. Most days she did a full day's work around the place. When I drove away she always stood beside the drive smiling and waving me off. She was so strong, so robust.

Although the evening is now cool and I'm tired from my meetings and driving and the previous late nights in Auckland I'm reluctant to move from the verandah. And so we sit on in the dark talking of this and that, of Ben and his ambitions — I'm going to be a professional musician, Mum, I can't be anything else than that — ah now, Zoe, Ben knows already his own place and understands the necessity to defend it, you have done so well to teach him that. We talk about Tom, about other plants I might cram into our matchbox garden, about the writer I interviewed last week, the next book I'd like to write. We talk about the two ancient apple trees in the orchard which should come down if we can bear to order their execution. About Eliza's oak which must be trimmed. We talk about the wine and the weather and Mrs Samuels' operation for varicose veins. About Prebble and Peters and Shipley and Clark — having a woman heading the government hadn't made the difference we'd naïvely imagined. About Maori land claims.

In the end we're silently looking out into the garden. The pinpoints of white daisies, the pale roses which gleam in the dark. I yawn and shiver, a wind has sprung up. Evie says, Zoe you're tired, cold as well, we must go to bed. She stands and places her hands on the rails of the verandah resting her body against them, leaning out towards the garden. After a minute or two she turns, smiling to me, 'I've been so fortunate,' she says, 'such wonderful fortune, Zoe...'

I wake hearing the sea, late in the morning, go to the window and see Evie below me clipping the dead heads off the roses with the secateurs. I wave and call to her, does she want to come for a walk with me down to the beach? She calls back no, she wants to carry on with this, if I like we'll have lunch later in the garden.

But when I come down the stairs she's out beside the kitchen door waiting for me. She's changed her mind, she says. The roses can wait until the afternoon. She walks behind me down the track and we walk along grainy sand, over rocks to crouch and bend over the rock pools, we dip our feet into the sea. This is where you taught me to swim, Evie, this is where you taught me to row. Remember this is where I first fell in love, Evie — well in lust. This is where I wept those great shuddering sobs over Alice. Where we saw the dolphins. Where you told stories. This is where you held my hand that first day you brought me down the track. You said it's where your mother liked to come, Zoe, and I looked into your face and I saw your eyes bright with tears. Remember, Evie? Oh Evie I remember.

You say you're a little tired, perhaps we should turn back. You walk in front of me on the way back up but you walk slowly, tentatively, I ask if you're all right and you say yes, well just a bit puffed, as the track gets steeper it's hard to catch your breath. I take your arm as we reach the top. You lean on me and I feel a jab of uncertainty but you straighten as we reach the orchard and we walk slowly through to the garden. You talk about the beauty and profusion of the late roses this year.

When you first stagger I believe you're bending to the roses. Then I see your hand clutching at your side.

I'm not quick enough. Not quick and sure enough to catch you before you fall but I'm here, darling Evie, kneeling beside you on the earth, here lifting you, cradling your head and shoulders, holding fiercely onto you, oh my grandma please don't die, oh God please don't let my grandma die. I am here holding you, Evie, here, keeping you back. I am here Evie. I won't let you go.

Tom and Ben came. We buried Evie with Hannah and Joe and Grace. We walked down to the sea and waited for the dolphins.

And they came. A great swarm of blue-black bodies spinning, skimming. We watched them dip into the ocean, soar above the white froth. Ben walked forward and stood at the edge of the waves. He turned back to us, his face washed with tears and wonder.

Tom took my hand and held it tightly. 'That's some celebration, Zoe. A celebration of living.'

But I couldn't think of living. I could only think of death. And I wouldn't cry, wouldn't grieve because I couldn't let Evie go.

I performed marvellously. I repeated all the platitudes I'd ever heard about old people suddenly dying — *never ill, so wonderfully healthy right up to the time she died, it's how everyone should go, a good life then pow, a quick merciful heart attack, didn't suffer.*

Thank God she didn't suffer.

But I suffered. Oh God I was suffering, because inside my body was a large, dark, festering, gnawing mass of loss and guilt and sorrow — *Why did you leave me, Evie? Why didn't you tell me you weren't well? Why did I take you down to the sea? The walk was too difficult. I relied on you too much, leant on you too hard, never listened properly to you, never watched out for you and oh Evie how can I manage without you here?*

I couldn't cry, acknowledge the hurt. Outwardly I recovered immediately and managed everything marvellously. I made decisions about the house. The Samuels were ready to go — of course Evie had left something to them and she'd given Sam his car long ago.

I found Lucy. Sometimes I visited the place, but only briefly and mainly to ensure everything was adequately functioning. I worked capably, my articles had a new edge, a tone of cutting cynicism the editors liked. Then Ben told me he'd won the scholarship to study overseas and I was hit by despair.

Grace and Evie and now Ben. Everyone leaves me.

My voice is bitter. The sound frightens me. I've drunk too much whisky.

'Darling, it's the way life is. People die and children grow up. It's tough. But, Zoe, could I remind you I'm still here? I'm not going anywhere.'

'I know. I'm sorry. I just feel so… I feel so alone and bereft. I feel like I'm in a black hole. Drowning in a hole.'

And although he doesn't entirely understand he comes and holds me and I cry at last, great shuddering sobs which frighten us both.

I tell Ben how immensely proud of him I am and clutch him tightly before we watch the plane rise and roar off into the clouds. I lurch from assignment to assignment. I ask awkward questions of awkward people knowing the stories I write will be consumed in one sitting and out of date and forgotten by the next day.

I don't care any more. My anger and concern and passion have gone. I just purely and simply don't give a stuff. I'm in a void I can't crawl out of, immersed in fog which doesn't lift. Does Tom know? I smile at him, we make love, I laugh at his jokes readily enough. Sometimes we cook dinner together and invite our friends. I see him watching. I know he's careful with me, waiting for this to pass. He takes my hand, rests his hand on my body as I fall asleep. I miss a period.

I'm following the track down to the sea. Because you followed me down here that day I couldn't see if you walked more slowly than usual or if you winced from pain. I couldn't hear if your breathing was shallow or more rapid than usual. I walk the same way as we did, along the sand to the rocks and I bend again over the rock pools, put my finger gently into the centre of the anemones as you showed me and feel that softness tighten and suck.

The wind is blasting up from the Tasman — Are you warm enough, Zoe?

I'm at the edge of the rocks. Sometimes I'd sit up there on the sand watching you swim, watching your body skimming then bobbing and floating on the waves. You seemed so far out. I wondered if I could rescue you if you drifted too far.

This is where Tom and Ben and I stood watching the dolphins. I couldn't let you go that day. Could not see, Evie that your stories were not only of living but of death and loss as well, could not see that joyous interlinking of light and darkness and growth and decay and loss and recovery your stories told. I crouch down on the rocks, feel the hardness beneath my feet, feel the salt-spray, salt-tears on my face, feel the wind press and tug against my body.

You're right Evie. Nothing ever is lost.

Today I leave you behind me and walk alone back up the path.

26

I come shivering into the house, haul myself up the stairs, fall into bed and a long, dreamless sleep. I wake hearing something unfamiliar. A car on the gravel outside.

I'm hurtling downstairs and out the door, hurling myself against this man standing by a car, this man in his T-shirt and jeans. Rubbing my cheek against his stubbly chin as he curls one arm around my body and at the same time takes his bag from the boot with the other. He places it on the ground, pulls me hard against him, then holds me gently away to look into my face.

'Here you are, Zoe.'

We're walking towards the house, me babbling that I phoned and phoned, I started worrying, I know that's stupid but I did, I almost came home, why didn't he tell me he was coming, what if I'd already left?

He says sometimes even he is propelled into impulsive and irresponsible action.

'Propelled? What do you mean, propelled?'

'I thought you might never come back. I thought I'd better come up here and find out.'

'Oh Tom.' I butt my chin against his arm. 'Of course I was coming home.'

Too chilly tonight for the verandah but we build up the living-room fire and cook a meal together in the kitchen. A celebratory meal, I say, this is a homecoming of sorts and we open wine and taste and slurp and chop spinach and celery and chervil and garlic and sweet white onions for Evie's Kitchen Garden Soup, spoon in the egg yolks and save the whites for the omelette. Oh the glory of cooking, of eating. Soup poured over bread anointed first with olive oil; then the omelette Evie taught me to make with sweet peppers, tomatoes, cayenne and ground black pepper. So lovely to cook and eat together again. I'd almost forgotten how much fun this is. Sharp cheese and the last of the grapes. All swilled down with a mellow Chardonnay redolent of gooseberries and rosemary. All the time talking, talking.

So warm up here, he can't believe it. This house. So beautiful, you forget until you come back. Our house? Still standing. The new curtains arrived. He's had to get in coal and wood. The plumber finally turned up to fix the shower. The garden's missing me. And then there are our friends to gossip about and our children and the Auckland motorway, God how do people drive on it every day and stay sane? — the traffic getting up here was... oh we're talking about everything. Well now. Almost everything.

We drink coffee and brandy in front of the fire. Talking. Talking. Then watch the fire.

It's what we do when cautious of causing hurt or offence. Too cautious to communicate our own truth or hear it from the people we love. We silently watch the fire, afraid to tell.

But now that I'm no longer afraid I stand positioning myself beside the fireplace underneath the high dark-wood mantelpiece. Beneath the portraits.

Tom looks up at me. 'You've decided then.'

I stand beneath the portraits.

This is Eliza. Eliza who left her native land and parental roof, the friends and the guides of her youth, and embarked for a distant clime as the partner of a Christian missionary. Eliza who built her garden in the Hokianga.

This is Hannah, the daughter Eliza yearned for. Hannah, who played her violin more sweetly than any imaginable sound, who gave birth to Evangeline, the new child for this new century.

This is Evangeline. Evie my grandmother. Evie the storyteller. Evie the gardener.

This is Grace, my mother, who wanted to live in Paris but chose instead to keep a child. So aptly named for her beauty and her elegance, Grace named me for Eliza, knowing the importance of naming wisely. Knowing that a daughter requires stoicism, courage and faith and naming her for a grandmother with those qualities.

Yes I have decided. For these are the women of my family and how can I deny them? How can I deny their blood, their courage or those patient teachings of my grandmother?

Evie. The gardener. Who taught me the connectedness of death and life, the wonder and the value of our living. Who held out to me on the palms of her hands those dry golden husks, the memories of past gardens foreshadowing those of the future.

'Yes.'

Tom is silent, looking up at me, then reaches up, takes my hands and draws me down beside him.

'I know what you've decided. And I understand why you came back here. But there is something you told me Evie said. What was it? The men in this family either die or go missing? Well, Zoe, I'm in very good health and besides that, I don't intend going anywhere.'

The wind is squally tonight and the waves high and shining like pewter in the dark. Tom is sleeping. When we came to bed he placed his hand lightly on my belly.

'I suppose you know already what it is.'

'Of course,' I say comfortably. 'A girl. Or even perhaps, a boy.'

And of course I don't know but even so I try out a name in my head. Evangeline. Evangeline Grace. For the mothers.

Evie. Evie Grace.

We're approaching the end of this sad, mad, desperate century. Even so I have discovered there are things worth salvaging. Those golden husks which must be gleaned and saved and protected.

I stand at the window watching this endless ocean lit by a multitude of stars, this ocean which roars and churns and spreads to the darkness and the gold of the Hokianga, to England and France and Ireland, to gardens built and lost and rediscovered.